The Loved Ones

The Loved Ones

Alia Mamdouh

Translated by
Marilyn Booth

Arabia Books
London

First published in Great Britain in 2008 by
Arabia Books
26 Cadogan Court
Draycott Avenue
London SW3 3BX
www.hauspublishing.co.uk

This edition published by arrangement with
The American University in Cairo Press
113 Sharia Kasr el Aini, Cairo, Egypt
420 Fifth Avenue, New York, NY 10018
www.aucpress.com

First published in Arabic in 2003 as *al-Mahbubat*
Copyright © 2003 by Dar al-Saqi
The moral right of the author has been asserted
Protected by the Berne Convention

English translation copyright © 2003 by Marilyn Booth

ISBN 978-1-906697-09-9
Printed in Egypt
1 2 3 4 5 6 7 8 9 10   14 13 12 11 10 09 08

Cover design: Arabia Books
Design: AUC Press

To Hélène Cixous

One

1

In airports we are born and to airports we return.

I am certain that my mother, Suhaila, uttered this sentence, though I can't pin down the day she said it. As she talked to herself, preparing for our departure, I heard it distinctly. Such things happen from time to time, when we are sleeping and she sits in the living room or when we are out and she moves around the kitchen slicing bread and assembling salad greens in a bowl. She bends forward slightly and then her short figure straightens, thrusting her slight body a step to the rear. She does her best work when she knows that none of us is watching her.

My intuition tells me—she would say—that they will come, like father and then son, one after the other they'll come and they will talk with me, even though I'm only a mother who shortens the distances between everyone else.

She believed in the truth of her intuitions. Her premonitions came as if she were a prophetess—and one whose prophecies never erred. Her intuition remained her best friend among friends. She measured out time between those who were living and those who were dead. . . . But, I would ask her, what's the dividing line between the two of them, Mother?

Nothing separates them, nothing.

But—

No buts.

My mother spoke then in a hushed voice as if she were addressing a ghost. We used to say—we women—that weeping and talking were possible as long as we were all together. Those things that happened drove us to recollecting things: No one is treating us with the proper kindness—we would say—and yet being kind is one sort of treatment when you are ill. No, we did not exaggerate; we just had plenty of intuition about what was happening to us, and to those men, and about what would happen later on, too. At times when one of us was away, far from all of the others . . . well, those were moments when we believed there was no hope for us. But as soon as we came together, even if all we talked about was other people, because we felt like gossiping and working the rumors, still we'd discover that one of us, or a few—no, all of us—were in need of some help. We were not women alone. We were three women, four, sometimes more. Maybe two in franji clothes, looking like the trendiest Paris fashion, and a third in skintight blue jeans with all sorts of fancy stuff down the legs. And then there was me in a pleated skirt, a long one; it makes me look a bit taller. A skirt always paired with a loose blouse to conceal the size of my chest. Sometimes, joking, I would say to them, Just imagine, now—what if we had the moustaches, hair on our faces like theirs, what if we were to wear a husband's hat and what if instead of those drivers we were the ones to drive them to work? But they don't laugh at my laughable words as I am expecting them to do. That's when I shift my body from one position to another, going over to sit on the floor and supporting my back, in my usual spot (you know the spot I mean). I move the pillow so that it is behind me—that pillow, the one covered in Indian cloth with the sequins and tiny mirrors and silver threads; it does make my back prickle slightly but I don't pay any attention. Yet I cannot maneuver my legs and back quite as I should be able to move them. My women always figure that I am ill—well, that is what they assume before they come to know, for instance, that just the night before I got a beating worth its name. Knowing *that* is not simply a matter of intuition, not in this case,

Nader, because just the fact that I am there in front of them scuttles their doubts and suspicions. I may be standing or sitting; my skin is tinted and my cheeks are rosy as usual with the bright rouge I use, my eyes—already large—made larger by the bluish gray eye shadow I put on my lids to camouflage their bruised swelling.

But not a single one of them gave me a word of advice on how to resolve things. We all seemed to be more or less in the same fix as we talked about some subject that, it was perfectly natural to discuss, all of those matters, call them whatever you like but don't label them a tragedy. For it is laughable, yes, what a joke it all seemed! As if these things had happened to someone else, not to us, as if we were seeing them on a video and we had no feelings of anger about the events themselves, and no resentment toward *them*. For us it wasn't a matter of losing respect, in the way that a person loses personal honor—that's the least of it as far as I'm concerned. This might be what distinguishes us women from them. Of course it was a problem that upset and worried us, but it wasn't one that could force us to say their names—not enough to drag those names from our lips! We would dredge up the name of so-and-so, and then we'd talk on and on about someone else, and move to a third and a fourth name and so on and so on. Even an intense thrashing didn't dislodge me from my submissive state. As for those words—pride, dignity, and sobbing until a very late hour of the night—those words are meaningless. Our sense of hurt and vexation arose from our pity for them; that feeling wasn't a consequence of anything else. What's amazing is that we look to be women who have forgiven everything: the intense pain, those particularly humiliating slaps to the napes of our necks, and the army bats. Sometimes the pistol would be out of the drawer and aimed straight at one of us in a matter of seconds—after all, pleasure gripped them and would not let go whenever they saw us primed to escape from them. Those things we would tell each other, laughing together; but the horrific images of it all would come back to us to stun us all the more. How could we not have fled? How did we go back to them? How did we go back, smiling into their faces and concealing our anger behind the high walls? It wasn't a matter of being just stupid or silly. After all, we would refuse to sleep on

3

the very same bed or perhaps even in the very same room. We did not — at all! — stumble over our clothes when trying to escape, as they imagined. No! To the contrary, we were good and ready. We bore up under it and we mocked them until it tired them out and they stopped. We had to handle it by acknowledging that what happened to us in private rooms, concealed from all eyes — to be specific, from your eyes and then there were also the eyes of servants and drivers — was just some excessive and misplaced energy, and it was not something to boast about, of course. Granted, it was a mistake, but it was not a sin or even a scandalous social ill. Don't try to apply labels — it all comes down to the same thing. From my point of view, being beaten granted me a license to sleep from pure exhaustion. It drugged me as my condition was getting worse, but there wasn't a single day when you saw what was going on. I never let you see it. As women, we were all fenced in by barbed wire and very high walls; all of us lived in the same neighborhoods. We rode in late-model cars. We colluded with each other and covered for each other. But no one ever said in our presence that what we were going through was actually caused by our severe and remorseless husbands.

Can you imagine? One of those times your father tried to call the ambulance after I had fainted collapsing into his arms. When I awoke I was like a deranged woman. But what possessed me was my fear about what would happen to *him* if such-and-such should happen. He was the one who shoved it all aside. A day came when I was even able to tell myself that when and if he abandoned all of this foolish and illicit behavior I would go back to the folk dancing that I loved so much but which my very nature had come to despise for his sake, back when I was studying theater in the Fine Arts Academy. And now here I am and you are seeing me jiggle my body as I have fun with your little Leon. I bend and sway every which way; he is in my arms and I'm like a woman possessed. It used to be that I danced as a way to ward off this and that, packing into my body every new move, every added gesture and bit of imagination. I was ignorant of myself and my body: what I wanted was to look better than I'd looked the night before. Later — years later, during our time in Paris — I would tell Sarah, who was my Iraqi housemate and co-

4

conspirator in life just then: It may be that dance is the dynamic energy that puts life into the world's weak peoples. But your father, coming home at night from the military base, looked as though he had been far away, somewhere beyond the seas. He resembled one of those corsairs of long ago. He suffered; maybe he was more in pain than I was. I would look into his eyes ignorant of everything except that he was in another and unknown place, and that he was suffering from an ailment in his endocrine gland, or in his brain. Likely his suffering had to do with his inordinate sexual needs. In the beginning we didn't touch each other, not really. No caresses. He did not look directly at me, didn't look for my reactions. He was bashful to the point of being completely shamefaced, and too decent for words, so proper that it always seemed as if we were meeting each other for the first time—and I loved that way of his. He hovered over me, agitated and uncertain, like a wounded bird both stunned and thrashing, one wing sticking out at an awkward angle and the other held tightly against his body. His feet would get tangled up in the clothes which he'd shrugged out of so fast and tossed onto the floor, out of the way, he thought. He would all but fall and that would send him into a fit of very ugly cursing. He had this ridiculous way of moving his hands, clownish, and vulgar, too, which galled him but he couldn't keep them still. I would be standing there in front of him watching in complete seriousness. He would jerk the coverlet up nervously and dive underneath and in seconds that irritating snoring of his would start as if the noise and its timing had been precisely calibrated by him. I'd stare at him as if he were on the brink of death. I would turn out the light and practically leap into bed beside him. His manner when asleep was extremely seductive and it had its own kind of power over me. But it was never long before I would again be my passive, weak self. When I was apart from him I would hear myself saying quietly as I shut the door, He is my Superman—strong and robust, certainly fertile, full of lust and always able to do it, again and again. Forgive me, Nader. But you must let me raise the curtain for you on those years of our life that are now over and gone. So that you can see us the way we were. It was always as if we were doing daily exercises, each of us with our own particular routine, in order to present to you—to you specifically—a particular image. We each wanted you to see the best possible image of our separate selves. As long as an exception was made for certain fairly vile parts of it, and for some of the stupid little stuff, I would imagine that we were deserving of at least your silence although probably not your sympathy.

Your father was in his mid-thirties and I was still a fresh young thing, twenty-four years old and from a middle-class family, with a father who was a recognized theater producer and a mother who'd been principal of an elementary school and had gotten early retirement for health reasons when she was no more than forty-eight years old. So there was enough time in the future for me to have a daughter by him. Or even two.

She rose to stand at the big window that overlooked a small garden and the neighbors' homes. She took a deep breath and exhaled a forceful sigh. Some memory came into her mind: she spoke again, her voice fragile.

We didn't turn into passionate lovers right away. It wasn't like the love stories you read about or hear of. Later, though, Nader, he started calling me the Deadly Bullet and I called him the Hunting Rifle. We teased each other and joked around in that sort of way, making use of all those things of the moment and devices and equipment that surrounded us, whatever we saw in the streets or on television. It was more than just a few flower vases and the public gardens. Our love letters were always dipping into the military dictionary. After all, he was a courageous and daring officer, an athlete who had graduated from the Military College, the prize product of his middle-class family. He was my mother's relative, but a distant relative. The day he came to ask for my hand she was the one who refused; my father insisted, though, that he was the one for me.

He used to stick the letters we sent to each other during our engagement—we weren't engaged very long—into his cartridge clip and so they smelled of gunpowder, and every time we extracted those little scraps of paper the traces of it sent us into spells of hysterical laughter.

She smiles and for the first time I catch sight of a satiric twist in the way she moves her lips. Her sarcasm has always been bitter but quiet. She turns but does not look at me. She walks over to the table calmly and goes back to work arranging the tablecloth. She straightens every edge, stoops and peers below to make sure that it isn't crooked or hanging too low on one side. Suhaila prefers such details. She stands straight again to observe everything carefully from a distance.

It's your turn, now, Nader, she says. Put out the forks and spoons, and the plates, and don't forget to change the water in that vase. Don't set it down right in front of us as if we're at a farewell party. Put it over to the side—we still have plenty of time before going to the airport. Is Sonia done in the bathroom?

Two

1

In airports we are born....

I repeated the words to myself again and again as if I were at Leon's bedside, chanting the phrase to him in my usual singsong tones that would make him go quietly off to sleep. It was hard to come up with any other locution but the fact that there was no other phrase was even harder. When the French security policeman at Charles de Gaulle Airport started to study my temporary Canadian papers I was suddenly uneasy to the point of alarm. I was afraid, in fact, my fear acid-like, fully able to scorch my skin and then burn all the way to my heart without emitting the slightest telltale smoke. That fear has been with me all my life; I don't know where it came from or when it will ever leave me alone. It has always been there for me to follow in its wake, winding through the cities and people and houses in which I have lived. We have stuck together; we're twin-like. My mother says, No, it is not like that. My fear—she says—is arsenic-like: I put it away, stuff it into whichever pocket is handy, and it's there to be sucked on and swallowed.

On the edge of collapse, I clutch at the wooden barrier that keeps me from moving forward. I have come to know ultimately that my blood will stay with me, loyal to the end as I push it away, trying to cover it up and hide it as if it's a sin or a physical handicap. Arab blood. I stand to the rear while everyone here stares at me, giving me cryptic looks. I'm no longer in love with my own good intentions toward the other.

The policeman stares me in the eye, uncovering my anxiety.

Your eyes, Nader—they carry responsibilities, exclaims my mother. And they're due some responsibility, too. Put your eyeglasses aside and let me see you as you are, whether your flaw is nearsightedness or the squint of being farsighted. This is your gift to me. Do not retaliate by hiding your eyes from me. I want to make sure of something: are they dry or are they tearing over as you say goodbye to me?

That's the way Suhaila is, demanding a concession from me, demanding even that I look at her as she wants me to, and even in the moments when we part—and we're addicted to the game of these separations, for hundreds of weeks, I think. I can even explode in pure anger and yet hide it so well that she completely fails to notice. For me, utter misery was not a matter of being expelled from paradise, that heaven of queenly motherhood to which I clung in the belief that it was the very center of the universe, the pole of existence but which she—in her severe, even ruthless, way—disregarded as we grew further apart. For I figured that in my case, this paradise of the mother was not even there. My own mother. An absence.

It all seemed a laughable exercise in futility as I tried to place the policeman's gaze. His stare was arrogant—that was the word. We were alone facing a battle that had to be joined even if it were to be fought solely with "white weapons." Words, just words. Is there anything out of the ordinary here, Officer? My name is Nader Adam. I changed it. That was also for the sake of the other. My French isn't too bad. But his gazes were equipped with magnifying glasses that put me on a giant screen, making me thousands of times bigger so that I looked as if I should be in a cage or a cell, as if I required a guard, chains, locks, and keys. Gripping the wooden rampart between us, I answered his questions. When I turned around to look behind me I found that I was alone. That's what made me feel embarrassed, ashamed. Now, how strange was this! We had exactly the same skin color. His questions weren't able to pierce to the depths of my secret Arab self. And after all, my answers were cooperative.

"These are my residence papers for Canada. That's where I live and work. Here's the file documenting that I'm about to get my British citizenship because of my marriage."

He examines me, his gaze steady and firm. A young Iraqi guy, he is thinking. All that this young Iraqi guy wants is a foothold, or maybe two, in order to see himself worthy of this lucky break, the two blessed citizenships that he'll very soon possess. Two lucky young fellows, the parts of body and mind all back together once again after having been driven apart by torture, by a miserable and deprived existence, and by the international organizations that hem in this young man in the long journey of discovery. Standing still or walking, he tells himself the lie that he exists, that he is here. He believes in his own presence. But without having to hear it from anyone else he feels that he isn't coherent or solid. He is clever, though. He senses that he is incomplete, but he is trying. He is not a hero and his body can't handle such superhuman efforts as these. He is not capable of being a fighter, a possibility that did strike his father one day and remained with him all through these years past as he tried to blow courage into his son's limbs, repeating in his hearing day and night, You are my recompense; you are the payment that I can claim for the days to come. I did not attain the goal he had for me. Nor would he attend my wedding, that occasion which meant that I was soon to grasp, with my own two hands, the sacred wreath of those two divine nationalities. So here I am now in front of you, sir. My smile is not a swindle and my quickness is hateful to you as I stand on the stage. This is not the theater of my poor grandfather and mother. Confused, all I've wanted is to obtain some role in the next season's program.

"Where are you *from*, Mister—you're Iraqi, aren't you? That's where you're really from, oui?"

With the tips of his long fingers—the nails are clean—he grasps the file that holds my papers. No absolution from Iraqiness for me, then. Even poison won't absolve me of it.

I smiled. If luck were to be on my side, if I were to see Suhaila once again, I knew what she would tell me when I related all of this to her. Don't you see, my darling? That he's sicker than we are? And more tired—as well as more tiring—than we are. All of those who wear official uniforms are sick—yes, w-Allahi, you just have to ask me.

2

One day you will go back there. That is what she said. Not to the same places, once seductive, that put me where I am now. You'll go back, she said, and she went on saying it. But I did not believe it, for which road would I choose in the end? To leave, to journey, to live in fright and leave all the instruments and acts of reprisal and revenge behind my back? Or would I take the path of forever answering stupid questions as I moved from one airport to another? Or, even if I were to obtain the nationalities of the civilized world—every single one of them—what then? What then, after everything had been stolen from me, even the scraps, the refuse?

What happened in the course of it all? The reason I am here has nothing to do with my occupation as an electrical engineer who works in a Canadian-American firm that produces, equips and sells spare parts for all the world's electronic gadgets. And she—is she this woman, the very mother who stopped all contact, who stopped writing and visiting, for no reason? Who had neither an excuse that was convincing nor one so trivial that I could quickly dismiss it?

"Yes, Monsieur, I came for her sake. She is in a coma. None of her friends has told me the date it happened, not exactly. Here—this is the address of the hospital. Here are letters from Caroline, her friend, sent by email, inviting me before—"

This conversation was hurtful, and because of it I was all set to let out a string of toxic language in his face. If Suhaila pulls through this, here is how she will describe me: Here is my son who was incarcerated by the blunders of his parents, people who lost the gamble and went astray, each going bust in his own peculiar way; my son who always shows up when it's too late. The days go by and as they do, he does recollect that he must keep his despair about these parents within the boundaries of a reasonable notion of "despair," and that he must not let his sadness become too strong for him to bear. Nader, she said, you will go back; and I did not believe her. Did she believe, or not; forget, or not? Whatever the case, she went on repeating the same things.

I won't forget, Nader. If I stop remembering, my self will get the better of me and take me to a place where I do not want to be. This self of mine contains more fright and more ferocity than other selves do. Yet I'm not capable of hanging myself—this self of mine. Maybe such was the fate of your father, but I cannot do it—it's that simple. Not at this age—I am not up to killing myself. I'm not defenseless, Nader, not unarmed.

But then she would say, almost in the same breath, Nader, I'm in worse shape than you think.

She was no longer capable of putting together a single coherent sentence. That's what Caroline had let me know a short while before. It did not worry me, however. I fancied she was playing with me since she has always been very fond of taking my breath away as a strategy to weaken me. For I am not, nor have I ever been, the noble and generous son; and no, I am not entitled to the role of the gutsy young hero capable of withstanding and handling her rapidly changing moods.

I heard the policeman's voice and the sound of his moving hand as he bore down on the file with his stamp. He raised his head.

"Do you know anyone here besides your mother, M'sieur?"

"Of course—her friends. Here, just a minute, please."

I opened my case of papers, pulled out the address book, and turned the alphabetized pages. "Asma, Blanche, Tessa, Caroline, Sarah, Narjis, Wajd, and—"

"Okay, okay, that's enough. I just want two. Choose two names, please."

"Blanche and Caroline."

Three

1

My son Leon was at my side, poking at me in fun with his soft fingers, pushing up the hem of my shorts and playing with the hair on my thigh as I read Caroline's email on the screen in front of me.

At this point — Caroline had written — Suhaila is captive to her own dismissal: she has admitted defeat. We don't know how long she'll remain in this state of complete isolation. She's in an indefinable place between depression and final despair. Not because of your wife. I worry about this: I worry that ever since her last visit to you, this is what you will assume. And it certainly isn't because of you. Don't take what I say as a sign that I'm against you. Look, the two of you, yes, you are one of the reasons, and likely we are another, and then, *her* — first and foremost, there is her. She is the immediate cause, the obvious one, but not the only one. What I'm saying might need some finessing, it probably should be more precise from all angles, but I'm passing it on to you exactly as I'm thinking it since we all need to summon our courage if we are going to uncover the causes of things when it's a question of illness or death. One day as we were drinking the wine she adores, in my apartment, and were looking out over the Seine, your mother said to me, Sickness is the least hurtful of pains. Haven't you thought, my dear, about the other kinds of pain, and the

13

miseries and troubles that one can't see, like waiting for a hug from a man, that man, him, him or another, why not?

Nader, I am just repeating your mother's own blunt language. Don't judge her—and I do know your traditions. I'm talking about a dear friend whose life I entered through the coincidence of Théâtre du Soleil, whose productions are written by the French writer Tessa Hayden. That's where I got to know her. There is no doubt that her friendship for me is priceless. Daily she menaces me, saying, It's the fierce sun of Iraqi friendship that will melt your Swedish skin slowly, and you will join our lovely gang.

She goes on, your mother. Even if I were to die after that embrace, she says, it wouldn't matter. She waves her hand at one of the scientific journals that I have subscribed to, repeating what she read there one time. Sciences drew her, and news of space and the astounding galaxies of the universe. She has always teased me. What a splendid thing it would be, she'll say to me, if we could be alive at a time when we can see other human beings coming to us from there. Let's hope they will re-educate us, give us a new education, that of the rational and the insane, the strong and the weak. This might be the ideal solution for the people of the world. She'll laugh, and I can see her continuing to chuckle as she nibbles on French cheese. Do you know, Caroline, she says, that the body of that man—most likely she means your father, because she never ever mentions him by name, she always says "he" or "that man"—or maybe he is some other man, any man, I don't know, but she goes on—I wonder where he is now? Is he in prison or did he die in crossfire at the barracks? It seems probable that he is somewhere beyond the country's borders. Perhaps he got married and had children. Who knows?

Your mother goes on talking; she doesn't seem particularly concerned or upset about any of this. His body carried secret love letters exactly as animals' bodies do, she says, but when she reaches that point she stops for a moment and then corrects herself. No—it was my body that carried those letters, in gummy, acidic secretions from warm places inside of me, to swirl out and enfold him in grace and the charm of a coquette. I was like an animal in heat—a radiation that drenched me completely, that came over me only at moments of anticipation or confusion, that might seep into me at those times when I was on the edge of breakdown. What could I do but galvanize that substance and keep it always vigorous to keep me in a state of passion—for such were my only letters to him. She would tell me, then, that she had sent tens of letters to the Red Cross, and to the Yellow and the Orange! Smiling weakly, she would add, her voice wry, These outfits hatch themselves everywhere, running the length and breadth of this globe as if the folks who spawn them are specialists in the running shoe industry. Every day she would sit down and write out those opinions of hers as if it were a sacrosanct duty. By the way, the name of that substance is hormone discharge. She would write each letter of it in a different style and a new color; she records things like a professional. I think it renewed her mental powers to do that. To me she would say, That substance, Caroline— it's the only matter in reserve I've got left. It is my last opportunity to stay alive. She wanted—she really wanted—him to hear that, to read it, even if he objected, or you did, to all of this loose talk. She no longer cared about *that*, at least.

She gets up slowly as if she's about to perform the prayers. She puts on her chosen recording of the repulsive gypsy singer. She detaches herself from me and from everything around her and now she is a being beyond anyone's ability to subdue or control. Later, on the point of bursting into tears, she whispers, The body dancing is striving to keep secrets secret, but all people think about is letting the secrets loose.

2

The airport corridors loop and coil endlessly. Dragging my suitcase behind me I shuffle down them like an elderly man. I don't peer into the glass or through the steel—this place, after all, is yet another one of those residences to which we moved at some time or another. I have kept my fund of fine names for its architecture, every possible way of naming beauty and expensive elegance, but when I am actually here I feel as though I'm in a prison cell that closes in on my chest.

I had the strong sensation that everyone who walked by me could hear the sound echoing inside my ribcage: yes, surely they could hear my loud heartbeat. I waited my turn in the taxi queue. I gave the driver the address written in my pocket diary. I was completely incapable of speech, so much as a single word. I sat scrunched up in the left hand corner of the back seat. My head, slumping back against the seat, was heavier than the barbells on which I used to train every day in hopes of strengthening my muscles. I kept my scream inside of me. I felt sharp pangs in my belly. Everything in existence seemed to parade by in front of me—my parents, me, and the entire world—to settle in one enormous barrel below which the flames were beginning to shoot upward. Whenever they calmed down those tongues of flame always blazed again; and the recipe is always tucked away inside the cook's pocket. There are no old recipes that are right for us, ones that will satisfy our hunger. But there aren't any new recipes either, recipes for which we're waiting, knowing they'll show up and so we can keep ourselves happy just by imagining them. We are afraid of sepsis if the ingredients are measured any differently than usual, and of vomiting if we eat the whole meal. I have lost my appetite and my ability to swallow has gone as far as it can. I'm no longer capable of swallowing new truths or new catastrophes either. In the mirror the driver's cold eyes keep tabs on me, his gaze as hard as rock. And I long for my mother's food. Bewildered, ineffectual, I feel as if I have come to search for a vacant position and now here I am, suddenly employed but not sure how, on my way to record my name and address at the syndicate.

Whom will I come upon first? Blanche, Caroline, Asma, Narjis? Or Tessa of whom Suhaila wrote on the day she met her: Tessa—a species of being unsuited to descriptions or qualifiers. In our beautiful Arabic literature, storytellers used to launch their stories by saying, There was once a certain place, toward which we will set our face. That's the sort Tessa is—she's worthy of all of us setting our faces toward—she's a destination in herself. Nader, I expect you will encounter her one day since she lectures in literature, theater, criticism, the novel, and poetry in the universities of the United States and Canada as well. I will tell you about her sometime.

3

I put my hand up to my face and ran it over my rough skin. I hadn't shaved for three days. I always found it annoying to perform this stupid repetitive task simply so that I could appear to be in the prime of my youth. For Suhaila it was a matter of overwhelming importance. I would be a bit stubborn about it but before long I would give in to her desires. Whereas with Layal, the Lebanese girl, I'd find all my plans changing the moment I faced her, trying to confront a personality that I found very forceful. Layal would exploit my strained nerves, trying all means of irritating me. Once she stripped me of all my weapons I would yield to her. She was the first girl to put an end to that shy adolescent boy—here in this very city, years ago—so that he burst into young manhood, no longer listening to advice or putting up with complaints, lost among furtive embraces and hasty touches and stolen kisses in the side streets. Those kisses were taken from girls who didn't stretch any helping hands in his direction. The girls in particular! This blossoming young man vied with an awkward youth who associated with silly girls but made no further effort at acquaintance or real friendship or sex for that matter. He groped and stumbled; he suffered; and he resorted in desperation to the secret act.

Being in Layal's presence would transform me, even if only momentarily, into a raging wind. For a few paltry seconds the claims of male pride would be satisfied. But she would close me down, roughly, and so I would stand there completely impotent as she stood watching. She was freer than I. I was determined to appear to her in all my elegance, my face shaven and my clothes pressed, cologne drifting from me. But she was resolute about treating me as if she were my boss, and she would storm at me.

What's the meaning of this, Nader? I don't like your shaven face. Your skin is so clear that it makes you look too sweet, like a bit naïve. I really like you better aimless and lost among people, a little crazy, oddball, not looking like yourself. So that I don't know you at all and the nearer I get to you the more you separate yourself from me—I get dizzy trying to follow you and I have to work really hard—and that's what I want!

Suhaila, on the other hand, would stand me there in front of her even though I was already twenty-six years old and my hair was beginning to thin. Seeing its long coal-black locks flying across my forehead and down into my face, she would tie it back for me in a rubber band and tug me forward a little and sigh. Would you tell me, now, how such respectable seriousness can come together with such youth in a single face? Now, would you just tell me that?

I loved to really make myself sly and clever in front of her as I also worked to do in Layal's presence. But Layal! No sooner did she meet me in Paris, long after those years of stupid pride, than she let out a dramatic sigh in my face and gave me a firm hug.

You've always been attractive, ever since adolescence, but I never imagined that you would truly fascinate me like this! You are aware of it, aren't you? Don't you think your attractiveness is your major talent?

What's the use of appeal and youth when Layal isn't with me—when she isn't my lover or my wife or a friend of mine? A relationship without clarity, so much so that I could not even say what it was that we had had between us throughout those years. My "respectable seriousness" had held no attraction for her in that past—to the contrary, it brought me low from the start and it still does, because it appears in the wrong time and place. Nor has my gravity been of any help since I have become a married man. My mother did not take Layal's characterization of me seriously; she couldn't consent to it. In my first visit to Paris after graduating from the university she would beam a little-girl smile into my face. You're very sweet and nice but you don't look like someone who inspires confidence! she would say.

It wasn't a description of my traits that I had ever given any thought to. All I wanted was to disappear from her life, to make my own way, even if my back were to stoop with cares or my forehead to go wrinkled and my hands rough with cracks. Suhaila makes me look at myself and so I forget her a little. My faraway mother—that's what she is, and that city, Paris, took from her and gave the takings back to me. I would become stronger: my backbone would firm up, my bones would grow strong, and my manipulative abilities would double, while Suhaila wilted, and was diminished, and grew smaller.

All of the cities to which we came, leaving other places behind, stole something from her. What it was I do not know, but I would witness it in those storms, in the long spells of silence and the feelings of aversion as she shrank from what lay around her. As for that torturous suffering: she called it the mask that has settled permanently into place, turning into a sort of regime in itself. I see that right in front of me, face to face, as she starts to look more and more like charcoal briquettes that someone left outside. When I come near I can see that she was once aflame but the fire has gone out. Layal, too, was much changed the last time I saw her. She had finished her university studies and gotten a master's degree with honors and then had begun to work toward a doctorate. Somehow or other she had dampened the flame; now she seemed quieter, deeper. Layal, almost Layali, Nights, had become a single layla now that Beirut and Paris had taken from her, and from me, all of those nights.

And now, here I am, returning to this place. Was that inclination of mine a love gone astray or was it a patent misery whose steep price I was still paying to this very day? I don't know. Layal had made my blood curdle with fear: in my dreams I faced her in one-to-one combat. Awake, I would not be strong enough to lift my head in her presence. I look like I'm falling asleep as the taxi driver leads me to my new destiny. I have traveled from Montréal to New York. I tried to sleep on an uncomfortable seat until the Concorde flight to Paris was announced. Much earlier, I saw Sonia's anger as she read the price of the ticket but a look from me had silenced her. Among the many words that came crowding into my mouth not a single one came out. She noticed. She was alarmed at my silence for she no longer knew what she ought to do. Like my grandmother, Suhaila suffers from high blood pressure. She takes medication and reduces her salt retention with long walks. And yet, she treats herself carelessly—perhaps as I already knew she would—and as if it is of no consequence. Isn't that so? No, Caroline responds, that is not true at all. She's playing tricks on you. She is doing it to try to provoke you, and she has gone on provoking you for her own sake as well as for yours. It's amazing, Nader, how like my mother she is. In this one respect, they are peas in a pod. Mothers in general are alike when it comes to this sort of situation. But this is purely *her*—to the contrary, she is coming up with new kinds of artistry in the service of health and bodily strength and liveliness.

How is that?

She has a great deal of enthusiasm for following lectures on maintaining a fresh and varied diet, Caroline explains. Her spirits rise every time she reads or hears about some new idea—everything you could possibly imagine. The fragrance of the honey that alters her troubled mood: she chooses the finest sort from stores that specialize in organically produced food. She practically breathes in vegetables and seafood, and she keeps track of all different kinds of river and ocean fish, not to mention fish that comes from lakes. Your mother laughs, Nader, when this comes up. She says that fish have discharges like women do and to eat them makes us as strong and frisky as newborn fillies.

Don't you see, Caroline—your mother says to me—that one's enjoyment of the world grows many times over when one has the pleasure of sipping or swallowing, exactly in the way bodies lap up the gestures of dance and the notes that make up music. She began saying that a lot in our hearing—when I was around, and some of our girlfriends were, too. She would go into the little kitchen in the studio next to the Théâtre du Soleil—Tessa put her there. I told you, of course, that Tessa arranged it so that she would have a decent stipend, for the time being, as a non-permanent member of the foreign acting company. She rolls up her shirt sleeves, puts on that striped vest over her own clothes, puffs out her chest, and launches into it. Mood and mind will change for the better—there, Caroline. Get in touch with Blanche, Narjis, Hatim, Asma and Wajd, because today I'm going to rob the World Food Bank. I'm a thief, my dear. We have to learn how to steal good things from within us, as long as the gods are as stingy as this toward us. All we can do is to compose our own sources for our health and amusement, for our short lives. My saliva runs just thinking about the dishes I'm intending to make for Nader, Leon, and Sonia, and for Tessa and all of you. I am playing tricks on the illness and on age. Maybe these are ruses whose only benefit is more dishes washed and more swollen hands, but they ensure whatever remains, whatever there is, whether it is days or seconds. They are a warranty that I can spend my only remaining wealth—what lies in my imagination, and in my senses, the intuition I have. Once again I'm consuming the world. Instead of the world consuming me.

Four

1

Sonia is beside me, the child is asleep in his room, and I'm packing my suitcase. Her face is confronting me but I'm trying to avoid looking at her.

"Yes, Nader? Did you say something?"

She has come closer and now she is facing me. She's a bit unsteady. She tries to hug me but I've got my head bent, apprehensive for myself and for her. She tips my head upward with her hand but still I avert my face from her gaze.

"Do you want me to help with anything?"

"No, no thanks. Just sit down, here."

But she didn't. She stood behind me, encircled me with her arms, brought her chest closer and began to rub her breasts slowly against me while at the same time she was turning me around to face her. Turning me to her chest. After Leon's birth I would tell her not to get upset or tense as long as she was nursing him; otherwise, the milk didn't come out so abundantly or freely. Maybe she felt shy or embarrassed or did not know what she was doing. Or perhaps she wasn't very happy about the whole business, worried that it would cause her breasts to stretch and sag. I would wake up in the middle of the night and begin feeding the baby and washing and cleaning him. There were his feces, which I would easily take care of, and then I would wipe his red behind, put on salve and see him in front of me refreshed and crooning. Maybe I was like my mother in these things; if I had had milk I would have nursed him too. I'll say that to Suhaila and I'll bet she'll laugh. But Sonia doesn't laugh, not at all. She isn't scowling but she is a little down.

Good-looking—Sonia's that. Dark skinned with lovely, flashing large honey-brown eyes, a wide forehead, straight nose, and taut lips that are rather thin and dry. A very slender body that I worry will snap in two in my arms. Her steps are slow, as if she is an elderly woman even though she is still in her thirties. Her chest rises and falls and I surmise that she will be fast asleep very soon. This body was at its peak state four years ago: elegant, lithe, attractive, flaming the moment I touched it. But what first drew me to her was her sense of cultural identity. Like me, she's from the East. She speaks English with the fluency of its native speakers who colonized her country as they did mine. And so we were a blend of things: in us were combined three of the world's most ancient civilizations. She was Arab and Persian on her mother's side and Indian on her father's side. I thought that our difference would be our freedom: that it would keep us from misunderstanding each other if any problems should arise between us. Are unlike cultures more able to approach each other, more receptive to mutual understanding, than those that have always been linked and close? Why did various sorts of misunderstandings arise between us that I wouldn't have imagined happening had I married Elizabeth, my English classmate at university? Our friend William married a Palestinian woman and they're content, in fact they're happy overall. Is a Western man more apt to compromise, to give something up, or better able to adapt than is the Eastern woman, or the Western woman who marries a foreigner? We are an emotional people. We descend from cultures where emotions are the decisive factors. They, on the other hand, are more rational and calm—the opposite of us. I was thinking all of these things when Sonia's frightened voice reached me.

"But, Nader, in case, I mean, God forbid, what . . ."

We aren't strong enough to look each other in the eye. I'm

dripping with sweat and I feel a sort of resentment or spite, though not just against her.

"Nader, we're alone in Montréal and you know the rest of it. You mustn't leave us on our own here for long. Do you think it might be something serious?"

She looked like she was about to collapse and I grabbed her. Holding her, I stared into her face. She was very pale. In fact, she didn't look at all like herself. Her emotions are very strong but she has drawn apart from me.

Our love swings back and forth as if it is just eluding us. Both of us. It is a love we wrap in acceptance and apathy, a love teetering on the edge of the chasm and liable to plunge off the precipice because it carries the affliction of dizziness rather than being carried by the giddiness of a happy love. I will say I love you out loud but I say it without feeling that those words are lodged solidly in my heart. This has been a love not of the powerful and intense kind that could make me ill and deprive me of sleep, but nor is it of the weak variety that leads to forgetting such that I would have to consciously watch over it to preserve it from complete collapse. My love is a light thing, as if it serves to keep a void at bay. And so I do not attain the longed-for ideal nor is my lack ever reduced. How was it that this happened and why only now am I seeing it? Was my love feeble from the start or did it sometime ago grow weak and wither away without my noticing? Why do I feel so dull when I am in her arms? Run-of-the-mill, gauche, and clumsy, and my heart wants more than what I—or she—can supply. My appetite for sex has diminished to almost nothing. I don't know when that happened. I have come to a place where I no longer know, no longer desire, and no longer need. I love my imagination when it roams wide and deep and she's there next to me, but she prefers other things and I don't know what they are since she has never described them to me. For example, I don't like porn films. I bought a couple of them, yes, that happened, and we watched together but they didn't get me going. Of course I'm not discounting porn films in themselves. But they really don't do anything for me in the way of pleasurable and untroubled sensations. In fact, they caused me to forget myself and my own pleasures because instead

24

I became absorbed in what I was watching. I told her that I love guessing games and the imagination—I think it is all less boring that way. But she keeps quiet; she doesn't trust what I'm saying. And then I am troubled, but I don't let her notice. That is the way I have been in this relationship. I will go to sleep and wake up sensing that my own fluid has drenched the sheets beneath me. She has not dared to comment and I no longer care. In those moments I have had the feeling that we are merely a married couple who stare at each other just like every other married pair in the world. She and He!

When Suhaila arrived chez nous she sensed that something in the air. Not because she is four years older than I am—that's a trivial factor. Later, after Leon's birth, Suhaila decided to proceed by simply taking my breath away. Uneasy, I heard her out.

Nader, she said, inside of you I see a mother, a sister, some kind of soothing feminine touch. You're a gentler, nicer mother than I am, you're better at it than are a lot of my friends, not to mention the aunts. I see you as one of those good and useful women—you wash the little one and you are regular with his bottle and you make new and varied foods on Sundays. You're good at organizing what has to be done in the household—cleaning, keeping the garden nice, paying attention to décor, hanging pictures, fixing electrical problems and spigots and broken appliances. You turn the rugs and do things I no longer remember, and you do all of it with the generous chest of a nursing mother who is never tired or fed up. Where do you get all of this patience?

Suhaila puts her finger right on the wounds, and she doesn't stop there. Her voice has a sly quality to it.

It is not just that fatherhood is an instinct in you. It's a gift, a matter of will and stubbornness. Everything you touch turns to fatherhood. The kitchen knife and the paving stone, the flowers in the garden and the flour in the cake mold—even when you want to appear naïve, just as you are doing right now, acting as though you don't know what you are doing, to fool me or to put her off the track. I can't help but wonder when I see these abilities bursting out in you; and they come from somewhere you know but we don't. It's as if you were born a father and the only thing you are suited for is to be a father. Damn you, how did it happen that you are better at it than we were, we — your parents, whether we were together or each on our own?

I went about closing the suitcase and I set it down upright, ready to go. I tried calling Paris one last time but I had no luck. Where had Caroline gone off to? Suhaila had praised her lavishly but near the end of her letter, my mother added an odd line: I don't know why she stirs up my suspicions — but I prefer a friendship like this because it keeps my mind constantly alert. My mother went on to say, Caroline is the one who trained me in the wonders of that pale man, Bill Gates. One day she stood there opposite me as if we were adversaries in a state of war. Her palm, out in front of me, was very white, thin, and marble-like, and so still that it might have been narcotized. Her arm all the way up to the shoulder was every bit as rigidly unmoving. She trained me, and she swore by Bill Gates, by instruments, and numbers, and symbols, and new inventions, and all the different technologies. As she gazed at me, the very man seemed to hover before me: C'mon, Suhaila, shake off those old terrors of yours, and don't answer me saying that the smell of paper affects your body and your mind too — it may well be that the hanging gardens of Babylon never did exist. Come on, close that old mailbox of yours and come to the blessings of the internet. Throw away your ink pens and your airmail stationery and your heavy envelopes — toss them all into the trash. Suhaila, do you hear me? Where have you gone? Are you with me? You know, Nader, Caroline is not a monochrome person but what is strange about her is that her actions hardly vary.

2

As I pace around the room everything shoots through my mind in a matter of seconds. The mixed marriage: is that the flaw, the cause of the disorder? We speak English at home and French at the firm. And Arabic — I speak it with Suhaila when she comes; and as we do so we get the definite impression that Sonia is uncomfortable, even irritated. We are very fond of our language and we converse in it, but we abandon it when she is with us. When she goes to the bathroom or goes to sleep early, we pounce on Arabic as if it is the food of paradise. We joke, we quarrel in it, we put on airs and we remember the city and the world and the old house. Suhaila refuses sometimes to speak English. She says to me, *She* should have learned Arabic, not just for your sake but also for hers. It isn't nice, this look she has in her eyes about our language. True, English is the language of the strong and powerful these days, but does that mean we must bury ourselves and our language in the ground and stand watching while the worms eat us? And what about the children, Nader, will ...?

Suhaila feels that Sonia, in spite of the fact that she comes from the East—even further east, which suffered as we did from the dominance of Great Britain and its arrogance—still stumbles between a sense of superiority and an inferiority complex which she holds simultaneously. My mother goes on. It's not up to me, she says, to counsel you on a psychiatrist for her, or for us. I don't have diagnoses that explain how we hold on to a partner when thousands of miles of complexes and illnesses and disparities separate us. We— your father and I—were from the same country but the nightmares and harshness and pains drove us to living in a permanent state of war. And here we are, you and I, together now. I cook and prepare and write down recipes for you, recipes for Iraqi and Arab dishes, as if I am infusing my Iraqi breath, my very soul, into the fragrance of our food, but onto her tongue and my grandson's before I put it on your tongue. Food is the language of sympathy. If mutual understanding or communication between human beings is hard because of language, maybe food offers some merciful solutions to us, we children of this earth.

She would sing and dance with Leon, erasing the borders between them. With him she repeated local Iraqi expressions as if to offer him the ancient tablets of Mesopotamia, the scenes and texts and numerals of our history. She paid no attention to the resentment appearing on Sonia's features but rather plowed on, inventing games, movements, and other means of amusement. And the child in the end was drawn to her. The two of us—Sonia and I—faded into the background, part of the crowd. I wasn't in my own country nor was she in hers, and we weren't (in either fact or intention) compatriots. Perhaps it was merely hopes, desires, and a sort of courage and fear jumbled together, about being a failure as a married couple. For in our case, clinging together as a passionate twosome who had come close to drowning in love (as they say) meant water that hadn't even crept over our toes, not really. And these were two lovers who hadn't exactly made it to the furthest frontier of anything, let alone passion. Conditions were ripe for evasion more than they were suitable for coming together, and it may well be that the quarrels and the anger we had buried in our hearts were preferable to dialogue.

Little by little and as the days have passed—and then the years—my ignorance of her has grown even vaster. It is possible that she feels the same way. And here we are facing each other now, performing the rites that marriage, any marriage, requires; the pressure and intimidation. As for flight and abandonment, they will come. Why rush it?

"By law, Sonia, whether here or over there in England, you'll receive all the papers—the will we wrote together, if I should die, or if I don't return for any reason. Everything will go naturally as long as it is according to the law. Come on, don't hold back your tears if they're there. My mother always said, The dead surround me more than the living. Why did she say that, Sonia? Was it to remind me of my father or of myself? Am I dead in her eyes because I am here and she is there? Is this the essence of death?"

A little scream escaped her. "God keep you, you'll come back to us safe and sound."

I went on, my timbre that of a computer-generated voice. "You'll find all the accounts written out, the mortgage, what we owe on the furniture, the car payments. In case I'm gone for a while it would be useful to have all of the financial recordkeeping written in a hand that isn't shaky. You would have to seek out a lawyer first."

I explained to her the tasks she would have to take on. My voice was firm and my words were a little stern, and I felt the energy draining out of her, minute by minute. She burst into tears. I was calm, almost empty, talking as if I were reporting in to my boss. I didn't get anything wrong; my voice was clear and my sentences cold. I didn't repeat a single word and I deliberately made do with the smallest possible sum of feelings, all in a voice that sounded familiar enough, a voice I had heard before. It was the words that filled my throat to bursting and threatened to choke me even as they jumped awkwardly from my tongue. I was talking about my own death to keep from getting myself mired in the death of Suhaila, to keep myself from thinking about her passing. The idea of death pulling a fast one on me was the ultimate hope with which to thwart the reality of Suhaila's absence. And so . . . these were the only precautions I took before leaving Canada on my way to Paris.

Five

1

The traffic has gotten heavier and the driver has withdrawn his attention from me completely. The taxi is making snail-like progress: we slow to a crawl and then move ahead, and finally we come to a standstill. As we venture to cross the vast square in front of the Arc de Triomphe there escapes his lips a stream of curses against "this reckless extreme generation." He waits for a flock of flying cars to pass. For the first time I straighten up and lift my head to really look at my surroundings—at the Arc which so stirred my curiosity and amazement as I squeezed Layal's hand to keep her from any sudden flight. She was carrying a long-stemmed flower. My crimson bloom. The sight of the Arc, dazzling me. My throat and mouth let slip a smile that quickly turned into a quiet laugh that separated me from this loved one of mine, as if I were an archaeologist or historian of ancient structures whose only desire was to savor all of this splendor, having not a concern in this world but to enjoy it to the utmost.

Today the Arc's face is beset by wrinkles and it is merely a spartan and frugal structure as remote as can be from questions of pride and glory. And Suhaila? How did she like it? Did she get any pleasure from it or did it make her sad, or did she always look the other way as I am doing now? The traffic has gotten worse and the clamor of it is fraying my nerves. My mother's faint voice sticks to the roof of her throat as I hear her mutter, echoing the driver.

Watch carefully, Nader. Those young men will kill themselves in the act of shouting for victory.

She waves her hand toward them and her eyes get watery. She follows the crowds on the television screen, utterly sympathetic, able even to put herself in their midst, roaming about in their shifting masses. Nervous and furious, the driver is giving me his side of the story just after a car bearing diplomatic plates has all but careened into us. Unlike her, he is full of words. She had not been a seasoned observer of what went on around us. But she began to learn, gaining some new insight four or five times a day. She meant to acquire new skills that would enable her to distinguish between Victory and other labels. Her powers developed and she began to reveal a most eloquent tongue, as if she were on the stage of my dear, beloved grandfather's theater. Little by little, she came to occupy the leading spot in the sitting room in front of the screen, as long as father was absent. And when the television broadcast dwelt on inessential, marginal topics, which was likely to happen now and then, she left the room to meander down the long corridor. Restless, she would go out into the garden ringed by towering trees and barbed wire like that which enclosed the army barracks. Repeatedly she would say that magic word, and when she got tired, she would sit down on a settee in the garden, swinging one leg over the other. As it appeared to her one day, Victory preferred to stand on two strong feet. Whenever this insight came back to her, she would bristle and stand rigid in military fashion. As she swiveled her head—as I am doing at this very moment as we pass by the Arc de Triomphe at long last—she would commence straightening her spine and then would tilt her head upward and stand at the ready. She would appear utterly eccentric as she tugged her long skirt at the waist to adjust it, pulled the blouse tight below it, and took a deep enough breath in preparation to usher in that Victory. Yet her body would appear fragile indeed, even limp. Where had that strong firm body gone, the body that never a single day knew illness? She used to show me photographs of herself on stage. She would tell me, It's not physical activity that sends the blood rushing through all my veins; it's the force of art.

She would stay there, at the theater, on stage, long into the night. And that is when the battles would erupt between them. Between my father and her. I imagined sometimes that they were performing roles in a play with me as audience. But no sooner would I see her afterward, see her so sad, than I would understand that this had become a matter more troublesome and perilous than before. She stopped going there, ever, and my grandfather became my father's Enemy Number One. From the window of my room on the upper floor I would gaze at her downcast face as my father was spelling things out for us, having returned from the base at the end of the night. It won't be long, he would say, before you hear and know the very latest news.

She would try to plant her feet as firmly on the ground as he did but she was not strong enough. And there we are, she and I, repeating after my father like a chorus, twice, three times, four, and he shouts with us. Louder! Louder!

Louder than this clamor and screech of cars. I could see her haplessness within her sweet, mild demeanor as she remained determinedly gentle with me to help me get over every hurdle. I was fifteen and she wanted so much to forewarn me, to provide every precaution even if it had to be surreptitiously done. She herself neither retreated nor advanced. There she is: putting her finger in her left ear, she shakes her head as if a fly has gotten in and she doesn't know how to get it out, and so she starts rubbing violently, uncharacteristically. Startled that I am suddenly there she flares up.

How many times have I told you that I can't put up any longer with these childish things you do! My nerves are not what they used to be, Nader. That's right, I don't hear as well as I used to and I'm still at this age. I'm not that old. It might well be that those sounds ruined my ears. It might be better to be deaf.

Suhaila tried to teach many things very quietly but my father preferred a loud voice as he recorded his objections to the two of us. Several times in the space of a single day we would be triumphant; all she wanted was to catch her breath in front of him so that at least she would not be charged with an offense when it came to the Reckoning. He would not accept her dozing off in her chair, wouldn't accept her thoughts wandering even a little way off; and so she was terrified that she might give way and collapse in his presence, seeing Victory's steam wafting from his nostrils. When it was time for his breakfast or lunch or dinner, we sent double meals to him at the base. It was laughable; he was getting fatter and she, thinner, right up until the day we left Baghdad. And so the days were passing and the victories were mounting; and my parents separated. They started sleeping in separate rooms. They didn't concern themselves with me or the state I was in as I witnessed those battles between them. Each one changed in his own way. Suhaila, losing control of her nerves for whatever reason, slight or significant, maintained her silence and went into her new room. And he—he would lose his head completely. He suffered more than she did. I was aware of that fact, especially when he followed her from one place to the next, and without any letup. Later, after she had shut the door, I would hear his nightly sobbing. It pressed hard against my ears. I would feel very sad but there was nothing I could do to bolster him. I did not even dare to put out a helping hand. I don't know why that was the way things were.

In a weary voice the driver says, "The hospital, Monsieur. There it is, directly ahead."

2

Abruptly I returned to the present. I found it difficult to move even slightly and I had to drag my body out of the car. I stood on the asphalt street in front of the broad entrance gates. I averted my eyes from the driver's face as I paid the fare. I hoisted my suitcase, slung my attaché case on one shoulder and threw my raincoat across the other. The sound of an ambulance siren as its driver spun out of the main driveway gave me a fright. My tongue was like wood. The actual entrance to the hospital was narrow. The red tile was slightly dirty from car exhaust. Odd, unmatched bouquets of ugly artificial flowers stood in grey plastic basins. The door swung open suddenly in my face. To the left was a white and brown wooden counter and behind it stood a slightly plump, tawny-skinned woman. She gave me a sweet smile: at the sight of her white teeth, my fear and apprehension left me. Her appearance of lively interest perked me up, too. This was a good omen.

"Good evening," I said as I walked up to her.

We understood each other quickly as she read the papers Caroline had sent to me.

"Aah, your mother, Monsieur, what terrible luck . . . you've come from a long way away?"

"From New York."

"Ah. Are you American, Monsieur?"

The naturalness with which she spoke appealed to me. She sat down on a low computer chair in front of the screen and began to search for the name and hospital wing, the unit and building.

"Good—here she is, the Iraqi lady, Suhaila Ahmad."

She summoned me up there again, and with what sweetness! She pointed straight ahead, and when she saw me staring stupidly, she came out from behind the wooden counter neatly to stand beside me.

"Come, Monsieur, let me show you the way to her. That building way over there, behind the tall trees, emergency unit, room 44. Bon courage."

I felt as if my tongue were literally tied. I bowed my head and walked away. A feeling of nausea went with me and it seemed to me that I smelled its odor in my mouth and clothes. When I asked one of the nurses in my path where the building was she pointed it out.

"There. The last building, where you see those doctors standing."

She disappeared swiftly behind the gardens planted with flowers and trees hanging down like parasols. I couldn't hear any sounds of rushing water as I used to hear in our garden when I went out of the house in short trousers, shirtless, to lie on the grass which had gone yellow from the intense heat. The earth under my feet was not firm and I had had no sense that my roots were firmly, deeply planted; they could be uprooted, it seemed, at any moment. I avoided the faces of the guards at our front door who would replace each other regularly, though I did see their necks from behind, fat and thick. I heard their voices chasing me in the night more than by day, and I turned my back on them. I annoyed them with the voice of Bob Marley, the Jamaican singer whose portrait I had hung on every wall of my room. I turned up the volume on his voice when he was singing the song whose lyrics I knew by heart. *No woman no cry*. I used to sing it to my mother. Rather than her weeping, though, I was the one who was crying and she did not know. My father and those pals of his, those military, spoiling-for-a-fight generals, would get angry at the extremes in my behavior, at my clothes, my haircut, anything and everything.

I'm dripping in sweat and I can smell myself; I don't know if the stink is too disgusting to bear or whether my sweat is the odor of that earth which they call my country. I feel as though the air here picks up the odor of Suhaila and carries it to the other riverbank of the world, navigating all the pronouncements of lying and hypocrisy; but that same air returns and settles in my nostrils. It is the same air that gave me lessons to help me understand my new situation: that I was in a region neither mine nor hers. Suhaila says, This is what they metaphorically call cosmopolitanism. I don't know what this word means. Why do you keep harping on this particular word, she asks. I don't know either. As if mothers knew everything, she muttered.

Later—many years later—I knew, thanks to my imagination or perhaps without its help, that their use of me was not metaphorical.

I sat down on one of the wooden benches facing the door that would take me into the building. My joints were betraying me, from my fingers gripping the briefcase strap all the way to my neck. I lowered my nodding head and tucked it between my shoulders, overcome by a sense of terror at what was to come.

Six

1

For the first time I looked at my watch. It was nearly four in the afternoon and it was the twenty-third of August. The hospital wing, directly in front of me, seemed inviting; it seemed to be beckoning to me that I could enter it safely. Come in, Nader; come on, get on your feet, move! She is indeed here and she is more than you can possibly handle. Everything is up for grabs and you can't trust any of it: the advice, the East, the West, the last resort of internationalism. Calm down, cool down, be a little colder; you must not trust to feverish intensity, and zeal is a path that will steer you to mental chaos. Leave a space between yourself and her. Yes, even your mother—you must always put a distance between yourself and her, a space where you shrink back into yourself and keep yourself at a remove, and then your blood will have a chance to simmer down before it hardens and congeals. And then you will fully deserve that label of foreigner.

I rested my back against the bench, reached for my bag, took out my handkerchief and began to wipe off my sweat. Suhaila is no different from other women even if her nature is incompatible with theirs. She always liked to talk about a variety of things and she crammed many stories in as we sat at the dining table. I would observe her when we went together to the supermarket. Only there did she lose her patience.

All of these prices are written on the merchandise. They are thieves here! She would say this and laugh, but then she would take me by surprise and go out by herself, traveling long distances by bus, simply to see herself in small and different shops—Iranian, Lebanese, Indian—where she could bargain.

Hah, I want to test my skill in commercial affairs, she would say calmly when she encountered me in the evening as I was returning from work.

No, mother, that's not quite accurate.

She would look at me and smile. Fine, Nader. No. It's that I don't like shopping in supermarkets. They destroy my concentration and sometimes I buy things I don't need. In little shops I feel like I'm in my own hometown. I know what I'm looking for. Please, don't take me to the big store, because it costs me a lot of tension and pressure on my nerves. Son, I am no longer what I was. Can't you see me as I am?

∽

I did see her. I envisioned her as she was sending me clippings from old newspapers, quotations from writers and playwrights whom she liked very much. A few letters she had written to me, times she was angry at me, that she hadn't sent. At the top of the page, a few words of consolation on the suffering I would be in for. She began sending me recordings of very old Iraqi songs, older than her, older than the generations that lived before her.

Mother, send something more rhythmic, songs with tambourines and drums. I can't stand this wailing and moaning. I want to learn old Arab dance like the kind you do.

But she would insist, and she never paid attention to what I said.

Ya ayni, precious as my own eyes, these are not poisons that you need to fear will kill you if you hear them. My dear Nader Effendi, Mr. Nader Sir, I don't know how to explain this matter to you. Believe me, you are atrocious. Imagine, when I hear you talking or you write to me and ask about our country, I feel as if you are wearing a vest so tight that you can barely breathe. Your hard breathing puts me in mind of someone lifting heavy loads. Your voice on the phone is miserable. It isn't your own grief or pain, exactly; I swear I imagine sometimes that you are taking pleasure in the misery of others. I hear nothing from you but scolding and this is how it always starts: we cut off communication. Sometimes it lasts months. I don't hear your voice, I don't read any letters from you. I can hear you sometimes, criticizing your father and his government uniform to the supermarket owners. Those people, you say. How rich they are and how long are their lives.

Nader, don't toss out the letter that I enclosed with my letter to you. It came a long time ago but I did not send it to you; I didn't want you to feel any worse or any more alone than you already are. Read it slowly and forgive Aunt Ferial for what it says. She didn't mean any hurt or disrespect. She is much more apt to make fun of herself than of anyone else, you know her well, or have you forgotten her as you have forgotten so many things there? Please don't make a copy of the letter and send it to the children of Narmin and Tamadir in Austria and Denmark. Leave them, like you, bayn bayn, up in the air a bit. Maybe they are in a better way than you are, these days, who knows?

∽

Today it's the twenty-eighth of March. Your birthday. Suhaila, your being away is a foolish, lazy thing—how frivolous and changeable you are, girl! That mother of yours takes great pleasure in repeating these traits in our hearing every time we visit her, especially on this Esteemed and Unique Day. She longs to add new words, ones she has never used in the presence of any daughter, but no sooner does she see us in front of her than she forgets; or she cannot find those words, perhaps. In front of us—specifically us, who are considered your only friends—she's bound to make us take sides against you, to feel envy, ever since that, and then ever since. . . . But she shuts her mouth; she swings her head to right and to left, she murmurs the basmallah, In the name of God, the Compassionate, the Merciful, and she seeks God's refuge against all the devils!—us, of course. Her face goes tight and yellow like a squeezed lemon; she seems to be staring at us from every angle, fencing us in, to force us to show a little courage, to get something good to come out of us, though she doesn't know what it will be, as if we are pelting you with stones or breaking a rib in your chest or your back as you-know-who might have done in the old days. But we stay silent while she moans and groans from the heaviness of the pain in her liver and her permanent constipation. As for the high blood pressure, it's a craftier visitor than are the other kinds of pain. It knows its allotted time and comes, and takes away with it the dollars that Diya sends. Your mother now reminds me of one of your father's characters, one of those years, when he produced Yusuf al-Ani's *Wasteland*. What she says about the tears that are always pouring from her eyes is, They're all I've got left now, ayy yamma! Yes, indeed, my tears, always true to me, they are! Wouldn't even know how to betray me if they could, and they keep me company. No, no, now, I'm not shedding no tears over Diya, and not over her either, not over me, no-o-o, it's just, I have nothing else left to comfort me.

She blows her nose and talks to herself. Get yourself up and make tea, she mumbles. Make it the way she does, the same way, tea with cardamom. Shay bi'l-hayl.

The cardamom is in my pocket every time we set out to visit her. Each and every one of us—and niyalik alayna Suhaila, your happiness is ours to fulfill, Honey!—we each take one corner of that place. It has all turned into dens for the rats and the black and gray spiders. We sweep and wash; we air out the place and open the windows as wide as we can. Your mother is the one who gives us the strength that'll let us get through the next eight or nine years of our lives. She trounces us every time, as we go around through those rooms. Bushra carries off the sack of barley and then later she gives us loaves that look like hedgehogs—that's only the shape they are, that's all—and the food, well and good. But the shijar—your Lebanese friends call it kusa— that is what really preserves our lives, that squash, keeps our years in hand so that they won't flee from our grasp. Gives us questions and answers, that shijar. Girl, do you remember that man we saw in the National Theater, standing next to your father? He wanted to jump on every one of us, he was that aroused and it played havoc with his personality. It was you who turned to us cackling as you said, Even the dumb zucchini imagines himself a real stallion.

For shame! Zucchini is neither a fruit nor a vegetable. No, shijar doesn't even have that distinction. It is a species without honor or personality. When we cook it, any of us, we Iraqis, we would rather lower the curtains against the sunlight. We don't wash our hands. We sit down at the table and fasten our attention on its cowardly fragrance. How can we come to an understanding with this dish of shijar, Suhaila? We defeat it at one swipe—we swallow it then and there. We don't leave any of it on the plate. That is the ideal way, as its life is short. The minute we pick it up it has left us. About some of it Narmin says, and she is not joking, See, it looks just like our men's things, after the war. We're charmed by her simile, but she doesn't laugh, as I do, in the beginning when I'm treating it delicately. I'm soon pounding it, though, and shouting. I'll grill it! I'll burn it, kill it, we all hate it, and the first one is—Suhaila.

How is it that we no longer care about zucchini though it's become one of our loved ones? We discovered—I did, and Bushra, in particular—quite a few ways to cook it. And to actually enjoy it. If you were here, you would see how pleased we are with our glorious invention. We have offered it grandly to the matriarch who hadn't been able to stand it before. How could it be, now, that she accepts it so delightedly, her eyes watering? She is that happy! After all, the kitchens are empty except for shijar. That was the dearest and highest fine to pay which made our laughter erupt, our jokes on ourselves and on you and on the whole world. Zucchini gave us energy. It chased away our sense of failure and sparked enormous appetites, testing out the strength and liveliness hidden deep within each of us. So, from two o'clock in the afternoon until nine o'clock at night, true good fortune with those homemade goods has been our ally. We have learned new things about ourselves and about other peoples of the world. We could even predict the next day, through the life story of this hollow and barren squash. Shijar was our Leader, the leader of every household, a coward who required no elegy. Meals with that leader were a material witness to the highest stage of self-denial: we would eat our midday meal and proffer the emptied plates as if we were awaiting revelation at the Leader's hands. After our stomachs were full and we had wiped our hands of the divine grace of it, we would make a place for sweets, the royal dish that puts us in a condition of overall aversion, by creating a true curfew. After eating it, we really could not go out and about! Sweets, sweetie, provision our intestines with unbelievable amounts of gas, with that smell that never leaves the memory no matter how hard we try or what we do. Your mother—what a dear she is, ya ayni! She is so very embarrassed, you know she's like that, whenever she happens to let one out and we're right there. She drags her feet to the bathroom but even from there we can hear it all, a wide vocal range, as if her body has got its own private drain. We turn on the radio or Narmin starts singing in her lovely voice to flummox the sounds of your mother's gut. Sweets, sweetie, guess what they are? The sweet is your mother's invention: a raw onion cut in half and sprinkled with a layer of cinnamon and brown sugar. We put it in the oven for a quarter of an hour until we can't stand the wait any longer. We don't leave a crumb or a sliver of anything—nothing stays for the next day. Not even the contents of our bowels are held back for the morrow. After all, the two substances hold nothing in common, and no one holds them in common.

It is not a complicated business nor is it a catastrophe, Suhaila. So don't hem us in with haloes and heroisms, and don't start in with insane bouts of loud concern for our sake. Your mother is living first class. Your father left her for the home of that actress, the little demoness. He produces those stupid, superficial little plays to showcase her and then he labels them folk theater. The esteemed master, your father, has gone through a sea change. The plays of Shakespeare, of Yusuf al-Ani and Salah Abd al-Sabur, Peter Weiss, Lorca, Ibsen, Strindberg, Molière and the rest, have disappeared forever. We—and anyone else who still breathes—we do not go to his theater. People grieve, seeing him plunge to such depths of triviality. What reigns these days, as I understand it, is *The Rhetoric of Triviality*. Have you ever heard any such thing being used as a title for a play? The run of this particular play has lasted longer than the years of our lives, and it seems likely to keep playing until our grandchildren see it, having pushed our children to flee. Don't let this surprise you, Suhaila. We heard that your father married the actress but we couldn't pin down that bit of information. What's the difference, I wonder? He still sends some expense money to your mother, along with your money and Diya's. So she simply scoffs at everything and everyone. What's this they call hard currency, shu! Look, she exclaims, it's just very old, worn-out, crumpled paper. Huh, what am I going to do with all of this money? Where am I going to spend it? Who'll I spend it on?

She hands most of it over to us. You've got more claim on it than me, she tells us. I opened a savings account for her in Iraqi dinars, which are exactly like shijar—no taste and no utility—and another account in dollars. By now she may well be richer than you and richer than many women here who are her age. But she's just the same as ever; she hasn't changed in the ways that so many women have. She's still our mother; she's everyone's mother, with those black prayer beads in her hand, repeating "In-the-name-of-God-the-mighty-dear-and-wise" before she turns to her everlasting occupation of sewing. To her heaps of heavy wool, and of thin fine wool, and of the ancient stuff from which we catch smells of medicine and memories and sweat from long ago, of men and our monthly periods and crying and laughter and boredom. She takes apart all the old clothes that sit next to her and sews them back together in new ways. Fortunately for her, she no longer smells the odors of those first years, twenty years or more ago, when bodies were fresh and fashions pretty and enticement was a divine blessing. These days, she isn't afraid. She is like a dedicated smoker: her smell is unbearable but we love her. She hasn't washed for a long time, because she can't; and sometimes she says, I don't want to.

The cursed woman, she adds. She used to send me shampoo that smelled like peaches. If only she'd send some now, at least we'd have the smell of peaches even if we can't eat them. They say the fruit these days is all blemished and poisoned? Is that true, girls?

This is when I can't keep it in any longer and I start sobbing. I shout curses at you and I say awful, unfair, things: If I were to put you in the frying pan right now and fry you to death, it still would not quench my thirst for revenge.

We leave the house in the evening, each of us clutching some part of you, from the residues of you that we still have, from the friendship that was orphaned. We put your mother's words aside; we turn those words inside out, and in unison (but everyone at a different pitch), as each of us is getting into her car, the gas propulsion taking effect without anyone to watch. Ayy, I did learn how to drive, finally, yes, I did, learned that even if I were to forget my own name, Ferial, youngest of all of you, the one crazy for sculpture and drawing, sewing and décor. It's me, now, who screams in a voice higher than the Eiffel Tower and all the towers of the world, in front of my self and them, in the street where your house sits, and without any well-founded motive, Suhaila. Me, I scream it out: When will you die, my friend, why don't you die? Why haven't you died yet? What are you waiting for, billahi alayki? Usually people your age, women your age, I mean, Bushra, and Narmin, Azhar, Tamadir—they have died, one way or another, and that was a big help to us. We got something out of it, of course we did. Some found it a superb way to save energy and thereby ascended to the highest of ranks. One group died immediately, early. Died while combing out their hair. Fine, then, it was all over for them when they were at the beginning of the road, so in terms of principle they are above everyone. As for us, as for everyone who is waiting, it's all the same. Well, no, but it's no worse. After all, in practical terms, we're not knocking ourselves out to get there.

We did not understand your letter, my dear. It took a very long time for me to go begging to my brain, as your father always used to say. I didn't understand this alluring proposition of yours. Did you say you are going to get operations going in Europe and the Americas? That you will embark on a personal and dazzling sequence of actions—as you wrote, a string of actions that's engraved in the memory, that belongs to the long-ago era of struggle? As I understood it, you are planning to go and pay visits on some of the masterminds around you, clothed in our venerable national dress, the Sayi and the Hashimi styles both. You will offer them all the old stories with all the necessary explanations and at the end of the evening you will collect lots of signatures written out with elegant Parker pens. It is all to be a better means of bringing us back to the human fold.

We excuse you—you do mean it all perfectly sincerely, I know that. Here is a bowl of shit, my lady. My dear, to the words your mother finds to describe you, one could add stupid. You are truly stupid. If only you would come down to earth a bit, deal with that self-importance of yours, and your heartaches on behalf of us, and your contradictions, and also your hesitation, because I can say, as a general rule, We are here. We are present and accounted for. I mean, we can shine our own shoes, and we're capable of opening our front doors to receive some guest or other—a guest we're expecting, not the other sort. We go to the salon to get our hair done; when we open the old photo album we're seized by a sort of impotent joy. Back in those days, as we waited for our husbands, sitting around in those evening gowns that we can still see in the album, we knew perfectly well that before long we would be beaten to a pulp with canes and whips. Those photographs of ours—which we keep close by, as if we are in a secret meeting or a party assembly—we take with us to the kitchen. Or we place them carefully on top of unoccupied pillows. Our odd, unfamiliar forms that peer from the album are all that we have got left. Even so, we are living better than you are and better than they are. That is how we live. We live, coming and going, however it happens, this way or that. I think we are living in utter art: we take hold of our days with our own firm hands and we pass the iron over them and we do not send our clothes to the automatic laundry. We still smile into each other's faces and full in the face of the United Nations, the Confused Nations, nations more confused than we are, and the Short-sleeved Nations. Nations, nations, nations—we are their extra workloads, their overtime, and their vacations cut short by dollars. We are the ones in demand from all the gentlemen of the world. It is a bewildering thing, Suhaila, my dear; I don't want to say to you, So long, see you soon. What I do want to do is to boast a little. As long as you are listening. This little tendency to strut has cropped up in me recently. So here you are—I'm duty-bound, you see, to not let you off the hook. I am duty-bound by cleanliness, companionship, and the holiday friendships of our children, every Sunday and Friday that they spent together. Your friends' children became my children, like Nader. When we ate gaymer—I miss that thick Iraqi cream of ours!—and dry bread dipped in homemade honey as we made our way to that very island, Jazirat Umm al-Khanazir, the fishing and bird-hunting paradise, Pigs' Mother Island, across from the Baath Party residences. A thing of the imagination but it isn't strange or foreign. With that curiosity of ours which is constantly moving and shifting, we always feel that we are on our way to that island. It wasn't simply some wild, uninhabited ground plumb in the middle of the lackadaisical Tigris River. I can say to you, appropriately and frankly and with typical Iraqi liberality, that we abide there throughout all the seconds and hours and years that pass. We do not punish anyone with stoning and we don't fish, but we're there. We've grown smaller and less numerous than our children who fled as soon as they sensed that the fishhook might find them and sink into their flesh just as it found their fathers.

Get yourself far away from us, Suhaila, and stay away. Keep your resounding ideas and your proverbial sayings and your throbbing, pulsing actions far away from us. I beg you not to waste our time with one farce after another. Because, you see, we're no longer who we were. I won't press it on the rest of our little and loving group. They might write to you, as you asked at the end of that letter. Before you now is a golden opportunity—one—so don't let it slip from your hands. Who knows, we might even come to trust you if you make use of it. Suhaila, to all appearances you haven't gotten sick in a century, you haven't darkened the doors of any hospital, neither government nor private-sector, you battalion-in-one of Don Quixotes! It is within the realm of possibility that if you were to get yourself out of that chronic lethargy of yours and go into that world, you would get the reward of repentance. No. Of curses. Curses be upon you.

Seven

1

It was nearly five o'clock. I headed toward the building. There were a few steps rising in front of me that I would have to tackle in order to go inside. I didn't feel up to it. The silence was unbearably heavy and oppressive. Hospitals are self-sufficient cities that a person could inhabit endlessly without stepping outside.

I headed toward the elevator and stood in front of it. I did not think about Suhaila. What came to my mind was my office at the company, my table piled with papers, the file drawers I had forgotten to lock. The lemon-yellow cologne bottle with its piercing aroma drifted into view; I had put it in our own office bathroom. Every time my eyes fell on it I could barely keep myself from following through on an intense desire to open it and swallow a few drops.

It was fitting that my thoughts were on perfume as the acidic odor of my sweat and fear expanded. Fear has a forceful smell unlike any other odor, and all the perfumes in the world can't get rid of it. The elevator arrived and some doctors and ordinary people shuffled in. It was large, ample enough to hold our coffins as well as ourselves. It stopped at the fourth floor but I was in the very back and I ended up returning to the third floor. I stepped out onto the hospital floor, a waxy thickness of light blue. I noticed the door to the stairs that would take me to the fourth floor. I started to climb, trying to shake off more of my fear with every step. I opened the door with difficulty. It was strong and heavy and swung closed on its own. I fixed my eyes on the floor's shininess, from which rose that stinging smell particular to hospitals. When I raised my head, the light was strong in my eyes. It was one of the old buildings and they would be getting rid of it in the coming months. I had read that at the hospital entrance. They do this in Canada and the United States, too: they get rid of the buildings that are not very high. They say that these buildings do not suit the times. I began to work out in my mind the French sentences that I might be using in a few moments, I thought, as I saw briskly moving women— nurses and doctors in pressed white uniforms and low sandals. Their caps were starched and everything was topnotch and moving along according to established practice. My leather belt sagged loosely across my middle and I was finding the burden of my raincoat annoying. I began to cough. I wanted to hear my own voice. I started to feel slightly dizzy; I halted and almost threw up. The corridor was long, longer than the one in the armed forces regional headquarters where my father's activities had been concentrated. And it was longer than the road we'd covered together between here and there, longer than victory, failure, laughter. Talking to myself I caught a glimpse of a blonde woman sitting outside one of the rooms, something in her hand. Must be a book or a newspaper. In my state of unreality I didn't want to be in any doubt about who it was or the fact that this particular person was here. I came nearer and the features formed of a second woman sitting a little further away. Was this Blanche? She had changed, gotten heavier, but she was still attractive. I approached them: two blonde women, gleaming with the afterglow of Suhaila's luminosity.

"Nader—it's Nader!" called out Blanche in a warm Iraqi dialect, as if she were scampering behind me across the roof of our house in Baghdad. They hurried toward me although Caroline's approach showed a bit of that reserve associated with her native land, which matched her high-imperial English.

"Finally! You're finally here, Nader."

I wasn't really aware of what was going on until I was in their arms. "Caroline, and Blanche, right?"

2

If only I were to lose consciousness this very minute. If only I were to hurl curses at her, just her: Suhaila. If only I were not Nader feeling perennially scared that he would receive an email one night, saying: Come and take delivery of your mother's body. Come, come. For today she is the daughter and I am the agitated father in a hurry who is urgently entrusted with her affairs. I wonder who it was that invented mothers?

I stripped myself bare in their presence even though that is something I do not like or want to do. I did want to cry, to sob aloud, but not in front of them; that is not at all to my liking. Blanche reads me like an open book. But now she stopped staring at me. If only they would go out now, and go away, really away, further away than my mother is to me. If only they would return home. If only they would leave me alone with her. I have come, so you go now. Right now. Blanche's hugging was a little more elaborate than necessary. She understood the state I was in well enough. Enfolded in her arms, what could I do? I was not going to make things worse or delay this process more by breaking down.

"Nader, there is still some life in her." She grabbed my head and gave me a kiss. I don't know where the feeling came from, but I was leaning toward believing her. I was equipped only with this suspicion of her, as if she were simultaneously holding on to me and hiding Suhaila away, at least for the few seconds she could sustain it; but, I felt instinctively, it was all for my sake. Caroline turned her head away from us and began to mutter in a faint voice.

"She's in a coma, this is the fourth day. Don't be frightened when you see her. Be strong for her sake and for yours as well. If it weren't for her condition getting worse so rapidly we wouldn't have considered getting you to come."

I began blathering. She put her hand over my mouth and I saw quiet tears coming slowly from her large and pretty green eyes.

"We took turns being here. We are always here, all of us who are her friends. Even if she isn't aware that we're here. Between us, we came up with a schedule. Caroline took almost all the time since she does not have family responsibilities as the rest of us do. She is truly a rare friend."

"And—"

She took my hand. "Leave your bags here, next to Caroline."

She took them from me. She slipped my attaché from my shoulder and tugged my coat out from under my other arm. She dragged the suitcase over to Caroline, who now came right to me, eyes wet, nose red, and lips chapped.

"Go in, Nader, go in to her, this is the only thing that matters, the only thing that has to be done in the end."

I stood still as a statue. She handed me a box of tissues. One of the nurses came over to us.

"This is Monsieur Nader, her son."

She smiled encouragingly into my face. I was exerting unbelievable effort as I put off even looking toward the room with the number 44 on the door. Now there was a trio of women trying to push me gently but determinedly toward her and exchanging looks among themselves as I, meanwhile, couldn't pull myself together enough to even lift my head and look straight at them. Suddenly my spellbound tongue was untied and I said in a barely audible voice, "I'll do it. I will do it."

I turned my back on them and dropped onto one of the seats. Huddled there, I put my face in my hands and felt only worse. Suhaila does not know how to tease or take things lightly. If she had only tried to make jokes, if she had learned how to banter, then I would have been a little more at ease. She used to repeat in my hearing, It is no longer any use, Nader. I have sent many, many letters to humanitarian organizations on the subject of the Iraqi prisoners. We do not know who is responsible. No one can pinpoint the responsibility for that frightful occurrence. Is it the army high command, or the international disaster relief agency—in other words, in some sense, your uncle? Do we have to wait longer than eternity to know how these things happened?

Is this the reason why her relationship with my uncle Diya cooled, or was it for reasons I am ignorant of to this day? I was counting up my tears: a drop, two, three, scorching my cheeks and then plopping into the palms of my hands as if I had just come from a funeral. I would have preferred it if these two friends had not been here and were not observing me in this way. What the situation called for was some courage on my part: that I be amply obliging and decent in order to please and reassure them, and so that I would appear heroic in front of them. But I am a coward. I am afraid, in fact I am utterly terrified, and I don't know how to communicate successfully with them. Fine, I admit it: I am deceitful and crafty, and how long I have been throwing a sop to my mother! I've done it often, and a lot, so that she would feel good about me. No you don't! she says. You are clever; you are a little smarter than your father. But I don't know what it means when she says such things. I don't understand her. And so she picks up the thread of her insinuations.

You don't know where to set down your other foot, Nader.

And the first one, mother? It is still hanging there between the earth and the sky!

No—it is somewhere else altogether. You don't know how to reflect.

But I work like an ox and the routine they have over there is almost killing me.

And here, also, in this wing of the hospital, I'm feeling the same way. These people's gazes tear at my flesh just as that routine does. Their minds will not be at rest until I've thrown myself from the window to prove that I am the son who deserves her. I don't know what is to be said on such occasions. The whole thing is more than I can endure. Was the mother really there, was she a real part of the past? Or was the past entirely and completely the mother?

3

A mother and a son: two spies. One of them spies on the other at any hour, whether they are amidst the crowd or entirely on their own. What have you done to me, Suhaila? Where did you get this flair for cunning? Your war began before I was born and so I was afflicted with its seed from the start. I carried it with me in my glands and testicles, in my knees and forearms, so that I would be adapted to the climate, according to need. And you are a mother without ... and without. I chose for myself an innocent name so I could earn my bread and to all appearances be well-mannered and decent. I conceal my rebellions inside my throat. I bite down on them with my teeth so that they won't turn on them or on you, but what happens is that they turn directly against me.

My name is Nader Adam and I did not go off to the war, but the war stabbed me in the chest and back and never took its eyes off me. My war never dozed off. So, on the day you let loose the reins of your imagination to tell me those stories of yours, I had to make fun of you. I uncovered you from the beginning, and I uncovered him, too: my father. It amazed me, your proud way of concealing those secrets from me: your beating, your disfigurement, your teeth being broken, and your premature deafness in one ear. You were beat daily to the point where you became infatuated with being treated that way, insistent and passionate, as if it were the only way to earn your daily bread. And so I left you to imagine that I was better behaved than you had been accustomed to from me. I had learned to control my nerves and conceal myself in front of you, and in front of him. I would see him every day getting thirstier for that act until you became like pliant dough between his hands. Your wars, as the two of you anticipated, were what would spread peace and calm and security over me and over nearby homes of neighbors, close friends, and your wider social circle. And I was powerless before the two of you; I didn't know how to handle you. For the war was not outside as the two of you fancied, and as you compelled me to imagine. It was played out upon me, acted before me. I would see it in every inch of every room. "Suhaila"—all of Suhaila—that was what was now before me. I pulled myself together enough to stand up, and like someone in a trance I walked into her room.

When I saw her from behind the polished glass I did not scream. I didn't see spectral death peering smugly out from between the sheets, and I did not understand it as a presence that would soon be on hand to take her from me. I was strangely calm as I looked steadily at her. A tangle of medical instruments hung above her and lay beside her and upon her. I wasn't completely certain that it was even her, Suhaila, and I don't know—did I want her to be alive so that she could see me or dead so that she would finally become my mother, all mine? From this moment on, I decided, I would simply call her "her" so that things would not start seeming jumbled in my head. This sleeping woman, in this position—any lady could imitate her, any woman, or any mother in the world. But it isn't my mother, it isn't Suhaila.

Her gentle, pretty face, her face of long ago: that face had not been contorted with frustration or illness. To the contrary, it had been able—and it had remained able—to punish me. The right half of that face held the accusation and the left, its execution.

Two thin plastic tubes flowed with liquid medicine and nutrition into her arteries. She wore a mask attached to a long silvery oxygen tube fixed to the wall, closed with a plug and locked with a copper-colored catch. And so I couldn't properly see her cheeks, which looked as though they had sunk into two hollows. I saw her from behind the glass, a gown of hospital green covering half her ever-large chest, a white sheet over the rest of the inert body. Finally I entered the room, leaning for support on the sound of her slow breathing.

Eight

1

Had she been blind I would have exchanged positions with the woman in there so as to leave her in a position to long for me. I would be the one who would make tea for her, who would buy the newspapers, and give her the help she needed. I would be the one who watched closely and constantly to make sure that she was cleaned, who fed her with my own hand and left her feeling full. I would massage her toes, clip her nails, and experience the feeling that she was not at ease about my serving her. I would dress her in her nightgown brought from home and tuck her woolen shawl round her shoulders and reassure her that my version of chicken and macaroni would not disappoint her, and that I was capable of carrying her to her favorite chair. Well, no — I prefer not to be her cane, for the smell of motherhood seizes my head in its tight grip, and I feel the pain of it like a blow of the cane. I invent things to say, cute anecdotes, jokes. She withdraws more and I come nearer but she pushes me away until I am fully outside. This is my one opportunity to look at you as I want to, to give you everything you want. This is the best that it is in my possession to do, the best I do; I watch you, I talk to you and you remain silent. A flow of roses, carnations, narcissus, tiny buds on the point of opening, give off a slight perfume as I come nearer.

I come right up to the tubes and see the liquid moving slowly. I have not stopped looking straight ahead.

I can't see you clearly. Who are you?

By the time I was close to her I was trembling. I did not speak to her, did not breathe into her face. Her hands were open and spread apart as if she were about to fly away. Or dance. Her mouth changed shape, changed position, twisted to the right side a little, looking contorted. I knocked into the one chair beside the bed as I forced myself to move forward, even closer to her than I already was. I raised my head; the clouds looked low behind the window. In that moment my life appeared to me like the cloth covering that table in Montréal: the more she straightened and adjusted it the more weirdly it hung, and the dirtier it got the more she cleaned it and then draped it in front of my face so that I could not but see the holes and the stains. At that, I make it appear as though I am polite and even complimentary, and she does not know that part of my life which is wreckage.

Blind—no, no, I don't want that, but I do want her to see no one but me. I make a silent plea: if only she will not doubt and mistrust me, and remain blind, only so that she will live at my side, with me, that she will be in the other room, in the apartment next door, in the nearby city, like a phantom, a mirage, or a secret, for a particular reason or without it, with me there but always incapable of catching up with her. For she does not need me. Was all that happened to her a kind of retaliation, a punishment visited on me for my diseased intentions? I knelt there, next to her; I could feel the anger taking hold of me when I sensed my eyes overflowing with tears. I began to kiss her, once, twice, again and again, beginning from the dry palm that was so cold in the way hands are. I said, We will talk to each other. We did not do that before; and the time has come now to do the things we have to do.

Suhaila must make the first move. She must show the slightest movement, across her fingers, and I will press gently back, in the beginning, and then more strongly, and more firmly still. I repeat random words to her. Sun, moon, palm trees. My mouth kisses her palm; I wash it with my tears; I breathe between the spread-out fingers. Hands are the best channels for letting through any flow of words and warmth.

2

"Her voice went away completely," Blanche said, "and night before yesterday the danger returned. The doctors tried hard to preserve some life force there, any amount of energy that they could preserve, perhaps for your sake, Nader."

Al-Thuraya. The Pleiades. That is what I'll call you, instead of Nader.

These were Suhaila's words, one day, and she added softly, This is your first and real name. In the beginning we were thinking it would be a girl. She would be my companion, my dear companion, the moment she emerged from her place of safety. A girl-child whose beauty would come from the strength of the mix between me and your father, from the secrets of the kisses, the particular foods we ate, the shapes of our caresses, the hours of bathing at dawn as we fondled our tender bodies. Your father was sweet and gentle. That was in the beginning. He was a distant relative of my mother's and a part of him was still unspoiled. I don't remember when it was that that man went bad. When it was that he was corrupted. If you were to ask me, I would tell you that possibly it happened when the patrols to the north started. You don't believe that, of course, nor do I, but. . . .

She would pick up energy as she threw herself into telling that story. She would tell it time and time again, laughing shyly. Here she was, in her past. I want a girl that no one can steal from me to take to the barracks, she says. A little girl I can bob in my arms, lapping up her fresh flesh. As I'm bathing her, I look at her and it gives me pleasure. Those first, warm feces from which hot steam rises; as I remove them, all I can do is cry. I cried—I bawled and squealed—when faced with that extraordinary and simple thing on the second day after your birth. I saw the first, the primary, truth at that moment. I beg you, don't mock me, because this thing has nothing to do with either modesty or exaggeration. The story always returns, it's always retrieved and reclaimed; and I used to want to turn that story upside down. To turn her upside down, and kiss her, and smell her, and call her Thuraya. I love definition, and I retell all the details when you are with me and I'm wholly ensnared in the insolence of motherhood. But not even motherly insolence can embrace all of the aspects that enter your mind (and they are all true) when you are witnessing the first emergence of a child, coming from the furthest unknown, coming toward you, and you can touch it. And these reactions and needs are first and foremost for your own sake and not for the child's sake. This was the only way to create hope. Isn't that right, Nader?

That was what she used to say in the old days as we sat surrounded by a few candles with our glasses of red wine in front of us. She would revert further and further into the past.

To her health, al-Thuraya al-Nadera, the Rare Pleiades, to your health, Nader, Rare One. Imagine, I did not even cry as you were coming, but the tears were there on that night as I pushed Thuraya another millimeter from her position. The struggle of it bound me to her more. My backbone just about splintered. The doctor ladled her out. I talked to her in a low voice, lying there, ahh, if only you would spill out of my mouth instead of coming from that difficult place! If only it could happen that way ... the mouth would be perfectly acceptable. The story will be told again; it will be told a second time and a third but it will no longer sound strange. What of the mother? Why did she not lose her mind as she stumbled in the end on her anyway—on Thuraya? Why did what we had between us come to an end in the very moment of separation? It ended, Nader, and it is not possible to explain why that is so. Even though you were so long in coming I did not lose consciousness. I wanted to spy on myself as you sucked on me. How was it that my egg did not take the wrong path and so did not put me on the path to death? You slipped out with the rapture of music, yes by God. You did not wound me, as happened to friends of mine who gave birth. As for that blood, it warded the danger away from me, and away from you. I didn't wait a moment to take you into my arms. I passed you across my body with all the mucus and sweat and secretions you held. Nader, that was all I had; that was my savings book and my compensation strategy. As for the milk, my milk and my ample breasts, that is another story that I won't ever get tired of telling you, even if it consumes centuries of time.

3

I heard some sort of movement next to me, a hand patting my shoulder calmly. A practiced hand that was attempting to rouse me, an inflection as light as Suhaila's heartbeat. I don't know if it really seemed to me that I was hearing a woman's voice speaking Egyptian dialect or whether my hearing was simply distorted. I did not answer. I didn't say yes or no. I was squatting down, on my knees, encircling her with my arms and fighting off a man's pride. A son's pride. I felt that suddenly I had gotten very old; and this woman's shadow was blocking me from the light. She put her hand on my shoulder and bent down in front of me. At first she didn't say a word. I was tasting the saltiness of my tears. I grasped her arm and got to my feet. She was facing me. Her face was fresh and good; I felt myself on the point of collapse. She drew away her hand and saved me from confusion. She led me outside the room.

"Wajd. Dr. Wajd."

"Naam, ayy . . . Yes, hello."

I really could not utter much more than a moan, my chest heaving. I threw myself heavily into the first chair I saw. Blanche, Caroline! And there were faces I couldn't make out clearly, ones that I had not seen before. There was a tall, dark-skinned man who was smiling when my eyes fell on him and who startled me with his Iraqi speech.

"I'm Hatim and this is Narjis, my wife."

A woman was approaching me. She put out her hand with a pleasant spontaneity like her husband's. I tried to stand up but I could not quite manage it. They came closer and stood on either side of me. Exhaustion had dictated its terms to me by now. Wajd said in a friendly voice, "You're shivering, Nader. Are you cold?"

I looked over at my raincoat. Blanche brought it and draped it around my shoulders. The three or the four crowded round and tugged at the right sleeve. I gave in and put the coat on. I felt like I was going to crumble into tiny pieces and collapse at any minute. I did not dare to speak and I didn't know how in the end I would say anything at all. They moved away from me and I saw Caroline coming up, a paper cup in her hand.

"Drink it Nader, it is orange juice. We have other kinds, pineapple, lemon, peach, what do you prefer?"

"Shukran."

My hand was shaking as I lifted the flimsy cup to my mouth. I started coughing violently and droplets of juice spattered onto my face and coat. Caroline handed me the box of tissues and as I swiped at my face I began staring at all of these people who were now gathered in a semicircle around Dr. Wajd and at a distance from me. I touched my coat with a cautious hand. I sensed a voice shouting at me.

Come here! Come and stand in front of the mirror. Don't blink your eyes like that as if you are sad. No, I am not angry at you. Here, take it, try this one.

The coat was the color of wet sand and proved to be exactly my size, as if she had designed and sewed it for me without having to refer back to the precise measurements of my body, which she had memorized every time she embraced me in farewell and in greeting. She stood scrutinizing me.

The way you have of hurting me is beneficial most of the time, Nader. Do you know how it's useful? I will tell you. Whenever I think about blame, about blaming you, you chase me out of your world and you belittle my stories. You incite me, without meaning to, maybe, so that before you I appear weak. Yes, indeed. You like weak people—like him, like your father. You prefer those who turn round themselves and don't know how to stumble across a ray of hope. Fine. This is an important matter. You rescue me, in the end, from myself. Not from you.

Looking into my eyes, she adjusted the collar carefully. She was behaving as though she were a seasoned employee, a skilled seamstress at an exclusive clothier, and I was simply an obnoxious customer.

Yes. There, that's it, just right. The belt isn't necessary and you can pull it out from the back.

She fastened the coat so that it looked perfect and then began undoing the buttons calmly. She leaned her hand on my thigh as I am doing now and then knelt on the floor in front of me.

Go on, now, walk up and down, and leave those buttons undone. Doesn't that look nicer?

I hadn't noticed until this moment, among all of those friends, how dirty the coat had gotten and how dusty its color had become. She bought it as a gift for my twenty-fourth birthday. I had never had it cleaned. I kept it hanging next to my clothes and when she arrived for a visit I would wear it. And then I would leave it hanging there, mocking me as it swung back and forth in the closet. I would tug at it angrily and shove it to the very end of the wardrobe in the way that I shove my body back into the depths of the chair before slumping against the headrest. The raincoat was one of those old, classic models. My immediate associations with the style had to do with retired men from an earlier time in the century. It was expensive but I never liked it. Wearing it, I looked like an old man standing in a graveyard, receiving condolences for the loss of someone dear to my heart.

Nine

1

Detaching herself from the group, Caroline came forward.

"You'll come with me, Nader, after you have had a talk with Dr. Wajd. You can relax for a little while—I live alone. And we'll have a light supper. I'm not a great cook as Suhaila is, ya?"

She stopped and then, in a low voice, she went on. "You have to pull yourself together. Come on."

I lifted my head. What were they talking about? The look of apprehension on Caroline's face grew more anxious. Her voice was trembly and her words were a bit abrupt and disjointed.

"Thank you, Caroline. Today especially, I'd like to be alone."

She did not insist. She didn't even say another word. She walked away from me and in a moment came back carrying her bag. She put out her hand, a key ring dangling from it.

"Keys to the apartment, the mailbox, the storeroom, and the outside door."

I lifted my hand to take it, mumbling my thanks.

I won't be late, Nader. Here in Brighton, the American Film Festival begins today.

Hearing these words in my mind, I recalled how Suhaila would toy with the apartment door keys as she held them. It isn't an apartment, really. It's a single large room that she partitioned cleverly and appealingly. She put up a curtain of thick oriental fabric and over it she hung photographs, silver necklaces and traditional earrings from back home. Whenever the curtain was moved the silver jingled with a pleasant sound that echoes in my ears to this very moment.

Give me a chance to look at others in a darkened amphitheater, she says. I can sit there and not move, and this way I bring to light their scandalous secrets. I'm tired, Nader, of my secrets, the secrets I conceal from you most of all, my stupid trivial secrets, my sick secrets. For an hour and a half, two hours, I sit next to a man and a woman whom I do not know until the light and the silence and the outside world fade away. Your real mother fades away and the second one, whom I don't know and neither do you, triumphs. There I become a person who does not break out in a sweat over what is appropriate and what is not; who is not seized by conflicting, contradictory feelings that I cannot control or overcome. I become a spectator and that is all. Why are you afraid for me to cross those barriers, my dear? I have gotten tired of occupying the lead role in whatever is at hand. Yes, Nader, in that hidden and out-of-the-way spot I become another woman, not the mother and not the wife, not the free woman and not the slave, neither the Iraqi nor the foreigner. I am no longer a mature, sedate, self-possessed woman. And you are always insistent when I go out: Be careful, mother, you say, not to lose the key. It would be easy to lose since you hate carrying a purse or a wallet. And put that money deep in your pocket. Things might slip out when you take off your coat.

But my words only provoke her more and she is thoroughly annoyed with me. She answers in an irritated voice, telling me that she can't bear and won't stand for orders and instructions like this. But I keep talking and I don't let her finish what she's saying. I stand in front of the door, blocking her way.

It isn't a matter of the key or the wallet, mother, but of you. When you leave the cinema you return here shaken and hypnotized, and I can barely even talk to you. As if you haven't even left your seat in that big theater even though we both know perfectly well that everything taking place in there is deception—meaning, it's nothing.

Then her eyes take on an odd gleam and she answers in a firm voice: Nader, how can I find a way to make you see that this nothing has an appeal that it is impossible to understand rationally? I am in the most urgent need of the kind of emotions that these nothings produce. In those halls, by means of the theater—and here is the role of the show itself—I am really and truly me. Just stop this and let me go. You just cannot be exactly *you* always and in every place or situation.

2

I had to notice and acknowledge to myself that Suhaila, now, was a sweeter being than ever before, even if she did not sense this. She was the one responsible now for this face. She had been in an odd state of perplexity that had gone on for some time, and this had confused all of us in the beginning—me, the Vietnamese driver Ken, and the French lawyer Monsieur Alain. This bewildered demeanor of hers seemed incomprehensible for someone of her age but she didn't pay any attention to our concerns. Then, this might be her last opportunity to be my mother—and to be herself—without asking for any help or aid, not from me and not from the women whom she had called, in all of her letters, the loved ones.

I calmed down, overcome by a sense of clarity and peace that were inexplicable since I had had no reassurance: I had not been able to stand up and walk over to the circle that closed and opened before me as faces and forms came and went. Only Caroline went on standing by herself at a distance, for everyone else was speaking in Arabic. Her head was bowed and she seemed to be staring at an empty space that was expanding little by little. She raised her hand, wiped her eyes, and blew her nose. If only I were able to go over to her, I thought, and put my hand on her shoulder and thank her with my touch and not with words. Apparently wearied of standing, she fell into a nearby chair. I observed the backs in front of me each one looking very different from the next. Voices were hushed and the same gestures kept reappearing.

Narjis and Dr. Wajd were the most talkative. I took off my coat, put it to one side and began to dry my sweat. One of them should turn in my direction, call me, and come over and talk to me; this waiting was the worst thing possible in my present state of mind. I had not had any practice at this and I had no energy except to think about the urgent duties that were to be put before me.

When I got up to find the bathroom everyone's head turned toward me but even then we spoke only with our hands. My face in the mirror looked toxic, as if darkened with the aftereffects of poison. My eyes were puffy, my nose red, and my lips chapped.

Will she live so that I will talk to her once again? An additional day, a fragment of a quarter of a day, an hour completely unrelated to what would happen next, a minute, an instant that would fortify me and draw me to her? She would begin from my neck, she always kisses me there, she calls that sunken spot magharat hanan, a little love grotto. An eternal, never-ending task awaited her but with a push of my hand I would end it, scolding her. I never could bear that which filled her eyes and I would want to blast it away completely.

Mother, I'm too old for such things. I wish you would stop— please stop!

I would go away—and I would leave her talking to herself. No one knows what she was thinking. But soon I would hear various sounds coming from the bathroom. She would begin there; she would empty the cabinets slowly, scrape the dry soap along the edge of the bathtub, polish the mirror and the basin and the washing machine, change the towels, and begin mopping the floor. She was always entranced, even seduced, by the soap bubbles, the fragrances of jasmine and musk. That was how she would talk herself through long spells of anger and tension that would suddenly leave her to craft a smile on her face which a little before had been almost lost forever. She would not stop until her hand was swollen and blistered. When I tried to go in to her she would wave her arm up and down to stop me.

Those I'm speaking with, they're better than you are. I'm saying hello to them, welcoming them here. They are not as sly, not as distant as you and your father are.

Everything she held in her hands became an easy and delicious task. She worked as if she were singing or dancing, for she was blessed with a small body, thin and short, a build like a fan of feathers — light, soft, moving in all directions with ease.

Listen, Nader. To lighten my tension and unease, from inside my body come a dancer's moves freeing themselves to help me. I don't know where they were hiding, believe me I don't know. Before now, I never learned to accommodate them; in fact, it was always the other way around. The more practice I have at something the more lost I am and the more I lose. It is better for these movements to emerge of their own accord. We slice bread, swallow food, dry the laundry on the line, and cover our bodies in coats. These are movements that show us how to face death so that he does not dare turn his face to us. We leave death bewildered about us, unable to find a way to reach us — he doesn't know how to even begin his work. Dance is what keeps death guessing, eternally confusing him — even if they are wretched steps and movements like those I make.

3

She used to sing, too. Her singing would reach me as I reached the bottom step. Her voice was hoarse from smoking and coughing, from the late nights and all of her pacing during the day. Her voice is not pretty but it carries an edge; it mocks you. About her voice she says, It is made of the tobacco and the aged wine I consume at Caroline's and Blanche's. You know, Nader, I'm an Aries. A ewe, that is. Ferial is the same sign. We used to fight some of the time, and your father would separate us with an attempt at a joke: I am the ram, so now shut up. Ferial would answer him in a low voice, Ajib shlon araft? Amazing, how did you know? As she said this she would let out a sturdy laugh. But I love goat — its milk and cheeses, she would add. This animal is the one that triumphs in the end, even if its victory is a slim one.

Suhaila devoted herself steadily to those consumables on the few evenings we spent together. She was more interested in them than I could bear and I would show no admiration for her voice or her way of singing and dancing. I would get angry and feel embarrassed when I had to see her dance in front of me. Her image would abandon the realm of mothers to join that group of women of dubious pursuits, and this scared me. What if, one day, she were to present some man to me and tell me he was her man? What would I do if that were to happen? But that's something she would only talk about sarcastically.

Imagine, Nader, imagine that I did not take your father with knife and fork, or one bite at a time, but rather took all of him in one gulp like snakes do. That I swallowed him whole and he settled inside of me. Where, I don't know, though — and this is what confuses me.

She drains her glass and mocks my father again, makes fun of the man and of me too so that I get even more frightened. She was not like this before, when we were still in Baghdad, or even after that when we first arrived in Paris and lived in my uncle's apartment temporarily. Back then, she was not capable of any conversation however fleeting or simple and no matter with whom. When I would say to her, Mother, the weather is pleasant today, let's go walk in the garden by the building, she would turn her head away and not answer. She would not know how to respond or how to put things or ideas in their appropriate places. The words would come out from between her teeth slowly and with effort as if she were dragging them in from a very distant location. This would put me into agony but I would press her. And then I would feel as if she were answering for my sake, and only for my sake, to keep me from becoming even more upset.

I don't know anything, Nader. There is another person inside of me, who walks and breathes, goes into the bathroom and washes and goes to bed but doesn't sleep. I am chasing after my self and I want to meet her again but I can't do it. I can't bear the idea that I have lost that self forever. I will go on waiting for it, Nader, do you understand me? I beg you not to get angry with me if I am unable to make you happy or to put myself and those around me at ease. Do you know, I feel that I am not right but I'm not wrong, either, I am not afraid and it isn't that I don't care. I feel like the strengths

I had in the beginning, in Iraq, have left me and will never come back. Even if I was passive there, as you and your uncle say. When I eat I don't have any sensation; is it wood I'm eating or garbage? Everything is something else, every person who meets me is less, smaller, huger than I imagine the person to be. Nothing has a single perfect form and there is no question that has an answer and there is no good answer, one that's ordinary, mundane. I don't know if I've been expressing what was inside of myself, really, fully the way I feel. It's easy to make me out as a liar in all of this and more, but I know one thing which remains the strongest to this moment and you must believe it: when you are with me I don't feel miserable. That's right. Yes, Nader, this is the one truth in my life. But I don't know if it is helpful in any way. Even if I've been wrong, don't confuse me or embarrass me, and don't accuse me by saying that that lawyer was flirting with me. Did you notice that? He is just a nice man, but what is the point in this whole subject anyway?

But she is my mother. And she is more involved with me than I can bear, and I don't even show any pleasure at her Iraqi songs, which cause me unbearable distress. We're sitting at the little table and she seizes my hand and raises it to her mouth and kisses it, surprise kisses on the palm, and I yank my hand away immediately, disgusted. Her voice falls in droplets onto me and so do her sudden tears; for she doesn't know when she will stop talking about him, my father, and she doesn't listen to me, either. I let her talk on while I follow the figure of Elizabeth, my English friend, in her new dress. I am not able to distinguish very clearly between the young fellow infatuated with the love of that very devout girl and the love of my mother toward the last person in her life, because it does come into my mind that she still sees me as a person in the middle of the road, someone who is between son and husband, between the real person I am in front of her and that absent one who throws himself into captivity and escape. And she was so very confident of her issue that she would stay up all night, in front of her innumerable files on the prisoners in every site on earth, while the driver, Ken, would bring her some novels and promise that one day he would fill her in about him and his mother, in Laos and Cambodia, and about the gypsies and the native Indians.

She was afraid to get too close to the Arab prisoners and specifically the Iraqis. She knew that if once she were to enter there, she would be captured, spellbound; her throat, she knew, would become congested with blood and curses. Coming back to the apartment, she would rearrange the area that was mine as I followed her like a tethered bull going round in circles as one year cycled into the next. This tethered bull never came to a stop, neither in the cold nor in the heat.

The door opens quietly. Dr. Wajd comes in and finds me standing here in this state of mind. She comes up to me.

"Are you calm enough now so that we can talk a little?"

I turned. My calmness was only a result of some sort of aversion I had to all of these people.

"She—is she dying?"

"Where do you get these dark thoughts from? Not everyone who goes into a coma is at the end."

"And—"

"Should we talk here?" She put out her hand to me. "Please, if I may." She took my hand as she opened the door. It was a motherly gesture and my immediate reaction was to sense a danger signal in the air. I slipped my hand out of hers. We walked along together. I was thinking of all the surprises waiting for me. Was the end near? And would she parcel out the cataclysm in installments to me? Our friends sit silently, each one submerged in private thoughts. A new face, unknown to me an hour ago, surprised me. The owner of the face rose and came to me, taking me in her arms with a gesture that truly flustered me. She was sobbing. Dr. Wajd introduced her.

"This is Asma, friend of your mother's. She is the one who told us everything that happened. Haven't you noticed that the number of friends is growing?"

Asma's voice had that fervent Iraqi ring to it.

"God's mercy is wide, Nader, and you are a believing man, my dear. Come on, come sit here, come over here next to me."

I was dragging my feet leadenly. I sat down beside her. My emotions were a jumble. And every new face pushed my emotional reactions as far inside of me as could be and then I had to recompose myself. My embarrassment and tension were at their height as Wajd concentrated her look on me. Blanche sat down next to Caroline. Lifting my head, I saw Narjis and Hatim. They were silent. All of these emotions told me nothing. Wajd must report right now, she must talk to me. What was she waiting for? She approached me and I made a space for her next to me. I swung my head to look at her. In real fear.

"Now, really, please, I'm listening, tell me what you know."

Wajd smiled and the conversation began in a way I hadn't anticipated.

"Suhaila told me you tried to put together a band when you were at university, and that you write a diary, or memoirs. And do you still love photography? I've seen some of the photos she has. She'll say to me, Nader's better than anyone else at getting candid shots. And, all right, before this or beyond that, you're an electronic engineer; but clearly it isn't just numbers that appealed to you, and that's a brave move on your part.

> Life is not the nightmares
> that come to us unbidden
> in the middle of the night as we sleep
> The nightmares are what you
> yourself will tell me right now.

How often Suhaila repeated these lines of poetry in my presence!"

I was getting more uncomfortable, swallowing my saliva with difficulty.

> "No, this isn't me but someone else
> I'm not capable of standing this much pain
> For the sake of someone the moist breeze blows
> For the sake of someone the dawn light is rosy
> We know nothing, and it is all the same"

I didn't listen to the rest of the lines. She had memorized them only because my mother had repeated them so often in front of her.

They were my lines, ones I had written down when I first started university. But Suhaila had come to repeat them instead of me.

I sensed the seriousness in Wajd's voice. She spoke as though she were tutoring a little boy. I sensed equally that all of these women here were poised to play exactly this role. I wasn't used to this. But I wasn't capable of steering clear of it. They would judge me based on the ten years—or was it twelve—that I had spent walking atop a tightrope, next to my father, unable to figure out the enigmas that made him up. Meanwhile, Suhaila grew more distant from me year after year, so that I retraced my steps to the beginning, fearful all the while that I would never truly encounter the person she is, as long as I appeared—in her eyes and likely in the eyes of all of these people—unworthy of confidence. I dried my tears and suppressed some things I might have said that had nothing to do with any of them but only with her. I really wanted to be alone with her, and far away from them, in case she were to suddenly awaken and launch into words of blame as Wajd was doing now. I did not seem to even have any perspiration left inside my body. Not only was I covered in dried-up sweat but I discovered that the shirt I had on was showing signs of serious wear: I noticed how worn the fabric of the sleeve was when I opened the cuff and pushed it up. Suhaila does not like such doings in the least.

Nader, you aren't a teenager now! You just can't—

It was as if she carried around her reprimands in the pockets of her nightgown or her coat, and whenever she needed to, she just dipped in there and ladled one out to me. Where's your necktie— that would make your Adam's apple a little less visible. It is so very prominent on that neck of yours.

But right now it is Wajd who is going on and on. "Worry and depression—all very common among people, all people, especially women who are on their own. Such women are contributing in a major way to the generally high statistics on depression in the population. Being alone, feeling one's needs frustrated, having no steady income, and so not enough money to be comfortable, and then add to that the plunge in self-esteem. All of it doubles the pressure on one's nerves. Moreover, your mother is without a permanent partner—and then what about your father possibly being a prisoner or missing or … and what about your country being ostracized, maybe. The violence Suhaila faced from your father, I don't know if she told you the details or not—all of that caused her to suffer nervous and behavioral problems. She wasn't working with me on her problems for very long, because very soon we became friends, close friends. This was my mistake, of course, more than it was hers. It's very common in psychiatric medicine. I was the one who failed, failed with her, because I shrank the distance between therapist and patient. The funny thing is that I began seeking her advice on some of the issues I have."

"And now, doctor?" I said it impatiently, and then came to an abrupt stop somewhat nervously once she could hear the rising tone of my voice, which caused everyone to turn in my direction. But it was as if Wajd had anticipated this, for she wasn't in the least surprised, it seemed. She simply went on in a low voice, and I felt ashamed of myself.

"Suhaila didn't see it as anything serious. But her sensitive nature was causing discomfort for her and also making those around her uncomfortable and uneasy. When she got to know the French writer Tessa Hayden who was involved in writing for the theater, she wondered whether, since she is the daughter of a major Iraqi theater impresario, performing a role or two on a French stage might conceivably allow her to become a different person. She did some folk performances for small audiences and worked with a few Arab and Iraqi directors based in Europe. She seemed possessed by the spirit of ancient Iraqi dance, from the rituals of the Sumerians to the dances performed to this day. She considers dance a means of liberation and a way that she can exorcise the rejection and ostracism directed at her, first and foremost, and also at her country. Tessa became a source of support and fair treatment to her as her life was changing direction in this way. But she continued to lack the language, although she was not too concerned about it. She went on repeating in our hearing and in Tessa's that dance was her language and it encapsulated her sense of modesty and humility. It was her humble gesture toward her fellow human beings. It was dance that made art the point of universal convergence. She ended some of those evening performances with a gleeful and spur-of-the-moment touch. She believed that dance strengthened her resistance or her immunity to the harshness she had been suffering and that it gave a person more of the strength one needs to make the choice between life and self-destruction. That's why she has been so addicted to it."

I all but pounded my head against the wall in front of me as I seized Wajd's hand and shook it insistently. My voice reflected my constricted throat as I burst out.

"Doctor, I know what was confronting her and it is what continues to confront all of us. I hope that you can see that now I do want to know. Only now, in fact. Do you believe she can get beyond the danger stage, the condition Blanche called the zero point? What does all this mean? Please, please tell me."

"Along with the dance, she was searching and asking and taking things down and sending letters to humanitarian organizations. She knew there was no point in any of it but she went on doing it. She didn't know who was responsible for what happened then and what is happening now. The terror came very close to her and she acted according to its dictates most of the time. She would get lost in her own thoughts and wouldn't listen to me or to the advice of her doctors and friends. She would not follow anyone's guidance."

I could not make out exactly what Dr. Wajd was trying to get at. This conversation had gone beyond my capacities. But she went on with a patience that vied with my despair. Outmatched it, in fact.

"Of course she was treated successfully for the high blood pressure, and on a regular basis. But her condition has to do first with age, and also with how very strong her reactions to things are. And even though we—her close friends—we know how much care she takes with the basic demands of health by walking and exercise and reasonable nutrition, yet she has not been able to stop that awful smoking, and—"

Suddenly she stopped. She seized my wrist. I felt as though I stood accused, as she followed my reactions with her eyes. Now here she was opening the police report file; now here I was, appearing before her bench and before all of them: an outlaw son. Had I played my role as I ought? Or had it been purely a matter of obligation and duty? Had I reached adulthood—the age of right guidance, as Arabs say—in the gaze of these women who were Suhaila's loved ones? Had I become an equal citizen such that I could obtain their approval of me, at the outset at least? For I had lost the distinction of being the one whom she would recognize and take to her breast. Now the issue before me was straightforward and complex, simple and difficult at the same time: had I come here solely to strengthen the confidence held in me, confidence in myself?

4

She had deceived me, malingering. And she would deceive me more if she were to lose consciousness before she could hear the rumor of my arrival. I had not come solely for her sake but for mine as well. I had not been capable of ruling out this journey for myself, forbidding myself to take it for the sake of Leon and for the new child we were awaiting and for all of the questions we would encounter concerning this and that and whatever else we might have to face. Wajd still had hold of my wrist and the darkness was spreading inside my eyeballs. I felt as though I would drop in a faint if I were to remain here even another minute in front of these rows of watching eyes.

"Naam . . ."

Wajd did not take her eyes from me as I repeated, in a voice that was growing louder, "Naam, now Wajd, tell me, what is going on?"

There was silence for a few moments. I murmured, "Yes, Doctor, I am the ugly son, the harsh, self-loving, disobedient son. What we are obliged to do now is exchange roles, in front of you and of all of them. Hmm?"

I went on, my voice now capable of a stronger, louder presence. "Yes, *me*, a word not like any other, not like *her* or *him* or *them* or even *all of you*, all of the women here. Rather, *me*, I, ahh, yes, this is perfectly evident a thing for all of you. You are her friends, women and men, all of you are her friends."

She tried to stop me with her own stillness. She was trying to protect me from something but I didn't know what the essence of it might be.

"Nader! It's neither you nor her nor us. Why do you talk this way about yourself and others? Why?"

"It's owing to her. To my wife. And it's probably thanks to me, too — I'm her son. And thanks to the country, the father and captivity, and the war. It's thanks to insanity and stupidity."

I stopped suddenly. I would have liked it better had there been a megaphone in my hand so that my voice would pierce every corridor there.

"I want out of here. I don't want to see you. This is hideous and it is more than I can stand."

Wajd stood up and all the rest did likewise. Quietly Hatim came up to me, grasped my arm and stepped closer. He touched my cheek and laid his hand on the crown of my head. I sensed that wafting from him was a special fragrance of fatherhood. He was a father and for a moment, I had the sensation that he must be a new sort among fathers. He must be a good, sound father, truly there, not a mere image in one's head. There, in his care, his hands on me, I trembled, my body expressing the state of utter haplessness I had reached. I was in a stupor; he spoke again.

"I know, Nader. I know."

I buried my head in his chest. I was not embarrassed by the rising sound of sobs that went on and on. Why had Suhaila made me love the two extremes of yes and no? Like a peasant, planting seeds only to uproot the green shoots later. Why? Why?

Hatim pulled me away from the group. He was holding my palm in his warm grip. Our hands conversed amiably and acknowledged a mutual understanding as complete as could be. I would be a better listener if I stayed silent; I would know then what he wanted from the touch of his hand. This was after I had reckoned that if he were to utter a word I would hear it more accurately than would the women over there. As I sensed that I grew comfortable with him. His steps were strong and firm.

"Do you want to sit down apart from them or would you prefer that we go to a café somewhere nearby?"

"I can't take any more reproaches, Ustadh Hatim."

"Please, call me Hatim. Just Hatim."

I lifted my head to look at him. He was quite a lot taller than me. I saw his face in the patch of light coming from the large window at the far end of the corridor. He had an attractive look to him, and his features were telling me that he would understand me. I don't know why I had already intuited that he would make no accusations against me nor would he issue an unjust ruling. He would not cast the responsibility for Suhaila's illness onto my shoulders alone. His gaze was steady and concentrated, emerging from his light-colored eyes: were they brown or gray? I could not tell. Because of this and many other sensations he did not remind me of any of the acquaintances or friends of my father. Yes, he was Iraqi, and he was similar-looking enough to many other Iraqis, but he did not resemble my father. I imagined him as the shaykh of a tribe from the south of Iraq, wearing a zabun covered by a woolen abaya encasing his athletic form. As I tilted my head higher his elegant hand was poised to signal for quiet from the entire group. Everyone was paying as much attention to him as I was. I saw him as a man of nature, of the desert, born among the sands, with the ease desert men have in their walk, their gestures, and the flow of their movements from one stance, one action, to the next. To me he looked like a man of courage, more courageous than I was, to be sure, and more courageous than my mother, than all of the women here. His courage would reach over to me, lending me the strength to pull myself together in his presence without it causing any feeling of grievance or resentment on my part. He is a person who smiles through his eyes; he understands what I mean without my having to say it directly. For the first time here, I smile, as I hear what he is saying.

"Come, let's go to the café which is very close by; let's go have some cold beer and refresh our eyes with the pretty girls. Don't tell me that you don't like such things. Looking at young women on the sly attracts you, doesn't it, even if you're standing right next to your wife and even if she's a beauty queen . . . hmm?"

We headed out, Narjis's voice in our wake.

"Hatim—just a second, please."

We stopped and turned as if of one accord to wait for her. It was the first time I had seen her walking straight toward me. For the first time I truly saw her. Her beauty would take your breath away and make you overlook so many things, so many of the bothers and concerns that surround us all and would normally lead anyone to despair. Suhaila had not said much about this pair. There had been one sentence in one of her letters: If World War Three breaks out, these two friends will be the safe haven and shelter.

They surrounded me on either side. The compassion and warmth that they radiated enveloped me in a sense of peacefulness.

"Hatim, if the two of you have to go to a café then why don't we simply take him home? We can have dinner, and talk, and later on I can take him to his flat. And if he wants to he can stay with us tonight."

She was speaking cautiously but in a voice full of emotion, her Lebanese dialect flavored with beloved Iraqi tones. As I heard Narjis speak, Layal appeared in front of my eyes. Gazing at her face, I was more bashful at her beauty now than I had been at first. She looked contented, or something more than that. Joyous at something—her husband, herself, her friendship for Suhaila. Her happiness dispelled the anger that I had not yet been able to fully shake off. They were awaiting a response from me.

"It isn't possible today. Perhaps tomorrow, or another day. I'd like to remain alone today. Thank you."

They smiled at me. I admired very much the picture they made as lovers, as they moved and conversed in that very quiet manner. I even felt their happiness seep into me. They aren't like us, like Sonia and me. But is joy prohibited inside hospitals? No sooner do we enter the dark corridors than orders are issued—from what source I don't know—commanding us to bitterness and grief.

Ten

1

At that moment, Blanche, Wajd, and Asma came into view. Caroline was the last to appear, walking slowly far behind. They gathered around us, a closed circle. I pictured them in my mind as female soldiers at the ready, fully equipped and perfectly capable of vanquishing the enemy: Suhaila's illness and my helplessness in front of it. My morale rose as I looked at them. I was beginning to feel that they were capable of defending me as well, and indeed of defending life itself. Each one of them looked as if, unbeknownst to the others, she had made a private vow to defend life. How is it that those women are so able to draw on their imaginations to invent whatever it is they are able to do in order to guarantee that Suhaila will emerge once again, from whatever place she is in, on any day and at any moment, and in the company of any one of them? Life appeared at my side: strong, vigorous. Each of us wants to accept and embrace it in our own way. I listen to the hidden-away laughter that issues from them so gracefully and sweetly to grant me a measure of peace.

With all of them as his audience, Hatim made an announcement. "Dinner is chez nous tomorrow." He stretched his head a little outside the circle and his warm voice added a few words in Iraqi-accented English.

"Miss Caroline, tomorrow we will eat Iraqi food and I will be cooking. Even if we are speaking Arabic—everyone in the group speaks French and English as well. Don't worry, and please, do come, for the sake of Suhaila and Nader."

She was standing there nodding her head. She came up to me, put out her hand and we shook. She seemed to be hesitating between going and staying.

"I put some vegetables and fruits in the refrigerator, and milk, eggs, and bread. The flat is clean but it is quite chaotic. I could not do anything about the papers and books and newspapers. It is exactly as it was when Suhaila left it. This might be a bit painful for you, but it was not. . . . If you feel in need of anything, do ring me at home, even if it is very late."

Even before extending her hand, Blanche jumped into the conversation. "So then, day after tomorrow, lunch or dinner will be at my place. What do you prefer, Nader?"

"Thank you, Blanche. I must stay here, even if she is not aware that I am here. We'll see quite a bit of each other from now on. I'll be here all of the time now instead of all of you."

My eyes filled again but I kept myself together. Hatim patted me on the shoulder.

"I'm not able to say thank you, but that's what I've been feeling inside at every single moment. In Canada, and on the airplane, and here among you. I don't know . . . naam, believe me, I don't know."

∽

I turned to Dr. Wajd as if I had newly become a completely different person.

"I'm sorry—please excuse me. Apparently I wasn't very firmly in control of my emotions. Five hours of flying, seven hours' time difference, the night before I didn't sleep at all, and her—when I saw her it was as if she had come to an agreement with herself to be against me. You as well, all of you, I felt you were all against me. I was expecting something to happen, not a miracle, not a stroke of luck; I don't know what to call it, perhaps it is something completely futile.

Maybe I felt as if she would lift her hand and slap me the moment I touched her. Now, Doctor, I am back to repeat my question and what I'm worried about: Is she going to improve? Is there any hope?"

Wajd stepped closer. She took on the tone and lingo of the medical profession.

"Right, Nader. There are two sides to it, this condition. I am very sorry to tell you this four days into it: she is in a medium-intensity coma. This in itself is not such a bad sign, but how long will it continue? To be honest, we do not know. Most likely she will come out of it and will begin to show some signs of activity. It is possible that she will regain consciousness but with substantial losses. We are not able to pinpoint the extent of loss at the present time. Not until she has completely regained consciousness. And that takes considerable time."

My lips were trembling.

"But what are the possible losses, Doctor?"

"Paralysis in the limbs, which is a possibility but not at all certain. In any case, her life will not go back to being what it was. She'll need intensive care—constant, continuous—and long treatment, and she'll get physical therapy—that's amply available everywhere. This aspect of it does not worry me at all."

"And . . ."

"She'll require therapy to train her how to regain the normal functions that she will have lost. In most cases that takes months or perhaps even longer."

"Will she know me?" I could not keep the pleading out of my voice.

Everyone started to murmur gently, exuding everything from encouragement to disgust at the way I was insisting. Wajd responded. "Yes and no."

As always: no and yes. Does that make sense?

"How is that, Doctor? Please, I have to insist on hearing more details."

"Most likely she will regain her consciousness but that in itself might take some time. She will be able to recognize you, and everyone, but she might make mistakes at first. This will be the hardest thing for you. For all of us. And for her most of all. What I fear, Nader, and I say this in good faith, is that she might have no desire to get better."

I was stunned. I caught my breath at her answer and had to pause but then I went on. "And what is the second possibility?"

"The greater likelihood is that she will know you and others, perhaps without any difficulty, as if she is steadily and completely regaining her consciousness, but then it might recede, become blurred, and she would leave us once again."

"But how could you have come to the conclusion that she might have no desire to get well? Is an invalid in her condition able to take a decision such as that?"

Everyone smiled but their smiles looked pained. I didn't understand the secret behind these grimaces.

"Love, Nader. I am not going to say any more because I don't want you to get angry all over again."

I heard Caroline's voice again. I had not been aware until this moment that she was still standing apart from us as if she already understood everything that had taken place and was still taking place between us. Now she came close enough to face me directly.

"I wrote to you and I said that she is plagued by a sense of abandonment. Rejection. But you did not write back, Nader. It is not that we want you to take on more than you can stand. And it may well be that not too much time has gone by. It may not be too late, you know."

Like a thunderbolt, Asma intervened, looking as though she intended to fling her arms around me.

"Nader, my son, everything is written, and this is Suhaila's destiny. I'll take you to the mosque, my dear. Pray there and offer your hopes and pleas for her. I'm sure that you don't even have a mosque over there in Canada, do you? And by God, every day I turn to the Creator of the Heavens to take away this distress from her and from our country. She'll get better, and just about now you'll see it, my dear. Wa hassa tishuf ayni. Shnu hiya ghayr raghba?! What do you mean, Doctor, that she doesn't want to get well? Your mother's a strong one, she'll come out of it and she'll be standing tall. She'll come back, Nader, believe it, by God's mercy. His mercy is vast."

Blanche's voice was calm. "Do you know, every day before coming here I go to chapel in the Latin Quarter. I light candles of all colors in her name. I kneel and say prayers for her and for our people there. And when I come here afterward I hear that things are better than they were yesterday. I can't imagine Suhaila ending in this way. I know her, we all know her. She has a will that has never budged. No, Dr. Wajd, what is this hypothesis of yours? How did you come by it? She's never come to despair, she's never lost hope in God's mercy. She would say, Despair is always there, but this is not the time for it. Isn't that so, Hatim?"

Blanche turned to Narjis then and addressed her before anyone else could speak. "Tell Nader about her, perhaps this is more necessary now than it seemed earlier."

Narjis turned to me. In her I sensed an ability both simple and powerful to ease the deep pain Wajd had left in me. Her words brought back the reasonable self that I had nearly lost.

"Tomorrow, Nader, we'll talk in more detail. It's a mistake to discuss everything at once. Don't burden yourself with a heavier load than you can bear and don't let your spirits get hopelessly entangled in all of this. Suhaila has an ability to endure more than you or we can imagine. It's in her power to make treatment possible and successful, and to get to that point quickly. The first stage, of course, will not be easy, but she is capable of making a safe escape from this. I won't talk any more about it now, because you need to get some sound sleep, but I know Suhaila. To put it simply, she will not permit herself to remain immobilized."

Hatim's voice was firm and convincing as he put the finishing touches on what Narjis had said. "She's a fighter, Nader. All right, now, get your bags and let us drop you off on our way. It's late now to have a beer and spy on the pretty girls. And anyway, she is sleeping."

"Thank you, Hatim. But I want to stay with her, alone."

Eleven

1

I hoist my two pieces of luggage and head toward her room. I have never before had to endure pain as heavy as this. Yet it is an old pain, drawn from earliest childhood and from the few feet of ground on which I stand. It is a pain that I drag behind me; and so it never leaves me. And after they have all gone away I stand before her. Alone with her. The nurses have been very kind and pleasant, very generous with their welcoming gestures and smiles. They brought me a light supper, most likely her supper, but I didn't give it a glance. My insides were empty but I was not hungry. After they gave up hope of me, they entered into conversations among themselves. Danielle's ill dog and Charlotte's insolent cat which had made her lover Thierry flee from the sight of massed cat hair on plates and sheets. As for the third one's man—I don't recall that nurse's name now—he had abandoned her to sally off with her closest friend. Every so often, suddenly becoming aware of my presence, they would turn away from me. They came in to her from time to time, performing their duties with expertise, turning to me now and again with sympathy etched on their faces, for me, who still does not know why he cried so much in front of them all. All of those women.

If your father had cried one time, just once, Suhaila always said, then he would have been spared. He would have been spared to enjoy the rest of his days in better shape, happier. But he was a stone.

She cried in his place. I don't know if he deserved this, she would add. Did he deserve to have me replace him in this, or in that? Who can stand in for someone else?

She glanced right and left; we were in the kitchen, making food together.

I have this tale in my head: that we got married in order to act out a play and put it on record in front of my father's theater. His shows were dwindling with every day that passed. That was because of the censorship. We are such different people, Nader, which can be beneficial as long as one doesn't destroy the other. We differed on small issues as well as the big and complicated ones—and then he would get it into his head that whatever the issue was, it had no merit in the first place. He had arrogance enough to allow him to picture himself as the most worthy of human beings. Pride of that sort is a defect that eats up the one who has it: suddenly such a one no longer sees the other, no longer sees us—and yet he is there all the time, watching us. His first act is to punish himself cruelly. Poor wretch. That's your father, Nader.

"Why don't you go and walk around the city for a bit?" suggested Charlotte gently. "Is this your first visit, Monsieur?"

My mood had improved slightly. She was, after all, still alive. But I shook my head. Charlotte pressed. "She's sleeping. Go, and don't worry. Her condition is stable. This is the fourth day, and as long as she is putting up resistance, she'll come out of it, perhaps for your sake."

She laughed in a way that reminded me of children's laughter. I gave her a big smile. This set off a chain reaction of smiles between us. What I yearned for, though, was to rest my head against that body, to give her a kiss, to talk to her on my own with nobody else there, as it had been in the past, and to stretch out next to her without demanding her love. I used to tell lies for her sake so that the image she had of me would not be shaken and I would retain my status as an amiable, kind son who remained first in importance in her eyes. She would find me out, though. No one was better at expressing qualms about me, and I hated the way I would feel so stupid and trivial in her presence. I would try, and I had always tried, to hide my sneaky side from her. But she was always impeccably sweet and sympathetic. She would take me in her arms as if I were still a child, and that would make me all the more uncomfortable. Then I would get angry and imagine that she no longer had any need for me, and that all of my scheming had led to nothing more than a beaming smile on her face as she looked at me. And now, here she is in front of me. I see her and I am grateful to her. At this moment, she is here, present to me more than she has ever been at any time in the past and ensconced in a new space of quiet, calmer than she ever was. There are no guarantees, when it comes to her, except when she is thus, suspended between my tears and my fear. I was this sure of her: as if the two of us were not at all good for each other except in those very things that were the means of separating us one from the other.

2

Her hands are limp as the liquid pumps its way in. It embarrassed me too much to ask Blanche or Wajd about how she urinated. I observed, I searched, but still I did not fully take in anything. It was all very practical and coherent and unassailable, but for me it was unknown territory. It was as if the illness alone had allowed her to trump me, by means of the promise she had made in my presence one day.

I am fortunate to have you, Nader—but you, no. You don't see things in the same way. I put you before me, before everyone, and yet you are always in such haste, never pausing. You have turned flinty, as stone-cold as he has always been. You are al-Thuraya, the Pleiades, and I send signs to you hoping you will understand and respond. It's no use, though.

I do respond but she—no, she doesn't. Every evening I write to her. Here is what I tell her: You have become an enigma, Mother.

And I don't like riddles. You have given me no help, Mother, neither in the past nor now.

Her love for me is a lone sentence embedded within an incomprehensible theory. It's a single line of text in an ancient book. It's a local dialect which she is determined that I will strive to acquire, scampering after it as if I am a clown, and it doesn't matter if he breaks his neck as long as he reaches the end of the rope in concert with her intentions. But I didn't send her those letters. I would write them, slip them into file folders, and tell myself, One day she will stumble upon them. She will discover them herself. So I brought them with me to Paris. Her motherhood consisted of the minimum requirements of motherliness as mothers perform them. But what am I to do with this regret? It is far bigger than I am. I should have told you about the snow and wind that we get in Canada, how we store all the various sorts of bone-chilling cold—what we call in Iraq jamharir—in our bodies so that the Iraqi sun does not flicker and go out. That sun which devoured one's flesh and heart. I did not love Baghdad's heat—nor do I like Canada's iciness—but God was there, near me, and I love God. I see Him in the eyes of the neighbors and your friends, Ferial, Bushra, Azhar and Tamadir, and in your eyes, too, and in the eyes of the peasant. As for here, the gods are frozen and I do not believe that someday they will melt. You are not listening to me. You listen to Iraqi songs of weeping and mourning, and you begin your bouts of weeping in an inaudible voice. But I hear it.

Inside of these songs I rattle the bones in my chest, neck, and spine. Nader, you will lose out, because you did not even attempt to listen to them. Strange, when I have seen you shaking your head in time to your songs, ayy of course they're gorgeous, and I do like to listen to them with you, so why don't you let go, a little, give in, for your own sake more than anything else? Please, please, don't watch me in this way, as if I am a monkey in a forest and you are Tarzan, almost.

It was ten o'clock in the evening and I was still gazing at her. Afraid to say "for the last time," I repeated to myself, "for the last time today, the last time this evening." Her body lay flat and inert before me. She could no longer evade the years as if to outline new faces with the heavy makeup she put on to stand on the boards at the theater. She never did announce that her body was approaching the age of retirement. She loved her body and warded off anything that might cause it to sicken. She put it in a handsome frame, and she would always say, Look, Nader, my body is laughing as I make ready to play this role. I wonder, when do our bodies ever love us as we have been capable of loving them? When do bodies pay us back all we have done for them, all of those old debts that our own efforts have incurred for them as the years have gone by? My body was my obedient servant as I bounded through the Arab theaters. It said yes to me and I always knew at once that it was not mocking me. It would get a little angry if I tired it out with exercises but it would comply. My thin body scares me as I make my way through life. It dances and acts and never settles into a single position or place. For it I light fires made up of all the texts and plays that I perform and that my father produces; and so the theater seems more pleasurable than life itself.

Her eyes traced the path my steps took as if she wanted to run her hand through my hair, which was crinkled from sweat, and to massage it. Now I was apprehensive, following her with my eyes: How will she come to know me now? How?

Charlotte's voice breaks through my thoughts. "Are you leaving, Monsieur?"

I want to say to this nurse, She is showing signs of movement, she has moved. And it is more than I can handle. I stay motionless and I watch her. I don't raise my eyes from her. Dry-eyed, I call her name out softly, my stares enveloping her.

"Don't be in too much of a hurry, Monsieur. Don't come too early tomorrow morning. Everything is as fine as it can be. Take your time. She is sleeping."

What shall I do, when she is here and then gone, now present, now absent? The combined smells of the medications, the flowers, breathing, sweat, the folds of the curtains, the faint light near the ceiling, and me standing there, stretching my head this way and that; what should I do with it all? The faces of Leon and Sonia appear but they look different, so that at the end of the day I do not know who to obey and who to resist.

By email, Caroline had continued to relay to me Suhaila's misgivings. Your mother is afraid she will break, explained Caroline, and so she reverts to *there*. She returns back home, even if this means that her fate will be a concussion or complete muteness or paralysis and destruction. Paris she calls "the period of recovery from Iraqi jaundice." What do you think, has Baghdad really been so close by, I wonder, so accessible to her, as this? Dance has been like bodily instinct for her. I imagine, Nader, that dance is her watchman who keeps her Iraqi, who makes sure that her revenge will be complete, not lacking in anything, even if it were to forcibly afflict her with the madness of pride. Whenever I have said as much to her, she explodes in my face with a sarcastic response.

What pride, Caroline? she exclaims. Be precise, please! It is hunger that turns one into the most cowardly and abased creature possible. You stand at the back and wait for the blessings of the Paris municipality's meals. One day when I was standing there, Saad happened to pass by and see me there. He was one of my father's protégées as a well-known theater director. One day my father trusted him with a good role and he performed it perfectly. We clapped on and on for him from the gallery. We came from backstage to stand beside him and offer our congratulations. On that evening the true Saad was born. When he saw me in the Paris queue he dropped back a little and hesitated, but seconds later he came up to me in a state of sheer embarrassment. I was standing in line waiting my turn, following the rules. I was not quarreling with anyone in the crowd of elderly pensioners and I was not dying of shame and subjugation. I didn't even show any signs of anger at that moment. When you are brought as low as you can possibly be, you do not think about the enormous price that you must pay later on. You forget the laws of humankind and think according to animal instincts. That was the time and place I was in, and I was perfectly capable of going on with what I had to do. I wasn't concerned about who might see me even if it were, for example, Saad. I know those people there—we had encountered each other through long months of coming to this

86

building. Saad stood beside me without exchanging even a word with me. He picked out for me the best of what the glass-fronted refrigerator unit facing us held: a slice of cold fish, a small container of lettuce and tomatoes, bread and biscuits. And the sweet: then and there I remembered my mother. She had such lovely names for foods: kings' eggs, the bride's palms, the masters' horns. How it all piqued my delight and got me to regain my sense of fun as she clapped her hands at me, saying, Wonder of wonders! What has happened to you? It's nothing more than a little flour and sugar, eggs and oil and butter. What could have happened to you? Wipe that sweat off your face, eating like a wild animal! God give you strength and health.

The sweet in the Paris municipality's meal looks very much like my old shoes, your mother told me. Leather spotted with little blisters, some empty stretches, its color that of the viscous coffee at the bottom of the cup. What's the harm, I said to myself, I'll take it. It is misplaced pride to reject a blessing, and this will come in handy for the hard times, at least. When I open the refrigerator door I will have a sense of food security. I will make double-sure first that I have eaten all of the real food. After the confection one must enjoy a Nescafe. A tiny packet of it and another of sugar, during airplane flights. A meal isn't complete without some bite to it. Saad put everything in a plastic bag that was small and thin and transparent and that bore the emblem of the Municipality of the 15th Arrondissement. The food of the municipality is quickly digested: God give it long life. As I belch, my mother's voice will come back to me. Afarim, Suhaila, good health—you ate it all. Awafi. May you be strong and vigorous!

Saad and I walked together down the street to my apartment without either of us saying a word. When we reached the main entrance, I gestured to him to come in; he was more confused and uncomfortable than I was. He stood facing me, took my head in his hands, brought it near to his mouth and kissed me on the forehead. He raised my hand with an unforgettable gesture and kissed it too. I cried at the time, cried as hard as one can cry. Saad's conditions were worse than mine were. Caroline, have you ever stood waiting for the plastic bags of the Paris Municipality? They are meals I went on eating for months, eating and thanking God that France has laws that deal fairly with the hungry and the very poor, the sick and those who live on the streets, and that it did not abandon me. Paris: she was generous to me, as are all of you.

3

I felt intensely thirsty as I was coming out of the main entrance. I don't know why Hatim came into my thoughts, his face and his eyes as he was saying goodbye. I had the feeling that he had never in his life taken medicines or tranquillizers. I wanted us to be friends. To eat together and tell each other jokes and he would not ask me anything, nothing about my secrets or my life. He would leave me alone, to tell whatever I wanted, how I wanted, and I could be quiet when I wanted to be. He would say to me, Hey, would you like another beer? But no sooner would I start talking than I would forget myself and would sense that his heart was splitting in two on my behalf.

The apartment was a short distance from the hospital. My uncle Diya had come from Germany when things got too burdensome for Suhaila, after she had been moving surreptitiously between university housing and the actors' studio next to the Théâtre du Soleil that the playwright Tessa Hayden had made available to her for a specific and limited period. Crowding into it, though, were actors coming from all parts of the world to play their various roles. They would be there for the whole period they were rehearsing and throughout the performances themselves, which might go on for months. Most of what my uncle sent to her Suhaila would transfer to the administration of my university and into my own account. Sometimes she did not pay her bills and the telephone service was cut. One year the electricity was cut off after she went on ignoring the letters from the utility company. Since it was wintertime, the heater did go on working until spring came. She did not write to my uncle because she did not want to cause tension between him and his French wife, who never did take to my mother.

But Ken informed my uncle in his own special way and he came to Paris.

Caroline did not ask me about my uncle, and she did not repeat her invitation to me. She did not look anything like Marianne, my uncle's silent, uncommunicative, and hard-to-make-out wife. We did not take to Marianne; neither I nor Suhaila felt comfortable with her. Caroline was silent all the time, distant, her expressions suggesting heavy suffering. She would get to her feet, pace for a few minutes and then sit down. It was as if she had decided not to pay any attention. To be present but only that, without having any direct contact with anyone else.

Rue de la Convention is a very long thoroughfare. Here is where Suhaila fell as she was on her way to the post office. Tak, tak, and no one noticed her. This was the first thing to happen; it is what set everything off. In her first letter, Caroline had this to say: It was very hot that midday.

It is possible that here is the very spot where she fell as she was crossing the street, in front of the post office building, which I am standing exactly opposite. It was three o'clock in the afternoon.

Caroline went on: It is as if one were watching a frame from an old black-and-white film. A small woman in her fifties, thin and short, wearing wide-legged pants and a light short-sleeved cotton blouse, carrying a large bag in which she has put a small wallet holding her French residence permit, a checkbook, and another small notebook, old and wrinkled and mussed by fingerprints, containing her friends' addresses and telephone numbers. Your mother, Nader, still writes the Arabic numerals in foreign form, not the way we write them in Arabic, and she always says the same thing: These are our numbers, ours. Fine, you took everything and you left us the zeros. Do you know, Caroline, my dear, that zero is an absolute number? If it gets all mixed up with sums it raises a ruckus that will reach the skies. It will become the marker of envy and misunderstanding.

The numbers were written in a smooth hand and needed no special scrutiny to make out. But the names, Nader—most were written in Arabic and that's why everything got mixed up. They knew who she was, of course, but how were they to contact her acquaintances and friends? On the other side of the street, the story was told a second and a third time. Three black youths took it upon themselves to take charge. Did it ever occur to you to imagine such a situation involving such pain and suffering? Her body—and I'm imagining what it looked like in that fix—would have been remote, strange. Please, I beg you, do believe in her intuitions, and trust me with what I am about to tell you. One day she narrated it to me, in a joking manner but she was not joking, as if she was telling an ordinary story about another woman. What if, in the end, events really were to unfold just like this? she speculated. Would it be so hard to imagine that, Caroline? I beg you, believe it! But don't threaten or scare Nader with it.

This is what she kept on saying, always returning to it, seeing incidents and people and faces and cities. She would cover her eyes with her hand as if trying to rid herself of an unpardonable sin that agonized her. She would say, I know them, all of them, and as well as it is possible to know them; and that is the only thing that I cannot avoid seeing. She was taken to the emergency room with everything she had with her. And then, how did we find out, Nader? If you had been in Paris at the time and had seen all of the chaos, you would have been hard put not to laugh at that aspect of it. I beg you, Nader, to come; it may be your last visit, and this way she will see you and you can talk everything over with her. Her voice still torments me whenever I hear it: al-Thuraya. That's what she calls you. Don't you see these Pleiades in the front room of your apartment? she asks me. More beautiful than that rose crystal! Don't stare like that, with those doubting eyes of yours. I am talking about my blemish and illness, my star and my sun, about my eternal loved one. Listen, if I die, don't pass on to him all of these things I've said. He will say that they are just stupid ravings. She's a mother more suited to other children. Not me. That's what he'll say. How is that, Suhaila? I ask. Her face seems on fire as she answers. He does not understand how to be at ease with love, how to get along with it. My love. I'm not talking now about being a son or being a mother. I am talking about difficulty. Injustice, prejudice. About the fruits that having children yields, so bitter in the throat. About bringing a son into this world, a child who wounds you in your most vulnerable spot, who rejects you, but through this child you are made exceptional. A newborn without hope, you leave him to someone other than yourself, to them, all of them, but not to yourself. You leave him with peace, or with war, with quarreling, and the striking of swords. You love him elaborately and you spend time loving all the tiny, trivial things about him, and your love is endless. You try every way of calling to him, you use everything that is to come and everything that has passed, you try successive attacks and competitive ploys, you wield a cane and then a whip, you invoke luck as bad as hell and luck so good that he feels free to satirize you as a mere belly, a womb, a couple of breasts, and mucous, sweat, milk, and shit all pouring out—and my pleasure in him is ever insatiable. He is a masked son. He is absolutely my opposite. And all he has to do, at the end of the day, to shatter my own status as his mother is to fall into some kind of harmony with me. I have no role then, Caroline, except my own ruin. Like an uneaten, and now rotten, piece of fruit, I will drop off the tree. He knows that very well but he denies it. Ayy, he is a clever one, and a handsome one, too, at least in my precipitate eyes. I do not have a love for valuable treasures, and certainly he cannot be compared to any wealth that it might be in my capacity to possess. His meaning for me is that utter and conclusive deprivation that allows no further words of explanation.

That is what Suhaila says, Nader.

⸎

The situation had grown critical. Caroline told me that the doctors and nurses tried all of the numbers, starting with the first letter in the alphabet.

If no one answered, Nader, they went to the next, and then the next, and so on. No one seemed to know Mrs. Suhaila Ahmad. An explanation, then a few details, a quick description of her appearance, a few words about how she was now bedridden and that it was urgent and critical, but still nothing positive happened. Can you guess what the problem was, Nader? Your mother did not write down any of the numbers that she knew by heart, the telephone numbers of all of her close friends. She recorded those who were more distant and those most peripheral to her life. Lawyers, dentists, eye doctors, cosmetologists, internalists, bone specialists, workers from the gas and heating companies, plumbers, electricians. The airport and the ambulance service, hotels, other airports, L'Assurance maladie, and Sécurité Sociale. Numbers in London and Moscow, Baghdad, Amman, Cairo, Dammam, Damascus, Beirut, Canada. Someone's number was dialed, a man's voice answers, hesitating a little: yes, he does remember this name. He met her in one of those symposia convened for the sake of Iraq ... but he doesn't add anything more. And when the caller persists, he answers, Yes indeed, he does know one of those women, so perhaps they were friends—they had come to the event together. When was that, Monsieur? A year ago. And the name of that lady? Might be Asma, he thinks, if he recalls it correctly. She works as an accountant in some private firm. There they had the thread and could unravel it, and that is how we emerged from home and started arriving in droves and in turns at the hospital. I stayed the first night, observing her the entire time and cursing you, Nader. Excuse me, permit me to say this, I cussed out you and your father. I cussed out both of you as I saw her declining. I disbelieved my own eyes, which never left her. The first friend to arrive was someone I had never met, Sarah. One day Suhaila told me about her. Sarah is a sketch artist who breathes in colors instead of air. Hard to make out, very odd is this human being. Her bearing—the look on her face, the way she seems to live her life—she piqued my wonder and curiosity. She was compelling in the way that a dark painting draws you and you can't get it out of your mind. Nader, do you know Sarah? When I saw her at closer range, I realized that I was seeing one shape that death assumes. She was trying to give us a living sketch of it. Her behavior in public is unbelievable. She was quasi-stoned or drunk. She was not insistent or intrusive as she looked at Suhaila, and she did not seem afraid as I was. She felt that she had arrived later than she should have done. True, she was quite late, but that was not the most pressing matter. After all, she had not even hurried. But she was dripping with sweat, you would not believe how much of it, and she took out a fabric handkerchief from her bag and began to wipe her forehead and her cheeks and the back of her neck dry. She had a sense of confidence about Suhaila coming out of it that I will never forget as long as I live. She did not actually say so, but her manner, as she saw Suhaila lying there in front of her, made it clear enough. Doctors were coming and going; but the distance between us did not get any shorter. She was completely wordless. I was afraid of her and I tried to step back, out of the picture. But she wasted no time coming up to me, and she muttered something without looking directly at me. It was as if she were addressing Suhaila face to face. The price of knowing death is life. She said it in limpid French and then added as she wiped her face dry, When I die I won't be seeing myself die for the first time. Abruptly she raised her head to me. She was utterly sincere as she said to me, I don't want to know what happened. But, believe me, she'll come to. I swear that she will regain consciousness. Do you get it? This sleep of hers is upsetting but it is just a daydream. Excuse me, but I do not have the strength to stay here. I am in worse shape than she is, and she knows that. You are Caroline, bien, thank you for being here, in place of all of us. I can't. No. . . .

Nader, who is this Sarah? Come, leave everything, drop it, forget it all: the quarrels, the mistakes, the stupidities. My God, what is it that I am writing to you? Do I have the right to say all of this to you? It is me who is not strong enough to stay up until ten p.m., and who gets up at six in the morning. I do yoga for an entire hour. I light incense in various corners around the apartment and then I set to what gladdens my eye and mind: the computer Suhaila hates as much as she despises and fears blindness. Now there is a funny story that she will tell you. I am sure of that. Nader, I have just now discovered that you are a being who really was living among all of us, especially her and me. I feel as though I know you well, and I shall be able to put up some resistance to you if you start any nonsense against her. The important thing is that you show up before more time passes. Please.

Twelve

1

I stood in front of our building. To all appearances, it was almost entirely vacant. On many floors all of the windows were shuttered. Only the top floor was lit—ah, yes, that was the apartment of Madame Angélique. Everyone had left for summer holidays. A groan came from within my body as I touched the metal bars on the outside of the front room window. It had been my room at one point. The neighborhood was neither working-class nor wealthy; it was an utterly middling area. Next to us was a little place whose owner said it was a hotel, and my mother would respond, Don't believe him, it's just a dive and not even suitable for long-term stays. One day the owner decided to rent the apartment facing us on the ground floor and append it to his pensione. Customers started showing up in droves night and day. Germans, Turks, English, Americans. The building's entryway came to look like a sports arena. It started to get on Suhaila's nerves and the noise bothered her. Doors opening and shutting, voices raised, dogs barking, the sharp click of high heels, heavy feet kicking doors, their owners drunk. My mother sensed danger, as one of her letters informed me.

Nader, she wrote, I spent some of the money your uncle sent us. I put heavy iron bars on the front window and I painted it black myself. All for the sake of achieving some sense of security. I know money doesn't buy this, you say as much to yourself every day; it's just to be able to get some sleep and continue one's journey. Nader, do you hear what I am saying?

I was startled to find a shiver run all the way through my body; that had not happened before. I was punching in the numbers of the security code. This was something new, too. Caroline had written the number out for me in one of her letters. Lifting my head and preparing to drag my suitcase inside, I was so confused that I dialed the number on the house telephone and waited a moment: after all, she was inside and would soon answer. To the right were the mailboxes, with her name written there clearly. I opened it without thinking. There was a piece of paper from Caroline, written in a nervous hand, saying that she had paid out the month's bill for the electricity meter.

I opened the inner door, which swung shut behind me. The door to our apartment was directly in front of me. I felt my sweat pouring down, down the center of my back all the way to my feet. I turned the key and the door opened easily. The light switch was obvious; I pressed the button and light flooded the small entryway. What faced me first was a soaring wall mirror and someone was staring at me. The sound of the telephone made me jump. It was ringing in her little room, and I rushed in. I put on the light, glancing around hurriedly as the ringing continued. The bed was made—that wasn't her way—and the nightgown she wore at home was on the pillow.

"Hello?"

"Hello—is everything quite all right there? Please, I do hope that you will not make fun of the way things are arranged. I am lazy and Suhaila knows it. How was she when you left the hospital?"

"I don't know, Caroline. For a moment, I thought she was beginning to move. Maybe I just imagined it, or perhaps my sight was blurred by the lack of sleep. I was certainly hoping that some such thing would happen."

"Uh—"

"Thank you so much. I just arrived, and I came right to the telephone."

"Your wife rang. She was very anxious but I think I answered her concerns and soothed her. Nader, are you all right? It has been a long day, and a very hard one."

I put my hand on the small bedside table to support myself and sat down on the bed.

"Thanks, Caroline, for everything you've done, all of it."

"And, tomorrow . . ."

My hand brushed against her nightgown. I pulled it forward and put it across my knees. "I'll be at the hospital early."

"I'll be there, too." Her voice was faint. "Have you been through the flat?"

"No, I haven't been, not yet."

"I hope you have a comfortable and restorative night. Do sleep well."

"Caroline, I can't do other than thank you. I feel that I won't be able to return the favor."

Catching sight of a tissue crumpled into folds between the nightgown's sleeve and bodice, I faltered. I repeated my thanks several times. My gratitude sounded more like apology.

I replaced the receiver. The phone was on the floor near the bed. Next to it sat a small stand holding a triangular clock that threw out a light in the shape of an odd bird about to ascend and circle into the distance. I had only to press on it to see part-images of the bird in the form of pendulum swings of light flying along the high ceiling.

My clock was a gift from Narjis, wrote mother. On the day I started dealing directly with the French administration, struggling to get onto the Sécurité Sociale rolls after they had lost my file three times. Nader, have you heard of Amma the Great Mother in India, that legendary personality known for generous love, help, and purity? Narjis is even more than that. She is my mother, even though she is younger than me.

That is what mother had written to me one day. It was not long after all news of my uncle Diya had suddenly stopped. None of us had any news of him—not my mother, not the lawyer, not Mr. Ken. Directly in front of me now was the television, a Sony, which my uncle had purchased before leaving for Africa and his new place of work as a legal counselor working for the United Nation's disaster relief program. Steadying it into its place on the middle shelf, he had said, I like the Japanese best when it comes to products and traditional wear.

The kimono, Nader, is irresistible when women wear it in films, said Uncle Diya. The women of that country, Suhaila, carry a magic and a mystery—and where they are hiding it we don't know. Is it in deep silence or in still more powerful respect?

He turned to me and began ribbing me. Nader, start planning out a strategy right now to marry a Japanese woman. She won't shut the door in your face if you are late coming home in the evening.

It's the same room. If I had Sarah's talent I could draw it. I could draw the empty spaces between objects as she left them. A table of medium size with the hue of dark gold wood, with little drawers that, most of the time, do not open as they should, its surface unmistakably imprinted with the traces of hot tea cups, coffee, and wine. Ashtrays next to the bed, on the floor, on the table, on the shelf, different shapes and sizes but both large and small, deep and shallow, of various styles. She smoked then and she still does.

We have not been able to handle her on this, Caroline wrote. She quits for a few days but then backslides for months. Joking with us, she declares, A cigarette has better morals than some human beings have. A sigara is honorable and she doesn't practice deception. She's the only holdout—even if that defiance only lasts a few moments. A cigarette understands what is going through your mind, especially through those long, harsh days of winter. It only takes moments for you to realize how much you love your solitude when you are sharing it with that sigara. Listen to me, Caroline–this cigarette is my loved one. She thinks as I do and she does not leave me in the lurch.

I was still holding her nightgown. I got up slowly, turned around, and spread it out on the bed. I smoothed out the sleeves and the collar, and then the whole body of it so that the hem hung down straight. I knelt down and buried my head in the soft weave. Mentally I was at the absolute end of my rope. For the first time ever I was in a complete collapse in solitude and I was making noise. I was starting to wail, and loud enough to be heard. I cried without shame or embarrassment and without trying to suppress the sound of it. I cried so freely that I was sure my eardrums would explode. I caught the right sleeve of the nightgown and plastered it to my face, clutching the left sleeve in my mouth. I could hear myself sobbing as I buried my head in her lap. Clinging to the robe, catching myself up in it, I could find no one beside me who would calculate my tears and hold me to account for them. There was the sound of the telephone again. It was Sonia, most likely. Sitting in front of the dining table playing with Leon, and she wouldn't waste any time.

"Nader, love, how are you and how are things there? What's that?—you're crying? The sound of your voice gives you away, but I know that you don't want to confess. Nader, what is it? What's going on there? Is—"

"Nothing new, Sonia. I have been back in the flat for only a little while, and I'm not certain of anything. There's lots of talk, details, information, medical terms and mental health jargon I haven't heard before. It's all had a pretty big impact on me. I have this feeling that I am going to burst from the roar of it before I can even go mad."

"Please, please, try to go to sleep right away, if you can. Have you seen her friends? Were they with you the whole time? You must try to calm down and take it a bit easy since they are there with you. Nader, please, please do not leave us full of worry about you. One of us has to hold together. I am praying for her and for all of us. Nader, the baby and I are waiting for you. He wants to say something to you in his own language—here, listen to him. There ... can you hear? Dada I love you."

"Fine, Sonia. Thanks for calling. Take care of yourself and Leon."

I turned my head away from the phone and shifted my position. I tugged at the small and expensive carpet, pushed it under myself and leaned my back against the bed. The wooden floorboards were old and dark. I stretched out my legs. My sobbing started to subside. I blew my nose and folded my arms over my knees. The pain was welling up from there and erupting where Suhaila was. Does the pain know where to head? Piles of clippings, newspapers and files. Papers, notebooks, brown folios large and small; it seemed likely that

Caroline had arranged it all this way. There were three stacks and on each had been placed an ashtray, a book, a flower vase so that nothing would scatter or fly. My eyes traveled upward and I saw those same shelves. They had been empty at the time of our arrival years before, at the time when my uncle was preparing to leave Germany first, having already sent his wife and his son Ziyad to the south of France where her wealthy family lived. Marianne retained her own peculiar ideas, most of all about Suhaila whom she treated rather coldly, making her distaste obvious. We did not live here when we first came to Paris by way of Turkey. When my uncle left us and went away in the early seventies he and my mother did stay in touch regularly. My longing for him had become indescribably intense and I imagined that when he first saw me again he would take me in his arms as he always used to do, lift the sleeve of his blindingly white shirt and tease me—Hey, Nader!—as he had always done in the past. He used to balance me on one arm and act as if he could not breathe as he repeated his usual phrase: I'm going to go on making sure that you sit on my arm even if you reach twenty.

The way my uncle had of announcing his love was quiet and affectionate and sometimes contradictory, the opposite of my father, except his emotions remained hidden. I did suppose at the time that his feelings would have remained unwavering toward me, at least. His objections to my father's treatment of Suhaila were constant and incessant. He objected to almost everything, in fact. He had graduated from the College of Law and Political Economy with honors and opened a law office in partnership with the top graduates from his year. After only a few months there, however, he dropped everything. His resounding arguments for the defense and his successes had made certain people anxious, my father among them. My father scoffed at him, at both his ideas and his personality. Later on he was offered many positions: postings in the judicial diwan, a governorship in one of the southern provinces. Choose as you like, Diya, he was told. My father would repeat those words to him in an unnaturally loud voice as if to ridicule his brother-in-law: Don't you see, we hold the likes of you in reserve for times of need. Now the time has come for you to work on our behalf. It is the only sure cause there is. Otherwise. . . . My father did not complete his sentence. Suhaila was sitting in her room trembling and not a sound was to be heard from Diya. As he was leaving, we caught a glimpse of his shadow. It looked as though he had been pummeled all over his body, battered as my mother had been. Later—years later, when we were in England—I learned that he really had been subjected to beatings. At the time, he had confided his suspicions to my grandfather: I feel like I'm being followed. Watched. There was someone shadowing him when he visited his fiancée, Nihad, and as he returned to the family home. My grandparents were afraid for him. But the surprise was in wait for my father most of all. I heard his screech all the way from my room on the top floor. Your brother, the honorable effendi, has fled. Do you hear me, Lady Suhaila, or has the deafness reached your other ear as well?

Was my uncle a courageous man who was turned into a coward at my father's hand? No one dared ask my father or anyone else about the matter. My grandmother sold an orchard that was in her name on the outskirts of Karbala and began smuggling money out to him. She always found channels for bribery—relatives, military men and civilians, businessmen and artists, and friends of my grandfather's, whom she would lure with substantial commissions. My grandfather, too, exerted himself on my uncle's behalf. While away on theater business and to stage plays in Arab countries and the socialist states, he sent off whatever he could get in hard currency. The phrase came to echo in my ears: *hard currency*. I would hear it for months at a time, and years; I read it in the newspapers and heard it on radio and television. Did hard describe the conditions of those who were strong and rich, and soft the lot of the lazy, the failing, and the poor? The idea itself was hard for me. I was embarrassed at my inability to solve the riddle even though I was so excellent at math and at the sciences in general—and the sciences were said to be very hard! As long as these matters had to do with currency and money, and all of these words which seemed to adhere to each other, it all afflicted me in some sense. It was very complicated, the impact on me of all of the events taking place around me. There was the day that Suhaila whispered to me that I could study in Paris near my uncle if I wanted to—but after I'd gotten through secondary school exams. Because, she said, there was plenty of hard currency right now. She said it in a most theatrical manner. The images crowd in my head; I dream when I'm awake as well as when I'm asleep. During the period when I was finishing middle school and going on to high school, I was learning foreign songs by heart more efficiently than I was memorizing the revolutionary writings which were declaimed to us in class. As for the guitar, my father used to ridicule me savagely about it. Instead of qiitaar he would call it qathra—dirty. It spoils revolutionary understanding, he would add. And it weakens patriotic sentiment.

But Suhaila and my grandfather stood up for me. She sent me to a Bulgarian teacher who taught at the School of Music and Ballet. She did it without his knowledge. Time elapsed; my father would come and go, and we would receive our orders. He never retreated nor wearied of it. I told myself, One day, someday, I will not carry through on anything that my respected father means to have done. My attitude was that laws and commands existed in order that we not comply with them every one and to the letter. At the age I was then, being apart from the family meant either carrying out drills with light weapons or receiving orders and preserving the principles of the revolution. I didn't understand what it meant to be revolutionary. Was my father revolutionary? He was the badge that let me gain entry everywhere. His chest was decorated with medals and his shoulders were covered in stars, many and glistening, as he marched ahead, while I often advanced more slowly than the other students in my division and year. I would move on, and draw away, and go in a direction contrary to them; and I would discover that the longing that motivated me was to echo the songs of Bob Marley and the Wills Brothers, Elvis Presley and Jacques Brel. These singers' lyrics were simple; they were sympathetic and free and they didn't fill me with fear or ennui. Their songs spoke of things that were always on my mind: traveling to new cities, innocent love. I memorized Bob's words and they moved me. *Me don't dip on the black man's side nor the white man's side. Me dip on God's side, the one who create me and cause me to come from black and white.* And I loved God more than my father. I would hear the word revolution in some of those songs as if it were meant only for me, and as if it were meant to keep me happy. No one was compelling me to do this thing or that. I believed that revolution meant pulling together the elements of my strength in order to triumph over my weakness and incapacity. And that it wasn't a question of military training alone but of being sound in my ideas and natural and free. Whenever I saw and heard my father talking about the revolution I had the feeling there were pebbles in his mouth. He would start to look gloomy, sad, and angry. He would pace around his room, his hands behind his back and me in front of him with my head lowered.

What are these qatharat that fill your head? What are these impurities? As long as he was at home, the prohibitions doubled from one day to the next, for when I was in front of him I appeared stupid and a failure and would have always been so even had I been top of my class and my school. Later, and in a whisper, Suhaila commented, Nader, you are strange, and I am afraid that your fate will be like his. Like him.

Like whom? I did not understand exactly—my uncle, my mother's brother, or my father? Ayy, Nader, your uncle who fled and immigrated, leaving everything behind.

But my uncle was not my ideal nor was my father. I loved them, of course, but in some way that I could not make sense of. When Diya escaped I was very unhappy. I felt that there existed some sort of competition between him and my father, but surely the issue was nothing more than a story in the air or some mistake that someone had made. No one in the family said anything about the real reasons for my uncle's flight. In the beginning, right after it happened, I persisted in trying to find out what had gone on. But I failed. Later I would tell myself that possibly my uncle had not believed strongly enough in the revolution—but was my father really any more of a believer? To this day I have not found the answer to this question.

Sitting here, I see a cockroach on the wall, a reddish blotch that has completely stopped moving. His moustaches are lean and wary as he falls under my gaze, into my hands.

What, I wondered, should I do now? I stirred, slowly, and got to my feet. I walked out to the bathroom. I had the feeling that the cockroach was freer than I was.

2

I was trying to avoid encountering Suhaila in every object that surrounded me here, but the little things pursued me wherever I turned. Although I was very thirsty, I didn't make for the tiny kitchen and its fridge. I didn't stick my head into the other room, my room which Suhaila had transformed into a sitting room where she could welcome friends. I stood in the miniscule bathroom. I turned on the spigots full blast and listened to the gurgling sound of the water in the faucet as I took off my clothes. The plumbing still took its time. Nothing had changed here; and I wanted a more forceful gush of water. I wanted it to clobber my head, my knees, my chest, all of the hidden places in my body. I was gripping the cold water hose and pouring the icy water over my head, passing it across my face and shooting it into my eyes. I was wishing I could sleep here, right here inside of the clean pink bath.

Everything—you require everything in such a hurry, Nader. Food, a bath, lessons. Even as you are consulting with the university doctors, you evade them and leave hurriedly as if everything is your doing and you are afraid that someone is following you. We are here, my dear, and no one is going to reach out and take you prisoner. Linger for a bit, be patient—why, why do you stint on water and food and likewise on emotions? Hmm? Why?

She would find a label for every sign she saw in my face. She would follow me with her eyes and it would irritate her when I didn't answer. In Brighton she would go into the bathroom and talk to the water; her glances as she closed the door unnerved me. I knew that she would climb into the large white bathtub that was sized generously for her small body. And when she would stay there, I would start worrying and would soon be at my wit's end about what to do, as if she had gone in there for the express purpose of committing suicide. I couldn't hear her voice or any sound of her, as if she were concealing it deliberately to torment me as much as she possibly could. How strange she is. I would knock on the door after a time, gently at first, then hard.

Mother! Mother, are you all right?

She would not answer. Just like that, to upset and anger me. Only she could shatter me like this, breaking my resistance. Only she could cut in on my sealed-off self. And so my anger and my craziness would erupt; and then finally she would answer, in a voice full of affection, Don't worry, dearest, you know how I like to stay in the water.

Why won't you say anything to me? Why don't you answer when I call you?

She would bathe more than necessary, and I still do not understand the reason for it. I suppressed my words, bit my tongue, and cursed her under my breath, on that evening and many nights to follow, due to this and for many other reasons. This relationship had to end, I thought—let her go somewhere and not tell me where she is. I am an extremely high-strung person. The things we would fight over might be silly, but it all would pulverize me, and she deserved my anger. I wanted her to share everything with me; it seemed enough for her to realize that the love between us could endure some gullibility and silliness, even some sneakiness and cunning. It didn't seem too much to ask. She ought to be aware of that.

The steam rose as far as the gray metallic shelves that sat to the left of the bath. Atop the shelves were lined up bottles of rose water, tubes of face crème, and hand lotion. There were smaller bottles of various colors that looked like thimbles—on the shelves there in Brighton and here as well. I had merely to pour a few drops into the tub for the room to be suffused in ocean spray carrying the fragrance of equatorial rain forests. Fine, fresh odors, as if they were hers. I had only to enter the bathroom in her wake to forgive her everything.

Barefoot, I stood in front of the fridge, my mouth hanging open with thirst. It was packed with various French and Arab cheeses, butter, and both strawberry preserves and apricot jam. I saw tomatoes, watermelon, cherries, honeydew melons, cans of beer, apple and orange juices, Lebanese bread, and a baguette in a paper sack.

Caroline, as a woman of the West who has a relationship with us, with the East, seems like us, my mother mused. Like Blanche, Narjis, Wajd, and Asma. She sits on the floor and she and Blanche have a competition going when it comes to smoking the narghileh. When one of them blows the smoke high, the other chuckles and says, No good—mine's highest. Sometimes she eats with her hand when she sees us doing so, especially tharid al-bamya and dry beans. She's like a child when she sees the dining table—yum! she says, and she begins taking off her jacket to get ready for what she is about to confront, the Indian spices and hot pepper blends that Diya kept sending from Africa and the combinations that I come up with according to my mood. She goes with me to the Arab souqs—Moroccan, Tunisian, Lebanese—every Wednesday in the popular market. I buy and she licks her lips imagining what I will cook. She puts herself in the proper frame of mind for it. She even prefers leftovers as we do—these dishes are always better the next day.

Caroline had also stocked the kitchen for me with all sorts of imperishables: canned peas, green beans, and corn; bags of brown sugar cubes; varieties of tea—jasmine, mint, and lemon. Suhaila used to wake me at six o'clock in the morning with a whispering in my ear. Yallah, Nader, hurry up—breakfast is ready. Toast, eggs like lynx eyes, tea. . . . She didn't like anything labeled express or fast; she would fret, standing in front of me, as if giving a speech. An illusion, Nader, ayy w-Allahi, it's a cosmic illusion. And then she would laugh before finishing her sermon. Everything express will crumble to nothing. It's as much of a trial to bear as any other humiliation.

She was enamored of making tea; she loved the process and put as much energy into it as if she were beginning to write a book or play a role on stage: boiling the water until the steam rose to coat the kitchen window and, a pretty sparkle in her eyes, opening a small green velvety chest. That's where she kept the tea, loose, free, not in bags. Even dried herbs won't stand for being imprisoned, she would say.

Scooping up a small fistful, she would put it in a glass teapot sitting next to the one on the flame and cover it with a tea cozy—a cap with ears. Leave it there to rest until we are absolutely frantic for it; until its aroma drives us insane. This is the way your father likes it best, too, tea with cardamom. My mother taught me this way. She would open the cardamom pods slightly and place them in the teapot. Your father always made fun of the English and their anemic, sickly tea.

Then Suhaila swings around and turns her gaze on me. Everything has its own proper time, Nader. This is the value of things. Sometimes I see you as a wayfarer who stares only at the highway ahead, who doesn't stop on the road to look and think properly about his changing surroundings. Other times you astound me with your ability to observe and appreciate, as when you're going into the kitchen with me where we'll prepare the dishes you love. You truly confuse me!

Here and now, directly in front of me, the water was boiling. I found a cup and slipped a teabag inside. I watched it, observing how the hue of the water changes gradually into a fiery color. The color of my face. I closed my ears to Suhaila's instructions. I drink fast; that's the way I eat and study, too. I tore off a piece of Lebanese bread and put a cube of cheese in the middle. I didn't feel that I had really had enough to eat but I wasn't hungry, either. I swallowed the rest of the tea and went back into her room. I pulled off my clothes and let them fall to the floor. I picked up her nightgown again, folded it offhandedly and stuffed it onto the chair in front of me. I raised the duvet and stretched out beneath it like a stiff corpse.

In the evenings we used to do some theater exercises. Your grandfather called me the General of the Modern Iraqi Theater, just so, to spite your father who had begun to be annoyed by my regular late-evening work—and I didn't know whom to obey or what to listen to: the instructions and admonitions of the impresario or the commands of the military husband? It's possible, Nader, that the headaches and illness began around that time, once I was convinced that my talent would be converted into mere scrap iron. I was in a pitiable state. It seemed to me that death was taking up position, lying in wait for me, ready to attack if I were not to act and dance. I would leave you in my mother's care and when I came back for you in the morning my mother would pursue me with incessant scolding and blame. Suhaila, Nader would not stop crying. He was afraid you weren't going to come back. But the minute I put your old nightgown in his hands he would start sniffing at it like a little animal. He would choke on his tears and start to hiccup, and finally he would quiet down and fall fast asleep.

Thirteen

1

I woke up in a state of exhaustion. All of those women, her friends, were in my mind. I had an image of them chasing me, running after me to grab me because of a sentence I had forgotten and then abandoned; a sentence I would not divulge. My mother is a wondrous woman and she is the one who has given me the occasional appearance of a beggar. Did she know this? She is a mother-tragedy and I no longer understand her; I don't know her. I wonder who does know his own mother?

The apartment closes in on me: the shelves are crammed full of books, recordings, piles of newspapers, dictionaries, and mute pictures. My photographs are above, all appearing to my eyes as if they are not me. There they are, as they were: the little boy, the growing boy, the adolescent. These portraits of me sketched the stages of my life, step by step, by moments and by years, in rows one after another on the wall. She used to study me, to review me as if I were a sequence of lessons, as I crawled, and walked, and fell, and stumbled among the pupils, on that island—Umm al-Khanazir, "Mother of the Pigs"—riding my bicycle, my hair flying and my trousers muddy. In the morning or at night; among the palm trees with my mouth wide open; on my bed clutching the guitar; at a small party in the apartment of her friend Wijdan in London; at the head of the stairs, playing songs; standing beneath the Eiffel Tower; in all seasons and in front of my green Volkswagen, looking guileless; or uncomfortable at the little stupidities of my unctuous English friend Elizabeth. And there was Layal, who is so akin to my birthplace—the place where my head first crowned to emerge from my mother's body—just as she is akin to the crowning question among all of those puzzles for which, to this day, I have failed to find solutions. I focus my gaze now on this one and now on that one, just as my lost and ruined father would have done. I chase every female on whom my gaze falls. Confused and caught up in it all, I seek amusement and I place no trust in fidelity—in the faithfulness of the girls into whose path I fall; and then I can no longer bear them, just as I can no longer stand myself. Standing before these walls, I rage, Pictures, pictures! Nothing but pictures of me. There is not a single photograph from my wedding, and there are no photos of Sonia or of my son. Why do you believe the photographs and yet you do not believe the one whom they portray? Why do you do that, Mother?

After covering the dark brown desk chair with a bright colored African shawl to hide its worn interior, I swiveled it round with a touch of my hand. I sat down. Lines of poetry by the Iraqi poet Badr Shakir al-Sayyab, by the Greek poet Cavafy, and by Abu Nuwas, that fun-loving and naughty medieval Arab poet, covered the wall in front of me, pinned up with tacks. Instead of reviving me, they dulled my senses. Lines of poetry on the ephemerality of existence, on the homeland, on unattainable love. I read while scooting the chair around within the few meters of what was a very small room. The curtains were of two different colors and types; the translucent ones were yellow. She had put these up first, wanting to let the light in. It was her intention that the second ones be of dark, olive-colored velvet, elegant and expensive, and that the hems be worked in green and yellow threads. She wrote to me about what happened.

The yellow curtains were Blanche's gift, do you remember her, Nader, or not? My father, Blanche once explained to me, gave me the nickname Kashaniya after a type of expensive Persian carpet.

My mother gave me the name Blanche. If you want the truth, Nader, she really is like Kashan Persian carpets. But I prefer the name Blanche: white of heart and soul and like a mountain of joy: every time you try to climb it and you think you've gotten up it, you find it still there in front of you, waiting for you. She—Blanche, this joy-mountain—reaches out a hand and pulls you higher. Like Narjis and the others, she tries to hide your failure, your stupidities, and your hesitation, because she believes you and she believes the women. Not right away, perhaps; it may be that you want to believe this more than anything. Those women have a certain immunity, a natural auto-protection against envy and spite. Don't laugh at me, Nader, and say that my friends are angels. No one is an angel, and in the first place, I do not like this sort of characterization. Really, though, when we are together, I do feel the worth of things, of thoughts and ideas, friendship, the world, poetry, drinking, and other things that I don't know how to explain or label. Ah, if only you knew what they have done for me. Amazing—haven't I told you that before? If you come to Paris one day and stand in this room of mine, and if you try to pull these green curtains, there is no help for it; you will find yourself repeating, Thank you, thank you, Caroline. This was her gift to commemorate my fifty-third birthday. Go on, push apart those curtains and let the light come into the room. Don't grumble as I did when I saw Caroline carrying an enormous heavy-plastic bag. It startled me when she said so gently, so quietly, Here, open it, Suhaila.

I averted my eyes from her, Nader. The sight had a reverse effect on me. In a tone far from joking, I answered her. If only you had brought me a head of cauliflower, Caroline, and an eggplant of the little, fresh sort, to make pickles and makdus, if you had brought French cheeses to die for and a bottle of cognac Napoleon (after his exile, of course), to digest the hours and the years. But I don't like velvet. I do not particularly like curtains in the first place.

Caroline laughed at first, sweetly. She didn't know, ya ayni, how to answer me. So I spoke again.

Look at me, my dear, daughter of the elegant and civilized North. From now on, I really prefer things to eat over other things.

Extravagant belongings like this. I don't even know how to use these. From now on and until. . . . when you're coming here, bring produce, all sorts, smoked fish, chicken, eggs from fields that are organically fertilized. Lots of fruit. Simplicity: shamam is better than shamaadanat! Yes, indeed, melon is lovelier than candelabras. No, not flowers—don't bring flowers. They are luxuries and I can't stand them anyway—they give me a chronic cough and an awful allergic reaction. Ya, Caroline? Now don't forget these instructions. Please.

My poor, dear Caroline! I did feel for her. On that early spring afternoon she went into a gloom I had never before seen expressed in her eyes quite like that. The curtains were spread out on the bed as if they were a sort of shroud. In no more than an hour, though, the storm passed. I was ashamed of myself, of how I had treated her, so I pulled down the old curtains, the brown and white weave. I climbed the stepladder and began to hang the ones she had brought.

Look, look, now, Suhaila, please, and do be serious. The room really is royal now. Isn't it?

The tone of her voice was utterly civil but I didn't thank her. I wasn't nice to her at all. And who said I prefer royals as you do? I snapped.

She knew a lot about us and about our homeland, my mother's letter went on. I did wince, Nader, seeing that her marble-pale face was now a flaming red. I came down off the stepladder. I pulled the curtains together so that the room was very dark, and it stirred up a host of feelings in me that left me seeing the room as if it were not mine. It is not my room and it is no longer a place of safety, a security zone. Drapes like this do not console anyone. This kind of fabric weaves one into captivity. When I touched the posh, heavy lining, I felt even more afraid. The room had somehow become permanent and unchangeable, and I felt it threatening me with something I couldn't know. I felt repelled, alienated, by it and by myself. Finally, I said to Caroline, We have to leave here right now. We'll celebrate my blessed birthday at your apartment. We'll invite our friends. I will do the cooking.

2

I threw the first window wide open and then I tackled the window with the iron bars that opened on the street. Finally the grating swung loose with a reluctant screech. The morning was gathering above the tall trees in the broad garden adjacent to the building. I stared at the scene with wide-open, unblinking eyes. I could do that; my tears were less furious today than they had been yesterday. Still, they were there: they welled up and rolled down my cheeks freely but I didn't wipe them away. I started to put on my clothes. My muscles felt tense and my movements seemed jerky. In the daylight, the sight of the overflowing shelves struck me forcefully every time I lifted my head and seemed to goad me. I couldn't help noticing massive files of all colors bearing thin white labels plastered on the spines and filled in with a heavy dark handwriting. Letters to International Organizations. Letters from My Son (just like that! She hadn't even written my name!). Letters from My Loved Ones in Baghdad. I saw a thick notebook on which was written the name Tessa Hayden in a different hand and ink. I saw long blue boxes lined up, looking freshly organized, as if she had arranged them very recently. As I was finished getting dressed I touched one. Dust rose from its cover. I paused before a violet-toned triple-fold greeting card to Suhaila, crisscrossed by lines and various colors. I read the message. I did not wait for you to answer me, my dear lady. Yet I wait; I anticipate writing to you as every new year dawns. It is not a question of duty. Don't get all bothered as you so often do, trembling like a teenaged girl. My heartbeat—that is what I want you to listen to as you are going to sleep.

My chest constricted; my heart felt the pressure. I turned my eyes away hurriedly from the top surface of the card. For a moment I felt afraid, as if I were hearing the footfall of my father's military boots. I drew out one of the files, a black one, and read at the top in her muddled handwriting the label Income Tax. I returned it to its place and pulled out another file at random. I read what had been written there in a fine hand. Canada Diaries. I shoved it back hurriedly. The table clock was pointing to seven. I stared at one object after another; I swiveled my head from this side to that. The garden was in front of me, its trees thick with branches. I took in the odor of the fertilizer that had been spread in the course of the night and still gave off a strong smell that I found unpleasant. I pattered around barefooted and stared at the papers and newspapers piled on the floor. I left the room and headed to the little kitchen. It was very dark; no sun ever enters it, and so she had installed a lamp that hung from the high ceiling; its strong beam all but grazed my head. I am taller than Suhaila although I am still short. My father failed to give me any of his fine height or his strong athletic build; my muscles are scrawny despite the exercises I do every day in hopes that I will not appear to be a grown man in a childish frame. Now, and slowly, I discover the arrangement of the kitchen: the stylish shelves, the pictures that hearten your appetite, some recipes. A set of scales, variegated plates, and pottery. Bouquet-like bunches of herbs hung on colored ribbons, giving off their aroma. She had hung them on the walls arranging them to look like musical notes. Smelling and touching revived me and worked on my spirits. I set the teapot on the flame. Here are Suhaila's fingers: the traces of her hands fill every niche. She would talk to everything around her and breathe in its air to invigorate her spirits. She made mental and verbal maps of the old country. She set them in front of her as well as finding a permanent place for them inside her head. In every home into which we moved she would find some way to regenerate her state of mind and lighten her longing for the country. She has a memory that never lets up. Before dinner and afterward, as if she is performing the prayers, she recites passages so precisely that one thinks they must have been engraved inside that head of hers. She puts up drawings. From kitchens the world over, from the peoples of the world, she translates the most famous dishes. She puts East next to West, the North in the South's embrace, and whispers to herself even if I am standing right beside her. These are not hallucinations, Nader, she says, nor the raving of a mischievous Eastern woman. The eye's appetite precedes the tongue's desire. You know that.

She dries off her profuse sweat as she writes titles that are as curious as can be. They are like addresses for things. This is a recipe for circling high, she writes, and far above and far away from the bastard hypocrites. And there's the meal of the Tower of Babel that drips fire. Here is a plate for sharp applause.

Suhaila loves all kinds of aromatics and spices. Ways to visualize things, pictures of tables and tablecloths embellished with lace and gold and silver threads, Arab-style coffee cups. Glassware for serving drinks, in particular special stemware for wines. Sometimes when she writes down amounts in recipes she gets some of them wrong, and then when she makes the dish it is more appetizing than the power of inspiration. In this miniscule space she would mix, and combine, and offer a running commentary. The place itself turns into a wonder when we prepare our own foods, she said. For the sake of a precious, delicious and little bite, we must please ourselves as long as we can't expect that from others.

The first thing she said to Sonia, on the day they were first introduced in Brighton was: Don't be stingy in your mind's eye when you are here in this amazing place. Try the tastes of India, of Iran, and of Iraq. Experiment with your knowledge, not as a chef and skilled expert, but to the contrary: as an impetuous, frivolous, out-of-control human being who wants to know and is ready to learn by trying things out. I may be the worst cook in the world, but I am the best there is at trying and developing a taste for the food of other people.

My mother was lying for Sonia's sake, to give a mental lift to this wife infatuated with her son. But Suhaila was every bit as capable of poisoning some guest if she couldn't stand him or didn't like him much. The cooking would look noxious. The guest would wish heartily that he could flee the scene, and she could be very sure that he would never return. The moment a guest proved to be simpatico, though, fitting into the family and appearing constantly at the dining table, her gruel would turn into the food of paradise. She ladled it out, and the guest was in heaven. This is precisely what happened with the Vietnamese driver Ken and his paramour, Sayyida Lady.

3

On one of my uncle Diya's trips to attend one of those conferences that were always held in the British city of Brighton, he met Ken. At first this fellow seemed an oddball. We could not make out his age. He was quiet and extremely polite. He would get out of the taxi and open the passenger-side door for my uncle. It wasn't really a taxi but rather a hired car; Ken owned it, and it was put at the disposal of conference participants. Diya was assigned to him. They quickly understood each other despite the reserved natures of both. As soon as Ken learned that Diya was from Iraq and married to a French woman they bonded. Twice Ken invited him home to his large apartment, or perhaps it was three times. He introduced Diya to his two children, products of his first marriage. His wife had died years before. Life is harsh here, he said, but we are able to find some outlets to give our existence a bit of flavor. The rest is not in our hands. Ken was Buddhist, and he had a unique way of choosing special dishes and of knowing how to find the spark that sets off conversations and penetrates the other person's mind to send it soaring into the distance, awakening the intelligence and offering as a cherished goal the attainment of calm and happiness and contemplation. In those days my uncle thought seriously about inviting us to Brighton and introducing us to this creature to whom he had given the charming name Enlightening Asian Moon. During one of those evenings at Ken's, however, my uncle suddenly stopped eating the delicious food before him to ask his host if it was within his power to find a place where his sister's son could live while he completed his university education. Ken gave Diya his characteristically placid smile but no immediate answer. After they had sipped their fragrant green tea, Ken stood up and asked my uncle to come along with him. Uncle Diya followed him to the upper floor. Ken was standing in the center of a spacious and well-lit room furnished in the English manner. In a low voice, as if he were revealing a secret, he answered Diya's question. Diya, this wing has its own bathroom and kitchen, both very small. It is possibly enough room for two people if we were to make a few simple rearrangements such as putting in a partition or curtain or an internal door. Don't worry, leave it to me. Your nephew will live here. Have you told me his name, though?

Nader Adam.

Will they live together? Pardon the question, but as it is right now the place would not be comfortable for two people for any length of time.

She doesn't know exactly. Sometimes she wants to be with him always, and other times she says that he has to bear the responsibility himself and it is better this way. But she will always be coming here. You, too, you must visit us in Paris. Right now they are living in a very basic apartment, one we own, my wife and I. I left it for them after I was transferred to Africa. And the rent, Mr. Ken?

It isn't high. Plus, I'll make it twenty percent lower, for friendship's sake.

Food?

He could be a companion for my son Ian and his sister Heidi. We will take a small amount from him as long as it is just him. It's possible that Lady, my friend, won't be very happy about this, but that isn't important.

Ken smiled—that smile which hovered between wonder and delight, and we could never tell which it meant. Lady is a somewhat inflexible woman, he told my uncle. She is strong-minded and a bit bossy, but there is one extremely important thing to keep in mind. If you fall into a real crisis you will find that she's at your side in a way that's truly rare. That is why I put up with her hard edges.

And so that is how I transferred from the Sorbonne after one year there which left me reluctant to continue. I went to Brighton and into the very different educational system of the English. The rents were unbelievably high. My uncle would work everything out in advance with Mr. Ken, and sometimes he paid in my uncle's stead if the money transfers were delayed.

When Suhaila and Ken met, she felt an immediate sense of trust. His sentiments were not on display but they were nevertheless real. When we were by ourselves upstairs, Suhaila said, Just imagine, Nader—this lovely man knows more about your country and about Palestine than we ourselves know. As for the upper floor, it had been transformed for me more or less into a place of security which was neither a permanent home nor the sort of temporary stopping place where, upon leaving, we would not know where we would be next.

With the passing of time, we became members of a single family. We would invite him for a light Iraqi dinner and he would invite us to his apartment when he was making Vietnamese and Chinese and Japanese food, its presentation as perfect as could be.

Have you heard the way he analyzes the situation, the war, the East-West struggle, the history of the region, and America's role in everything that has happened in his country and what goes on all over the world?

The tenor of my mother's words seemed to rebuke me. Mother, he's just repeating what he has read in the British press or heard from some of his Arab and foreign colleagues.

But he views it all in a really reflective way, without any extremism or provocation.

Fine. Better than me and maybe than you, ya? My voice was a little louder than usual as I spoke. She went pale and silent as we heard knocking on the door. Mrs. Lady was standing there. She wanted to invite my mother to attend one of the meetings held by the self-convened women of Asian origins group. If you are interested in this, she was saying, you can come. We will have a light meal— Indian—and then we will have a dialogue between members and new friends. Aren't you considering joining us?

That woman had given herself the name Lady in contrast with every lady she had happened to encounter in shops, parties, and the elegant invitations she received as a member of some environmental society. When they first met, my mother found her, as she described to me later, aggressive, Nader. She is a bit hostile. Her tongue is truly vicious and sometimes dirty. She pokes fun at everything; she can be devastatingly sarcastic. She is the polar opposite of Ken.

On their way to that meeting, which was specifically for divorced women and widows, Suhaila had to listen to stinging words about her foolish mania for searching out any and every means of learning my father's fate. When she saw the hodgepodge of Indian, Pakistani, and Anglo women, though, my mother felt a little more relaxed. A little while later, though, she had an encounter that staggered her. One of the women, on her way to the little raised stage, and in front of everyone, stopped beside Suhaila. She was a woman of color, in her forties, and she had an odd, even delusional, air. Lady explained my mother's story as a way of getting them acquainted. That woman laughed very loudly and directed her words, which everyone could hear, to Suhaila.

You really ought to be happy rather than sad. I wish my husband were dead, but he is in fine health and he's with another woman. And I work like a beast of burden just to stay alive. Yes, it's better when they die.

They were ascending to the podium, talking, squealing, winking, and laughing, and then coming down, hysterical, whooping, and talking in yet stranger ways about families and marriage. Could that be attributed to their being without husbands, or because they had a longing for men who would feel in their company as they did when they were with their buddies and colleagues? These were things my mother said to me when she returned from that evening, her thoughts disturbed and her mood very agitated and tense.

Sometimes we have a need to dole poison onto plates, she added, and offer them to some creatures. Sayyida Lady is one of them.

Fourteen

1

I had not even glanced into my room—the one in which I had lived for about two years. I had no desire to unearth that room from the past right now. The phone rang and suddenly a lump swelled in my throat. I leapt up as if some part of me had touched a live wire. I stumbled over the nearest pile of newspapers and documents as I went to pick up the receiver.

"Alloo . . . Alloo?"

It seemed a voice that I had not heard before. It was a jumble of loud words, tears and entreaty. The woman spoke very fast.

"Ayni, ayni! Nader, dear, your mother, O God, prayers for His messenger Muhammad, these are the pleas of those who love her, your mother's habayib, my prayers, by God . . . hassa rajaat, I've just come back from the mosque. I stood there and I opened my heart to my Creator, my dear, I told Him, it isn't hard for You, O most merciful, to bring her back to us, to her poor, poor son. Nader, yamma salayt . . . I prayed right at dawn in the mosque and then came right to the hospital, I'm there right now. My son, it isn't unlikely . . . mu bi'iid 'ala Allah, God may well hear my prayers, nothing's too far away for Him. Nader, ayni, come quickly, shubiik, what's the matter and why aren't you here, my son? It is Auntie Asma, Umm Hammada, haa, my dear, and Shawkat's on his way, too. Don't eat any breakfast, son, I baked khubz al-abbas for you. The blessed bread of Abbas, the Prophet's grandson! By his blessed grave in Karbala, that precious one won't look unkindly on our beloved now! Just listen to me, Nader, dear, listen, Suhaila moved the fingers of her right hand, ayy! I swear it, w-Allahi al-azim, by Almighty God, she did. Yimkin li-khatrak ibni—maybe for your sake. Yallah, my dear, goodbye, now. Maa salama."

I began to walk down the street. I didn't look at anyone. But the voice of Angélique, our fifth-floor neighbor, besieged me. From the side street she was trying to get me to stop.

"Hiii, Mr. Adam, ça va? C'est vous?"

"Oui, madame, ça va." I echoed her, my voice restrained. I was breathing heavily as I stopped opposite her. She swayed right up to me. The smell of wine welled up from her mouth, clothes, and hair. I felt annoyed and uncomfortable as she took my hand to walk me away from this neighborhood and that building. So her malady, it seemed, had worsened to the point where it was now unsupportable. What was I going to do now?

"When did you arrive, Monsieur? And your mother—how is she now? Is she in good shape?"

Her appearance was disgusting and shameful. She had lost her mental equilibrium and her face and form had aged greatly even though she was younger than Suhaila. Her clothes were filthy; there were bits of dried food here and there, holes on the sleeves, and rips on the front of her dress. She was carrying a mass of various-sized keys: she owned several apartments in the building. She did not look straight at me but continued talking in a nervous voice.

"Imagine, Monsieur, my mother too went into the hospital after she lost control over her organs and muscles and—"

I seized her hand and lifted my head to look at her. "Madame, yes, I hear you, but I must go, I must be at her side. We will see each other again and we can talk for a longer time. You know how highly my mother thinks of you."

Her voice rose in my face as she clutched at my arm; she started shouting ugly things at me. "Merde! Even you don't want to listen to me. Now don't look at me like that, I am not mad as people think

119

in this building. Your mother knows me better than them all. Don't believe anything that's said about me. Believe your mother and no one else. She's the only one who still speaks to me. She hugs me and we have a glass of wine together sometimes. They're crazy. Bad, wicked, merde. My father died, Monsieur, and my mother doesn't know me. And Jacques, miserable, wretched Jacques, left me and went away with a girl from Morocco. And Anne was separated from me, my daughter Anne, after the court ruling—Jacques took her, he stole her from the school door, he said she doesn't want to live with me any more."

She started crying and sniveling, wiping her nose with her hand, avoiding meeting my eyes. For the first time I looked right at her face. She was truly in a miserable state. Her movements were jumpy and she was pulling me this way and that.

"During the war, your country was getting hit by everybody, even France. I went downstairs to her one morning, very early, and I saw that she was crying even though she was not making a sound. I gave her a hug and we cried together in the hall. Your mother was more uncomfortable than I was but she didn't say a word. I told her she could go stay for a while in my village in the south, in the house in the country, but she just turned her head away to wipe her tears. She said to me, It's not your fault, Angélique. It's our fate. Monsieur Adam, did your mother tell you that? She didn't agree to go with me. She is stubborn, she said to me, No, thank you, I won't leave the apartment."

The smell coming from her mouth was making me dizzy.

"I will take my daughter back, that's what the court will order, and your mother will go with me as my witness. She said so and she is a lady you can trust. We will go to the house in the country together. I am on holiday. Air France is on strike right now. Didn't your mother tell you that Jacques left me, and stole from me? He stole my money and my jewelry and the credit cards. And he stole my daughter. Pig, bastard, salaud! For so long your mother kept after me. Leave him, she said to me, he is not good for you. But I can't, no, I can't do that. No, I don't love him any more, but I want my daughter. Just my daughter. He's crap."

Her fingernails were cutting into the flesh of my hand.

"Monsieur, please don't leave me. Your mother never left me. She waited with me for Jacques to come back at night. We would stand right at the door at night and talk. She'd watch the street with me and make it easier for me, and we'd look at all the cars passing. Do you know, Monsieur, I bought a new car for him? And suits, shares, bonds, and I put one of the apartments in his name? Jacques is about your age, Monsieur Adam."

She had me cornered between the wall and her arms. I had the sensation that she intended to sit on me and keep me there, and I could just about feel her insides erupting from her mouth.

"Jacques doesn't want to see me. He says he's busy. Fils de pute!"

Her voice was assaulting my ears by now like the screeching of some animal. Falling down on the ground, she was begging, cursing, and crying. The sound of her wailing and the smell of her wine compelled me to try to drag her into the little dive next door to the building. Her body was trembling as I carried and dragged her, and she held me caught in her arms. She was taller and heavier than I was. I tried to put her gently down onto one of the seats. I ordered black coffee for her and stepped back out of the place, her voice chasing me as I made my way to the hospital.

2

Angélique's face and voice pursued me. The image of that woman produced in me a deathly fear for Suhaila. I remembered my mother in our first days living in Paris, the image of her as no longer capable of holding a passing conversation, even a trivial one, with anyone, no matter who it was. She didn't respond to anything. I would try to lure her with the pleasant weather, inviting her for a walk, but she would remain still and silent. She did not know where to put herself in a city like Paris.

I do not understand what is going on around me, she would say. No, no, it has nothing to do with language. Language by itself cannot patch up what is around you. Language is just one means. It is as if I am without a memory, without a father or grandfather, without ancestors, without history. It is as if I had not been living before this. I mean to say, the question is, have I left my first self behind forever and I will never meet it again? I have been afraid, Nader, and I still am. But I am still waiting for her to show up: for that first self of mine, do you understand me? I beg you not to get angry with me. I really did not notice, believe me, that that lawyer seemed to find me attractive or that he was flirting with me. He is a pleasant fellow, a friend of your uncle's, and he means to show his concern for us. He is polite, he's warm, but he is a man as you are. He is like you, like your father, like all the men in every place in the world. You are all alike. But here alone is where I become your mother and I am no longer Suhaila. I have told you that before, I said it in a different way that I don't remember now. We change, and you have to notice as much, but in yourself first, and not just in me.

This was true and I felt the justice of it as I was entering the corridor of the unit where they put patients like her. Caroline's face was the first thing I encountered, a face that granted some of the repose I had lost this morning. She seemed out of breath.

"She moved, Nader. Her fingers and her eyelids showed some movement. Just a tiny flicker, and it is only the beginning, of course. Does it make sense? Did it happen for your sake?"

I followed her military stride down the corridor. But what is the use? I thought to myself. Will she know me, or not?

"Imagine it, Nader! The nurses and doctors said she must have sensed that you were there. It's because of you, see, it is for your sake, that this has happened. Ooh, she's coming back, she'll come back, Nader, you must believe that so that she will believe most of all. Isn't that so? Don't shake your head at me as if you don't believe it. Come now, it is possible that she sensed you, just you. The bonds of love, as Dr. Wajd said, are what we must be most attentive to. Nader, the fatigue of your traveling here was not in vain, aren't you confident of that? Come, now, go in to her. Put your hand over hers again—love runs through hands, by means of the pulse and the will. Go in, Nader." She pushed me toward Suhaila.

3

She looked different. She was Suhaila and at the same time, she was
someone else. She had not changed so much in the past twenty-four
hours, but I felt that she had begun to notice me, to sense my presence,
and that her body and mind were no longer the still emptiness that
illness brings. It was not simply a matter of communication or its
absence. Before many minutes had passed, I thought I could sense
that she was fighting the illness. I got very close; I stood above her
head. The pillow was blotchy with warm sweat, and a few drops rolled
off her dry lips. Whether it was the residue of her liquid nourishment
or saliva that had come back out I did not know. Her face looked
serene but there was something about her slumber that caught me,
something, I thought, that had no bearing on me. Perhaps it was
something very private, something that was hers alone, I told myself,
or perhaps it was something connected to her women friends. That
something whose essence I did not know, but which was clearly
there, surprised me and I couldn't account for it. It would not be
sensible of me, though, to be distracted by this, or by anything. I
must concentrate on her, must satisfy my craving for her and my
overpowering desire to touch her. I wanted to appear as a new son,
that I might really come to possess all I would be due from her, as
a good son. All of that closeness. All that she might be for me. For
those moments, this was enough to fill me. But all of these eyes
behind me and around me — the nurses, the doctors who came in
and went out and paid no attention to me, Caroline, Asma, voices
talking in Arabic and in French, voices muttering, sniffling, crying.
This day I decided not to cry. The tears were there in my eyes but I
pushed them elsewhere. I was trembling and I had the feeling that my
inner organs, my liver, the sites of life and feeling, had been shifted
from their usual positions in my body. The channels through which
urine was carried from my kidneys to my bladder now seemed to be
somewhere beneath my feet. I was about to pee on myself; nothing
inside of me was the way it usually was. Has she gotten to the point
where she is thinking about me, has she been waiting for me? Am I
really here before her, present to her? I touched her again and then

a third time. I felt love, that very first and primary of emotions, so natural, so immediate, always so excessive just before we part from each other. Her arms lay motionless along each side of her body. Her flesh was not so very shriveled as I had imagined it last night. It was soft, like putty or children's clay, and there were discolored patches. For the first time I was seeing all this quantity of spots on her cheeks and lower face and all the way down to the bottom of her neck and in the vicinity of her ears. The spots had multiplied across her skin. I put my hand gently over hers. I drew up the chair slowly. I began to study her. For the first time since the end of the war, it seemed, I was truly looking at her. Her face, there in front of me, looked so generous. Mother, all that is left of me is you. The fingers of her hand were all enclosed in my fingers. Her left hand and her right. And then I saw the twitch. I am definitely not exaggerating.

Now, and since last night, the layer of fog veiling my eyes has lifted. I hear the steps of one of the doctors coming in. Perhaps he is the senior doctor here; perhaps he is the one in charge. I sense him behind me and then he is in front of me. There is something happening and all I have to do is believe it. Otherwise, it will all be—

I tried to stand up as my head went up to attract his eye. Her palm was still between mine. I suddenly caught sight of a plastic sac at the bottom of the bed, connected somewhere but I didn't know where, its color that of iodine, the yellow liquid dripping slowly.

"Bonjour, Monsieur!"

"Bonjour, Monsieur!"

No, he could not be the doctor in charge. He was a young man and his features gave an impression of nervousness. He is slightly older than I am, I thought. Waiting for what he would say, I am sure I appeared bewildered and lost. To me he seemed very young, someone who would not be able to really supply me with the truth. I put down her hand and got to my feet. He began to read the metal clipboard hanging on the side of the bed. When he spoke, his voice showed little concern.

"Good, good, everything is going as it should."

"How so?" I had the sense that I had not spoken very clearly.

After a moment, he came closer to her and I moved out of his way. He lowered his head and began to study the sac at the bottom of the bed.

"Very good. The kidney is working slowly but there is no call for worry."

"And the pressure, Doctor?"

"Stable. Things look better this morning than they did last night."

I followed his eyes, coming closer as he examined her eyelids and fingers. He touched them. He tried to raise the upper lid and I saw a flash of white. He closed the eyelid manually. He put his hand out to hers and began to move it in his. He opened her fingers and folded them in with tiny movements. It appeared that something was successful but what it was I did not know.

"There's some change." It was as if he were talking to himself.

"What is the meaning of it, exactly, Doctor, please?"

He lowered his eyes and looked away from me. He set her hand down, took out his stethoscope and began to check her heartbeat. I don't know why it was, but I was feeling that his responses were merely gestures to quiet the worry of a big child. I tried to shrug that off as I faced him squarely. Two new faces appeared in the window that opened on the corridor: a pretty, delicate young woman rubbing her eyes although the tears refused to stop coming, and, next to her, a handsome dark-skinned youth who was staring at everything around him, an expression of bewilderment and awe on his face. I found Caroline and Asma facing us in the doorway as I followed the doctor from the room. I wanted more information before he went away.

"But, Doctor, do you know who I am? If, if—please . . . if she were to move, would—will she remember who I am? Please, will you tell me?"

I had gone completely pale but I stayed in control of myself as I saw the doctor's smile. His teeth were small and white, and his smile was sweet. The feeling flooded over me that he would understand me after all.

"Do you want her to remember who you are, first of all?"

I did not understand. I wasn't accustomed to such pointed, challenging questions as this.

"I want her to come back. To come back, first of all."

He set about asking more questions, and answering; he spoke about things I did not know, matters of which I had not the slightest understanding. I believed that he was being harsh; indeed, that he was being harsher to me than she was. She was still in a coma and this morning would be no better than last night. After all, though, on the telephone Asma had told me that she was beginning to recover. And Caroline had pushed me into her hospital room, exclaiming, "She has moved!"

Neither Asma nor Caroline would let me go. They were firm in their insistence that I should stay near her. Hopefully, my presence would help her to come back to herself more rapidly.

"Today, it wouldn't be right for us to leave her for even a second," said Asma. Nader, dear, wipe those glasses of yours. Zayn, zayn—that's better."

If Asma could give me a sweet, gentle smile, her eyes were still on the point of shedding tears. The young woman whom I had not seen before this morning came up to us and spoke to me shyly. "Shidd heelak, Nader, gather your strength. I'm Nur and this is my fiancé Ahmad."

They were about my age or perhaps a bit older. They put out their hands and each of them took hold of one of mine. "You'll be seeing that she has friends of all different ages," said Ahmad.

"I took today off from work," said Nur. "And the weekend makes three days. I'll stay with you here until you are really tired of me."

Sometimes hope is unmerciful, exactly like despair. But despair doesn't deceive, and so you cannot blame it if an hour passes, and then the hours languish and finally the way to hope is lost. It is too hard for me, this hope. I am not strong enough to bear it. I cannot imagine it into existence nor can I make it bigger than it really is. Asma was huddled at a distance from us. In a nearly inaudible voice, she was reciting verses from the Qur'an. With her exhalations, she was fighting desperately to animate her friend. She thought it was the only right and proper way to go about this, and I was supposed to believe or otherwise I would lose first my equilibrium and then my patience. Asma is a woman of patience. Patience is her superogatory work that commences at dawn and continues until the following day. Asma searches for patience and, if she stumbles upon it, she strews us with as much of its bounty as she can. Whenever I see her in front of me, I have the feeling that I am stepping over my own threshold. Now I hear the light thud of her footfall again next to me followed by the rustle and crunch of bags. She is opening them and taking something out, diffidently but calmly. "Nader, honey, here's the Bread of Abbas. I know how fond you are of it, and *she* doesn't make it very well. I made the dough last night and I baked it first thing this morning. Your mother says, Hammada and Nader are so like each other in their sympathy toward others, God keep you both, my son. Yallah, come on, sit down here, come on, now."

She took out a round of the filled bread. Still warm, it gave off the fragrance of Iraqi spices. The warm, flat bread encasing fragrant lamb attacked me in the face and whisked me off, over there. That I was Iraqi suddenly held some value even if it remained a hidden worth, kneaded into a loaf of bread that intensified my sad loneliness and compelled me to survey this road that linked Suhaila and Baghdad to this generous hostess. I took it from her hand. She had already turned to Caroline, Nur, and Ahmad.

"Come, now, dears, taste the real bread that comes from homes. Ma biikum? What's wrong with you, why are you all so shy? Come, come closer." She offered a loaf to each of them and then turned back to me with a smile. For the first time here in this place I was seeing a true Iraqi smile.

"I swear, by her mother's wedding Suhaila never tasted bread like this—ya, Nader dear? I made tea, it's in the thermos—I know you really don't know how to make yourself a proper breakfast, love." She set about pouring the tea into plastic cups and handing them round.

"Hatim and Narjis, there's their share. Blanche, Dr. Wajd, here, Nader, and even Sayyida Tessa, if she comes, her cup is waiting for her. I baked maybe twenty loaves, just about. The meat is halal, son, halal, North African meat."

Caroline sat quietly next to me, taking bites and swallowing in silence. I sensed she was feeling a sort of happiness and I guessed that soon her emotions would expand to include me. Ahmad came up; our eyes met as he swallowed.

"If you need anything you really must ask me, or Nur. We have a car, we know people, doctors too. They are from home, from Sudan and Syria, and we have friends in the fitness and physical therapy and natural medicine centers. I can say one thing: she will pull out of it. You can be sure of that. You just have to be strong and let your patience do its work."

I had finished the first fatira without even realizing it. And I had been imagining that I had lost my appetite!

"Strong health a thousand times over! Now eat, eat, God keep you, my dear, you have to get strong to face these difficult times you live in, all of you young folks. Ya ayni! Eat, please now, eat some more. Kul, kul!"

She took out another loaf. She swirled a spoon around inside the plastic cup and handed it back to me. Caroline, Ahmad, and Nur set a pleasant tone as they ate. With their good cheer, they were trying to break the inert silence and dispel my sense of waiting.

Fifteen

1

Commotion along the corridors. The faces of new doctors and nurses. The sight of equipment I had not seen before. Suddenly, everyone seemed to be in her room. We got to our feet hurriedly and collected in front of the glass pane that separated us from her room. She was no longer directly and wholly in my view but there were openings in the curtains, and they allowed us momentary glimpses of her. She was still lying on her back. The pillow under her head had been pushed slightly back. They were touching her from every angle and no one turned their head to us. Someone put a hand against her forehead and another opened her eyes. Arms were moving back and forth as if they were stroking her. They replenished the intravenous liquid. The nurse bent and straightened up holding the sac of urine, which she put into a deep metal basin before attaching another bag. They would remember something that needed to be done; I could see them retracing their steps. Amidst all of this busyness the nurse suddenly caught sight of us peering from behind the glass and she stopped in her tracks, turned to the pane, and pulled the linen curtains tightly together. Suhaila disappeared. Ahmad drew a few steps away and Asma followed him.

"I think they are changing some of the medical instruments," said Caroline gently. "They are checking everything and soon they will tell us what is going on. Don't worry."

"Didn't you notice that they didn't ask any of us—not me, not you—to go in? What is the meaning of that? Is it a good sign or a bad one?"

"I think she has started to move. What I mean is that she has moved in a particular way. They saw it by means of those instruments they have going. Nader, she is not going to move the way we do, not at the moment. A flicker of her eye is enough, or her pulse getting regular, or her blood pressure returning to normal. There are details we're not even aware of."

"Monsieur Nader."

It was the voice of the nurse named Charlotte. She was sticking her head out of the door to Suhaila's room. Her face was calm and her voice did offer a little measure of confidence.

"Come in, please, Monsieur."

They cleared the short path between her bed and the instruments and team of doctors. I didn't hear anything at first but I did notice a doctor who was older than the doctor I had seen earlier and had a more serious look. He was standing next to the young doctor. It was the older doctor who spoke to me.

"Do you want to speak in English, Monsieur?"

"As you like, Doctor."

He smiled slowly, as if we were in a university class.

"You may have as much of a look as you wish to have, Monsieur."

I lowered my head slightly as I gazed at bottles, tubes, and wires. The doctor shoved one hand into a pocket and came closer to me, in an affectionate and sympathetic gesture.

"It is premature for me to tell you that she will know you right away. But I must say that we have something little short of a miracle here. From the medical perspective, this might have been expected to happen after some weeks at a minimum, that is to say, after her condition had stabilized and then after a gradual transition, over a period of two months or more, until she reached the condition she is in today. The attack she had was certainly very serious. When she came in—and I won't hide this from you—her condition was hanging between death and paralysis through half her body."

"Can you explain the situation to me, Doctor, please?"

"I don't know whether you have gotten some basic medical information. It is indeed a complex case but I shall explain it to you as best I can, Monsieur. A surge in her blood pressure set off tremors in the veins that send the blood to the brain. There was a hemorrhage and it stopped. But you must realize that we certainly do not know precisely when it stopped. In the veins and arteries, there are certain types of sacs that contain blood and when there is swelling there is increased likelihood of tearing and excessive bleeding, and this leads to such a condition as we have here. Those sacs do have a charming name: mothers of blood. One of those mothers can become paralyzed, meaning the artery is blocked. Then the condition is as you see—a state between some loss of consciousness and a true coma."

"And ..."

By now, my entire face was wet with soundless tears.

"She is out of danger, Monsieur Nader. Furthermore, even though her eyes are closed she can hear us. It is possible to limit the blurring that afflicted her eyes with the rise in the pressure on the eye that can harm the optic nerves. This is a possibility and it is the grimmest one at this point in time. But the surprise here is that her blood sugar level remained moderate; if that had shot up her condition would have been very poor indeed."

I was standing there shifting my eyes between her and the two individuals remaining near the bed, for the nurses had moved back slightly out of my way. On the other side of the bed, the doctor bent low and began to examine her left eyelid. There was a tiny flicker on the outer edges of her eyes.

"Take her hand, please, Monsieur."

For the first time, I feel so truly afraid that I cannot find the strength to touch her. For the first time since childhood, I am feeling that no one has the power to separate us. My head has remained fixed on the palm of her hand. These movements of the fingers resemble a mother's first language, the earliest and elemental mother tongue. These tremblings speak in Arabic. We exchange greetings and words, as-salam wa-l-kalam, in the intimate way of words between members of one family. Do you hear me well, mother of mine? We make another exchange, one role for another. It has never happened before that I speak and she does not answer. And today is no different: she does not refuse, she answers, but so very weakly. I look at her and the palm of her hand speaks to me. Her language has not become clear yet; I do not know what the words mean but that does not matter right now. I look directly into her face. I lift the end of the tube that is pumping oxygen into her lungs. The palm of her hand seems to want to remember my name. My name is between her fingers, it is within them; I gather in my name, letter by letter. Here it is, my name: it is the first time I know the location of my name, the first time I love my name and want that name more than anything. I begin to sweat. She has begun to sweat, too. Our sweat answers for us. I lift her hand to my cheek as I study her face. I watch the movement of her lips. Her hands are moistened by my tears. In hospitals, nothing saves us—nothing brings us together—but the water welling up from our eyes.

"Congratulations, Monsieur."

That was Charlotte. Danielle followed suit as they left the room.

"Visits will be very tiring for her. It will be best to allow only one person in the room at a time, and only for a few minutes."

Standing behind me, the doctor was speaking in a low voice. I straightened up slowly, not comprehending exactly what he was requesting.

"Things will be confused for her, of course. She will need a lot of time in order to make out images, to see things clearly. That is how she will feel at first, confused, slow. We will be near her to make sure that she is not startled—since everything will look to her either hugely magnified or very miniaturized. All we can do is to try to manage and organize what is around her, or perhaps rearrange everything. This means all of you, in the first place. Her son and her friends. Just as it is with numbers, we must rely on fractions first before we can move on to whole numbers, and everything must come in comforting and moderate doses. You are the one who will help us through this process, as well as those friends of hers whom you think are appropriate to have here with her in your absence. But it will all happen in stages and through different intervals of time."

His words were firm but sympathetic.

"Should I go out now?" I asked.

It was as if they had diagnosed her with a simple sleep problem, and so this was the way she slept. It is her eyes that are my security zone. If she opens them, I will know her. As for her, it is still early. The doctor nodded. "The light is hard for her, too, but so is the darkness. Raised voices but also quiet ones. Both noise and silence. She will find being alone and the commotion of people equally distressing. At first she might resist responding to treatment if she senses anything disturbing."

"Such as, Doctor?"

"Psychologically, we don't know. What I have told you is the extent of what we can be quite sure of, what we can count on in order to ensure that the first two weeks will go as they should. And then, through a bit of trial and error, we can come upon the right code for her new life."

Pacing across the room as I watched, he stopped by the window. Only now did I notice that the window treatment comprised both blinds—very thin strips of metal—and curtains of heavy fabric lined with oilcloth. He moved the panels gently aside and a bit of soft light came in, falling on his head and glasses.

"What about food, Doctor?"

"She'll want to refuse it at first because she cannot open her mouth quite as she could before. With your help, though, she may be able to accept some types of food. What foods does she like best?"

"Everything!"

My reaction to his question was emphatic and it elicited a smile, the first one I had seen on this doctor's face. I smiled, too. The doctor prescribed the duties and responsibilities that would fall on our shoulders. As he stood in the doorway the nurses came up to gather round him, as did Asma, Caroline, Nur, Ahmad, and a woman in her forties whom I had never seen. Her skin was pale, she wore glasses, and her eyes held a crowd of words. She was carrying a cardboard carton in which sat a pot holding an odd-looking plant: a whole tree in itself, fully mature, short but with many thick roots that held it sturdily deep in the soil. I had the fleeting sensation of Suhaila as this tree, this tree as Suhaila. The woman walked right up to me, holding out the plant.

"Good morning, Monsieur Nader. I'm Simone, a friend of Tessa Hayden's and your mother's."

We shook hands. I had taken the tree and I was supporting it's heaviness with my other hand. Caroline came up. "She is Tessa's secretary and her good friend."

"Hello, Madame. Thank you very much."

The doctor stood in the corridor giving his instructions and the nurses wrote things down. When two new assistants arrived, the circle widened to make room. Silence came over everyone and all eyes were directed toward the doctor. We walked over quietly and stood in the group. The doctor's tones were calm as he directed his words to all of us. He would look at those friends and then turn his gaze to me, singling me out. I sensed that he was putting some confidence in me. No one answered, no one asked. He was the sole director here. We had only to begin our work, each on our own course. His voice was decisive, his words as terse as telegrams. I didn't understand most of what he said. There were strings of medical terms, all very complicated. Where was Dr. Wajd? Why was she late? When he made as if to move away, Madame Simone walked quickly toward him and caught him by the wrist as only a long-time acquaintance would do. They walked away to stand off at a distance together. She leaned her head in toward him and then I saw her lift it. Their voices did not reach us. I studied the plant as Caroline came over to me.

"I expect she is talking to him about Suhaila. Maybe she is passing on Tessa's instructions or recommendations."

Sounding flustered and upset, Nur broke into the conversation. She was wiping her eyes on a handkerchief as she turned to us. "I think they are talking about Suhaila. Will she be moved from this section to another place?"

"It is a bit early for that," responded Ahmad.

Asma returned to the glassed-in wall and stood motionless there.

She had not stopped praying and reciting verses from the Qur'an for a moment. The nurses were reentering the room and they lowered the blinds completely. Asma came closer, her face still full of emotion.

"So now they will start in washing and sterilizing and cleaning. Akhkh, if only they would let me in, I know what-all Suhaila likes, hmm. I know what would do her some good. A long massage on her forehead and rubbing her hands until she opens her eyes and sees me—first of the loved ones."

She was quiet, looking at me. Through her glasses I could see the soft and compassionate gaze.

"What a lovely tree," Caroline commented, to take the burden off me. We craned our heads to look at the elegant lavender-tinted card and in low murmurs began to read what was written there. *To Suhaila, my friend with her deep roots in the Iraqi soul, roots so like that of this tree. We are calling you. Hear our voices and prayers. Come back to us—we are all waiting for you.*

"What moving words," said Nur, coming closer to me. She took the card over to Ahmad who began to reread it.

"Bon courage, Monsieur Nader. Your mother has passed the critical, vulnerable stage of her illness. But according to the doctor's explanations we must be careful not to disturb her."

I turned to Madame Simone. So did everyone else.

"Thank you for coming, Madame, and for bringing this beautiful plant, and I want to thank Madame Tessa for the affection and kindness she has shown."

My voice was shaky. I could not go on. Simone held out a small card. Her voice was very warm.

"Please do call Tessa. She left quite a few messages for Suhaila and for you on the answering machine but she didn't get any answer. She is still in the south. She will be back in Paris on the fourth of September. If it were not for Caroline, we would not have known of your arrival from Canada. Tessa is directly in touch with the team of doctors and the hospital authorities. She will talk with you. Don't worry, please. Your mother is not alone—you must be confident of that."

Her words moved me. "Caroline will tell you ..." she started to say.

"I do know of Tessa through Suhaila and Caroline, of course. Thank you, thank you very much, Madame, for coming."

I felt completely incapable of expressing myself. I was gripping the plant tightly and I was sure that I would burst into tears at any moment. Simone was sensitive to my unsteadiness as she held out her hand to shake mine. We were all muttering inaudible expressions. After shaking hands with everyone, she went away.

"Come here, ayni, come over here, Nader, dear, and sit down, now. Come, dear." As she spoke Asma was reading the card. She sniffed at a bud that had opened on one of the tiny tree branches.

"I will be the one to carry it in and put it near her head. In a little while." I made my announcement and sat down on the first chair that offered itself. The base of the plant's vase was square, made of an unfamiliar material, adorned with Chinese motifs and portraits. It was not pottery nor was it plastic. I don't know what it was made of. It was dark green and edged with a frame matching the protective wiring. The plant was indeed a tree, with a trunk and leaves and roots. It was not a copy of something else. It was a real and original tree in the shape of an open fan. Its branches were not new but indeed looked quite ancient, strong, and harmoniously arrayed. The branching trunk, the tree's whole form, leaned toward us. There were blooms reaching upward as if they meant to stretch to the crown. I had never seen a tree like it. Holding it, every time I turned my head it kept its balance and grace, accommodating itself to the movement of my hands, its heaviness shifting to the rear and downward, settling into the palms of my hands. So now I had seen Tessa with my own eyes before meeting her. I considered how noble and good her sentiments were as she spoke to me about my mother.

"She will come back, Nader, she will come back. She is just away, just traveling, as if she wanted a bit of a break by herself in order to come back renewed, to accustom herself and fit in anew with us. And with her own self."

I was still holding tightly onto the plant as if it were a connecting cord between me and those roots of mine that had been severed. I held it gently, as if it harbored a part of my mother's soul, of the spirit of my homeland from which I had so long been absent.

Caroline took note of the state I was in. "This plant doesn't like a lot of water," she said. "We water a plant such as this with just a spray of water or a slight misting, a couple of times a week. It will yield flowers the color of pomegranates. You can eat them; they taste like sugar. Simone told me that just now."

Sixteen

1

My mind was on Sonia and Leon. Even so, I also recalled my father's face. I thought I had forgotten that face, but it seems that I had not. It was not possible to forget that face. He should have been at my side. All of these faces coming and going and the hands that went with them were always carrying something or other. These people's gazes were tender and their feelings sympathetic, and yet . . . it wasn't them I wanted as I walked all the way down the long corridor. The few patients in this wing stayed here for days without visits, without family or friendships. How amazing were these women who were Suhaila's beloved friends! I saw the nurses coming out one after the other, carrying a bucket, sheets, towels, clothes, and other things I didn't know. What did they do inside that room? Their eyes seemed to bear some message—a mission, I thought. "She has fallen into a deep sleep," they said. "You should hear her snoring!" The tone of their voices was a little mocking. They were confident in a manner that carried over to me. I got up and went into her room.

"This is the way she will be, Monsieur. She comes to, and then she goes away. But she is coming back more than she is absent."

She was quiet. She would camouflage things for me, feign something, put up barriers as she always had before; she would leave me behind. Don't be like this, Nader. Your words hurt me. Why do you always try to cause me pain, hmm? Why?

And then I would leave her; I would run off. I would tease, and be harsh, and mock. How was it that she taught me bribery and we began to toss it back and forth? Nader. Look, son. I have made your room grow. See: it is bigger than it was before. I took space away from myself and added it to yours. Don't you see? Your area has gotten larger—come and look.

What she said did affect me but I would distance myself. So, you have made it right, then, I would say to her. You've done what you should have done before.

She felt she was giving me this space that had not been a space, either for me or for her. She beautified it, aired it, and cleaned it. So that it will be meaningful, Nader. Why are you sad, my dear, as if your eyes hold some sort of regret? Is it because I changed the look of the room for you? A place becomes dear to us, for it has witnessed our lives' worst moments and also the loveliest of them. It is the place that occupies us, not the other way around, and so we must grant it something, though I don't know what that may be, something so that it will help us, so that it will not be stricken as we are with illness. We have an obligation not to abandon that place and leave it to die as so many places around us have died.

She always tows Baghdad into whatever places we have lived, to be able to endure things, to stay alive and not die. If there is one thing that felled Suhaila, it was Baghdad. And the wall goes up between us.

I do everything for the sake of what is best for you and then you blame me for it. I am not your enemy, Nader. Your father was not your worst enemy, either.

Oh, what to do with good mothers! They repeat those laughable expressions with astonishing facility: for your own good, what is best for you, what is in your interests, or for a higher good, as my father always would say. Good, or what was in our interests, was the end of me and the end of Suhaila, as we dragged our feet from one place to another, from exile to hospital, from the place that is beloved to the place to which it was a mistake to go. All of her loved ones, all of those beloved women, will applaud and say, You are right, Suhaila. And when she awakens she will look at us. I crave a soft touch from harsh sons, she will say.

But what is the use of it all when I can barely hear you, and when you block your face from me, and you say, Go away and eat yourself!

I am left to become like that beggar who used to show up at my grandfather's house in Baghdad, obsequious and cowering. If he ate, he acted ill, while if he remained hungry, he looked mortified at his own shadow and fell into even worse shape. Now I have become the begging drifter who waits for the feast day gift of a strange donor whose name is My Mother.

With the passage of the days and the years, I turned into a beggar of a superior and distinguished variety, for I would design the realm that beggardom encompassed. I would amass videotapes of the American films from the forties that she loved, so that she would not leave home in the evenings to go to the cinema houses. I would bring her the forms from the central library in Brighton so that she could document her research on prisoners and spare some time for me. I would search in the flea markets for antique wine glasses and jazz and blues records and take them back to her. I would always return from the university at a run, leaping up the steps, short of breath. I would be carrying a bouquet of roses and some fresh vegetables that I had bought from the Pakistani man. Meanwhile, she was huddled inside, worried and depressed but with no trace of tears in her eyes.

I have used up all my tears. I used them all up on him, on them, all of them.

I would see traces of him on her as I went into my room, the bathroom, the kitchen. Cleaning myself up, I would make trouble for her; I grumbled in the way she did, as a means of getting nearer to her. Her mood would change. I am at your service, dearie, she would respond. I am your servant and you are so full of yourself, Nader! Yes, w-Allahi, full of yourself! You handle egotism very well indeed—you do egotism one hundred percent.

She would repeat my name, saying it over and over. Nader, Nader, Nader. If only I had been younger than I was then. If only you had been my mother and I had been your daughter; if only your father had stayed on as the first and last man tethered to me, and united to my body, taking the threads of me and not being so quick to criticize every last thing; if only my milk that nursed you had run in your veins like blood; if only, if only . . . then you would not talk to me in this hard way of yours!

She was immoderate in her love and she coerced me into accepting her extravagance. She wanted to hear that she exceeded all bounds; she wanted to hear me say to her, Let me see all of your teeth when you smile.

She provoked me into anger by using her love. With it she made me oblivious. There is no one like her for loving excessively.

"Na—."

It is her.

I started. As if stung by lightning I jerked my head up to look at her. The eyes were half open. We were together, face to face.

"Yes, Mother! Yes, I am here, I am here beside you. This is just a temporary thing, Mother. Just a little accident." My voice grew stronger, louder. "We are all here. I am here and so are your beloved friends. We are all here together."

I noticed the white hair at her temples. Those signs of age had assaulted her in the time since we had left Baghdad. One day—that was when we were in Brighton—she had said, I will not let it go completely white. I will color it and appear in disguise. There—what do you think of that?

I will be the one to return the color to her hair, here! I will do that, with Blanche's help. And Asma, Nur, Narjis—all of them can help.

She always looked so pretty as she left the house before I did, heading to the main library. Mr. Ken would be waiting for her in his car at such and such an hour; and he would bring her home before I returned from the university. In the evening, she would prepare her papers. That is also how she began to work with Monsieur Alain. A French lawyer, he was a friend of Uncle Diya's. Monsieur Alain's features were very reassuring. When he saw us standing before him in his office in an old building at the Opéra, at four o'clock in the afternoon, he told us immediately that he had strict instructions from my uncle to the effect that he must watch over our life and future.

Immediately after Uncle Diya left for Africa, however, the mission turned into a difficult one. Indeed, it became an alarming mission as far as I was concerned. The relationship between us—between Suhaila and me—got so tense that I would not listen to any advice whatsoever. My uncle's prescription resembled a stimulus by injection with the sole remaining hope. I was the one who would take over guard duty for my mother, as if she were a waxen body on display in a darkened hall, waiting for my day-long ministrations in order that she not melt from heat and neglect, in order that she not rot. I was not very keen on this; my uncle still considered me an adolescent who wasn't at all serious about life, and he thought that all he had to do was to engineer some ongoing discipline. And so, by means of this monsieur, he would admonish and reprimand me. My uncle's monsieur always directed his words to me particularly. He asked me about my studies and my experience in practical things. Carpentry, construction, gardening. His conversation was gentle and affectionate, as Suhaila commented later on. But his way of getting acquainted provoked me. He would ask the same question numerous times but in different ways to test my state of mind, my abilities, and my way of thinking. It is true that he did not offer me advice quite in the way that Suhaila did, but neither did he give me a serious hearing or afford me a chance to organize my thoughts and ideas in a way that suited me. He was like the Party representative at our school in Baghdad: in his presence, I felt like I was a failing student. It was my mother's wordless persona that excited his admiration, and first and foremost he wanted to attract her appreciation, though had he gotten out of bounds it would have stirred up only anger. She was wearing black, and a lead-gray shawl covered her neck and hung down over her shoulders. She wore low-heeled shoes. She chose her apparel with absolute care as if we were going out to meet one of those foreign ambassadors, for she had a strong preference for the classical look. In the beginning, I used to imitate her. I wore a full suit, which made me look older than I was. I was approaching sixteen at the time. I didn't know the niceties of how to behave. My English was laughable and the monsieur was skilled at heading me off, steering me away from the bold or off-limits responses that I used to prepare in advance as a way of showing off my budding masculinity. For my mother he would attempt to play serene musical compositions as he chatted to her about concerts, evenings of dance, and various waltz tunes, enumerating for her benefit the theatres, halls, and troupes whose names he mentioned in passing.

We are right here at the Opéra and we can reserve tickets now for the coming performance. What do you say, Madame Suhaila?

He irritated me by not including me within the orbit of his interests and concerns. That was his way: directing one invitation after another to her, suggesting that these were places to which she really ought to go, and in his company. It was not as if she was lacking basic knowledge of these venues. She was both satiated with the theater, after all, and thirsty for it.

Of course, sometime, later on—why not? We will go one of these days, she would say to the monsieur. I adore the theater but I prefer to settle in a bit first so that I will know the ground I am standing on. Thank you, Monsieur.

I recalled what she had said to me about her readiness to return to dance, perhaps to come up with an imitation of certain ancient Sumerian and Babylonian dancers. This was after she had been subjected to my father's abuse. She was on the point of telling all of this to the lawyer, I believe. In those years, when we were still in Baghdad, I would return from school in the late afternoons to find her massaging her legs, rubbing them hard. I would notice some bruises on her body. But what she had to say about them left no room for further questions from me.

Just imagine, Nader! I nearly broke my hand while I was going up that wooden stepladder to straighten your wardrobe shelves. Do, please, stop collecting those posters and all those recordings and the pictures of Bob Marley and those bands whose names I don't know. What is this—your room looks like a shop where one goes to buy posters and cassettes.

In the evenings when I was around, she tried to move normally, but it was clear that she felt extreme fatigue. As she went into her room, my anxiety about her would stick to me like my shadow. She was acting in front of me, acting for an audience composed of me.

She was acting for him and for herself, too. Is what I was seeing now acting, as well? Did she talk with my uncle about those things and then did he retell them in the hearing of that lawyer, Alain? Was the monsieur's task to treat her, finding a medical diagnosis that would help her to sleep and dispel her fears? I used to answer him in her place.

You see, Monsieur, we tried to form a musical band of guys in Baghdad. My mother agreed to let us turn one of the rooms in our house into a practice studio but my father vetoed the whole project out of hand.

When I told him that I played guitar, a little, he was astonished, but he also seemed to like the idea. For the first time I witnessed that quiet and agreeable smile of his. It all seemed like a couple of friends sitting around and chitchatting as a way of getting to know each other better. But then the conversation changed: the apartment, income, whether it was better that I remain in the Iraqi school or go to a French school, whether Suhaila could enter one of the municipality's French language-study schools and many other things. It was nearly eight o'clock in the evening and all we had to do was sign the proxy authorization. It had been read out loud. None of us commented on it or added anything, changed or struck out anything. What my uncle had set out there was correct and suitable, and my mother said, It is fair. She had transferred his inheritance and a little of hers to his account outside the country without my father's knowledge. It is yours before it is anyone else's, Nader, she told me. When I heard her say this, I had the sensation of having become as old as my father. But I would not be as he wished me to be: a beneficial, serviceable revolutionary youth. I had seemed an ordinary enough young man; I would chase pretty girls and they chased me back as they did others, these girls from those parts of Baghdad labeled by my friend Husayn as Qusur al-Fawq, the palaces of those above where men of high status and high salaries lived. Everything in those palaces worked automatically: lights, beds, doors, and bodies. As for that amazing story we heard one day and began telling it and went on repeating it for a very long time, whenever we heard the rumors going round that such-and-such a minister was seen landing in his private helicopter by evening at the home of his new wife. . . . But Husayn said to us, No, she isn't his wife, she's, yaani, you know . . . and he did not go on. I wished I could ask my father about that story as we were eating dinner, for instance, or watching television. I would gird myself to launch into it but I didn't dare. I was afraid that if I began I would suddenly be clueless about where we were heading and where we would end. We would go our separate ways—perhaps forever? I was preparing myself for leaving him. He was capable of leaving us, Suhaila and me, for entire days and nights. When he resurfaced it was not our prerogative to see him, and so we might well be apart again. There was no hope that I could have a real father who was really there, who would open the door to me and talk to me calmly about small things, simple things, silly and ordinary and non-revolutionary things. A father who would talk to me about himself, about me, about the sweet young boys who are completely unaware of the electric current their bodies emit when they come in contact with girls, about the tears that I would want him to hold back for me and not let them pour out far away from him and her. When I start to cry, I do not let up. I don't know what I am to say and I can't call him Papa. When I mouthed this word, it simply felt to me like those strong kicks that would send me back to the hard floor. I used to count the times that I had called to my father, as if I were a cashier counting his money; and then I would know how very bankrupt and ruined I was.

I heard my mother's voice a second time. "Na—"

"Mama. Look at me, now, I'm here, right beside you, Mother. We all want you to come back. I will play and we will all sing for you. Meet the day, Mother. Show that you can move something. Please."

Here is the only chance I will have to say what I want to say to her. Only with her illness is this a possibility. I let go of her hand to get up and walk. I pace round the room. Mother, you are my mother. You are without heart. Talk to me a little. I have tried to come near to you. How long and how much I have tried! But you have not made it simple for me. Why, Suhaila, why? Here I am cursing you again.

Seventeen

1

We worked out what each person had to do. It all seemed to fall into place without any deliberate or formal planning. Every morning I showed up telling myself that this would be a morning unlike other mornings, previous mornings. The eyelids would go up, she would look at us, and she would close them suddenly. She would sense us: she might move her head in our direction as we stood around her. One of us would grip a bunch of flowers in one hand and bring them close to her nose, and we would all believe that she was breathing them in with her eyes. We would read the gift cards that came with the flowers. Every day, Tessa sent a bouquet different from the one she had sent the day before. Suhaila, we love you always, she would write. There were flowers whose names I didn't know, always bright and cheerful. Giving her a kiss on the cheek and then laughing into her face, Blanche would say to her, "Not all of the flowers are from Tessa. These are from my daughter Maya and my husband Salwan. This one is a single, lovely red rose that hasn't opened yet, and it's from Jalila, the Tunisian—do you remember her? She's the woman who wrote the anti-American banners in French and held them up in the demonstrations. Here are bouquets from your neighbor, Madame Morino and from Clara, the residence supervisor at the

Théâtre du Soleil. Even from London—your colleague Dr. Hafiz sent a huge flower arrangement and a lovely card that says, Wake up and rise, Suhaila. Rising fresh and new is your distinctive quality and you have a reputation for it. And here—look at it with me, Suhaila, here is a sketch on very elegant paper. Sawsan has drawn your face all veiled by the light of the sun. And here are bouquets from Ahmad, Nur's fiancé, and from Hammada, Asma's son. Where are we going to put all of these flowers—hmm, my dear? Please tell me?"

If Blanche came in I would stay with her for a few minutes and then I would leave. I would watch the two of them from behind the immense glass wall. Blanche would bend down and whisper into her ear and she would try to smile but she could not really manage it. Her jaw would curve slightly leftward and her smile would retreat and we would know that she had understood. Blanche would press on but without constantly looking into her face. It was her ear that spoke, and her hand, and Blanche always remembered to hold her hand and to start there. I don't know what she was telling her or why Suhaila would listen with all of this attention. My mother was regaining her consciousness slowly and acquainting herself with us one after another. When Blanche would laugh and I could see her teeth, I would feel a little jealous. Coming out of the room, standing in front of me but before I could ask she would give me a cheerful response. "The third week has passed now and the time has come to color her hair. We'll do that—me, Asma, and Narjis."

Seeing my astonishment, she went on. "That's not all. There's another surprise—I'll tell you when the right moment comes."

She always spoke with such sincere devotion and feeling. She wasn't explaining the things she intended to do as a sort of duty. Everything she did was done in her own particular way, which kept us from feeling that any of it was beyond her capacity or endurance. She never glanced at her watch, and the two of them seemed to understand each other through a spontaneous and childlike interaction. We would sit next to each other, Blanche and me, after Asma had gone in, and conversation would begin.

"I told you she would regain consciousness. We all told you that. I suppose that you didn't have any confidence in what I said. I am like Suhaila—I catch sight of the unseen with my intuition. I knew she would wake up from her coma even if, in the beginning, it was all very difficult for her and for you especially. Everyone who loves the world as she does, as I do, and as we all do, dies and then returns. She understands life in this way, Nader, and we must not complain too much about that. Just think, as I have been seeing her during the past few days as she has been regaining consciousness, she has been moving her organs and limbs in secret—that is how it looks from outside but I think that she has been moving more than we have. Where did this inkling of mine come from? First and foremost, it came from her, Nader. Ayy, death is a truth but some of us were ignorant of life. Coma: why do you see it only in the medical sense? After one of these evening visits to her, Narjis's comment was: She is more ensconced in life than we are, because she is trying to speak to us in a language we were not accustomed to before. We are the ones who are having such a hard time reaching her and not the other way around. This vacillation between death and life, Nader, is her attempt to talk with us, and with you, and perhaps also with your father."

When I don't see Caroline, I miss her. That has never happened before.

"She left early," Blanche tells me, "to get to yoga on time. That might be the only imperative as far as she is concerned, and it is sacrosanct."

"And the internet?"

"The internet is His Majesty. Suhaila says that Caroline is lacking friends. Like us. She is quite reserved. Her only inquisitiveness concerns that screen and addressing the world by means of it. Did you know, Nader, that one day your mother made a slip of the tongue. She happened to mention that she writes diaries or memoirs about being here as well as about being there. She mentioned Caroline's name and her training on the internet and your mother's own resistance. We were at Narjis's at the time. She turned to Hatim—she really respects and likes him, and his daughters. Concerning Narjis, she kept saying, This one is the gift of the gods here. She is the daughter of a family who live by a particular slogan: "Concern for the causes of the people." It was not enough for her to be a member of the Lebanese Communist Party; she was determined to have a stronger connection, and so she followed her destiny through all of the organizations on the far left. She wrote for Lebanese and Arab magazines and came to Paris to resume her studies, wanting to earn a doctorate in sociology. She didn't abandon political work and the struggle for human rights. In fact, she became active on quite a few committees, such as the working committee to free Lebanese detainees in Israeli prisons and the working committee on Iraq. She is a type of activist that is nearly extinct now. She considers herself a fighter and doesn't expect to be paid anything for her work. She offers it as her modest contribution to resisting the negative facets of Arab political reality. She is a truly rare sort who regularly says, in our hearing, I am shy. I don't like big parties or occasions and I try to avoid the limelight. Political work cannot be accompanied by an expectation of returns or by personal and individual interest. If it is, the concept of struggle itself is in danger. Some people still consider struggle to be a means that must offer some compensation, a means of material or spiritual profit.

"And Hatim—well, here is what Suhaila requested of him: If I die in this city, my dear friend, she said, please sing the songs of Husayn Neama and Dakhil Hasan in front of my grave. She was laughing although Narjis seemed uncomfortable and perhaps annoyed. You know, Suhaila has depended on Narjis in everything connected with the agencies and bureaus of the French state: taxes, guaranteed health care, social welfare, your building's residential association, and other things that I cannot remember now. Narjis is the one who organized the files for Suhaila, wrote letters for her and sent them to official headquarters and the organizations concerned with prisoners and refugees. She called her the sadiq amin—the loyal friend, as we say of the Prophet Muhammad—no malice, no jealous confusion, no meanness, no pride or self-delusion. She would keep on saying things such as, I know I shouldn't go on praising you—and in your hearing, too—but I feel as though your honesty and dependability and purity are too much to be expended just on the research and struggle you do for the sake of Iraq, Palestine, and Lebanon. Leaving your place, on my way home I reflect on how some of your qualities seem impossible in this age. Tell me how you bear it—you might as well be a man of religion from the earliest eras.

"She is quiet for a few moments and then lets out a faint laugh. She persists: But why a man? A woman of religion, a Greek wise woman—a physician. She sighs at this point as if she has located the meaning in it all. Why didn't you study medicine, she muses, like your father—hmm, my dear? You are a doctor, a specialist on all the chronic illnesses of the Arabs.

"Narjis is embarrassed at this praise. Her pale face goes completely pink and she turns it away. Sometimes she gets up and leaves us. Her pretext is the kitchen, and so she asks us, Do you want your tea with mint or jasmine?"

2

"Do you like this combination, Nader? Suhaila would mix things together more than this, much more."

Blanche would bring with her all kinds of appetizing sandwiches. Sometimes she made them at home and sometimes, because she had so much work to do, she would buy them from restaurants—Chinese, Lebanese, Turkish. Today, she put down in front of us paper plates holding lettuce leaves, tomatoes, slices of red and green and yellow pepper, fiery pickled vegetables, cucumbers and tiny eggplants, cabbage and cauliflower and green beans. Over all of it she had scattered green and black olives. It was all arranged beautifully and it made us hungry immediately. Now she stood there, her hand out in a welcoming gesture, saying in a laughing voice, "Eat, Nader. Eat, and stop inspecting me like that! Food is one of our basic pleasures, come on, don't act as if you're in a boarding school dining hall."

She began to eat, for food brought joy to her heart. I could see her growing more beautiful as she chewed—as if she were eating for the first time. She had in her mind's eye something much more than this little table that she had crafted in seconds inside the hospital. I joined her, slightly embarrassed at first but then changing my mind and taking what she offered me. Her generosity was simple; she didn't record how many bites one took. Generosity with Blanche is a kind of virtue. When I said as much, she reacted skittishly. I looked at her out of the corner of my eye as I pushed bread into my mouth. To taste food in the atmosphere of the hospital made my nervous tension even worse, but belligerently I went on seeking the pleasure it could give me.

"And Hatim?"

"What about him?"

"What does he do? Is he a writer and researcher, like Narjis?"

"In addition to writing and researching, long struggle and longer exile, he writes folk poetry and sings. You excused yourself from coming to their evening party and so you missed the chance to hear him. His voice is lovely; it's astonishing when he sings the Iraqi abudhiya. Hatim is interested in everything that has to do with Iraq's cultural legacy, from myths to costume and ancient folk dance. He has provided Suhaila with the best sources that exist on that heritage, from his memory as well as from his library. Suhaila conjured up Babel and Sumer for Théâtre du Soleil in Tessa Hayden's presence. Suhaila performed it, a routine of just a few moments, during an evening show. Tessa and Suhaila gave the piece the title *Dancing in the Silt between the Two Rivers*."

"We will get together next Thursday. At first, I felt uncomfortable with all of you, almost ashamed. I felt as though you were all watching me. I could sense many pairs of eyes following me at a time when I was completely exhausted. I tried to pull myself together as much as I could and to concentrate on making sure that Suhaila would pull out of it safely and return to consciousness, even if it turned out to be very tough indeed."

"It didn't paralyze her, though, Nader. Wajd says we are now at the stage where her treatment won't extend beyond a few months, perhaps four, perhaps six. At first, she will have to use a cane, but even this she won't need later on. Don't you see, now she is with Asma, this woman—here is how we describe her in Iraqi: Put her on a wound and it recovers. Her faith moves your heart and makes the danger evaporate. Listen, Nader, your mother doesn't believe much in luck; she's caustic about it and she says, Luck is good for good-for-nothings—and there's no relation between friendship and luck. But my response to this was to tell her that we are lucky in our friendship. She smiles and doesn't say anything immediately, but then she adds in a low voice, Friendship doesn't come down from the sky. It is rooted in the earth and it is up to us to make it come up and to tend it so that it will persist and flower. Where is the luck in what is between us? Most times it doesn't come when called. But you and the rest of the clan didn't ignore my call a single time."

"With the girlfriends only. . . ."

"Eat, dear, eat. You are her son and her country. Eat, and don't invent things that can only give you pain."

She offered me all sorts of delicacies; I couldn't help noticing how marble-hard her hand seemed. On the finger of her right hand, she wore a silver ring bearing the shape of a crescent moon, at its center a turquoise. I don't know why I pictured her in Suhaila's guise, standing on stage and concealing her face with an orange-colored silk khimar, practicing the initial movements rapidly and exploding seconds later into laughter and weeping. I felt that my powers of observation were not what they ought to be; I sensed that once upon a time, her beauty had been striking. Swallowing that morsel, I said abruptly, "I am going to film Suhaila while she's like this. Hmm—what do you think? It might be a bit severe, perhaps distressing, but it is important for me."

"Do you mean that it would be a kind of treatment?"

"It might be something of the sort, but that wasn't how I was thinking about it. If she would watch the film in the weeks to come I think it would hasten her recovery."

"And she . . . she might not be very happy about someone surprising her in circumstances like these."

"She will see these images when she is better, when she is fully up and getting around. She will see her body and her form. She will see the strengths that she does not know she has, and we do not know either. This will be the best of witnesses to all the pain and agony she has suffered."

"But it is possible—I think perhaps it is certain—that she

wouldn't welcome this. It might remind her of what she wants to forget and what she hates thinking about."

"We won't tell her in the beginning. We will film her while she's asleep. Awake, too, but in that case from outside, from behind the glass. Did you say that you are going to color her hair? There are dyes in crème form that don't require washing and drying."

"I know—I know that."

Did I want to use the camera to protect her from obliteration? Couldn't this be considered as a kind of treatment even if it was a ruthless one? I regret now that we did not have ourselves photographed with my father. We have a few pictures of him in military uniform, medals on his chest, wearing his cap, or, sometimes, bareheaded, his bald spot visible above his slightly narrow forehead. I have a couple of photos of him where I am in the picture, too: a child of four, and we are with my grandfather at the theater, my mother standing on stage performing one of her roles. There is no photograph of all three of us, though, and there never was. After the war, I read: The image is a dangerous thing: it is the opium of our society. There, images were everywhere, even in unexpected places such as the façades of theaters, cinemas, and bars. On the day I went into our apartment in Paris and saw the photographs of me from childhood to the present, I said to myself, My mother doesn't love me as much as I love her. I don't put pictures of her around our home in Canada yet I still feel her presence, and much more so than my presence stays with her.

All the plates had emptied—we hadn't been paying attention. She noticed my worried glances. "Don't worry about Asma and everyone else. I brought lots of food. I put it in the refrigerator in this unit before I came in here."

I smiled into her face as I saw Asma coming in and out, her hands lifted. They were glistening with oils.

"So, how are things going?" asked Blanche.

"Allahuma, prayers on the Prophet Muhammad, I rubbed her shoulders and arms and neck—I did it, instead of the nurse. She nodded her head and gave me a look that was all tenderness." Asma looked happy in spite of her fatigue.

"Don't you see? From where I'm looking, Suhaila isn't disappearing, nor is my father. They transform themselves into a secret or a puzzle—and then they're even more present than they were before!"

"It's as if you envy Suhaila or your father," responded Blanche, "for the conditions they're in now."

"Why do you say so? That didn't enter my head at all, and that wasn't how I was thinking about it. I think Suhaila has many spirits. One time I see her with your spirit and another time with the spirits of others, and many times with my spirit. If I do take this film, it will be one of her faces. Should I take it with sound or without? What do you think? Your voice or mine, or Caroline's voice, or Hatim's, Asma's, Nur's or Narjis's or maybe Tessa's. Why not? Why not have it record all of our voices? Right now these thoughts have come, while I'm with you. Voices talking and folding into each other, in many languages; music, tambourines, flutes, various religious chants and hymns. Imagine, right now I am noticing that we have three faiths among us, and several languages and peoples and states. So, here we go: Hatim's daughters play and he sings and you chant from the Holy Book and Asma recites verses from the Noble Qur'an, and Tessa, I don't know, would she agree to read from the Torah?"

"Maybe she'll read stanzas from the Song of Songs," said Blanche, giving me a smile full of meaning.

"And Sarah, the Iraqi artist, do you know her? I'm thinking, what if Sarah was to draw her?"

Blanche answered without looking at me, a touch of fear in her voice. "Ayy, Sarah, yes, of course, I do know her. Listen here, though. Do you mean that you want to film me with her, here, right here? Please don't, please, I don't like seeing myself in any film. No, please leave me completely out of it. I can add my voice to it, and—"

"You're at the head of the list, and there's no getting out of it, Blanche, please. Do you know? I'm thinking about playing for her, on the guitar. She always liked my playing a lot. She would sit and listen as I played—over and over—the Spanish songs she loved. I never did succeed with the Iraqi melodies. She would forget herself as she listened to Spanish music. Those gypsies, she would say. Their voices and their wailing, they are like the pain and wailing of Iraqi musicians—Nasir Hakim, Dakhil Hasan, Hudayri Abu Aziz. When I would ask her about those three—who were they, and what did gypsies have to do with them?—she would bite on her fingernails and answer me with a shake of her head. Think about it, Blanche. All we are trying to do is to make her listen to us and respond to us. So—what do you think?"

"If we move to the private sanatorium that Tessa arranged for her, then everything might be possible."

3

"I didn't know I was so hungry. I wasn't feeling hungry at all."

Blanche got up, opened her large and heavy black bag, and took out something wrapped in colorful giftwrapping. She stood in front of me, her whole face laughing. "If you knew what this was!"

"Wine?" The tone of my voice reflected what I saw in her face. She let out a loud laugh but quieted down immediately as she caught sight of the passing nurse. Asma came over and joined us.

"What is making you laugh so loudly that we can all hear you?"

Asma sat down next to us, the scent of oils drifting from her.

"Thank you, Asma."

Taking off her glasses and setting them down next to her, she began wiping sweat from her face.

"Thank you, Asma," I echoed in a soft voice. I sensed that Suhaila was in safe hands, perhaps safer hands than were my own. I ought to feel reassured, I knew, but even so, I felt a dash of jealousy.

Blanche stood up between us. "You must be hungry by now. What do you prefer—duck, fish, or chicken?"

"And I know you only eat halal meat," she said as she moved away. Asma smiled. "Thank you, my dear. But don't forget the water, please."

"Is fish the most halal?" We both looked at Blanche.

"You know, Nader, my dear, this woman has done so very much

for your mother. Ayy, my son, and God give her good health. She does a lot of good and does favors for everyone and no one really knows it. Maybe your mother told you, she has an antique shop, a tiny shop in the eleventh arrondissement that she opened years ago, practically the moment she arrived from Baghdad. She was invited by UNESCO to be part of the international exhibition for antique carpets. Her father shipped her here, loaded down with all of those splendid and costly carpet varieties, the work of Mosul and Iran. Her father had retired from the army and gone into this trade with his brother. She had graduated from the College of Communications and was thinking about working in journalism. You know, Nader? I had arrived in Paris just the year before and had started a master's degree in political economy at the university."

"How did she go from communications to antiques and carpets?"

Asma sighed. "Back there they wouldn't allow her to remain outside the Party. Everyone who works in the press has to be one of them. Blanche says, I'm Iraqi and that's that, shnu hizbiyyeh, what does party have to do with it? Iraq is my party. There was no newspaper they were willing for her to work in. If you knew where she was appointed right out of university!"

"Wayn?"

"The Ministry of Agriculture, and in a unit that makes one laugh, ayy w-Allahi, the unit overseeing poultry and eggs and caging chicks and the proper feed for such creatures and all."

"How long did she stay there?"

"No more than a few months. Then she requested a transfer to the Ministry of Communications. At least that way she would be closer to books and magazines and the press."

"Did they say yes?"

"They said yes to her transfer to the Ministry of Health, in a unit just as laughable. In those huge fat registers, she was recording the name of every child who got vaccinated for measles, polio, smallpox, who knows, even dysentery! In the government hospital, she saw some things that a body would find really hard to see and she's such a gentle one, poor dear. You know, that's when she started getting terrified about needles going into the skin. She decided to resign and work with her father in carpets. She loved all the styles of old and valuable carpets. She would laugh and say, If the Generous One were to reward me with children I would name them after carpets: Isfahan, Tabriz, and Kirman. Ma sha Allah, she became a specialist in Persian and Chinese carpets, a magnifying glass in her hand whenever she looks at one. She sees the weave and can tell its age from the number of stitches. And the day your mother, my dear, was upset about the war, and your uncle's problems with that French wife of his, and the money stopping, she started thinking about selling your uncle's carpets. They were of several varieties: Chinese, Persian, Indian, and African. He had collected them through all of those years he was away. I think your uncle did not ask his wife for her opinion when he asked your mother to sell some of the small rugs. That's when the problems started between them—your uncle and his wife on one side, and your mother on the other. Blanche says that the small rugs or fragments are many times more expensive than the large ones."

"You mean, Blanche bought my uncle Diya's carpets?"

"She took them from your mother first and organized them all together at her place. What she told your mother was, I'll offer them for sale and we will see how much they will bring. She knew their prices cold but she wanted to take some time about it, hoping that perhaps the outlook would improve and she could return them."

"And then—and did you know that I had no idea any of this was going on? That I never heard these stories?"

"Suhaila plodded along with it, all of it on her own. She didn't want to give you any more worries or problems when you were going through some difficult days yourself—and your studies, Nader, dear, all very precious you know! But Blanche—God be pleased with her—I don't know all the details but Blanche gave her a lot of money. I don't know how much. And told her, this is just what you cleared on one of 'em."

"And my mother?"

"She believed it, dear. She always would believe. She didn't know that Blanche had put the carpet in her own home until things got easier and she could return it to her. And one day, after they'd become friends and there was plenty of bread and salt eaten between them as good old friends, and visits, well, your mother saw one of the carpets hanging at Blanche's. She was startled and it upset her a little and, well, when she heard the story and realized that the carpets were still there, unsold, she cried. Blanche returned all the carpets to her. I kept them with me in trust, Blanche explained to her. I only did that so that you would not have to sell them at a big loss. That's all."

"What about that money she got?"

"Blanche asked her to pay it back in installments over a long, long time. Things were getting a bit easier and your uncle went back to sending money, and you, dear one, you were helping her out a bit by then, and the whole thing was paid back. That is Blanche for you, Nader. You know that your mother calls her friends— Narjis, Blanche, Tessa, Caroline, and Wajd—she calls them little diamond nuggets."

I got to my feet feeling very abashed and embarrassed. I felt surrounded and a little trapped by Asma, the sixth little diamond nugget. I saw Blanche pacing in the corridor, carrying a tray piled with cans of juice. She was smiling in my direction and she nodded her head at me to suggest that I join them. But I was too tense for anywhere but Suhaila's room to be my only refuge.

158

Eighteen

1

My longings for Suhaila had come to feel like a swelling bruise on my heart. She had only to utter my name for me to erupt. Sitting beside her, I began to aim driplets of water onto her lips. I squeezed fruit and brought the juice to her mouth. Everything that was Suhaila became telescoped into a pair of wandering eyes that watched me, following every tiny step that I took. First thing in the morning, I was the first person she would see. I would open the large window to let her hear the sounds of birds. And my voice. I would come very close to her when I spoke.

"This is the fine air of September that you love so much. Tessa returned to Paris two days ago. She called and we talked for a long time and she will be coming to see you very soon. These chairs will all be filled soon with them, your girlfriends — your loved ones. With whom would you like us to start? Nod your head when I call the name of one of them. Every one of them has her place in your heart. No, I'm no longer jealous of them, Suhaila."

She tried to smile. When she couldn't do it, she kept trying, and I averted my eyes.

"Ayy, though, believe me, I *was* really jealous of them. That was so when I first arrived and saw them beside you. I felt that they were better for you, more useful, I suppose, than I was. Maybe they were better to have around in sickness and I was better in health. Anyway, I told myself so, to give myself a respite from their eyes. So that I wouldn't avoid or shun them as I did Wajd. I learned later, from Narjis, that Wajd was getting here every day at six a.m. and would read the latest bulletins on your health. She talked to the night nurses and did the urinalysis and checked your pulse and raised your eyelids and studied the whites of your eyes. Then she gave you a kiss on the top of your head and left for her hospital, which is an hour and a half away from Paris even by the TGV. The day before yesterday she requested two vacation days when she learned that Tessa had secured you a nice room in the sanatorium that specializes in convalescent care and physical therapy. Mother, in a few days you will leave the hospital for good. You will return to yourself and to us. Wajd said to me, laughing, Over the next day or so I am going to be emitting my wajd in Suhaila's direction. Your mother, Nader, loves my name, because for her it conjures up everything emotional and passionate. There is no stronger feeling than wajd. She kept on insisting to me, Wajd, you must live your name fully. You cannot take a vacation from wajd. If you don't do as I say you will get sick as I do. Pay attention, Wajd, and think about it: all of our wajd keeps us from consulting doctors and keeps us ignorant of maps that point the way to psychiatric clinics. It cures us of depression and so our solitude doesn't hit us with a bastinado. Maalish ya hilwa, you will lose customers but gain the profit of having yourself. And then I, Nader, I always answer her with the same words: I will fall in love and reveal the secrets to you, all of my secrets. But your mother responds to me, I don't want you to reveal or cover up or confess. Wajd doesn't demand all of these arrangements we make for it. For wajd."

"Mother, obviously Wajd has stayed away over the past few days because she listened to what you said. Heh, what do you say to that?"

I wanted her to smile, to let go and cackle. Why not? At first, her eyes were staring blankly but then they flashed with laughter for a trice as if she was processing that voice, the articulations of sounds and syllables and the meanings of the words. Next I could see her eyes fixed on my hand. I moved my hand to hers and her hand pressed mine faintly, delicately.

I do not want time to move: I do not want to be in a whole other moment of time. I want this time alone, and you here next to me, just about to say something, anything, any letter of any word, for—right here and right now—all letters delight me. We touch; I caress your palm and I feel you, although even touching never can bestow the abundant meanings that dance around one's mother. I long for you, Mother: do not hide your eyes from me. Tell me, what is my hand saying to yours?

Behind me I hear Asma's sweet voice. "Ahh, dear, now you are a little easier about things, now that she has started to follow what you are saying."

Asma leaned over Suhaila's chest and shoulders to give her a hug and to kiss her on both cheeks. She was reciting the holy verses and prayers, breathing them onto my mother to bring her vitality. Asma does that every time, as soon as she arrives and just before she leaves. And whenever she has come she has always been toting large bags the contents of which remain mysterious.

When Narjis comes she whispers into my ear, "Asma can knead prayers as if they are dough. She can say the no god but God with flour, raisins, sugar, and butter. She bakes it all on an Iraqi tannur that she crafted herself and has at home, even if it's the sort of communal bread oven you'd usually see outside. She puts it in front of your mother, and in front of all of us, as if it is the most appetizing cake that ever was—after she has recited over it to ward off envy and evil, to keep them away from us. You know, Nader, Asma got her doctorate in political economy, and with distinction, too. She was even awarded high marks for her adherence to rules of grammar and her composition and the professional way she wrote up her difficult research. Her dissertation was on the nationalization of Iraqi oil and its role in national development. She has two jobs so that she can pay the expenses of her son, who is an only child like you. We get together at the end of every week, Arabs and French and foreigners. Our association began with a few members, for the purpose of aiding Iraqi children, helping those in south Lebanon, and supporting

Arab men and women held in Israeli jails. Asma drew everyone's admiration for her discipline in examining and verifying everything even if it kept her awake until a very late hour of the night. Every one of us who is here finds herself in an extreme state of alert and finds herself doing what she can, anything and everything."

"And you, Narjis? And Hatim and the girls? Don't escape me, as you usually do."

"What do you mean by usually?"

"I mean that you will say nothing and then you will stand up and walk away. You will busy yourself with going in to Suhaila. You will arrange appointments and talk with the doctors and nurses. As always, you will shoulder the burden of making sure the medical analyses are organized and kept track of. You will notice the little lapses of this sort or that, and you will measure the progress in my mother's condition fully when it comes to nutrition, her pulse, the way she is moving and her sleeping and other things that I don't even know about. Do you realize that whenever I see you, I picture you as a doctor, or I think that you must have studied medicine and then without thinking about it you turned to studying sociology? Yes, that's the notion I have right now as I am talking to you and you are listening to me. I am strong and I can face danger. Certain words are not said. But I do know one thing. If it were not for all of you I would not have gotten through this trial. What would I have done without you women, Narjis? Without all of you?"

She gave me a bashful smile and began pushing up her shirt sleeves, rolling them up to stay.

"No, no, God forbid! What is all of this talk? You're beginning to embarrass me."

"You'll get up now, as you always do. I was hoping to see the two girls. I'm sorry, I couldn't manage it before this."

"You'll see them tomorrow, Nader. These have been very difficult days for you especially. The reports now are good. Her pressure has stabilized. Things have not gotten any worse and there have not been any added complications. I believe this is the best possible result we could expect at this point, and it is fine, because Suhaila will prevail over whatever difficulties remain. She will move slowly at first. According to the tests they've run on her, the nerves in her legs aren't all paralyzed, although the left thigh was torn badly, but even this is no disaster. Suhaila has unusual strengths but her forces were flung here and there. It is as if what happened is, itself, what will return her to order, for her sake most of all. And as you can see, here she is after about forty days showing us that she is a paragon of will. There is no question: the credit for this is due to you."

My eyes filled with tears and spilled over. "My mother's condition improved thanks to all of you. I am grateful to you all, because you stood by us and didn't abandon us."

Narjis fidgeted and mumbled, wanting to stand up, just as Wajd, Caroline and Blanche together approached us. She turned to me swiftly. "Tomorrow, Nader. And we won't accept any excuse. We'll come here and pick you up around seven thirty, is that good? I have to get home now. You know, this is the first summer we haven't gone to Lebanon — isn't that strange?"

I watched as they came toward us. I was wishing that I had the camera with me. I would have taken a picture that would unite me with them. They placed themselves under my direct gaze and Suhaila's which she was regaining little by little. She doesn't smile but she is trying to, and her face becomes all twists and she is embarrassed until the final image is finished.

2

The next day her three friends stood over her head. Narjis, Blanche, Asma. It was three o'clock in the afternoon when the hair coloring party began. Caroline, Nur, Wajd and I stayed outside the room.

They sought Suhaila's opinion, waving the tube of dye and the cotton in her face. Her expression was indication enough that she was very keen on this. Blanche had prepared her for this day. "We won't return your hair to its original color," she had said. "It won't be black. No. That's the color of the past — and it made you appear so severe."

Asma broke in. "You will have a different look, Suhaila, dear."

Blanche came back into sight holding a large wad of cotton with a very thick fluid on it. "This shade is the color of the Iraqi dates that your heart loves. It's a good color for you right now."

Suhaila was submitting to their hands very naturally while Narjis offered a running commentary to make the time go faster. "This is a new type of hair coloring that you find sold at the coiffeur's these days. It's actually a blend of plant substances infused with scents. My sister taught me how and when to use it—this stuff is especially good for emergency situations or when you're in a hurry."

Narjis reads the instructions and Asma sections Suhaila's hair while Blanche does the coloring, laughing all the while. They arrived each toting a bag of something. Starting the evening before, Asma had been saying, "We're bringing you a surprise. We're getting it ready." Caroline's head bobs and there is a smile on her face unlike those I am accustomed to seeing from her. She seems delighted by the proceedings but does not have the fortitude to participate.

"I don't know anything about these affairs. I don't know how to even up my eyebrows. There is a boutique coiffeur next to me that does everything you could think of, and when I need a change of mood, I go there. I am quite lazy, Nader. Suhaila knows that well. Imagine it, every one of them brought something for her. Narjis bought her a pure silk blouse and Blanche made her a silver necklace; Blanche is an artist with silver. Asma, my God, she said, I will give her a makeover. We all—every one of us brought her a gift and put it beside her head. Nader, this is only the preface. The doctor said that taking all of these medicines won't make that hair of hers lose its thickness or stop growing. But Blanche says that her hair has lost its gloss. Things will get better, my dear; after all, health before all else is a matter of will. Did you bring a new film? Now let's see, how many films have you taken so far?"

I used to collect photographs of Baghdad, Basra, and Mosul. My uncle and I corresponded by email, using a private address so that my emails would not reach his wife. He sent me pictures of the archaeological remains, the inscription-covered tablets, lakes, stands of date palms, men's clothing from the beginning of the century during the Ottoman occupation and then on through the British occupation of Iraq, women's dress in the cities, north and south, the first automobiles, and carts and carriages pulled by Arabian horses. I would seat Leon on my lap and point them out. I would pass the pictures slowly before his lovely eyes. I would talk to him about everything as if it were me who feared that it would all be forgotten. I would collect all the palm trees in a cluster where his eyes were focused and then, no longer captured by it, he squirmed, muttered and, throwing his head back, began to squawk. I would spell out Baghdad for him in all languages. I would sit facing him and try to stimulate him to repeat it and fill its letters with music. Bit by bit I would feed him the knowledge that Baghdad is a musical composition worth his singing. Leaning over and speaking right into his ear, I would tell him to repeat it. He listened to me, and sometimes he responded, and then he would slip out of my hands and flee and I would go after him and drag him back. I was a happy father, happy with Leon, happy with fatherhood. How often I buried my head in Leon's little chest or his belly. I could almost eat his little feet, I loved them so much, and I wouldn't know what to say to him, as if I had been very late in returning to him. Every time I looked at him, I saw something new. I saw a picture of me with my mother, of me and my father; I saw myself sticking out my tongue in the photographs my mother had taken of me in the garden, as if I were being recorded for an advertisement of a mother and her child. I had never seen a picture of myself smiling or laughing. Was I a child who annoyed others and disturbed the calm of their days? I photographed baby Leon's feces as he toyed with them. I photographed him bathing and crying, eating and stumbling as he took his first steps. I photographed him to escape from him and to return to him so that I would not forget myself. I took his picture as a way of joining him, of meeting him and meeting myself. I would develop the films and mass them in albums but not hang them in front of my eyes in the living room. To do that scared me: I was afraid that if I hung them up I would forget him. And I wanted to preserve, keep hold of, him. Time was going by and life was moving at a run and I was celebrating Leon's second birthday. Photographs do not preserve love, my love for my

165

mother, my love for Leon. I was awakened from my meditations by Narjis's voice.

"I am certain that you will not even know her. Come on, go on in."

I heard the sound of many footsteps—Caroline's, Nur's, Wajd's, and some of the nurses, rushing into her room. I went in last. Everyone was smiling: a smile of true victory beaming into my face.

I stared dumbly. It did not cross my mind once that we were standing in a hospital room. The curtains were lowered except for a thin sliver left open through which seeped golden light. I wanted to let out a whoop in her face and I wanted to burst into tears. She was a young woman beautiful as a bride–and she was this age. Heads bobbed toward her in pleasure. Every movement we made, every sound from our mouths, she heard, and she would turn her head slowly and evenly in the opposite direction so that we could see the lovely relaxed hairdo that enhanced the delicacy of her appearance. She was beautifully dressed: a blue blouse—her favorite color. I didn't hold back my tears; I didn't feel any shyness or shame as I had earlier. Narjis sensed the tension in the air and said in a firm voice, "Even if they are tears of joy, Nader! Please, we want smiles only."

Blanche put her hand to her mouth and let out a low ululation.

"Zaghariid only work in a loud voice, Suhaila, dear," Asma remarked.

Caroline went to Suhaila, bent down and kissed her on the cheek, and then moved to her head and hair. She patted everything gently. She did not know what to say but her voice made it clear that she could not rein in her patience. "All of you—you are such devils!" she blurted out. "How did you do all of this and how did you do it in such a perfectly short time? She is returning to us looking better than she did before. Honestly, I have never seen her as pretty as she is today." She turned to me. "It's quite important, this, Nader, all of this that is happening right now. You must feel confident now about her will to come back."

Conversations were going on around me, and I saw smiles as broad as singing and the room was scented with her perfume, the one she liked best of all, the gift of Caroline. The fragrance enveloped us as soon as Caroline opened the bottle and sprinkled a few drops onto Suhaila's wrist. Wajd was silent, unusually so for her, but her eyes held visible joy at what she was witnessing. She, too, was carrying something in a bag. She went over to Suhaila, bent down and kissed her, straightened and opened the bag. She took out a purple and white shawl and draped it over Suhaila's chest and shoulders attractively. "This is from Egypt, beloved of your heart." She bent down again and hugged her. My mother's eyes followed Wajd, circling round her. There seemed to be a trace of worry and discomfort there at seeing Wajd.

"I must confess in the presence of all of you, honestly, if I had had all of these lovely friends around me I would have finagled things so that I could be where you are now, Suhaila."

Nur began to tidy the flower bouquets and straighten the cards that had come with them. Nur looked just like a bouquet of roses. Ahmad had sent a lovely flower arrangement and a card on which he had written lines of Sudanese poetry from long ago. Nur began to recite as if she were singing.

> *So remember her*
> *and make my sad heart flutter*
> *in joy deep inside for friends*

Tessa's plant had matured and new buds had opened to reveal the scent they had hidden. Hatim had sent geraniums and had written a mawwal in Iraqi dialect for the occasion. Starting to read it, Nur stumbled a bit and her cheeks reddened. Even the letters were not quite like those of the Arabic she had learned at school. She gave it to Narjis.

> *wa-ykuul inta ward wa shloon tishtim ward*
> *and they say, you are a flower and how do you curse a flower*

Suhaila's friend Sarah had not shown up to see me. She had not even gotten in touch with me. But here, for the first time, she had sent a large bouquet of flowers, a kind unknown to me, and with it was an envelope holding a pencil sketch of my mother's face and bodice with a shawl wrapped round her shoulders. She had been drawn as a very strange creature. This wasn't Suhaila at all, nor was it my mother. Sarah had given particular prominence to her wide forehead while narrowing her eyes. Her nose was larger than in life and her lips were thinner. Beneath it she had written: Suhaila, you always reach for the impossible, perhaps because you know your own powers when matched up against a comparable void. I love you. Sarah.

Nineteen

1

At seven-thirty Narjis was picking all of us up in her little car. Hatim sat in back next to Asma and I sat in front. Caroline, Blanche, and Wajd were going by Metro. Ahmad and Nur gave their apologies. With the shyness of a young lover Nur said to Narjis, "Maalish, sorry. We'll come another time, when Suhaila is able to leave her bed, when she moves to the sanatorium, we will celebrate—we will dance the dabke and we will dance everything else and we'll sing. I promised Nader, and he will see it even if Ahmad gets annoyed! But today I will be the one who stays with her, even if she's sleeping the entire time."

Narjis drove very sedately, as if she were worried about my fragility. She made her way with gingerly progress through the narrow side streets while I was hardly aware of the rush of sounds. I had been in a state of high tension when I joined them, but my edginess was soon replaced by a sort of nervous anticipation and even hope. I found this group and this moment more affecting than I could ever have imagined. How could love's energy come together so, and shape such a perfect outcome among so many collective nerves? Asma's voice was gruff with awkwardness. "Nader, dear, Narjis did invite Hammada but he is a bit shy about everything right now. In sha Allah just let your mother be well and we'll have something slaughtered according to the Faith and we'll hand it out to those who need it around the Paris mosque. Now all of this will become a thing of the past, it will, and so soon!"

She meant to remunerate my presence with that of her son Hammada on the basis of custom, on the basis that we were old friends. Narjis intervened to dispel any possible unease.

"Diyala is fourteen and Quds is eight. They'll have in mind that you listen to them play the piano, and I expect that Diyala will perform some rap songs. She loves them. She buys a lot of rap albums and goes to parties where rap is the thing. Suhaila told us that you're a really good guitar player."

I answered with a shake of my head. "Well, really good is a little too strong of a description to suit my playing. I make an attempt, that's all."

I had bonded to a strange degree with this instrument. My playing would take me to frontiers and borders far beyond the limits of my understanding. It was not that those strings brought me immediate if short-lived euphoria as seemed to be the case with most people. Rather, as I was playing I would sense these songs drawing together the fragments of my self. Through playing the guitar, I seemed to shake off my feeling of still being that young boy who was just amusing himself or that adolescent whose voice had changed and who just wanted people to listen to his new adult timbre. Playing the guitar, I could live all of those things that I had never really lived. It had never been a matter of simply amusing myself and I had not perfected the art or developed it as well as I should have.

"Do you still play, Nader?" asked Hatim.

"Sometimes, just for myself, but I always used to play for her. It's only her. She was the only one who really did listen to me in a natural way."

As she once wrote to me: Nader, play whenever you are in a bad state. It is better that you please yourself in art than that you end up being a hypocrite and giving way for the sake of someone else even if that someone else is your wife. Please, please, don't lose your patience—don't burn your fingers with Sunday cooking or the work that has to be done in the house and garden.

"And your wife," asked Narjis. "Did she love your playing?"

I made an effort to change the subject somehow or other. "When a person marries, his previous life disappears forever. That doesn't mean that it is worse, or better. But it is different. That's all."

Suhaila prefers music to all other arts. She listens with intense attention and, whatever the circumstances, whether or not she is in my direct line of vision, her body moves. I think she feels that music liberates her from being alone and depressed. But I can always hear her saying, I am invigorated when I hear you play, Nader, and it is wonderful that you play. But, Nader, marriage is the reality. Marriage means living with another person when we have no idea whether that person is wrong or right. We have no idea. We don't notice it when, between one night and the next day, that person begins to follow a different path. Even the basics—every meal!—even those basics have to change.

I said all of this and I was laughing but everyone went quiet. Marriage had stolen from me my mirth, my youth, and my happy propensity for odd tangles and motley associations. I had changed and it was a transformation in which I had acquiesced. Viewing my image in the mirror now, from whatever angle it was, I thought I looked out of my own time, ancient somehow, a being from another age. At least I looked very old. I could still move at a run but I had accepted my new image so that my wife would accept it, too, and I did not change direction away from the route that her expectations followed. Before our marriage she had loved music and guitar, and she had been all enthusiasm for those late-night musical notations I would write down. She was dainty and sensitive and caring as she carried that instrument over to me wherever I might be sitting. She took care of my guitar, too, wiping it off gently as she returned it to its leather home. She embraced my playing as if I were the university's premier musician. As I engrossed myself in my art, working to polish my playing, it was as if I could feel my spinal column coiling and my fingers elongating to become more delicate and pleasing than before, and it was all so that I would obtain her approval which had precedence over my own. She fell in love with me and told me all she loved in me; and my guitar playing was the biggest part of that passion. What happened afterward? I find it hard to make out the reasons for that change. I don't remember who put the guitar in the garage. Was it her or was it me? The strings went loose and flabby from the humidity and dust and the instrument's body began to rot. I went in there one day and saw it in front of me, ailing and elderly. I touched it in the same way I had touched Leon on the day of his birth. In the same way, I considered him a part of me; in him I deposited my feelings, my joy and my sorrow. I could not see my feelings being thrown out like this, or put aside in a corner to rot. I couldn't stand seeing that instrument so dusty and ragged, imploring me. Angry, I slapped at it until one of its strings broke in my hands. But I kept on as if I had taken up a whip and was beating myself. I remembered my father when he beat my mother. I remembered fathers and husbands, mothers and sons.

I am the exact opposite of my father, I began repeating to myself. But was that really so? Somehow, I had gotten to the point where I expected to be against my wife. What good was it, then, to be with myself? Why had I—I!—faded away when the wedding ring remained right there on my hand where I could stare at it, feeling neither happy nor sad? I had bought it before my mother's arrival for our small wedding celebration. Mr. Ken was the only one present from Suhaila's world; even my uncle had not come from Africa for it. He had apologized fervently and sent a gift, a check for five hundred pounds sterling. He had said, Buy something that the two of you are keen to have, and please accept my apologies. My mother gave us her diamond ring, which had originally been given to my grandmother by her mother. I put it on Sonia's finger. Since it was too big for her ring finger she put it on a different finger. Suhaila hugged her, tears covering her entire face. How is that I could have changed as much as this? I felt that I had been robbed, stripped of all that was me. In that dark garage my nature was plundered from me, the original and simple being that was me. For the first time since our hasty departure from Baghdad, I felt no sense that to come here was to return anywhere, but I also sensed that it was not within my grasp to return there.

"Hey, Nader, you can get out. I'll park the car and catch up with all of you."

Everyone was very welcoming and warm. Caroline was standing

motionless in front of the massive bookcase in the living room, studying the French book titles and carrying on a whispered conversation with Wajd. I heard Caroline's laugh and Wajd murmuring. Blanche rejoined us and gave me a hug, beaming. Hatim's demeanor radiated sympathy and kindness so strong that it embarrassed me. He took my hand and walked me through the warmly lit home.

"Come, I'll introduce you to our delightful pair of girls. They are a little shy around guests and new faces."

I suddenly saw the piano as we went further inside. I glanced at it quickly, noticing how prominently it sat in its own open area, a special piano stool in front of it. We came up to Diyala who stood with her head slightly lowered, Quds hovering behind her. Hatim's introductions were informal. Diyala had the kind of good looks that make you instantly happy. I recalled what my father used to say upon seeing my mother's friends, Ferial, Narmin, Tamadir, and Azhar. He would smack his lips and swallow as he greeted them.

"Kull wahda abaalik keeka! Your sweet faces look just like cakes—you pretty things look sweet enough to eat!"

I never did understand this way of putting it. Ferial was pretty and I adored her. She mocked everything—my mother and my father, herself, life in general as it was for us then. She had a knack for poking fun at beauty—her own, my mother's, and beauty's own beauty.

I can prove to you that beauty is counterfeit, she would say in a laughing voice. It's false—it's criminal, because it is against us. How can I explain this to you, Nader? I don't know, w-Allahi, I just don't know.

Perhaps this mocking outlook was why her husband divorced her, or maybe there was another reason for it. I don't know if, like Suhaila, she was being beaten. Or whether perhaps she was the one doing the beating and then things went on from there. She was always doubting and suspecting everything. God's truth, she would say over and over. They would be in the right if they were to beat us every one! We are unbearable; I can't stand myself and sometimes I can't bear your mother, either.

I was very fond indeed of Ferial. She was always so much fun. Her conversation and jokes dazzled me. The minute she came into our home she would already be changing something around, some aspect of the décor, grumbling into Suhaila's face. This place is a wax museum, she would exclaim, not an inviting and comfortable home! Nader, go out to the garden and pick us some flowers, the nicest you can find, and come right back, hurry. Don't pay any attention to your parents or the soldiers at the door. I swear, flowers don't grow well here. They sicken.

Diyala's beauty was sending me sailing somewhere above the horizon and I did not know when or how I would once again land on earth. She raised her head suddenly and I saw her face all at once, glowing a warm pink. She did not resemble her mother: she was darker and her eyes were as green as Hatim's. Her name echoed an Iraqi province famous for sweet oranges and lemons. I felt as though the fragrance of those orchards was filling my nostrils. She put out her hand and shook mine. She was wearing blue jeans so long that the hems dragged behind her.

"Diyala."

She withdrew her hand quickly. But Quds spoke up so fast that she all but interrupted her sister, her voice forthright.

"I'm Quds. So, you're Nader, Tante Suhaila's son."

Her gesticulating hand grabbed mine and Hatim let out a small laugh. "She's a little demon. She is Suhaila's pet. They have fought every time your mother has been here. Quds gets a little angry and stays out of Suhaila's way, but then she creeps back in and stands in the hall, staring at her without letting her notice."

"Take me to Suhaila," Quds said. She still held my hand in hers.

The place felt familiar. The smell of food was there with us and yet my mother was not. Narjis, passing us on her way to the living room, could hardly begin a sentence without Hatim finishing it. He had left me, delivering me over to his daughters' care. Quds gestured at her sister. "Diyala, come on, start playing." Those smiles seemed to be a permanent feature on both girls' faces.

Asma walked by us with a load of utensils and Blanche trailed after her bearing a tray stacked with glasses. Diyala sat down to the piano after lifting the top and coughed a little as if she were preparing to face the audience with the obligatory gestures that would draw everyone's attention to the performer. She bent forward slightly over the keys. When she began to speak, her voice returned me to myself and to the present.

"I'm going to play some pieces from a group made up of French Africans and Arabs. I will give you some of their lyrics, first. You understand French, right?

> *How much malice in people's looks*
> *how many insults in people's mouths*
> *generations change but*
> *people want more and more*
> *they get sly*

Meanwhile, Quds was gazing at me steadily. She seemed now to draw nearer, now to draw away as she smiled and swung her arms to the words. I was afraid the two girls would notice the tears I had been fending off. I closed my eyes. She pushed me to sit on the floor with her. Love was capable of making Suhaila well again and of making her once again whole. That notion was what had led to my anger at Wajd on that first day at the hospital.

Diyala turned to me and said in a very shy voice, "Listen, I'm not a very good performer, I don't have the skill. Please don't judge me. But listen to this second one:

> *the system forgot us*
> *forgot us*
> *till elections come round again*
> *state grabs us by our necks*
> *with hopes strong as ropes*

"I love this one—listen.

> *state won't move no*
> *'less we got so many people on the edges*
> *their breaths weigh down the*
> *concrete of le seizième . . .*"

Quds suddenly perked up. "The sixteenth — that's the really bourgeois part of Paris." She blinked at her sister and puffed out her chest. "Nader, now listen to me. We will play something and you have to guess what it is. Can you?"

It was just as if we were sitting in the garden outside our house in Baghdad, except that Suhaila was not there calling out to me. What if she had come here with us? Why didn't we think of that? I had seen her today looking beautiful, more beautiful than she had ever looked before. It was a beauty, I thought, that had nothing to do with hair coloring or finery or the silver necklace and the silk blouse over her bosom. Her bosom: that was her primary problem, especially on stage. Her bosom was full and she was always embarrassed about it.

Diyala recited the poems of those marginalized people for us. She declaimed them as if they were missives directed to us all. As if we were the marginalized. In itself, this was a message for Suhaila. I couldn't imagine lovelier playing and singing. There remained a particular place in my mother's soul dedicated to that prisoner, recorded in his name, the plea mouthed again each day, even though that little place in her soul would remain empty.

She sang out in a loud, strong voice. "Visit me every year once, it's wrong to forget me wholly." It was the famous song of the long-ago Egyptian singer Sayyid Darwish, a song we all knew because Fairuz had also later made it popular.

Suhaila could scream just like me: if death were to strike down my father, he would be more secure than in prison. Members of the family would prefer visiting his grave to any leniency; they would prefer the relief of death to being granted leave to take on new burdens, those of hope and talk of tomorrow.

"There, what do you think, ya Ustadhu?" This was from Quds. O Professor! She said the formal title in very proper formal Arabic and in a forceful declamatory tone as she looked at me, as if I were a creature who had just now descended into the world. I longed to give her a kiss and to bawl out to her, "This is the most beautiful and inviting dinner of my life!" Diyala and Quds, each now positioned at either side, nearly touching my shoulders as I sat, tried between

176

them to lift me from the floor. Flanked by the two of them, I got to my feet and I flung my arms around both of them. I swallowed my tears once, twice. With sweetness as light and as lovely as the breeze, they were helping me to be better.

I was shaking and trembling as they held my hands and pushed me toward the dining room. But the soft and gentle voices of everyone gathered there gave me calm.

2

We gathered at the dining table. My attention was drawn by the silver flatware and the costly, precious china. The table was loaded with delicacies: luscious fish, hot spicy sauce, miniature pink shrimp, and an innumerable assortment of vegetables: artichoke, sliced avocado, radishes, carrots, lettuce, tomatoes, cucumbers, and chard.

Narjis, on her feet, was beaming, while Hatim hummed an Iraqi tune and Blanche tried to provoke him. "Hatim, today of all days does your voice have to burst out of its solitary confinement? For the sake of Nader and Suhaila—please!"

He was smiling and the mutual attraction binding him and Narjis was like a magnet attracting us all. It was a round table with space enough for six people. I felt embarrassed when I saw that Hatim and Narjis were not sitting with us. I stood up but Asma pushed me down lovingly. "Sit down, dear. Mu khtaar—none of us are guests here, it might as well be home and we're all family. Nader, dearie, why on earth are you as thin as your mother, shnu inta ma takul hunak? You must eat nothing over there! Why?"

Everyone laughed as I held out my plate, steering it beneath Narjis's hand, which was dishing out a moist, oily slice from the fish's generous front side. She moved among the plates distributing food onto each one while Hatim spooned on sauce. Caroline began to eat slowly, sending me messages with her eyes as if to tell me that she was as wildly in love with the food of the East as we were.

"Here no one pushes food on you, Nader. Consider yourself in your own home." Hatim spoke as he neared Caroline to offer her a slice of lemon and various pickled vegetables.

"This is a blend of different cultures," she said. "I love combining things like this—I'm different than the rest of my family who are all bourgeois, and I'm even different than my country. I have learned to taste and to enjoy the variety that Suhaila offered me the first day we met. And then the same thing was true at Blanche's and chez Nur. Suhaila made me feel as if I were in the presence of a Babylonian artist and now here I am and around me are those lovely dishes with every sort of appetizing thing! Poetry truly is Iraq's first talent and gift. Even if Narjis is Lebanese."

Asma answered her, smiling. "Don't forget, Caroline dear, that Hatim is Iraqi."

Swallowing the bite in her mouth, Caroline tipped her head up to look at us. "No, I have not forgotten. And anyway, with all of you around, all of you as friends, who can forget such things? I am going to tell you something about les crevettes that I see here in front of me, lying quietly on these plates as if they want me to reveal what happened to me and to Suhaila more than once. But before I do that, I will tell you what happened to me. One day Suhaila asked me to make her some Swedish food. Anything, she said. Soup, gateau, any recipe, even if it is nothing more than a hot drink. My tongue went dry; I nodded. Yes, of course, Suhaila. Sometime soon, I will certainly do that. And so she is waiting. She does not insist but her expression as she invites me to share her simple and delicious dishes truly embarrasses me, but I am unyielding. I did worry that she would call down maledictions on me and that they would strike home! My mother sent me a how-to-cook-Swedish cookbook and I marked some dishes that weren't very elaborate and looked easy to make. I drew on my own everyday training, as I was growing up, in food and nourishment. I discovered that we eat as if there are secret police hovering and at the ready to punish us. I really felt things were awfully dire as I read the recipe amounts. Our food holds no enigmas for us to solve! And my family comes from a class background that dictates meals strictly within the law. That is all we know. From my perspective I fixed on Mexican food as closest to the East, and so I made her that famous Mexican dish, chili con carne. It took me a while, practicing, learning to get it right, preparing. One day I invited her to dinner. But this is enough—I have said enough! I cannot go on and tell you about the outrage I committed. After the third bite your mother went. . . ."

Caroline turned to look at me. Her face, squarely opposite mine, was crimson. But courageously she plowed on.

"Suhaila went into the bathroom and without further ado the whole thing ended right then and there. I heard the sound of the water, washing off the long hours I had spent in the kitchen. She washed her face, combed her hair, applied her lipstick and put on some perfume, too. She came back into the dining room, sat down, poured herself a glass of water and drank it down all at once. She lit a cigarette. When she turned to me, I was in the worst state of confusion and anxiety you could ever see. Her voice was quiet but the sarcasm it carried was unbelievable. If you were not Caroline, she said, my very dear friend Caroline, I would be suspicious of you.

"I didn't say anything. She went on. Did you mean to poison me, dear? If I were considering murdering a certain someone, then I would surely invite you to make this cunning dish, for no one would suspect you. Caroline, don't you dare—don't you dare invite me to your kitchen again. I will go on inviting you to eat what I cook and I'm in God's hands! And you—your punishment is that you must invite me to restaurants—Italian, Chinese, Persian. D'accord, my dear?"

We laughed and laughed although we didn't know how we might make her feel better. But she kept on.

"From that day on I was in a permanent and public state of repentance. Usually I invited her to seafood restaurants in Montparnasse. Aside from their specialties, she loved crevettes. When I told her that this dish raises one's blood cholesterol—and wasn't she following a proper diet to keep it down? I would ask—her answer put an end to the discussion: Caroline, you must read Robert Wright's book on betrayal and faithfulness.

"When I asked her what that had to do with crevettes she launched into her own version of what she had read. Among all known species, she explained, shrimp and leeches are the only two species distinguished by marital fidelity. As for women and men, it isn't a certain thing. This writer—he's American and author of *The Moral Animal*—stirred up terror in men and women both when he wrote that multiple partners guarantee the continuation of the species. I couldn't help laughing as I asked her, Are you still occupied with the subjects of betrayal and fidelity, Suhaila? Your mother didn't answer, Nader."

I turned immediately to Wajd and asked her baldly, "What's your opinion, Doctor? It seems to me that people betray each other without having to make much of an effort—betrayals that the law doesn't punish."

Wajd was not her usual self. She was uncharacteristically distant this evening and her complexion had a pallid look. She smiled weakly but did not raise her head to look directly at us. As if she were wary of touching on some particular topic she mumbled from the corner of her mouth. "For men, betrayal is tantamount to existence and equilibrium. It stands in for power, influence, and a reputation for being strong."

My voice was hesitant as I asked again. "What about women, Doctor?"

She lifted her head to look at me. Her gaze seemed very sad. "As long as we're talking about Suhaila—she used to say that women are likely as unfaithful as men. Maybe a bit less so, or maybe more so, but whatever the case, they are very keen to keep everything hidden. And that's all there is to it."

Asma broke in with an attempt at dispelling the atmosphere of tension. "Hassa shnu hadha'l-kalam. . . . Now what is all of this soul-destroying talk? Women less or men more. Everyone thinks that they have been the victim of betrayal many times over, and the very person who thinks that might well betray someone else and not even know it. People betray people without being conscious of doing so. That's what they say in psychology, isn't it, Doctor?"

Wajd did not say anything. She picked up her napkin and began to wipe her mouth. Caroline was like the proverbial deaf woman at the wedding—she seemed oblivious to everything, even though

Blanche was translating for her. She turned to me, the gesture looking spontaneous and casual as if she wanted to put a stop to this sensitive subject.

"Your mother is harsh, Nader, very harsh. Do you know that?"

Narjis was setting her plate down on a small table nearby where she and Hatim were sitting but almost immediately she stood up, still gripping her plate. "Suhaila had fancies akin to those of some primitive people. For instance, that in a plump body there must be a delicate, 'slender' soul." She looked at Blanche with a sweet smile. "And in the slender body sits a big soul. So—Suhaila would add—ascetics fast long and hard and often in order to achieve large souls and acquire vast dwellings for them."

"Thank you for these lovely morsels, Narjis. Who cooked today?"

Reaching to collect the plates, Blanche remarked, "They are dazzling partners. Narjis stuns the fish with exquisite sauce and Hatim fishes it out and puts it on the platter and arranges all of the vegetables around it. He draws on his poetic culture and Iraqi sense of style, and she delights us with her impeccable Lebanese taste and elegance."

"Allah alayki, Blanche! You are all poets. My soul just flutters away with happiness when I'm listening to poetry or reading it. But, in the end, I studied economics."

Caroline answered her, sounding sure of her facts. "Right, you economists are at the center of today's world. You organize the financial chaos and you put life into the numbers."

The table had been returned to its pristine state and we were all in that post-feast state of somnolence. Wajd stood at the window looking into the distance. It looked to me as though she were mourning, or grieving, or pining. Was it decent or appropriate for me to ask her about it? She might just avoid me and wriggle out of it. She seemed wary of any approach, her eyes conveying a deep sadness.

"Where has your mind wandered, Doctor? How do you explain such distraction, in the language of psychology, when you are amidst friends? I wonder, are there special locations where the mind wanders? Do places exist that can ease the jagged edges of distraction and blunt the sharpness of frustration and turmoil?"

She turned to me, and I saw the look of pain in her face growing sharper, I thought, as if she were struggling against something stronger than she herself was.

"Will you go back to the hospital after we leave here?"

"Yes."

"Good. It isn't far. If we talk a bit on the way, we'll find ourselves there."

"About Suhaila, or me, or—"

"Or."

Wajd smiled, finally, though it was a tiny smile. We heard Asma's voice inviting us to drink Iraqi tea.

3

I realized suddenly that Asma was there in front of us. Steam rose from the tray in her hands on which gilt-edged Iraqi tea glasses sat.

"W-Allahi, I want to hide my face in front of you, Nader, dear—I am that ashamed. Hammada promised to come and meet you but it is always the same. He is forever embarrassing me in front of my friends by not showing his face. Ayy, he's a little shy, around a lot of racket and folks he doesn't know really well."

"I am sure that I will get to know him sometime. You don't have to apologize. We have days and days in front of us. We will see each other."

"But with your mother he's just fine, really himself. He comes out of himself, talks with her for hours at a time. By God, I don't know where he finds all these words to say to her! She asks him about the computer and then she says, Ayy, he's just like Nader. Both of you are programming engineers and you do all sorts of programming but you don't know shloon how to program things when you're having any conversation with us! Suhaila says, I only hear my rare one's voice rarely. Naderan. Rarely, only every month or two. Nader, my son, is it true that you don't have much to say to your very own mother? That you don't talk to her very often but you do sit there in front of that machine talking to it by the hour just like Hammada does with his? Allahu akbar, ayy shnu ash-shasha ahamm min al-walida! How can it be? That this screen is dearer and more important than your mother! And your mother brings out all her grief and anger onto Hammada instead of onto you. Ayy, he gets a little uncomfortable, my Hammada does, but he keeps quiet, because he loves her and holds her dear. He talks to her on the phone, complains about me to her when I am late coming home from work and I go to the co-op right afterward instead of coming directly home. We pick up medicines, pens and notebooks, and food for the children of Iraq. Nader, dear, you see, all of us here, everyone here sitting with you, even Caroline; we all work in some way or 'nother for the old country's sake. Min ajl al-balad, Nader!"

Wajd was aware that I would get uncomfortable, even irritated, if Asma or Blanche were to ask me what I was doing for the old country's sake. But it was Narjis who happened to be standing nearby and stepped in to rescue me after my face changed color.

"Nader!"

I heard my name said simultaneously in two pitches. One voice belonged to Narjis and the other to Quds who, standing stock still, was looking around the room for me.

"You passed the exam with flying colors, Ustadh," said Hatim. "You've got what you wanted—enjoy it! Quds wants to monopolize you. Come on, what are you waiting for?"

Narjis tried to inject some lightheartedness. "You're in such demand with the girls! Imagine, Quds said you would play guitar for them. They really are devils! They called their Chinese friend Hee and she brought over a guitar. Come on, no excuse works with them."

Narjis's deep blue eyes smiled into mine, shimmering with true nobility, a generosity of understanding that embraces all humanity. Visiting us in Canada, Suhaila had spoken of Narjis, calling her a life buoy. She accepts you with your weakness and your sicknesses, and she transports you to the other bank, said my mother. When she puts her lovely hand on your shoulder, that is all it takes to make you feel as though she already understands your state of mind.

As for me, I thought, I did not know whether she issued her finding when she saw me for the first time. Did she understand and absolve me without question or did she postpone a bit to see what would happen? I had been in a state of suspension, surprised by those true friends, until I could make it through the truly dangerous parts. These were the thoughts in which I was absorbed when I heard Narjis shout from just inside the study.

"Nader—your wife is on the phone."

But where had she gotten the telephone number? The impact of the surprise was evident on my face. Caroline, who had come to stand beside the girls in the corridor near the phone, noticed. "She rang last night, and I told her where we would be."

My voice was faint. "You're right, Sonia. I'm sorry."

"No, I didn't forget. How could I forget, my dear? All it is—is that I was waiting until midnight to talk to you."

"Yes, of course. She's making progress, getting better. But I'm greedy. I want everything to be over quickly. I want her to go back to being as she was before. And that isn't going to happen right away."

"No, not at all. It wouldn't be good for the two of you to come right now. What's that? I didn't say that you were pursuing me. Yes, of course you're worried. I know that. But I did not want to worry you any more than I already have. Of course I'm concerned about the two of you, Sonia. Please, this isn't the time for scolding and blame. Don't put questions to me that I can't answer in advance. How am I to know when I'll be able to come back?"

"Fine. If your sister is coming from London day after tomorrow, I'll be more reassured. How is Leon?" She put the receiver to his mouth and he began to talk to me in his incomprehensible language, babbling his repeated syllables and singing.

"Yes, she has shown some movement. No, not her whole body,

just her fingers and eyelids. She opened her eyes partway and closed them. That has been the pattern; she comes back, in some fashion, and then she is gone again. I don't know, as if she is playing with me. When she opens her eyes she doesn't look at anyone. She just looks into empty space, and it is a sort of strange look. It's as if . . . well, as if a person isn't himself, isn't the one we used to know. Basically, this is what I have to expect to see over the next little while. The doctor said that there is no cause for fear. That it is very natural to be like this during the first period."

"Completely. She was saved from the worst, and we all want to believe that."

"We'll go to her when we leave here — Dr. Wajd and I will go. Bye, Sonia, see you soon."

I put down the receiver and slumped back into the roomy sofa. Leon's voice was still in my ear. Daa-dee, BACK! I remembered wishing one time that I could have a womb so that I could give birth as Suhaila and Sonia and all the women on earth do.

"Is everything fine, Nader?"

I raised my head to Narjis. She was carrying plates of maamul and the Lebanese pastries that I loved so much. I stood up.

"Let me help you with those — please. No, no, it's all right, everything is fine, it is just anxiety."

"That's natural, isn't it?"

I don't know if I had been wrong to keep the details from Sonia. I really didn't want to worry her. But her voice today carried an additional resonance, something other than worry. Jealousy, perhaps — I was surrounded by women. I had not seen a wedding ring on Wajd's finger, or on Caroline's or Asma's. And Wajd wasn't "fine." She was still looking remote, impossible to reach, as if she had had a shock before coming here. Perhaps I noticed it because I had gone through something like it. Perhaps it was a relationship with a man that was going bad. But why did that particular possibility occur to me at this precise moment, with Sonia's voice still in my ear, with Sonia clearly on the point of collapsing and bursting into tears? The glass of tea was all but cold in my hand. I stirred the spoon slowly and heard my name ring out again.

"Na-a-a-der . . ."

Quds again. She was on her feet, prepared, waiting for me. She had changed her clothes; what she wore now seemed inspired by American First Nation styles. She had dyed her face in a rainbow of colors and put a feather atop her brow. She stood in front of me like a cannon primed, wanting me to say the word. Bewitching! She grabbed my hand and, without saying a word, planted me in front of the guitar lying on the long couch. The Chinese girl, Hee, and Diyala next to her, were waiting as if they were expectant hosts of an impromptu party. I gave a start, though, seeing that the instrument in front of me was miniscule, just slightly larger than the first guitar I had ever had, the one I played in Baghdad between my seventh and tenth birthdays. They exchanged glances and then turned to me.

"Here, Nader, ya okay it is a small guitar but it's the best we've got here. Come on, we'll accompany you, we'll clap and dance. I dance better than they do."

Quds made a victory sign and hung on to my hand. What could be a more encouraging incentive to play than this amalgam of sweet and flirty? My voice was no more capable of being heard than it was ready to decipher the clashing feelings working in my chest. Caroline stood up, camera in hand, and began snapping pictures amateurishly—tac, tac, a glowing flash and then darkness. I had to make these girls happy. Diyala was giving me furtive glances. Her eyes shone and I felt that in some way I was performing especially for her. Immediately I picked up the guitar. Diyala turned off the bright light in the hall and struck the pose of an emcee comfortable with her audience, who exudes unmistakable and earnest sentiments toward the crowd. I settled myself on the sofa.

"Play whatever you wish, Nader," said Caroline, the kindness spilling from her voice. I heard the warm timbre in Narjis's voice. "We will listen to your playing from over here. It is better this way."

The adults remained in the living room while the girls sat on the floor in front of me. Their eyes were following me closely, alight with intelligence, verve, and a delight beyond description. I began

186

to play slowly. I adjusted the strings and half-closed my eyes. A wave of pain that I cannot characterize swept through me. It was not the pain of earliest childhood or that of pure teenagerhood that has gone forever. It was the pain one knows who has never reached that promised ecstasy, for he has seen love slip through his fingers: my first love, my love for Layal. The pieces of music were like my grandfather's prayer beads. I had only to place my fingers on the strings for the tunes to detach themselves little by little and drop from my hands. My heartbeat was picking up the tempo and my fingers were pounding faster and faster. I was afraid of failing in front of them. And overpowering emotions pulled me to those first, original melodies, the ones Layal had so loved, the ones I had played for her without having to practice. *Love Story*. When Layal said, I am going to Beirut, I did not get it. I did not understand that she was leaving me. She said she would come back and I believed her. Perhaps she assumed that it was not really very important in the end, or maybe she simply forgot, while I waited for her in front of the cinemas, at the doors to museums and theaters, and in the cafés of Paris. Layal always seemed exceedingly wary of young Arab men, especially exiled Iraqis—those who had no street addresses for their fathers. Her only hint to me that she might be mine was a tiny shake of her head, a miniscule toss that threw me at first. Yes, here I began to repeat that particular segment of melody. I would whistle it in her presence and she would sway. We used to walk the streets and boulevards in rain and snow and gales of wind. I would follow her and call out, right in front of the passersby, as if I were an Arab poet-lover of another era. Look at that face of hers whose beauty has made me waste away. Tell her that if she's a beauty she's a vain and arrogant one—so that I can cloak my dignity in my ire. And Layal is always in front of me, always there ahead, like my father's whip. I imagined a whip uncoiling, exploding in her hands, and instead of throwing it elsewhere, she cracks it in my face. She stops me with hot tears and as I face her, her voice seeps out, separating itself from the sounds of rain and tears.

Listen. I am not good for you, I'm not right, and the same goes for you. I am afraid of this kind of love. I am afraid of you. No, let me go, I am not the right one. Go, right now, and leave me, go, leave me to myself.

But she fragments, scatters the parts of herself, and draws me to the slivers of her that she has left behind. Every time she wanted to separate from me, I clung harder, to the point where she would spring away from me, a leap backward exactly like Diyala's. This girl's face is as alight as Layal's was. How often I begged Layal not to let the tears flow but she did not answer. Her face closed up like the wall of a dam and her fetching brown eyes shone with something other than tears although what exactly it was I do not know. But she wouldn't say anything. She would not talk to me. She was intractable and callous and painful. I could not forget her severity nor banish her rebuking tone of voice as I heard the whistles of trains leaving Paris for Lisle where she lived and studied. She was going to leave early in the morning. I must kiss her before I die. That was what I was thinking before I saw her. I believed I would die if I did not kiss her. Seeing her, I did not die although I was not happy, either. As she walked along before me, my longing was tearing me to pieces. She would take a seat, smoke a cigarette, drink wine. The first time I drank wine, it was she who taught me how. And when she came toward me I would open my arms. I would want to gather her to my chest. With her at my side, with that slim body of hers next to me, I breathed calmly and slowly and I felt as if I were just awakening from a dream. I told her that her body was my summer. The moment she heard me say that she laughed but she had no words. I wanted to gather her in my hands as threads of silk are brought together and intertwined, and so to discover new desires that no one before me had experienced with her, or with me. But we did not talk. I went on watching her and burning, as she smoked and I sniffed and breathed in her smoke. I grabbed her, one day, by her hand and dragged her off. We got into the first taxi that came by and went to the apartment that mother and I shared. Suhaila was in Tunis at the time, attending a symposium on the theater. In my room, there was a single piece of fruit, a pear that my mother had put into a nicely etched bowl.

You are practically crushing me, she said. Nader, please, leave me alone, I'll eat it by myself.

188

I put the fruit between her lips, between tongue and tongue. I began to peel it, my tongue and my teeth reaching. I pulled off the skin, my tongue quiet between her teeth. I did not close my eyes or give any thought to myself. I began to push the juice into her mouth, inside of her, far down and inside. It bubbled and ran down her throat and I licked it and she was on the point of falling asleep and I wanted her to open her eyes a little so I could know her more closely. But she did not look at me. It was me who was fading from view. I was playing tricks on myself so that she would not distance herself from me when she was in my arms. She would withdraw into herself, moving further and further away from me. She would tremble, and shiver, and I would touch her. I would stroke her slumbering body, that soft body that made me dizzy but that was never obedient to me. It shrank away from me; it grew remote as if to refuse this communion. I believed her when she said that she would return. I believed everything she said to me. And no sooner would she stir, meaning to leave on the instant, than I would begin my flight from her. Without warning, I sensed myself rejecting her. She was slinking away; she was killing me with pure ferocity. This was not Layal, for whom I played songs I had learned in my country. She was leaving me and going to another place and what and where it was I did not know. Playing the guitar, I fantasized that she was listening, as the sweat beaded on my forehead and my clothes, as if she were saying to me, Go, Nader, go on your way. Work out your life far away from me. I have been fleeing from the war and you are coming from it. The war is between us, Nader. Why can't you believe that? This isn't something that concerns only you or me. We live among dead people more than we do among the living. . . .

The clapping rose around me and an adolescent hand grabbed me by the shirt.

"We recorded everything you played!" Diyala said this shyly, her expression a copy of Layal's face. Standing by herself, Wajd stepped nearer to me but remained standing. Her eyes said to me that she had heard and seen everything. She knows, doesn't she? I didn't avert my eyes from her nor did she take hers from me. As we exchanged looks I was trying to smile; I lowered my gaze from her, then. Asma broke the silence, her voice merry.

"Your mother didn't tell us you were such a wonderful guitar player. No, no, your mother did not let on! I'll bet in your mind you were playing for her. Tamam, Nader, that was wonderful, wonderful. Did you think about your mother as you played, hmm, my dear?"

She had a broad smile on her face as she went on. "What Hammada is missing! W-Allahi I will tell him everything so that he is sorry he didn't come and hear you."

"I'm a beginner, just an amateur."

"You were angry, Nader," said Blanche, "and you were working hard to keep us from noticing it."

I didn't burden myself with answering. I did not want to land myself in a situation that I didn't know how to get out of. Hatim looked me straight in the eye. "It is as if you are threatened by some danger as you play. As if you are in a little rowboat and are worried that you will drown. But the message got through, Nader."

I stood up, turning my head among the three girls. Each one stuck out a hand. I raised Hee's hand to my mouth and imprinted a kiss on it. Quds smiled as she put out her hand, offering me the yellow feather. I poked it into the pocket of my shirt. She did not say a word but she kept her eyes on me. And then she retrieved her gracefulness and turned in the other direction.

"Take it, there you are. Haak. If this drawing doesn't please you then you will have to come here again so I can finish drawing you. Your face was a little hard to make out as you were playing."

"He will come here again. Many times. He will still be here in Paris and we will see him often." Hatim was propelling them toward the corridor that led to their rooms. Diyala had an unending stream of words to get out, as I realized when she was standing in the shadows of the hall. There was a sudden silence and everyone was standing up or moving. Diyala wanted to say that the time had passed quickly. Was it a single minute, a second, or even shorter, or was it longer? Layal could be presumptuous and stubborn. She said she would come back one day and I believed her. It would have been better if she had not said that at all as long as she was not able to do it.

Wajd stood in front of me, her purse in her hand. "I will go with you to the hospital, Nader. I want to get back to her and see how she is doing, with you."

She paused. "Will it bother you if I go with you? I mean, do you want to go without anyone, to be by yourself there?"

I smiled at her but I did not say anything.

"Tomorrow, okra stew at our place. Please don't forget." Blanche was laughing as she offered the invitation to us all, grouped in the entryway.

"Nader, one minute, please." Narjis took me by the hand and we walked over to her desk. I saw files crammed full. Postcards, official letters, French and Arabic newspapers and magazines, books piled high.

"I want to thank you but I don't have the strength, I don't know what to say."

"Don't say this again!"

"For the loveliness and hospitality and the lovely girls. Narjis, I'm unable, really I'm unable—"

"Listen, Nader. We have a great deal of work ahead of us. Suhaila handed over to me a lot of files on the prisoners, on the 1980s war specifically. And, I collected files on the 1990 war for her, but there is a lot that I am still missing. Would it upset you to look through her papers for—here, take this, I wrote down what I want, because she wasn't able to give these things to me before everything happened, and you know the rest. We have campaigns ahead of us. Writing letters, petitions, recording all of the grievances, going to demonstrations, and collecting anything and everything for Iraq. Do you have the time and the desire to search these things out? Or even to work with us as long as you are here? This would be helpful to us and beneficial for you. And for Suhaila, according to my thinking. Give it some thought. Today is Thursday, and it seems likely that we will take her on Monday to the sanatorium. Did Tessa explain the details to you?"

"Yes, she explained it all. Everything is ready to go."

"And your work, Nader? And the family, and everything else?"

"Caroline and I have worked out everything with the head of my company, by email. He was very understanding about my new circumstances. If things are stable at the weekend I'll search for what you have asked for. Again, thank you, Narjis."

Diaries

The news this morning, yesterday morning—there is no change. They will strike the country again, and just like that, whenever they want, without giving us any timetable in advance! Soon, they say. Or later. Now. Could be any time. They have taken this as their special mission in life and their area of expertise, and they have gone all out, and now they are positively on fire with the excitement of it all. We are not alone as the targets of all of this love that they apply to corpses—and there can never be too many corpses. It is not yet quite the right time, intones the news announcer. When?—we are in December now, so ... in the New Year? Or before?

I snuggled into my very thick and heavy woolen shawl, took out a cigarette, pulled open all the curtains, stretched my legs out in front of me, and began to study the naked trees outside the window. I could not take that first puff, though. On my lower lip there was still a trace of a fever-blow. Latmat humma—that, I said to Wajd, is what we call it in Iraqi Arabic. It's a blackish bruise that has a mean way of developing. Suddenly it is making it very hard to talk, as hard to say anything as it normally is to swear, and a smile is even harder to manage. Layal called a little while ago so that we could comfort each other before the next blow descends, and to repeat her invitation to attend her doctoral thesis defense. My dear, I said, I can't do it. My face is all bruised. I feel as though it isn't my face. That fever-blow is marching in time across my skin and I am just following along—where to, your Lord alone knows.

Her enchanting voice came back to me instantly. Suhaila, you will be more beautiful than ever! Come, now, don't use that as an excuse. My mother, who does not even know you personally, hounded me to make sure you would be there in her place, and in Nader's place, too. Tayyib, come for his sake, then. Will you?

All right, then, I said. Tammam. I suppose that the leftover traces of fever are a pretty trivial case. I grant you that. But, you know, sometimes what is trivial sets the highest example for us.

She laughed. And added, to shut me up, Tessa Hayden will be there. She is honorary member of the committee. I'm sure you will forget those effects of the fever and all of your various woes soon enough.

⁓

Twelve noon.

I'm in a very bad way and it's unsettling. Annoying. It's not just a matter of the many and long years I've lived. There is something additional going on here. Something that is sneaking ravenously between my temple and my jaw and creeping in beneath my eyelids. It doesn't seem to slow down at all and it hasn't given me time or space to make up for the steady losses. Every day it strips a layer from me without even allowing me the meager compensation of being able to howl like a faithful dog over whatever traces of flesh and bone I can still find as they are coming apart and disintegrating. Incomparable courage there!

It is the fact that I have reached this ripe old age and I am now on the other side of the pinnacle; nothing more. The age of maturity! I stumbled over it in my path like an obnoxiously clever girl on her way to school, but I have always just knocked her breezily onto the main road and continued on. But then I would feel my teeth shifting in the gums. I would clench them, my jaws clamped together all night, and the moment I woke up I could see the blood on my pillow and my gums would be swollen. My teeth were the first thing to disappoint me. Dr. Nabil said it was a matter of inheritance. There's no escaping it, Madame, he said. I'm so sorry, but there is nothing I can do and I am afraid it is going to go from bad to worse with every year that passes. May God compensate you! And may you live a long and happy life! I started to keep on hand a supply of openwork lace handkerchiefs that I could put over my mouth whenever I laughed. And then I decided that there was no real need to laugh, either, and hopefully, if I could avoid that, it would keep the peripheries of my mouth, already seriously damaged, from deteriorating any further. I figured that a permanent frown and a serious attitude would produce excellent results. But the position of my nose shifted: it no longer had that pert and prideful lift. I swore to Blanche that things were better in Baghdad: its position was definitely preferable there. In truth, my nose apparently enjoyed a firm alliance with luck, back in Baghdad. It would go up a little, in disdain, and my sense of dignity would increase accordingly. At least I would die happy, as long as I couldn't live that way. I no longer remembered my parents' noses. Now I have completely forgotten the shape of them. Did they become bent and lowered from it all? So many things that could break a nose. . . .

Blanche makes things so much easier. Her laugh rings out and her response comes promptly. It's not your fault, and don't worry about any of it, she says. When I win the Lotto we will do the necessary repairs to whatever has been damaged. Blanche has more faith and more natural joy than I have been able to manage. When I am standing up, though, I have been working on devising all sorts of ways to make my bones grow. I have been compelling my backbone to stand tall in arrogant defiance. When she hears this from me Asma starts to laugh. And finally she asks, How can this be, Suhaila? And what do you mean by it? Billahi alayki, God help you, now answer me! Kayf? How in God's name does this help?

Asma, my pet, Usayma! Arrogance rebuilds the bone marrow, I answer her firmly. If you are modest and retiring you will find that your marrow has been consumed—that it is reduced dramatically. I can't stand modest bones. Asma goes on laughing as I go on explaining. Ayy w-Allahi, I swear to you, I tell her. You know, in Baghdad I was taller by at least five or six centimeters.

When did this meek, enigmatic and obscure kind of rotting begin to set in? No one answers me when I ask this question. Suddenly you don't come upon your own height. Ferial is slightly shorter than I am and so is Rabab. In the Academy everyone called us The Tripartite Alliance of Short Women, following the pattern of The Three Knights. The long and short of it is that my heart is open and equally is shut tightly. Today expressly I am in need of the epidemic of youth, that which in my case I concealed sadistically. The youth whose taste I have never known. That my illusory youth existed is proven only by the mature years I have reached. It began like this fever-slap on my lower lip; I annihilated it there in Baghdad when I was with him. I invented youth but I did not test it out as one usually tests inventions, in trials and laboratories. There was a time, in Brighton, when I told Nader (between us sat a pretty white candle and two glasses of wine), If you want the truth, I don't want to hide from life in all of his longwindedness. It is up to us to refrain from annoying life, life as old age. We must leave him to stumble over his own steps and then he will not know how to apologize to us. We must make him visible, all of him. We must proclaim him on our faces and put him where he belongs and not overdo our adherence to him. Then we can hope that he will grow ashamed of behaving so basely when it comes to all of the ways we deceive ourselves. That is what I said to Nader, but I felt rather embarrassed in his presence. I was too ashamed to tell him that every one of my desires was as rampant and foolhardy as it ever was. I had not stamped out even a single one; but that was because I had not yet discovered what my desires were. When I raise my glass high, chez Caroline or Blanche, I find it impossible to believe that I have lived, and I cannot believe all of the seconds that were mine to draw on and all I did was to draw back. I cannot believe that I was thirty-eight when the lord and master, the sayyid, went away and did not come back. I did not know whether he had fled, been imprisoned, killed himself, or been killed. The puzzle of his disappearance and the specter of the refugee camps tore my youth and my desire to live up at the roots. And now here I am squandering these years of living and pacing inside the maze of my life, so that I become an exemplary lesson to warn those who shall heed lessons. The enmity to my body intensified whenever the viruses of desire entered it, so I would vanquish them and exhaust my body by means of the volunteer work I did for various associations, and with dancing lethal enough to make me dizzy and faint. On the day we first met, Wajd listened to me with genuine intimacy. When the examination proper was over, we were heading outside together. She invited me to her apartment in the eighteenth arrondissement, where we drank wine and opened a few tins of food. She talked to me about how lonely she felt, and she was very open and spontaneous about it, too. Were we really so alike?

No, Wajd, I said. We are not alike. But in the end, we are two women alone in Paris.

She stopped talking and looked at me, and then she spoke before I could do so. Don't you see, Suhaila, that my skin has started to wrinkle? I feel it. My flesh is sagging. I used to be finer looking than I am now, much lovelier. I was infatuated when I crooked my finger at him. He was my self-esteem and pride. I was stupid. I did not ask him, Are you as in love with me as I am with you? For him I would summon and collect the words of the ancients and the moderns. I thought about him on the Metro, and in the trains that took me to the popular clinics outside Paris, and in bed as I teased my body so that his touch would pass across it and I would break out in sweat and sweetness. I never found it difficult or tiring, Suhaila, to talk to him night and day. I would tell him all the details of everything. Secrets, stupid little things. I got pleasure from finding excuses to talk to him. Every minute, it seemed, I loved him more than I had before. I never repeated the things I said to him. I wanted to take care with every word I said. He would use the secret powers of talk on me. I would whet his appetite just enough so that he would have a taste of me and would enjoy me, so that I was nourished by him. He was my good food; he was the nourishment I fed on and drew sustenance from. I wanted him to swim in my body, which longed for him and to float on my lips which were thirsty for his kisses. I wanted him to form bonds of sympathy with my youth before it began to decay. Yes, he is from North Africa. But there was some sort of curvature in his spine. There was something unsound there, some bruising. At first I wasn't alert to his deviousness, his artificiality. So be it, I told myself. I will take care of him, not as a doctor or as a mother but as a lover. I didn't lose patience and I did not give way. He was of some odd, maybe fantastic, species. It was not a question of illness; that is too simple. He would drop out for weeks. He would disappear entirely without having any reason for it; he stayed away in hopes of deceiving me. He was a famous bone surgeon.

I would laugh and answer her. Maybe he enjoyed breaking your bones. She would not pay any attention to my teasing. She would keep on talking. But I did not hate him, Suhaila. He was very weak and he would make threats.

She said that with such sadness. I would make excuses for him and love him even harder and more, she said. Sometimes it seemed to me that I loved him before I saw him. Don't laugh at me, Suhaila, and don't say I'm the doctor and you are the patient. Sometimes things blend into each other and people switch roles. And that is what is happening right now.

⁂

Three p.m.

I love Paris's summer: doubt besets its atmosphere at every moment. I put on big, loose flowing shirts and long narrow skirts so that I will look taller. Most days, I put my umbrella into my bag and wear my raincoat. I love the uncertainty that grips us from the month of June to August. A person walks many steps between the splatter of the rain and the heat of the sun. I become many creatures in that season. As for this cold which seeps into the bones and hands and feet, and into the heart most of all, what shall I do with it?

There is the phone again. Layal pleads and insists. I'll be there, I tell her.

Why am I here, in this very narrow and cold bathroom? My face in the mirror is inescapably close. I will take an anti-allergy pill now, right now, before I find myself in the lecture hall and the scratching and wrangling begin. I do not want to create any disturbance. Allergies are a stupid disease; they are "trivial," remarks Wajd.

197

Hayif. The general run of my sicknesses are trivial and apparently these are the ones I deserve. It seems that where I am concerned not a respectable illness is in sight. Even high blood pressure is a ridiculous malady that afflicts millions of people all over the world. I have longed to have an illness that would bear some resemblance to me. It would be a sickness worthy of me, and it would be my one and only infirmity. An allergy does truly cause inevitable suffering, as trivial as it may be, because you cannot really anticipate when it will show up or in front of whom, or with whom you will be when it does make an appearance. It begins down the arms, a preface to what will come. Next, there comes an itch in your armpits that descends to the soles of your feet. The itch I would get across my chest and stomach would take such forceful hold of me that as it swept across me I would try my best to vanish from everyone's sight. My back is the worst culprit, playing such tricks on me and treating me so very badly. It is like contending with a demon. I cannot reach every spot. I bought a mother-of-pearl backscratcher and put it next to my bed. My allergies have gotten worse here. This surprised me so much that I went to Dr. Sallumi, the physician to whom Arabs and emigrants go. How very nice he was, really. He explained the origins and causes of allergy.

It is the only illness that doesn't kill, he said. But still, it is a malicious one.

Examining my back, he was not as clear and concise. Does it make sense that a woman of your age would carry on her body a bloody map like this? he muttered. And then: Did you feel any pleasure at doing this? He began to touch my back. I shied away and stood up immediately. When she took me to him, Sarah had said, He is not bad. He will give you several kinds of medicine. Six at the very least, and one will be the right one. You will not see immediate signs of improvement, but do persevere with him. Use pretexts or use some charm, it makes no difference. Don't be put off by his revolting jokes. He is really a very good man.

But he is always picking at me in the most irritating manner, I say to her.

Eh bien? One day I will tell you about my other Arab doctor.

He would have killed to sleep with me, and that was when I was unconscious from poisoning. I smelled disgusting but he tried anyway. They all try. We are all projects for each other, but the men are always in such a hurry, more so than we are, I think. Why do you expect it to be otherwise, Suhaila? And afterward they will have a lot to say to us or about us, whether they got us or not. It isn't your problem. You are free to take it or leave it. Sallumi is not the worst of them. Can't you see yourself? You look like dead wood. You have dried up; everything about you is arid, desiccated, dry as a bone. All you are now is remains, ruins. Don't you trust what I am saying? What did you do to yourself there, my dear, and what will you do here? Look, they are just like us, young pullets with our feathers all plucked. Maybe they are not in such a bad way as we are. Maybe they are not as unhappy or alienated because at least they are clear in their minds about it. You don't seem to get it. Why don't you?

Sarah isn't very good at giving comfort. On that day, Dr. Sallumi gave me a long white pill, breaking it in half. Take this half now, he said, and the other before you go to bed. It will make you drowsy, but that's okay. Do you have a car? Don't drive in this condition. Go home right away. These pills are not to be combined with alcohol consumption. Do you drink wine?

∽

Four p.m.

I really must get my hair cut. Just enough so that it will look like it did three months ago. Where is the rose-pink card on which they have recorded the number of haircuts I have had? The coiffeur stamps the card and says with a feminine lilt, There you are. The tenth haircut will be free of charge. Each time I am there, I sit in front of him like a failing student. When I am on the point of losing my mind from depression and despair, I open those magazines and I point to one of the models. At the end of it all, I have a haircut that bequeaths me trouble and foolishness. I ask the coiffeur to shear off as much hair as he wants to, so that I will look a disaster. And then I disappear from everyone for a period of weeks or sometimes months, and I do not suffer in the least for it. Asma is the only person I see. When she sees me, she is always the first to speak and she is always forthright.

You are really overdoing it, Suhaila, why? Ayy, all right, it isn't as nice as it was, but zayn, it's fine, it isn't a big issue and yaani, it isn't horrible.

I flip my hair forward, brush it, and stare at some hairs falling into the basin. I shake my head to the right and the left and return some locks to the back. Combing out my hair with my fingers, I have seen that around my temples the gray roots are showing. It looks as though the dye makes no difference, as if I am dyeing air. Why is that?

Your hair is like sand, Sarah insists. Even the coloring slides off it. Stop this idiocy and go over to Sonia's genealogy—isn't your son's wife half Iranian? So, the only thing to use is Persian henna—it is so rich!

If Umm Diya had been standing there, she would have slapped me with the saying one always hears. Pigment shows no mercy to the cherished child of a people abased.

The Spanish dance director, who was roughly my age, said to me, The thing about you, Madame, is your short, compact, and supple build. And your slim legs, too. Bodies like this are treasures buried in clothing. All we have to do is strip off the layers and return these bodies to the earth. To the world, right here.

Hearing words like this, I was already seeing a brighter professional future for myself. Only days later, though, I would be stumbling over my feet at the slightest provocation and trembling from head to toe. I was clueless as to what the very next step should be. It was nonsense, all that praise. Garbage. I would stay away from lessons and the exercises led by that kindly lady, a friend of Tessa's. It was Tessa who introduced me to her and got her to take just half the usual fee for lessons. Do it for my sake, Tessa said to her. Later, after we had become friends, she made do with just a quarter of the fee, and that was for *my* sake. But with the passing of months and years my body ebbed, reduced from what it had been the year before. The facts were there before me in flesh and blood. It was not a case that required lots of additional evidence. One day, returning from those evening lessons in the School for Spanish Dance, I said to Narjis, with Hatim right there, The bastard has no shame at all! I was boiling with frustration. Narjis, that poor dear, was completely knocked over by my swearing. She fancied that someone had been bothering me, and between laughter and gravity, she exclaimed, Shu? Khayr in sha' Allah! You're all right, aren't you? What happened? Nothing bad, surely?

Before I could say anything Hatim jumped in with his usual slyness. His voice sarcastic, he addressed Narjis. He—who else could she be talking about—he is Age, isn't he? Life? He is the life span she has lived, and the age she has reached. Right?

We all laughed. The bastard moves along to his own music, I said. He keeps moving, so stubborn he is, and he is quiet. No screaming or moaning from him. And I can't even accuse him of overstepping the boundaries.

I press on my temples and all but scream. But I do not scream after all. What is the use of any of it? I was witless and the whips of the young republic curdled my blood while the husband swung the cane of obedience across my body and I did not even scream, not then. I look at my body, from the roof of my mouth, to the vivid redness of those lips—a color to dispel my fear. From my toenails tinted death's yellow, with the adulterated poison I was ready to swallow that I might sleep alone, to my small frame always there at any hour of night and day, my body ready to toil the moment it was necessary and always in his hands. My mother moistens the sheets at night—and you, Suhaila, at any time of day or night—with tears. What stumbling luck! I didn't have a care for the time still to come, the years still left, the men and youths, everything in God's creation. I found excuses for all of them. And I began to go to evening concerts with Caroline who always purchased two tickets. Foolish circumspection was my downfall. My footwork started to improve, day by day; my hair flapped against my forehead and bounced down across my cheeks. With kindly seriousness, the obverse of Sarah's way, that teacher made me aware that I should leave the little white hairs on my temples as they were. There's nothing wrong with them, she said in an affectionate voice. Everyone is doing it these days, she would often say in my hearing. It's moda.

She would say such things as she got the music ready for us, and the lights, and as she put film in the VCR. Come on, Suhaila! The final commotion around my face, a light dusting of powder across the nose which has shifted its position slightly, and one light line of Indian kohl, more gray than black, on each heavy eyelid. Caroline gave me this kohl one day; there was no particular occasion. I didn't put mascara on my lashes. Across my shoulders I draped the heavy coffee-brown and purple Afghani shawl, wrapping it around my neck. The final glance in the mirror. Beneath those eyes, the hideous blackness, the site of first and final revolt, or of blasphemy: that blackness smiles into my face and thwarts my will. The powder no longer delights either friend or foe. Sarah would respond to me in her usual manner. Her voice would be inaudible at first, as long as we were still inside the dance institute, but it would get louder and louder as we emerged onto the street.

You have to show some respect for the wrinkles and pockmarks, Suhaila. Even the light spots you should leave alone. It's nicer that way. Why don't you believe it? The droop of your lids, those crooked teeth, short or shrinking bones, your shriveling blood vessels and the dryness of your skin—if you want me to, I will spell out even more than this. I am a specialist in such things. Everything comes along and encounters no obstacle in the path. It all comes as easily as if it is gliding across ice. Listen, Suhaila, we will stay this age for a long time, longer than we prepared ourselves for in our earlier years. The years constantly renew themselves, and they suit us. Don't stare at me like that. Come on, come out of that illusion of yours and think about how you can serve your self instead of assuming that your body always serves you. You have already blasted apart those fortresses so don't walk in your sleep—in the sleep of your ghosts and specters. Don't raise the crown of your head high for all to see, like a single, strutting, peacock, and do not puff out that big chest of yours, because you are no longer particularly sexy. Ayy, you were beautiful—you were! But no longer, not now. The past will never return.

I kept up my smile and my air of unconcern as I heard Sarah out, for I do not put too much stock in anything she has to say. I smile at myself in the mirror. I squeeze myself into my heavy old black coat. I push all of my hair into my wool hat and tug the brim lower until it covers my temples. I shove my feet into low shoes and close the door behind me. Ya ayni ya Suhaila—you poor dear thing. Sarah is outrageous. She doesn't offer comfort or sympathy to anyone. In the first place, she gives herself no comfort. She is worse than I am.

∾

As I read, it comes to me that my mother wanted to cover over deficiencies and failure. It is for her own ears to hear that she wants to declare her undaunted progress. Amidst these bits of paper and notebooks that I have spread out, searching for what Narjis requested from me, it is difficult to distinguish between false and true. It is as if Suhaila is in front of me, anew. I am not the only one who does not know her; first and foremost, she does not know herself. Likely, she preferred this woman, talking and addressing her, babbling and being sarcastic and extracting from her head all of these farces. Suhaila lies. She means to lead me astray so that I don't have misgivings about her. She is doing this so that I will not stumble across her, the real her, neither in the world nor in these papers nor even in the afterworld. Is she simply a bunch of stories, merely stories that she tells? Stories that will leave marks on me, that will have consequences which she will not know, should I come across them and read them some day? How many lies will she concoct and how many lapses of the tongue will she voice?

Approaching these notebooks, I felt myself intensely cautious. I was afraid that I would run into a man. Men will break my neck as I collide with them in these pages. They walk fast and try to get away before I can catch up with them to learn their identities. Every piece of paper here is a guidebook. Every guide is a voice calling out to me, a call that is not lost and will not dwindle away or vanish. And I wonder what Madame Tessa Hayden will say should I meet her days from now as I am studying the notebook in which her name appears—alone of all the notebooks. This one was different, which intensified my anxiety. I sensed danger as I picked it up but then I took down the rest of the notebooks and lay them out beside this one so that my fear would dissipate. If Tessa tightens the grip around my throat I will go to a different one and put this one aside. I will burn it, throw it as far away as possible, and not return to it. But I began to hear echoes of laughter wafting from that notebook, rising and then growing softer as if Suhaila and Tessa were themselves emerging from it and standing in front of me in the middle of the room, to say in unison that today is a day different than all of the others, that day itself which went away and did not. . . . When I opened the cover I read immediately on the inside: To Tessa Hayden. Without any break, the first sentence was: Let's go.

Everything sends furtive glances your way. I have gotten accustomed to that, as you hover in the rows of seats with the students clustered around you. Ultimately, you can convey what you want to whomever you want. On that particular day, your choice fell on me, on that wintry evening that was so very cold. I was not alone. Caroline, as well as Nur and Ahmad, had also come. Layal had contacted them and invited them to attend the defense. I swear that she must have said to them something other than what she said to me, because deep within me I know somehow that they came for your sake. Me, with the latma on my lip, with my shadowy face, with my prim caution and my fear, with my country which would be blasted apart in the course of the day or perhaps in just a few seconds—I came to make you hear the vibrations left by that earthquake. With the dead, their chests weighted down by dust and dirt and humiliation and sickness; with the flags of the empire that flutter and the sound of the airplanes warning of the worst as they spew out white smoke: with all of this.

We are standing: we wait for you to walk by in front of us. What words will I find to say in your presence as I stumble along my way and trip over my own tongue, tucking inside of myself all of those who are still alive so that they will not slip away, slide off my features, eluding the contours of my face.

No doubt you will notice all of this in the expression on my face. No doubt you will believe the streaming tears to be genuine. Our tears were our unchanging weather conditions. No doubt you will take it all very seriously as I look at you. Caroline tugged at my arm a bit roughly, and said in a low voice, Here she is, she's coming, see, that one who moves as if she is walking on a ray of light. Don't look directly at her with those big eyes of yours. Close them until she goes by.

How do you want me to look at her, then? I like my own way of looking at people. I want whoever sees me to know that with my gaze I am stepping toward that person. That way I am already speaking before the words come from my tongue. Shush—I don't like your advice.

You shush. She's getting close, look! Look how elegant and beautiful she is.

I felt the traces of the fever in my eyes rather than on my lip. We were still standing in the long corridor at Université Saint-Denis. She reached us and went on. For a fraction of a second our eyes met, hers and mine. Our eyes traveled as far into each other as one can go, and acknowledged something. She knows me, I thought. I did not know her in that hour but I discovered later, in my state of illness, that I knew her, too. I knew that I knew her when I saw her in front of me. I almost let out a loud laugh: who reckons the number of times, who counts the number of months and years? She was strange; she had no age. She was sculpted from the East; no, she was pure supra-East. She was very tall, very slender, and very elegant. Over her shoulders she had draped an African shawl that was folded against her long neck and, between tightly erect shoulders, draped low on her back with its even longer proportions. The ends swirled in front of us. She seemed happy as we stared at the shawl draped behind her. Its tones were those of sulfur, volcanoes, and iodine, and on her head, I immediately noticed, she wore an odd hat, square at the top and round at the rim, with some handwork on it, and stones and tiny mirrors which, I imagined, would flash and sparkle whichever way she turned, so that we would always know exactly how and where she was moving. I was following her with my gaze. She arrived before the student—Layal—and the group of professors. She came for my sake. Why not? This professor with her slow, stately walk and her dignified carriage waits for the main door to the exam hall to open. She carries about her a certain magic. She bears the authority and integrity of the wise. She is exacting in matters of schedule and timing; she knows precisely how far this particular intolerance can go. I felt myself in the presence of a first-class soldier at the peak of performance and the height of glory, exhibiting the drills learned on every variety of firearm and an easy ability to leap over the flames of hell in order to defend the line of fire—and all with severe solemnity. I swallowed, privately repudiating the easy-going ways at our universities and the indulgent attitudes found among professors and doctoral students engulfed in the tumultuous wars of educational devastation in our lands.

So, what do you think? Nur asked me, her own voice filled with admiration.

I don't know . . . I swear that I have no idea.

Caroline jumped in. What do you mean by that?

I have not seen her yet.

You are always like this, said Ahmad, laughing. You never echo and you never hand back, a yearning.

Her face, it's—

It's what? asked Caroline, her voice insistent.

She puts me in mind of an unfinished portrait. Her face seems to be looking out from a painting that isn't yet fully realized. No, she is looking out from a book, from books, from somewhere far to the east, Far Eastern perhaps, but in the best of circumstances from among us, from our land. She is from there. From Babylon.

Winking at Ahmad, Nur commented, You claim everything for yourself, or yourselves. Even Tessa.

Everything that I am able to take with me, for me, everything is mine, everything is somewhere among my possessions. Why don't you believe that? Look at us right now. We have come here for the sake of Layal but we came for *her* sake first of all. Different nationalities: you are from Syria, Ahmad is from the Sudan, Caroline is from Sweden, I'm from Iraq, and Layal is from Lebanon. Every one of us wants a share and there it is gleaming like a pearl in front of us. But she . . . does she know that she. . . .

We went quiet expecting the door to open, though my gaze continued to shift here and there, distracted, and in my head reverberated echoes of writings, texts and ideas I had read, some of them hers and some about her or against her or supporting her when she pronounced her notorious sentence, I am not a feminist. That had been years ago. Recently she had set out her new theory on feminine écriture. Writing had become feminized, and she was proposing the feminine as two facets, intellectual and philosophical, confronting the dominant male in the edifice of patriarchal thought and its linguistic and philosophical structures equally. Such writing, she argued, was not solely the province of women who write but rather it was discernible throughout the writings of myriad eminent men writers, from Shakespeare to Jean Genet and Heinrich von Kleist. Reading her ideas I would applaud loudly, if only within myself. She has responded to my very own secrets! And here she is continuing to uncover that world and to probe its depths. She was attempting to take apart and expose the enduring patriarchal construction of Eve's rebellious role face to face with Adam's role as he played it, submitting obediently to the incomprehensible command of prohibition and banishment. For Eve responded to her own desire or, to put it more accurately, to her humanity, in the sense that humans are creatures who err. She dared take a risk; she gambled on rebellion by eating from the forbidden tree, while Adam's response acceded to the attractions of power and positive law and their conventions, even though both were put in place for him: they were not of his own making. He preferred the ongoing and stable existence of the system to the danger of rebellion, although rebellion quickly enough swept him along when he could not withstand its powerful magic. Thus, she argued, the regions where desire accrues are put in confrontation with the law, and the self is placed against the system, and the female is positioned as contrary to the male. And so it has been ever since the beginning of all things. She finds that this story of origins in humanity's legacy of knowledge is what has set the shape and development of the two basic paths available to humanity since its earliest dawn. One consists of submission and obedience to that which has been decreed, in return for reaping the fruits of blind obedience. Since the dawn of history, this path has granted men the status of prisoners of power and authority, sentencing them to be slaves to its conventions and victims in its struggles at one and the same time. Woman, meanwhile, paid the price of rebelliousness. Religiously instigated and patriarchal maledictions long pursued her, even if they could not imprison her desire or shackle her buried yearning for rebellion. And yet more significant, on the philosophical plane, is her relationship to the other, ever since her eating of the tree of knowledge led to her discovery of Adam as an other and different on the one hand, and to discovery of the principle of desire/pleasure entwined, on the other.

She continued her measured walk, quiet and composed, and I followed until Layal arrived with her set of friends. Nader was the only absentee. Nader, the naughty unfortunate who would have crawled on hands and feet to satisfy Layal. But Nader was not cowardly as I was. Nader is more courageous than I am. I am the most cowardly, set between the two of them, him and his father. This is not something that I will confess to in anyone's presence; I will not even acknowledge it to myself. Saying this, I hide my face from everyone and I say yet again that my cowardice is my sole courage. It is possible that I protected myself with it so that I could remain by myself, and thus mingle with, and even blend in to, the circles of colleagues, women and men, in this association or that, time after time, and so that I could go out in the demonstrations, and record, and criticize and accuse and call out and shout and press myself into the crowd of others in the streets and in front of the embassies of the great powers, filling my throat with imprecations infused with all the languages there are, knowing that all of this was no use and would produce nothing.

Come on! They have opened the door. Where have you gone off to, Suhaila?

Layal stood before me, looking like a paradisiacal nymph. She gave me a hug.

Did you see her?

Yes, yes. Come on, let's go in. Later. . . . I am praying for you.

I made way for the two of them and they went in together, Tessa and Layal. They shook hands and embraced and then each went her separate way. Caroline stayed close to my side. Without a word from me, she asked as we walked across the room to take our seats, So is she as I described her to you?

No, not at all. You are not a very proficient portraitist.

I took my seat beside her. Nur and Ahmad sat next to me. The hall filled up. The professors who had directed Layal's work sat in the very front of the room, facing us. In the center of the room sat Layal behind a table, her back to us. To the right and left were two rows of long wooden benches on which her friends sat. Tessa, honorary member of the committee, sat half a meter away to my left. She is a committee in herself, Layal had told me. Her remarks will conclude the discussion.

The student was at her most tense and most splendid. She had prepared her defense in advance. Nader was the one who would be defended today, whose case would be acknowledged. To my eyes Layal appeared magnified a hundred times, although today her elegance was understated. She wore a trouser suit with a vest, the dark green of naphtha, over a milk-white silk blouse. Her hair hung loose down her neck, swinging about her shoulders. A beauty I cannot properly describe stole from her. I had never seen her looking as lovely as she did today and I had never really seen Nader quite as taken with her as I was now. My God, where is Nader? Why had one of the two held back until it was too late for the other, too late by ten years? Both of them were late to leave and late to return. Nader acquired some wisdom and one day he spoke to me about it, his tone of voice unruffled, even serene.

Mother, it may well be that I loved her for myself only, not for the person she really was. I loved her out of my own self-ignorance, and I wanted her to pull me out of my fear. But she was more afraid than I was. She was like me. We were both fleeing from war and men, from women and cities and the family, from insanity and death, and each of us went in a different direction. I'm not demanding an excuse or apology for her, or for me, but I curse all the wars that turned us into rabbits.

And Layal, whenever Nader's name came up, would resort to evasion. Love wasn't at the top of the list, Suhaila. I would have implicated him in too much, and myself as well.

But, did you love him even for a day? I asked her once. We were in the apartment, the same one, our apartment that had witnessed ruin and broken passion. Their passion. She hung her head and the tears flowed. It was the first time I had seen her cry. She answered in a very low voice as if she did not want me to hear her clearly.

It is out of the question that I could love a man as I loved Nader.

I tried to keep back my own tears. I was shivering: I could hear the sound of the military marches and land-to-air missiles, and I could see the colors of fire in the skies over my country and hers—that besieged, surrounded East, from Palestine to Baghdad to Beirut. Here they were, the two of them, Layal and Nader, each on a different continent, between them the defeats and the crimes that struck them down and sent each one in a different direction. Not a single grain of sand would ever be returned to their possession. Not even one.

∽

Nur writes fast, translating summaries of what is happening, as we agreed on beforehand. No sooner do I raise my head and swivel it to the right than I see Tessa's gaze opposite me. My God, whom does she resemble? The resembled is more beautiful than the one who resembles, so why did I want her to resemble something other than her own self in order that I not go astray? If my mother could see her she would utter the basmallah and recite a verse for her from the Noble Qur'an and let out a string of admiring la ilah ila Allahs. And in the midst of it all she would turn to me and exclaim, Your father will send her a telegram to make her head hurt! He will be that insistent on having her come and see one of his charming plays. Suhaila, my girl, this woman looks to be honest and clean through and through. That's my feeling about it. It's a thing of intuition and belief. Like us—she's like us, ayy w-Allahi, she knows right from wrong, all right, she's a daughter of good folk, I can tell.

This is my first encounter with a celebrity writer who conceals her fame behind her pleasant, unassuming demeanor. Her smile is inconclusive, as if she isn't even smiling, as if she is merely remembering other smiles, recalling the first time she smiled after conflagration and terrors. Looking closely, I can tell that very soon she will smile. Afterward, she will smile.

When she stood in our line of vision in the corridor her form seemed to reshape itself; it seemed ever-changing. Big eyes that are always there in whichever direction my gaze turns. Why do I exaggerate and say again that we were exchanging looks bearing the strength of words not yet in existence? I look at her and I am bemused at seeing that she is looking at me and we are realizing that we know each other. We are the daughters and the women of those butcheries and disasters that bloodied us with wounds and death. As one professor stops speaking and another launches in, our glances take their time, accumulating out of that history smeared with blood, out of childhoods saturated with stoic waiting, out of Eastern mystical asceticism that I can see as a shining exemplar for her and for me, out of Andalus and from Andalus to Baghdad to Jerusalem without my choking over a single superfluous word.

The committee members take turns, each with his own path to pursue, while I run my eyes across Nur's translation. I read and I seek refuge from the devil in the way of my mother. I all but let out a loud, piercing zaghrada at the high-powered words showered on Layal and her thesis; but I cannot. I am fundamentally too shy. For my benefit, Nur writes: The committee is now recording its official judgment. The thesis is excellent. It is a strong and thoroughly considered work. They found no gaps in it that require specific discussion. Layal closed the circle completely. I think she will get the highest distinction possible.

At this point Tessa stood up. She began to speak about Layal, Marguerite Duras, and the substance of the dissertation. She pushed up the sleeves of her wool pullover, leaving the shawl across her chest, and began to move about in the space where she stood. She was using the space to fullest advantage. Her step was firm and she met the eyes of her audience. I did not miss even a second, listening to the timbre of her voice, to the very last moment, sensing danger all the while, all of the danger that I must reckon with as I listen to her. I was sure that we had talked before although I could never have imagined such a possibility. She inclines her head to listen and I run behind her. A silken veil wraps her short hair. I raise my hand, a first salutation to this hair which no dyes in existence can tint and camouflage, it is so soft. What if her lover loved to play with her hair? What would he do and where would he put his hand? Her hair has escaped its primary ties, its intimate family bonds: Nature. I will tell her when I meet her, very soon, that this hair is the childhood stage as she describes it in her writings, and that stage reached its essence in a single point of harmony on her head. It reached that limit when she was a child in Algeria and so—unlike me—she triumphed over the dye.

Applause resounded through the hall and my hands moved in spite of myself. But applause was not enough to satisfy them. I felt myself on the verge of the nonsensical itching of my chronic illness, the allergy; it would happen, I knew, if I were to stand very soon in front of Tessa.

Layal obtained honors with the committee's congratulations— there could be no higher distinction for a doctorate. The tears flowed without my being particularly aware of them. I didn't hide any of it and I did not wipe my face dry: they were more stubborn than I was. Caroline did not comment, but Nur, being Arab and bearer also of some of the distress I have borne, appreciated the value and meaning of this. Through the filmy veil of my tears she saw her own, anticipating them a few months later in an occasion just like this one.

I was the last to leave the lecture hall. We began to climb the stairs that would take us to one of the reception rooms where we had prepared a private party for Layal. On an elegant table, platters of Lebanese delicacies were set out: kubba, spinach pastries, cheese and meats, tiny meat pies, falafel, makdus, olives, pickles, and wine. I saw Marwan, Layal's brother, and he was bursting with pride. Tessa and the other professors collected around the table. No matter where I turned, I found that Tessa and I were somehow always approaching each other, certainly not by any prior agreement but rather with considerable wariness. Venturing that step forward, we were scrutinizing each other and holding back. What were we waiting for? I don't know. Layal stood still for a few seconds only; I hugged and kissed her and then she fled from my embrace. I sat down with my glass and a plate piled with good things. Tessa drinks according to her mood and whim, but eats by constant monitoring of what and how much. She plays tricks on the food so that it will not really enter her stomach. I estimated that her weight could not be more than fifty kilos although her height was over 170 centimeters. How could that be? Clearly, she needed to fatten up a little. If I were to stand up to greet her, I would appear to be overdoing it. A little too much formality. Odd—she doesn't eat like Caroline, or like me, or even like Blanche or Narjis. Mingling with the other thesis directors, she was extending her hand to someone but she was looking toward where I sat. Where will you go? May death be yours, O you who abandons prayer! What will I do? Here she is walking silently to the back corner where the coats are piled up. Her back is directly in front of me. This is the moment in which I come to know assuredly that she is the goal that fixes my eyes.

I stood up as quick as a flying arrow leaving its bow and walked toward her. She was raising the right sleeve of the coat. I put out both hands as if I wanted to help her with the other sleeve but then I faltered and hung back. No doubt she would find such a gesture far too dismissive of all formality. I decided to retrace my steps. Suddenly she turned toward me, just as I was raising my hands toward the edge of the wall as if I were about to fly. That was the best I could manage at that moment. She put on her coat and began to button it as my voice sailed ahead of me. I tried to avoid letting her gaze fall on my ill-at-ease confusion as I said in English, in a nervously cheerful voice, Stop.

And then the words that were churning inside of me spilled out. I am so-and-so, daughter of so-and-so. I'm an Iraqi actress and theatrical dancer. My father is a theater producer. I don't have a book to dedicate to you, nor a play that you can read, nor a film on videotape where you could view some of my best roles in the past. But I wanted to introduce myself to you. I don't know why! But, I thought this was the best way to get you to stop so that we could talk.

There was some sort of unspoken agreement, some sort of collusion between us. She was waiting for me. It seemed as though she had been expecting me. Our eyes met. I put out my hand and she extended hers. She took my hand and pulled me behind her without saying a word. At the end of the room, away from where the guests clustered, a few chairs were grouped. We sat down. She opened her bag, took out a red pen and a small notebook and began to write. She tore out the page and gave it to me. Name, address, and telephone number. She handed me the notebook and pen wordlessly but with an unforgettable gesture. I wrote down my information exactly as she had done. It amazes me how we spoke without uttering a single word. Nur, Ahmad, and Caroline were coming toward us. Raising my gaze to her, I introduced them one by one, stammering over their names. I did not hear much of what was said. I was watching her surreptitiously as she brought out her ammunition, which turned out to be openness and a capacity for listening that one would not readily have guessed were there. Her eyes bring together disparate expressions and her voice communicates tranquility and reassurance even if the words she is hearing are flimsy, as mine were, or oh-so-proper as were Nur's as she introduced herself and then her thesis proposal, or tedious as was Caroline's going suddenly quiet in her presence after having edged closer and interrupted softly to tell her about staying every Saturday at the Sorbonne to attend her session for graduate students. Ahmad broke in, too, making a comment about the thesis of his exquisite beloved as if his sole purpose was to announce that they were partners. Standing up to announce her departure, she said, Come to those classes whenever you wish. They are conversations, introductions, summings-up of events, books, ideas, and names from all eras. In one way or another they are steps toward perpetuating humanity and knowledge.

I did not say another word. Startlingly, she turned and hugged me. She had helped me out of my embarrassment; I was rid of my stutter. I hugged her back. I did not understand why she had made this gesture toward me alone.

✑

I am someone who often needs a long spell of time alone with my self. Right now, I did not want to share what I was feeling with anyone. I did not say goodbye to Layal—even to Layal. I did not speak to Caroline nor to Nur or Ahmad, not even to tell them that I wanted to leave by myself. I had a need beyond compare right now, which was to be in my own company. I felt that I was being stingy and selfish and yet bighearted at the same time. What I wanted was to be in touch with Nader. Alone. Yes, Nader was life, life and age, my life span itself as I have lived it. A life that was so definitively sundered and yet now was coming round again. We are the children of our children; and all of this love, so agonizing to bear, burns all of our capital out of existence and carves into living flesh without compassion. What was unanticipated was that I loved Layal now more than I ever had, for at the end of the day here I was, here, in place of Nader and of Layal's mother. Here I was as a witness to a small but decisive victory, a triumphal residue of all of those victories so hollow at their core, victories that indeed collapsed even as they came into existence. For the first time, I was witnessing an Arab victory in a foreign place and in a direction beyond and leading away from cannon and tanks, in a bewitching conversation around the revolution of children against mothers and fathers, in a rebellion of loved ones, beloved men and beloved women who were proud and perplexed. Layal's logic and intelligence were unassailable, her voice was hers but it was also different. The intonations in that voice were half Nader's and half hers. It is a voice that does not complicate or confuse the present in the name of the past. If Tessa had asked me as we greeted each other . . . she did not ask anything, but if she had said to me, Who are you, feverish frantic woman? I would have said, without a pause, Layal. Nights. I am the nights, al-Layal, I am all the nights and all of the Layals.

∽

One day we were backstage, he and I, in the Théâtre du Soleil. The producer was not reading the notes she had set down. She looked to me like a herdswoman from the days of the ancient Greeks. She was a big woman and the expression on her face suggested her penchant for sarcasm. I imagined her as a creature without a sex, achieving production of the greatest plays as she prowled the theater by night. Her hand, beckoning me over with a grand sweep, was very large. Her eyes, though, were eagle-like. Her intelligence was unnatural and not out there for everyone to see: she was sharp as if she were sleeping with him in front of us and letting us imagine what we could find in our imaginations. Her commands seemed physical movements generated through the energetic timbre of her fluent English. I walked over to her. She appeared to have eaten very well today; her food is not light like Tessa's who sat far away from us, all politeness and elegance and perfume, traces of sleepiness still on her features. She did not interfere at first. She left me in the hands of this trainer to whom she had introduced me two hours before, when I had come in through the back door to the theater which is located on the outskirts of Paris. I had taken the Metro and then a bus, and then I had jumped out like a monkey, walking the rest of the way so that I would not be late for this first meeting with the writer and the producer.

My name is Maria, and this is Faw, your dance partner.

She gave me nothing more than a cursory look; neither my appearance nor my build nor even my eyes seemed to interest her. She moved across the stage in front of us. Suddenly, it was as if she had gone into a spell of heightened consciousness that seemed to have a ritualistic gloss to it. In a matter of seconds, her force with words became physical struggle, a rocket capsule on the point of take-off. I felt completely paralyzed by alarm. With a fleeting glance I took in Faw's state. This Maria, it seemed, furnished him with a sort of blissfulness I had never seen among any people before. She repeated the gestures and movements several times for us. She had a way of emptying out completely whoever was before her to the point where that person would no longer have the slightest notion of personal, intimate identity. She wanted to grab us; she wanted the dream to shake us to the core, she wanted to set us trembling before anything inside, any part of our earliest, most fundamental selves, could settle. Indeed, Maria did not settle for anything; she was never satisfied; nothing was ever enough. She wanted the actor to disavow and disbelieve his own ability to clasp the fire such that

216

no one would hear his cry of pain. She said the words through dance and then her body appeared utterly delicate and transparent. Tessa and Maria did not let me get to know Faw anywhere but onstage. They would always prefer this kind of acquaintance, immediate and explosive. I forgot — or I repressed or ignored — all that Maria said. I slipped my arm into his and began to rise and soar and descend. He was bare-chested. I could see his blood vessels beneath the expanse of his body in my hands. I hypnotized him; I stuck hash cigarettes in his mouth and took deep draws on them myself, blending their fragrance into my breath as I looked into his eyes. His features became submerged in me and our bodies clung together. No space separated our organs. Both hands were extended, open. Faw gathered himself together like a bouquet of flowers that he meticulously arranged. Our fingers conversed and our limbs trembled together. Flying locks of hair, a neck twisting, shoulders bending and fire in the thighs. Faw was years younger than me, though by how many years I could not tell. This body was a deep watercourse into which I had only to dip. Music assailed us from both ends of the theater, ancient music that simultaneously pained me and delighted my anxious heart. In his body's particularity crouched the untamed harshness of Enkido and the divinity of Gilgamesh.

It is as if you are bent on atonement for something or other. I don't like repentant women. As he spoke, he nipped at the tip of my nose. He had attacked me from the first moment. He took my hand and put it to his mouth, then fell back slightly: Maria was between us.

Pull him to your chest as fiercely as you possibly can — no, more than that, with more force.

For the first time I hear Tessa's voice. My dear, she says in English, and then in French, don't mix up your cards, please. Put everything you have learned behind you. Go far away, so far that I can no longer see you and I do not recognize you. Spy on your own body, drain it drop by drop, burn it one millimeter after the next. Forget legend, and tragedy. Do not search for any solutions and don't be afraid of renunciation and pollution. Devastate and sneer at death, though not any one death; not your death or mine or that of your man. You must know that your only ally is yourself, alone, and your art. Faw will acquire only what you propel into him.

Suddenly Tessa was not there; she was standing a long way off. Who is Faw? Who are you? He enticed me but he was a liar. How did I find him in my path? He had come into my thoughts, someone whom I had put together in my mind before I ever saw him. I told myself, One day I will see him without exhausting all that is in him. And I can enjoy him to the fullest. I put my imagination truly to the test only when I was with him. My life was mundane as I made my way and kept my eyes on reality. And then he took me in his arms and I took him like one hypnotized and put him under my tongue, and so he slipped into every part of my body. And it began to sicken. This is what reality is. He made me dance as he wished; he screamed into my face; he gnawed at my life, kicked at my body, bombarded my fervor and fixed in place the glands that held my talents. Reality had gotten its revenge on me through law and principles, by means of government, officers, civilians, rows of medals and rows of generals, to the point that reality could take me perfectly for granted. I did not go off and fabricate ghosts and chimeras as some of my fellow artists did as they delivered resounding arguments against reality, opening fire on it as if it were merely a mangy dog and erecting electric chairs that would carry them off and into the world of dreams. Reality had not changed me into a valiant hero as it had them, even after that husband surprised me on stage, dragging me off in front of all of those workmates and friends, dragging me by the costume of the last role I ever played onstage. No one said a word. Not a word, not a sound. He caught my head under his feet and struck it with a practiced hand, and I did not protest as they did, wailing of woe and ruin. Perhaps, I told myself, it was just that he was shutting his eyes to reality while my simple presence spoke it out loud—and this was prohibited. Nader did not understand the reason for our separation, each into his own room, me and his father. Nader did not understand how it was that he extended the period of my convalescence and announced in front of everyone that I was very ill. Every time she goes up on stage, he thundered, her illness grows worse until she is no longer fit for anything. And then my sickness went on for a long time and it was true that I was no longer fit for anything. I began to despise my beauty and appeal. I began to do away with my youth and my longings after I had amassed them all for him. He mocked them, struck them down precisely like the finest of marksmen. A failure. That is what I was. I failed; I was defective; I grew smaller and smaller. I did not even have the strength to cry. Everything was coming undone and falling apart and I stretched out my hand and took the failure. I took the crude behaviors of that master. Whether he meant to or not, Faw kissed me imprudently, incautiously. He did not lay out a plan and then test it for viability, nor was the space of the theater the other name for the country. He did not retreat by even a step; he did not bat an eyelid. For ten years Faw had been awaiting me. With her own hands, Tessa prepared things I was not used to: perfumes, oils, incense, minerals, sprays that sent their mist across the stage and our bodies. I did not look. We sweated and perfumed ourselves and the salts of our bodies led us each to the other. Tessa guided us: the dew glistening on our skin grew heavier and our lips took moisture from our shimmering bodies. Breathing heavily, I would want to scream at the top of my voice and in my own language, Stop! Stop, Faw, please! It's enough. Don't overdo your act of refinement for my sake. I did say that to him in a voice he could hear. No one was surprised. I was not tired and my years were not pressing painfully on me. The Suhaila I regained was released now from reality and from the son and the father. That evening I appeared with that same hated body of mine, with the stinging and itching that had been. I emptied myself of those thorns as I fell to my knees behind Faw, smelling the incenses of his body, the sweat flowing from the hair in his armpits and down his calves. I got closer, awaiting our passage between the two rivers. I paid no attention to our instructions—let Maria and Tessa go to hell and let the final practice flop—it did not matter. In that moment, we turned in unison to each other. I drew my finger across his high forehead and dropped to his nose and then his neck so that I would not go shy or resist. Concentrate, Suhaila. Take him now in your arms and don't move apart. But Tessa's voice is there again.

Don't translate your dance. Just dance. Give in to everything that has accumulated inside of you. Come on! Leave yourself behind.

How can that be, when that master is waiting for me, to take me, like a digger of graves? and when I am driven to him like a corpse that is no longer fresh? He commands the darkness of the room and focuses the power of the light beam on my pelvis. Swiftly, so very quickly, in his clothes, those khaki pants with the cap still on his head, he undoes his buckle, not saying a word, not looking me in the face. He empties me out but he does not grow empty. I become a dreadful, fearful, emptiness. He is over me, above my past life, arriving from the direction of my pain. He comes in and goes out as if it is something learned by heart years ago, its newness forgotten; and my heart—my insides—churn. He pushes me away; I go to the bathroom and throw up. I lied to Nader and to my own soul, I lied to Blanche and Narjis and Asma. That is how he waited for me, that sick man, the civil servant, the hero, the vanquisher. I blame him and I curse him in my sleep and I follow him in my wanderings. To Tessa without shame, and to Wajd without fear, I can say: I am empty; I am desolate and damaged. I would love to love; I would love to be loved; I would love to be a beloved woman, a loved one. I love all of the words that waited for me but I said them to no one. I love speaking to an unknown one whose existence I could not be sure of. I love that hand that moves across my body without any regulation or command or target, with the excess that did not overflow and with the scarcity that did spill over, and with the men whom I left of my own accord, having slept with them one after the other but without ever really meeting them. With the naked civilians who possess nothing more than the authority of their weakness in its middling stature. With the weak whose forces have been depleted, who answer every time I say to them, Come, and bring.... With those who are weaker than me, with those who have been deceived and tortured, who make no distinctions between themselves and me. All of them slept with me and our tears poured out; we entwined our arms and fear held us captive. Tessa listens; my tears drench my face.

I want a single passing moment of any galaxy's passage, I say. There I will meet someone who will not be carrying any implement in his hand. Not even a flower. Only Nader will outlast me, Tessa. And his father. One night when he came home very late after receiving a promotion, I sensed that he could not do it. He began to mewl. He would straighten and then sink down again and he could not. He was filling his chest with air, straightening his back, trying hard and not looking at me. At me, who had been stripped bare of everything. I tried to hold him. He followed me into every corner. I did not try to conceal myself or disappear from his path as he scrambled behind me with every implement he could find, with ashtrays and porno videos, driving me away and rebuking me with his heavy cane, hurling flower vases at me, whipping me with his leather belt on whatever part of my body he chose. I was the free one and he could no longer stand it. He grew tired, collapsed and began to howl like an animal. And that young Nader on the floor above stayed in his room and no sound at all came from him. Tessa waves her hand at the girl who has stopped next to the sound system. Higher, higher! she says with her hand. The drums, tambourines, guitars and violins cling to my tongue as my lips press against Faw's cheek. The fragrance of me, and my first home, the dust of the earth that I left behind me, enter my nostrils. I breathe out into Faw's face in the very way I have not attempted before. I suck the water and cardamom as I always did; my mouth holds those little pods. My mother taught me that habit: cardamom seeds between the teeth and your man is made your lover. I chew and Faw goes back to sucking slowly. It is on the point of unbearable. I descend further, push far inside his mouth, and bite on his lips as fast as I can. I hear the flutes: those nayys release their melodies. My waiting has grown long, and Faw flows over me. He begins at my head, undoes the head veil adorned with the colors of turquoise and saffron, pulls off the skin-bronze diaphanous veil over my belly, dips lower, detaches the pink lines of my legs so that my body opens in his hands. I feel as though he is peeling me. His arm lies across my shoulders. I have found a response to my waiting. I have found my response. My large and groaning chest listens beneath the gentleness of his palm. The movements are tender, fresh: a movement for parting, for things scattered, for the evening breeze and for fidelity to Baghdad. A movement meaning anger and the pustules on the face of the country. A movement in the opposite direction, wide-eyed like eyes before makeup and after old age. Movements for the path

221

taken without guidance and we—Nader and I—talk in the rooms where we sleep, each one alone. In the mornings we freshen up our appearances and straighten our clothes and make it appear as though we are the happiest and most fortunate of fools. Faw starts in again, reaching upward this time, beginning from the fingers. You are very late. Come, come to me.

He dragged me by whatever remained of me. I want the years of your life to come to mine, your waters into my pitcher. I will pull the years behind my back and make them pass across your chest. I am learning you. I am learning the greetings of your people and I am drinking the bitterness in your country's throat. Suhaila, please— please do not falsify things to me. Come, more, more, for the cells of you will not break or wrinkle between my hands. Between my palms, your pale face erupts in fire and all of your years are my fortune. Your thin arm encircles me. Encircle me more. Harder. Embrace me, lady of mine, and let your chest laugh in my face. Aah—your little body, my harvest! Here, don't turn to Maria and Tessa. Come away from their texts, leave them behind, and do not listen to their instructions. Bar the way in front of them. Do not follow a single and ultimate road, and do not put up signs to the roads that you do follow. Come, move, don't tarry or hold back, turn to me so we can sleep together in the sex of the earth and the youth of the world. Here, I am gathering you up, and sprinkling you around, and murmuring your thanks. I spell out your hunger as I do the parts of your body, for I deserve you as I bring together the parts of me with you. We fade away. Fade away and don't even let yourself hear the echoes of the applause in the final performance. Come. Don't turn to the audience, for they do not know what has happened. Don't nod your head in gratitude to Maria and Tessa and don't listen to the fine expressions of admiration. Tessa will say again and again—and then again—what she said to me years ago when I was stepping across this stage for the first time. Fine, Faw, but . . . there remains something incomplete, something which the two of you have certainly not reached. Always there is an error somewhere, a repeating flaw. Yes, yes, a failure that shows itself anew in the heart, in the lonely inner place of the ephemeral body as it breaks. There is ever something that we cannot hold onto in all simplicity. It will never end. There is something here that the two of you have never faced. Always, at every time, it says to us, Come, begin all over again, come back, you two, you dear friends.

∽

Dear Suhaila,

Yesterday I read the details surrounding the knifing of Naguib Mahfouz, based on the opinion of the doctor treating him. Mahfouz's weak vision and hearing saved him from death, because if he had seen the assailant he would have been terrified and confused and that would have turned it into a far worse attack with graver consequences. So there are benefits in having poor vision and hearing, I said to myself. I say this to you as well, not just to myself; during our lives, I think, we have gotten the aid that nature grants to every creature in possession of a pair of eyes, for we have consumed our share of visual perception in many matters and deeds. I am no longer capable of taking up the magnifying glass and reading the weave of Kashan and Persian and Afghani carpets, of analyzing the stitches and the spaces between them, knowing the type of threads, evaluating the age and testing the sound, the has'hasa of the silk in my hands and between my fingers. I used up nearly all of the sharpness of my eyes for that beloved craft. Later I would sit down and draw on every one of my senses to read those books and reports on carpet making in nearly every part of the world.

Just a minute, please, Suhaila, while I get myself a glass of the wine that your heart adores. I have not done what I have done just to make the time pass. My feelings of pride have expanded every time I have read, because all of those who craft those fine and lush types of carpet, all of them are women. Amen, I said to myself, as if you or Asma were right here in front of me. I tried to establish the truth of this observation when I visited Morocco some years ago to attend the Festival of Carpets in Meknes and Fez. Wherever I went my mood soared as I saw their faces in front of me, smiling and beautiful and most distant from the honorifics of heroines. Just imagine, the one reaction they have to their situation is to protest their bad treatment. They know without any hesitation where to go and what to do, and that would be so even if their lives were to be destroyed by pain. Yet between evening and the next morning, they discover themselves by means of that lovely choice. They are capable of living from what they produce. They are able to work on their own even if they are not fully conscious of that.

I would meet with them in unofficial meetings on the margins of the arranged ones. We would eat together, to move further on our discussions of the book on carpet weaving which I still hope to write. I think about all the consequences of those long conversations should the book be published. My poor vision will be of some sort of benefit after all. You know? I think I will resort finally to laser to correct the wandering eye I've suffered from (but have I really suffered?) since childhood. Sometimes I walk in the street imagining that I have corrected my vision and that I see further, further than I am able, further than a fantasy tripping down the street that I do see in all its details. Then I step back from my ever-moving fancies and I echo the words of the poet:

I open my eyes, when I open them, onto much
but I see no one

Over there and here, both, there are things that one's being blind to— and I mean really blind, not metaphorically so—can be considered a mercy from heaven. There are people to whom this applies as well. But my problem centers on reading the carpet's threads so that I can judge the actual or approximate age. And this reading, as the French writer Céline put it, has made me one of those people who are good at issuing judgments on people quickly from the first glance and thus do not see anyone. But I do see that "anyone"— and two and ten anyones—within the ordinary course of everyday greetings, in antique shows and carpet exhibits, in concerts and plays at the Théâtre du Soleil directed by your friend the playwright luminary Tessa Hayden. My impression is that she freights her texts with radioactive material. This writing is what I love—it's uranium writing. Life after your trip to Canada! By the way, will you go to New York? How I wish we were with you so that together we could all win a great victory. Life remains for me an end to be attained, not a means. You are receiving in advance the profits from the years of your life, as you don't demand more than this Hatimish liberality in a city that never once entered the mind of the generous Hatim of Tayy, that early and legendary Arab poet, who is not the same Hatim, not our lovely dear friend, our Hatim. As you habitually do in Paris, you asked me about the draft of the book and how far I have gotten? Have I started? You said to me, Writing about carpets is also a creative art through and through, and why don't you believe that? About the pleasure of getting reactions to one's art, about . . . and about. . . . As if you do not know that I know all of this. Hear it from me, then, my dear friend, once and forevermore: I am a special case. My daily life in its particulars is a creative act that breathes and laughs, despairs, eats and drinks, loves, and walks on two feet. Wherever and whenever I shift my gaze around my apartment I see the different styles of carpets, and their images and the texts of small carpets and smaller ones and the large ones that surround me—on the walls and flung over the sofa and under the glass of the long coffee table in the sitting room. Then I can feel a netting of fingers and hands and arms enveloping me. I feel soft and loving hands, free and real, expressing their emotions and their selves, and they have done all of the hard work they have done in order to reach the treasure: freedom. And here I am following that call, their call, the call of those women, all of them. I lift my hand in tribute, raising a toast to their health, to the health of freedom. Those women are the substance of my novel and short stories, not on the walls alone but in my blood, with every step and every blink of my eyelids here in this place. For Paris, this magic woman, this jinni who connives with me, works with me hand in hand—this Paris provisions me every new day with thousands of cargos. I become umm arbaa wa-arbaiin, mother of four and forty, that creeping centipede with so many legs. I want to climb and struggle and reach the innermost point in the innermost hear of the city. Paris opens before me all of its saliva and sweat, all of the threads that it holds, and I live the days and years I have here in a state of agreeable and avid energy, provisioned with mellow feelings and eager appetite. Writing alone certainly could not provision me with all of this!

Zayn. Fine, you are not a writer even if you do write, using your body to enact what others write. We are alike in this quality. Writing is their bread, Hatim and Narjis and the rest of our friends who are writers and poets. Those people are prisoners of the temple. They are the sorrowful, deprived of the pleasures of touching the moment and feeling the pulse of the universe. As for me, I have been liberated from all of my bonds. I leave the threads of the carpets to lie in solitude along the walls and I enjoy them to the extent that I leave them on their own to turn toward all the corners of the world. I write my existence on this earth with the eloquence of the loveliest fictions ever written. The work of the household and making a living take only a few hours from me. I do these things quickly and competently because I'm so accustomed to them, and afterward I wander freely among my pleasure excursions and friendships and the life of a flaneur, and singing in my heart an abudhiya that went missing from its writer. The silk threads protect me from the herds of the treacherous. Suhaila daughter of Ahmad, you who confessed to me of an astounding innocence, that the seven minutes in which you danced with Monsieur Faw on the stage of the Théâtre du Soleil were tantamount to the story of your life, and I believed you, and I was not afraid for you as you were afraid of the reactions of Nader if he were to discover it. Ayy, Nader is here, your son, though he is in Canada, it is as if he is living in your apartment, in the second room. Go, Suhaila, travel in your feelings to wherever you can, to whatever you can do. Do only what agrees with you and pleases you. We can never please those around us, no matter how hard we try, and I'm the last one to be giving sermons. I have not begun writing anything for that book in which my belief has been strengthened by your insistent queries. I am coming back to my wineglass, I am refilling it, and I drink to you. To the health of those women, creators of the light coming from all the carpets around me. To the health of your light, my friend, at a time when you are with Nader and your newborn grandson Leon. Don't let your absence grow too long, please. For you, too, are like the Kashan zawliyya—the older you get, the more youthful and active you are. Your flaw is that you have no confidence in this.

I have just looked over what I've written to you. First time I have ever done that, the first time that I am on the verge of begrudging you this letter, putting it in an envelope on which I write my own address. It is a model of the sort of letters that I dream of receiving. But I will be noble and generous, as I usually am, to judge by what you say, and I will write your name on the outside.

Blanche

Dear Blanche,

Ja wayn awaddi al-hija witaatib ma'a man. . . .
If Hatim were here, he would have sung us these lines in his mellow voice on this glorious occasion. Where can I stow these words? To whom shall I lament?

As of a few days ago, I'm a grandmother! The whole thing took only a few hours of labor and then a very real child was born into my hands. The grandmother is experiencing a new sensation that the mother never had. I did not understand what it was that I held in my hands when Nader handed it over after a few hours in the hospital. For me it wasn't a grandson. What is this thing whose perception exceeded the powers of my mind? He is not a mere child, nor simply the child of my son; and it isn't in my power to produce the assumptions that others—other grandmothers and grandfathers—have made before me. I did not understand, Blanche, what was happening to me. I am not one to strut about in pride as I bring him close to my lips. He has a certain authority when he is in my arms, a power that compels me to alter all of my actions and behavior.

I was avoiding embracing this baby out of fear for my own state, not out of fear for him. As I watched him, I was afraid that I would somehow dwindle away into nothingness, breathing in his fragrance.

It was an indefinable odor that ran between us, a fragrance that sends into one's soul a sort of faith and devoutness that has nothing to do with any of the religions but rather with something whose essence I don't know exactly: it's a contentment that remains unfinished, a poetry exhausted of its powers, a mysticism akin to that of the Sufis who wore wool, but this mysticism is silken, not woolen. If only I were a poet, or a singer, then I would have thought of Edith Piaf when she sang those lines to her beloved:

> *Le ciel bleu sur nous peut s'effrondrer*
> *Et la terre peut bien s'écrouler*
> *Peu m'importe si tu m'aimes*
> *Je me fous du monde entier...*
> *Je renierais ma patrie*
> *Je renierais mes amis*
> *Si tu me le demandais ...*

Blanche, my days are not simply *going by* here; rather, they are developing and accumulating, like growing crystals. This is what led me to avoid getting into the game with Nader and Sonia of choosing a name for the newborn. I did not interfere in this at all; I simply could not do that. The name does not fix its owner's identity; no name does that, as you know. But as I was leafing through the Arabic dictionary that I once sent to Nader, an idea took hold of me and wouldn't let go: As they did not permit me anything having to do with the grandson, my choice fell on your name. As is common in the Arabic language, common in the way news is reported, in any male language: Do you always know the male before the female, or is there simply never any mention of the female? But I will transpose the image: Do you know that Blanche is the name of a sea located to the northwest of Russia. Blanche: the name of a valley—Valle Blanche, just below Mont Blanc where the snow piles high. But you are like the samovar full of coals. Blanche of Castile, Queen of France in the thirteenth century and wife of King Louis VIII and mother of St. Louis: after her husband's death, she ruled for eight years, and then she returned to rule for four more years during the early Crusader campaign. And finally, "Blanche" — my friend — is the name of a beer that tends to be almost white. This latter meaning is what has stayed in my mind; it is the gist. I think that when you arrived in Paris twenty years ago and tasted that beer, the flavor and color pleased you so much that you changed your name from Kashaniya, marble-colored, to Blanche, beautiful white.

Suhaila

Canada Diaries

Sonia has become a true woman—with the child in her lap. Motherhood leads me toward her in a way that no exchange of smiles ever has. I have come to feel that she knows what she is talking about. She notices the lapses in the house and in the order of things. I have begun to understand her old nervousness. Her presence is strong and so is her wariness, even if that has intensified just recently for the child's sake, and there is something of nobility in it. Her wise Indianness has encouraged me to draw closer to her, and her merry Persianness has made my body shake with joy. We came together, that is what I have imagined, woman facing woman, a lovely, real mother with all that means, to accompany the body that gives birth. With this sweet fragile newborn, it was as if I were receiving back my son from her. He is the very same child whom I took in my arms as if he were curtaining me, and veiling the years of my life imprisoned inside my body: and he gives them more glory and virtue.

I watch him and notice things. There is no use in kisses or tears or all of the Iraqi murmurings with which I came prepared. None of that has sufficed as I address him through the magnanimity of that beauty which makes joy public and strong and which neither his crying nor my singing or dancing interrupts. He is simply there and I love him, another being whom we love. We don't know how to behave in front of him until, in his presence, we become acutely aware of our own shortcomings. That is how we know that he possesses us and not the reverse. I have seen all the secrets of my life in his face, witnessing them with my own eyes, and I am allowing him to discover them, with me, little by little. My age has become a good thing in this life I have lived. I have become completely me, more myself than I was before. Whenever I bring his soft palm and his gentle flesh to my lips, the warmth from his hand flows and my soul comes to seem simpler and yet deeper. This child is my recompense as I come forth to him. His eyelids are lowered. I embrace him. This child comes from my imagination. He does not live in dreams but in the wakefulness of reality. He alerts me to my own slips and blemishes, and he rescues me from my failure and my losses.

⟳

Sonia is asleep, the little one beside her. Nader is at work and I am walking in the street. I was alarmed when I first saw these extremely wide streets completely empty of people and movement. What frightened me was the freedom, which I don't know how to handle. I felt like a person whose shackles have been removed but who has lost his folk. Like an animal's, my nose sniffs for the smell of the first place it has known, the one that is lost forever.

There is no solution to my depression; even the existence of this exquisite newborn doesn't provide an answer. I immerse myself in it until I sense that my blood will indeed clot among my pores. At times, my depression protects me even if by an inaudible voice and keeps me from feeling upset. I do not know how to be free. Freedom devours me and I am truly struck with terror. I am afraid: was it waiting for me all this time and through all of these distances I have traveled? How late freedom was! Freedom turned out to be out of reach and we were trying to sidestep its kicks. It was as if I were dreading that it would sweep me away as it has carried away others. I wonder what old people do with freedom? I clasped my hands together as if I were clasping my life for the first time and broadcasting a secret to an audience of myself. So, let us play together and whoever loses will lose. For the first time I become aware of, even attentive to, that region of the body. And the pains that Sonia feels do not turn my head. I smile, walking down the street. I am always walking. I walk especially when I am readying myself to dance. My muscles have grown hard and my steps flow over the even asphalt. I transform my walking into a dance. I search in my body for new regions and I sense my own transformation. I give dance my two feet, wholly, and I acquaint myself with my condition and the calls of my body. I call and always encounter something strange: ties of peace, bonds of fraternity chasing me as I am making adjustments between walking and dancing. It makes me feel as though I have just been born, like Leon. But these streets are here, they exist, with all of this natural-seeming unconcern around me. It is all spectacular. Yet I prefer the narrow alleys and the side streets that take me only there. As soon as I cross into them I will see someone beside me, a man or a woman, and I will feel the give and take of friendship. The ground slips away from me as I walk over it. It clutches hearts and minds as it pulls back from in front of you to be ready to equip your fear. It laughs at you silently: we are the territories of ourselves. Walking so much, I was tired. My feet were asking me questions other than those my hands were asking. The spaces of greenery are my hands, sprouting over my feet.

It is not envy or spite toward Sonia. I am free of that. It is a quality of anxiety that I don't dare to resist as I see her again with the child in her lap. It is something between admiration and respect. Something else solemnly pledged to the unknown drudgery that demands from you nothing more than modesty and silence. It drags me by my clothes and says to me, Don't leave the playing field, Suhaila. The periods of the game are not over yet. When it comes to most things my curiosity is feeble, and that did not change until after Leon's birth. I became someone who sticks her nose into everything, examining, spying, without twisting my head in the other direction. I want to see so that I may reel from the sight before me. I danced for the child day before yesterday when Sonia went into the bathroom and left him with me. I danced for him and for long stretches I left her behind me. I went all the way to Baghdad, and to all the women, and to the choicest men, cut down before their time. I danced, the suitcases in my grip and the country on my brow. I dance as Ishtar danced for Gilgamesh, wearing my simple clothes, picking up the flower vase from where it sits, as a gesture of coming together, of repartee and affection. And when I hear the soft hamhama of his voice I float on my tears. Leon will be redress for my tears and the years of my life. He'll be that redress more than his father ever was.

cdp

Faw rang. I was next to the phone when he called. Congratulations, he said. I'm longing for you. When do you come back? His voice was extremely buoyant with a tinge of flirtation to it. I felt as though my chest was bursting. You are my hard labor, I said to him. I heard a spirited laugh. I don't want anything stronger in what the two of us have together. But I do want that something stronger, I responded. He muttered something and didn't say any more. I did not laugh but I seemed to sense the color and size of my eyes change. I did not tell him, though; I didn't want him to get the wrong idea. I do not want anything unfamiliar from him. I want to keep him as he is, and between me and my self. I am not taking sleeping pills for his sake nor antibiotics, and I don't cajole my complexion so that it looks more glowing. And I don't like my imagination to go very far. I don't want to imagine us doing, or not doing, anything in particular. I can accept the idea of not meeting him again, not circling with him on stage, and certainly not making a vow to myself about being his alone. I can handle not feeling the sort of need for him that would kill me if he were to die before me. He is there, in his own place, in his country, there in the presence of his women and his body and his magic and his age and life; and I am here in the presence of my femininity and my sensitivity and my primitiveness and my stupidities. What happened, what took place between us could no doubt act upon the way our pasts and futures look to each of us. Endless and unspoken! So let him go away or go back, let him be in touch or bail out—it's all the same. I didn't give him the number in Canada and he didn't ask for it, and so without a doubt he got it from

Tessa. She called, too. The telephone is at my side and the moment it rings I answer, afraid that it will disturb the little one. If only Tessa knew Arabic—the local dialect; if only she could talk to Hatim and he could sing for her, ya binadam—O children of Adam!—in the language of the south. The sadness in his voice makes "people flee," as the saying goes. He is perfectly able to speak the dialects of the middle Euphrates and the south of Iraq. Blanche knows the dialects of the north and surrounding areas inside out, and when she starts to talk in Mosuli Arabic she becomes an unfamiliar woman. She blends Assyria with Babylon; it is all very bold and one can't begin to describe the scene. Why didn't she take up acting, this dear woman, why not the stage? Perhaps it would have been better for her than collecting antique carpets?

One day, sitting in that lovely and elegant apartment of hers, I said to Tessa that it is as if the objects there are not things but rather are salt and bread, water and air, and are standing or walking along before my eyes. And despite all of the books and recordings and paintings I see, and all the appearances of modernity, you—I said to Tessa—are so like a pagan being. I see you—instead of seeing these books—among rocks. Do you know that all these miniatures and treasures and silken veils from China and India, from Africa and the Orient, are nothing other than the rays of the sun, and you are inside the dome of your soul, listening to the music made by the breezes and the running sources of rivers and the trees of the forests? Do you realize, Tessa? Sometimes it seems to me that you do not work with your hand at all, or with your tall, thin body or your short and calloused fingers and clipped, worn-down fingernails, or your face like that of a bird with no name, a legendary bird. You don't write simply from the senses or only out of thoughts and concepts. Nor do you write out of intuition or your sinews. You write with all of these as if you have come here from an unpromised land. As if your throat has gone dry as you call out to your people and no one answers you. Covered in dirt, you are not soiled by despair. To the contrary, your spirit has recoiled in horror from oppression. You do not sleep, Tessa, for witnessing the disastrous cataclysms of those lands; of Palestine. But you do not complain of your affliction to God and you have no time to rest. Tessa, what are you doing for the sake of those and the others?

I invited her to my apartment months after we had met for the third time. I also invited the Iraqi-born playwright Nasim Salman after meeting him at Blanche's. I invited Caroline and Nur as well. That evening I made the most wonderful Iraqi dishes I had ever prepared—it was a meal I made, after that, only for Tessa's sake. That evening we talked about the language of ongoing communication among people. That new and lovely friendship returned me to far-ranging memories, to Nasim as he watched my practicing with Faw and then decided to write for us a short theatrical piece to be presented at Théâtre du Soleil between the acts and in Iraq's name. That evening I returned to years long past, to the theater festival in Iraq in the early 1970s when I presented my paper but did not present my dance or any of my roles. My father was upset with me but I didn't care. I told them about it as I drained my third glass of wine. As I was speaking to them, surreptitiously I began to shimmy my body. I stood up, sensing my hands saying, We are all from the East, even Caroline the Swede. The East is not the past or the search for lost time. It is the mouth of a river that pours out love even if it is a mournful, hot, and harsh love, one that squeezes the heart with the heaviness of its misery. I don't know why I feel that all of you are closer to the East, are from the East in the first place, I told them. I was drunk, bursting with life and feeling the hot Iraqi sun, knowing it had not befuddled my head but rather had made of it a fountain where the water of the two rivers met and rose. I was acting a role just as if I were on my father's stage. No police chased me, no husband was beating me as I bathed and swam in the Euphrates. For humanity stays interconnected by means of faces and dress and furnishings and gestures of celebration; through spontaneity and music. All of them play a role equivalent to the language of words. The function of communication is attendant on the whole of social practice more than it is represented in the spoken language alone. Tessa felt exactly as I did: what brought us together in the first place was the unspoken. Language sometimes breaks up relationships among people. To the extent it is an instrument of communication it may become an instrument of mutual misunderstanding and missed meanings. And then, all that is left are these gestures and silence and the touch of hands and the acuity of lively eyes.

I sat down, my glass empty and my speech winding up. This is what happened between us, Tessa and me. We didn't talk at all, but the communication and connection between us shone with words we had never before uttered. Isn't that so, Tessa?

When I put out plates and spoons, mouths were busy and tongues voiced their admiration. I started to talk again, my voice slurred with drink, directing my words to Tessa. If only you would agree about singing in all the dialects of the world, my dear. English and French are not enough. If only Babel would erupt again with tongues and anger and singing that sends its echoes far. If only the place where the date palms grow could be shaken, undone, so that it would spread to cover the cosmos. If only Christmas did not center on the Christian holy figure, the man, the prophet, but on the place as well, on al-Quds, the Holy, Jerusalem; and on Najaf and Karbala, on Mecca and Medina. It is not only Jerusalem in which the crucifixion took place. The crucifixion is all over the world and especially in our lands. If only all languages were destroyed and everything once again became the babble of Babel! Why isn't the theater this confusion of everything, Tessa, between scoundrels and vagabonds, human beings and the prophets? Your theater will be a cosmic adventure that will be neither spared nor left behind, and it will cause a splitting and a rending. I know, you are going to say that I am babbling because of the good wine. This is our blood, take and drink it. . . . My voice chokes and I swallow it into silence. Tessa laughs. She always laughs, and doesn't answer me.

❦

What do I do in Canada?

I dance on the stage of the earth. I see the calm lakes; they look like little food cans next to the Tigris and Euphrates Rivers. This is the theater of imagined lives: there are no spectators before me but the air, the light, the brush of insects in the air, and the sound of the

236

wind. No microphones and no loudspeakers but the whistling of the gods. The clothes I wear are as heavy as they are long and dark. They are so opaquely dark that I cannot even tell what color they are. From afar a faint light is visible, as if I am to be blessed by the illumination of a golden field of wheat; and one can hear the poundings of what sounds like a mortar and pestle, which I imagine to be the drumming announcing the performance in my father's theater. Suddenly many voices are erupting, tormented and sad, not moaning, not in pain, merely turning all the way around to face me. Dance is not enough, Suhaila, neither here nor there. Diya, your only brother, called, that's all. He sent a check for a thousand dollars as a gift to the newborn. He was afraid; he fears his wife.

We had arrived in Paris only months before. Coming across Turkey we were fleeing between terror and certain death. Such a flight was prohibited to us—to us, wife and son of a military man of an as yet unknown fate. As dawn broke I was still awake, conversing with my spirit. Nader was next to me on the other bed. I heard Marianne, Diya's wife. She was giving me a nickname that instantly captivated me as she announced it to Diya.

The khityara makhbula: the crazy old lady. I was not afraid of my new title. I fancied that all of my nicknames were ones I deserved. But she didn't stop there. Don't you see? she told Diya. She has begun to spread terror in the hearts of the two little ones. What does this lady want? She's your sister, fine, but it's too much—this air of hers, always this gloomy and mocking expression. She is a candidate for insanity as it is, and I have begun to feel afraid of her. As for you, your efforts at joking and clowning aren't enough to get around these sudden fits of hers. Diya, she is confused, and that's that. Just consider, last night for an entire hour she raved on and on, some nonsense I couldn't understand about prison and love, and then death and dancing. Then she was going on about the way her husband humiliated her. Her feelings seem to be a jumble of anger and understanding, showing in her eyes as he returns by night from the barracks. I think the two of them are not quite right, my dear. I know a little about what has happened in your country, even after you shut your mouth and refused to speak any more about it. Even the chirping of the sparrows had begun to frighten you when you arrived here. Don't look at me like that, please. Your country is somewhere else; somewhere out there, I mean, in that region of the globe, and I and my children are not concerned with it. We have nothing to do with any of it. And when you come through the door of this apartment you leave it far away, further away than the most remote galaxy in the universe. You know that. Has the whispering gossip of the home country, of your homeland nation, of family and folk, the sister and her son, started to come back to you? You must make yourself go to a psychiatrist. I thought the issue had been resolved. You are French now, my love, be sure you remember that. You will be buried here, having let go of everything for the good of your family. Did you forget that on the day our marriage was announced in my parents' presence?

∽

When Nader returns from work the table is ready, laden with the most appetizing foods. The only comment I hear from Sonia is, He will gain weight, Suhaila. Please. I have a response for her, though. But he is thin, like me and like you. We all need nourishment—and you most of all.

The foods I prepare for her are varied; they are full of calories and they are beneficial. I put them on a tray which I carry into her room. I thought I was forming more of a bond with Sonia than I had had before, but Nader would grumble as he sat in front of his plate, muttering as I ladled out food for him.

Imagine, Mother, that we at the company have the power to buy and sell everything, beginning with goods, continuing through ideas, and ending with people. You could say that we sell truths and illusions and we exchange them for each other, and because our company is half American and half Canadian, the American side takes from the countries of the world stocks and shares, hours of work, and minerals, and exchanges these for figures and fancies recorded in bank registers and computer memories. The whole situation appears laughable not to mention unbelievable. Daily, as if it were the national anthem that we've written on a piece of paper and put in front of us so we won't veer away from it or forget it, we recite our mantra. This is as per the instructions of the directors who have come to the company. It might as well be a sacred oath in the presence of a singular lord: Coming from Wall Street, we are the financiers and we are the ones who decide who lives and who will die.

Of course you do not know the name of that man who was a director of the Bank of Pennsylvania. His name doesn't mean anything to you. Shall I remind you or shall I be quiet?

I was pressing him, as I smiled—if only he would simply say the name without all of these preliminaries.

His initials are JP. But here is what is important. Could you ever imagine that they would make the same thing apply to our country? This is where my interest in politics was checked. And since the news about our country is not reassuring I don't listen at all, or if I do, it's without paying attention to details or concentrating on what is happening. There's nothing left here except marketing, Mother, marketing the heavens after the earth is already sold. The war was happening over there, over there where all of you folks are, over in the Orient and Europe. But here, in Canada and America, the screen offers us the golden age of the war of rumors. I don't remember who it was that said, At the present time this country no longer thinks of anything except what entertains it. Imagine, Mother, my identity here is completely a matter of what I do for a living. My occupation and that is the whole of it. I'm a commodity, too, Mother. Commodification extends to everything that might possibly enter your mind. For the real American buys American goods; as for the true Arab, he buys American goods, too. I have remembered what Ken said after the 1991 war when he was reminiscing, and we were there; do you remember what he said then? The United States reminds me of Great Britain and its control of the high seas in the past. The seas of today are the information necessary to control the waves, the sound waves of global communications media—in all forms. The US is the country that imagines it cannot be done without. Americans cannot deny their country being the most just among all nations in the history of the world, and the most tolerant, and the most desiring of continuous review and improvement. It is the best model for the future.

Ken called. It was a Sunday and so Nader was there to answer the phone. He began to laugh and to comment to us on what Ken was saying. Children are pearls hanging from the beard of nature. Yes, of course I will say that to Suhaila, of course. Yes, she is right here, next to me, and she's happy. Tayyib. Mother, it is Lady.

She was shouting and laughing very loudly. Listen, my friend. This child is for his parents—that's his ideal place to be. As for you, pay close attention. Don't be misled or dazzled by that ringing title of "the dear sweet grandmother," because one of these days you will wake up to find that all hands are stretching toward you, ready to force the tree of your life to stop growing. They are wicked. They will use you in all sorts of capacities for they love your weakness. Don't let your head bend and sway in ecstasy at this glorification of your new role. For that love is like morphine, and if you grow accustomed to it such love will deplete your spirit. Ho, there you are. Congratulations, my dear. Listen, we've sent a gift from all of us. When it reaches you it will make you laugh and laugh.

Ken took back the receiver, laughing. Don't listen to this pessimistic dame! he said. May God bless all the children of the world. With us or without us they will make their way. That's the world for you.

I sensed a sort of reverence in his voice. His laugh and his words offered me a kind of uninterrupted aid, advice, an injection of courage into my heart. Whenever the image of his good-natured face comes into my head, his voice begins to fade while his smile, or his laugh, surges out from a side of his mouth though his smile never does become any broader. Ambiguous, his smile is, somehow standing still, as if it is fenced in; it accumulates but nothing ever wells over to flood out, as happens with Lady who said to me one day, although it was not in response to anything I said, You, your people, do a lot of things in secret while out loud you go on at length about the exact opposites. Sex—it's important, it's necessary, and we must think about it. We do it all the time. We give ourselves and our partners pleasure. It is a beloved act and it is nice. I call it my water, it's that essential. It comes from me slowly, with the natural oils that strengthen my soul and my body and deliver me from maladies and points of weakness. I imagine that if the contents of our bodies stayed inside of us they might turn against us.

Then she turned suddenly and asked me, What do you think?

Who decides whether something is beautiful and how do we prove that it is so? Do its beauty and pleasure depend solely on what we imagine? I thought of the German philosopher Kant, the ascetic, the chaste, who dreaded to squander semen, saliva, and sweat because he thought that would drain away his philosophical energy and intellectual life, which he was so anxious to preserve. And me, for whom do I preserve my powers and the sexual potential I hold inside? I am nothing but an actress and dancer on her way to retirement.

～

One night years ago in Brighton, Channel Four was broadcasting a documentary about the Vietnam War. Demonstrations had spread throughout the world by then. Ken's face at that time is still before my eyes and I will not forget it as long as I live. He was at the height of his suffering. The smell of his misery filled my nostrils and his voice swung back and forth, between the here of Brighton and the there of Vietnam.

It was my mother, Suhaila, who stuffed me between her ribs and closed her clothing over me because she was so intensely afraid for us, as we all were being transported in trucks and trains loaded with corpses. She did it so that I would not scream or cry from hunger and thirst. I was more lifeless than a fragile, skinny child should be, as she transferred me from her chest to between her thighs, imprisoning me there, where I snuck looks at the ailing, bony, yellowish body pressed up against me, the whole way, which was crowded with American soldiers. The stink of urine and armpits and fear cut through my mouth and nose, and her pubic hair sprinkled her urine slowly along my palate. I would drink and then for moments be silent and still. I would drink and nearly choke from the stream of it and the blood she was hemorrhaging. We were an easy target, all jammed together, to be crushed like insects, our dead bodies to be tossed into the thickets and garbage piles or dumped at crossroads. My mother's pee was what saved my life. She inherited chronic bladder infection and a kidney blockage, and I inherited infections in the throat and a fissure in the esophagus whose effects are still with me. The urine contained pebbles and sand and a lot of blood that I swallowed and didn't pay it any mind. Who can distinguish in such moments between blood and piss? Years later, when I reached my tenth birthday and we were in England, I learned to shake my body fiercely. I pricked and tormented and pounded it; I split my flesh and made it bleed. Walking through forests and thickets that scraped my skin I would press the thorns of bushes into my body. I would sting my flesh with broken glass and sharp implements. I saw my blood run, in those fields. I swam in my blood and I propelled it outside of myself, repeating, Take it, and look, Ken. Don't you see those holes and wounds? Don't you understand? I want to filter and cleanse my Vietnamese blood of American sweat. My mother began to follow me like my shadow on those mad trips of mine.

You are a lunatic, she said. You are demented just like him. Like your father who went on fucking me as the sounds of the bombs and rumbling from the missiles echoed on and on over our heads. Blood was pouring from his ears and the bottom of his mouth. And his thing was spraying blood mixed with semen. I got pregnant with you in the mud amidst the moaning of the wounded and the dead bodies on every side. Every shudder of his body sent me all the way down to hell but he didn't care; he went on blasting apart my pelvis and hips, slapping, kneading my body with mud and bullets and the poison of microbe-filled dust. He would get up, naked, make his slack thing hard again, and start over. He would raise it high, and higher, like a missile; he wouldn't close his eyes but he would bellow when he saw the airplanes on their way to us. They aimed well and his skull burst apart, skudding through the dirt where I was submerged in blood and terror.

When Caroline called she was on the telephone for a long time. She congratulated Nader first, on the third day after the birth. On the fourth day she spoke to Sonia in her hospital room. She didn't ask to speak to me. She was very good at choosing appropriate moments when Nader happened to be present, when Sonia and the baby were awake. Strange — it is a matter of instinct, not just alertness and vigor. I truly appreciated her style when I could see that she was choosing her words with care, for she was easing things for me. She knows pretty well what goes around in my mind and what sorts of stories I will be likely to tell her and the rest of my friends there. In my notebook I've written down some of the bothersome things, certain inconsistencies; there is no time to sidestep them and it wasn't seemly to dodge them, at least not in front of myself. It was problematical: that Nader would cloak himself in all of the roles: mother, nurse, obedient servant and a man who does not know the meaning of neglect when it comes to affairs of the household.

He looked to me like something more than a son and a father. His masculinity made itself scarce and he became far less chatty. He was lavishly dissecting his new persona. He was a new man; he had become someone different. He was playing that role consummately and I was trying to fathom his new situation. That was in the beginning. He obeyed the call, Sonia's call, and the pull of this new, impassioned, ebullient emotion: being Abu Leon, the father of Leon.

Sonia would be able to write the history of that decisive stage in their life together. Without a doubt he became her particular project. No, it was not jealousy sinking its claws into me; these were fragments of theories on liberation, justice, and freedom, remnants of my own unclear, hazy ideas that I fancied remained securely embedded in my heart: Sonia is a woman with her head held as high as a fresh carnation on its stem. Authority is clearly etched on her desiring face; the halo of vindictive femininity casts its light all around her; and as such I hear her voice as she speaks to him, coming or going. She speaks to Nader. She gives him commands that he can't dismiss and she is constantly blocking his path. At first he tries to get around it but then he jumps up and says, Fine. Myself, I was going to insist on his release. Her authority had something supernatural about it, like the force of that legendary creature, the ghoul. I don't know where this comes from. I did not feel that way the day Nader was born and I had no knowledge of any secreted power, hidden somewhere and all I had to do was to wipe the dust from it for it to rouse itself, to flap its wings, slowly, quietly, and without much obvious force. I followed the path set out before me, with my newborn, and I was silent. I faded; I disappeared. I began to echo whatever that husband said so that I would obtain approval and reap satisfaction, or at least so that I would not face the likelihood of standing in the mouth of the cannon. Was Sonia here as an instrument of revenge for my passivity? Was she here to redo my training and thus to destroy the Nader I knew completely, as if she were conveying to him what I used to suffer, and then to publicly, overtly, push me irretrievably off into the corner? The general outlines of what I have come to believe over the course of my life, those issues and ideas and the ringing words that we repeated in the lecture halls and theaters and demonstrations and plays, and the roles we took on, have been made opaque, false, and futile. The damage and injustice of it all have emerged in sudden and sharp contours before me now, as Sonia has dared to stand above the unassailable fortress. She takes up her new stance before my ancient one and the scales tip in her favor. I look, I notice, I repeat; I dread to call out (and with her right there), Beware, Nader, be careful! Is it because you are my son? And so it is as if I am warning myself again, as if I am back inside one of those long-ago days. I am shattered slowly and the glass splinters fling themselves all the way to the furthest seat in the theater and on into the home and across the bed. Why am I so upset? I get angry, with my hand on the balustrade and Sonia's voice coming, elegant and eloquent; there is nothing that can curb its defiant canter. I hear her insistence, and the way she repeats things, gently, and then coquettishly, and then with that strength like an explosive device, and the magnetic appeal that she casts wide like a web-spinning spider, so that evil whisperings fill my head and spill over me like boiling hot water. Between us, what is there to divide us? There is her winning efficiency and my incapacity. By myself, I snarl and grumble, and then I surrender the flag to her while feelings of sorrow about Nader and myself fill me with regret.

244

Caroline's phone calls began again. In a word, she told me, this call is for you. What is this, Suhaila? When are you coming back? Two months you have been there, and I am sure you are sitting there collecting and going over all of your scattered parts, your faults and your great qualities. You will say thank you for this visit because it made you distinguish between artificial and natural light. Suhaila, what is the other thing you have become certain of? Do not swallow your pride in front of me and say yet again, I was unable to stand what was in front of me. Sonia became the general manager while Nader was just a simple doorman and gofer available for all tasks and services.

That will become your primary topic; it will satisfy your proclivities but it's also a subject that stirs you up. You must understand, my friend, the significance of the story which is so often repeated. From behind that curtain you are scrutinizing another man, as if you are on the point of issuing separation papers. Separate him from your self, then, please do. Do not put all of this blame on *her* for making what is in fact the best possible use of your son. What is worse than that, in fact, is that she is submitting the application to you and all you have to do is to fill in the blanks: your own shortcomings and your having gotten off track. Have you absorbed the lesson? This institution is full of faults and slip-ups. To remain was well-nigh impossible for you, not because of who you were, or because of your husband, but because of the war. Don't you see why I have never married?

Wajd would say repeatedly, It is not necessarily the case that depression is a condition peculiar to the wealthy and refined. Take Caroline, for example. You don't suffer from the sort of self-pride she has, but for you, feeling depressed is like a hoarded treasure.

The day I learned that Caroline had a master's degree in mathematics, I was stunned. And I laughed out loud when she told me. If you were an Eastern woman, Caroline, I said, you would have split my head apart talking about it and singing your own praises about the academic heights you had achieved, and you would have insisted that I call you professor.

What? she answered with a lovely quietness. But I got the equivalent of a doctorate in the philosophy of the Enlightenment from Durham University. As she spoke she was pouring out two new glasses of nicely aged wine. Her hand fluttered every which way in front of my face. Her nails, carefully shaped, were painted a dark silvery hue. The nails of an Indian fortuneteller, I remarked, and she laughed like a little girl. Around us were mounds of electric wires going to all sorts of advanced gadgets and pieces of equipment amidst which we sat: a television with a screen like those you see in the private theaters of French institutions; a digital large-screen plasma television and a VCR system for older tapes. I will give this to you, she said, on your next birthday. It really produces superior sound. It picks up everything. It's the only one I have kept from the old days — or from the second wave. Very high lamps sent the light upward so that it did not hurt your eyes. There were three computers, the huge original one looking like a ponderous old electric dumbwaiter sitting on the stylish black table with its huge, glistening screen. The smaller one she carries with her whichever room in the apartment she is in; it's like an obedient puppy that follows her everywhere. I envisioned her taking it with her to the bathroom as well. The third, smallest in size, she sticks into her handbag when she is traveling to some other country by air or train. Two printers, one of them the usual type and the second laser. A scanner for full-color images as if we are in a small institution or firm that depends on records, archives, and documents. Her library is a maze, a skyscraper in itself. I need an elevator and a uniform to move among these shelves, I told her. It was hard for me to remain inside that world for any length of time. It is simultaneously well ordered and chaotic, aberrant and overly regulated. I would require nerves of steel and advice from trained psychiatrists, plus an ancient prayer that I would proffer to assure that blessings would fall on me. She raises her eyebrows as I continue to flee from these presences. I feel, I say, as though I am facing an army of nice, pleasant enemies. She responds, laughing and saying, These are the seductions of knowledge. She sets me down inside symbols and numbers, lines, and languages, and invites me gravely, Come, write, if you would like to write. A button, two buttons, a light; and the information is all there in front of you in a second. Come on, start in. You can be sure that if you put your fingers there, no thunderbolt will strike you! And this is not a lamb shank that you put in the oven and forget while it roasts to a turn.

This, Caroline goes on, is where I establish links between me and myself and the world. But you are still out there roving around in the emptiness, in the deserts, addressing the stars with a sewing needle and expecting that your old moon will write your new history. Suhaila, my magic is stronger. This—this is magic, look at it and enter its world in safety, with confidence. I will donate my experience to you. Yes, slowly of course, and without a lot of to-do. I will give you a golden opportunity to make all of the mistakes, and I will appoint you an honorary consul in this world; but only after a year or two, when you've developed more of a backbone. She explains with the movements of her body, her hand, and her head. She is generous, lenient, gentle, tolerant, and courageous.

Look here. I am going to prepare a special binder I bought for you, she says. We will begin right now. Her words are like the prayers of a fervent intercessor. My feeling about it, though, is that this machine hates, and loves, and feels pleasure, and is a little harsh, but it never, never relents. Never retreats. All of these machines remain sleepless and vigilant, always at the service of her needs and entertainment. All I have to do in this situation is to disavow my own uncouthness and exaggerated caution. Here is the phantom whose price I have to pay from now on, as long as the Creator wishes. The gifted brain of this machine is computed in numbers with a long string of zeros. My natural ability is computed, beaten into me, with canes and bitterness and disappointment and failure. How long must I train for this? How long do I have to suffer? How long must I forget, and pretend to forget, and prepare myself to experiment, experience, and learn?

With the long explanation she began to yawn. She holds these secrets tightly in her hand and parcels them out to those, like me, who are in need. After a little, when I have left her, she will go into that well-designed bedroom, drape her Indian shawl around her head and begin her yoga exercises. Had she lived in the era of the Marquis de Sade he would have begun by pulling and stretching her, with all possible cords, attaching them to arms and shoulders, legs and belly and chest. He would have brought all of the candles on earth close to her face and surrounded her eyes with flames. He would have bedded her in an orgy that ends only to begin again. He is able to say to her, Come here! and she does not flee from his presence. I don't know why I had the feeling that she was in need of a whole host of such encounters, of such surveillance and control, of passions and love affairs, some indecency and truly obscene behavior, some uncertainty and lack of control that would mean all of her projects on these gadgets would be botched. There would be no man better than de Sade to animate the instrument panel of the Duchess Caroline and send it in all directions, moving his fingers to meet that marble-like body, with the hard push of a button stripping her of all her modesty and devilishness, without giving any consideration to her hellish iciness.

✍

I watch some of the American channels here. I wait for everyone to go to sleep and then, alone, I tiptoe into the living room. I don't know how to decode these talismans. Whenever I move from one channel to another I imagine myself in front of a scene from the theater that goes on for twenty-four hours. Suddenly one of the leaders of the Republican Party appears and I hear him bellow. Why should we concern ourselves with others whose fervent hope is that locusts will consume America? he demands to know. I remembered the incident newspapers in France had published and then Arabic newspapers had translated: Nine youths from Holland came for winter sports, said the news article. In a year of abundant snow such as France has not known since 1986, they chose what appeared to be an appropriate peak in the southeast of the country. Bad luck and lack of caution led to their deaths when an avalanche fell as they were skiing. But, over there, luck such as this had nothing to do with snow or an avalanche that commingles wisdom and senselessness. Over there, such items concern military targets. For at dawn on that very same day American planes were strafing the Amiriya shelter in Baghdad, as the newspapers wrote at the time. Later in the morning, four hundred—or more—corpses were pulled out of the civilian shelter. At the time, General Richard Neal stated, we are absolutely certain we struck the intended target; we do not believe that we attacked the shelter, which was not targeted. This was a legitimate target. We do not know why there were civilians inside the shelter, and we did not go to war to destroy the Iraqi people.

I woke up in the morning and went immediately to the window. Most of what I describe is imaginary. I make mistakes and then I say to myself, Fine, Suhaila. Perhaps this place is the right one for you, so don't go and leave it. And where will you go? Here thirst is not satisfied while there hunger is more shamefaced than are the words that express it, and any elaboration becomes meaningless. From morning to evening I work hard—my hard efforts are trivial and sick. I stare at the fresh greens and the meats, and at the frozen chicken and fish. At legumes, fruits, medicines, vitamins. At cartons of milk, household goods, pots and pans, all sorts of electrical appliances, for juicing and grilling, for doing anything and everything. At clothes, precisely engineered cabinets, chairs more essential and active than I am. Carpet sweepers quieter than an ice-covered tree in the garden. I listen to all of the parts of things, all the while searching for someone in need of a touch of insanity: those women, me, or those men, before we all start to rot and go thoroughly bad and insane. I do not want to be a useful member of anything here; this is not my home and the objects here are no affair of mine. I am not an extra part nor am I a whole drawn to them. If I move the flower vase from where it sits this is only to escape from what has been lost forever—the whole garden. If I cut the cake I know that they are observing me, six eyes waiting for one tiny piece of enjoyment and entertainment and satiation. I set in motion whatever is not requested of me. I set their intentions in motion and I carry out things they are not even able to articulate. They are watching to see how far I will go, under observation, under the microscope: my face, my gestures, my words, my irritation and bad mood. As for my silence, that is the heaviest thing weighing down on them, and on me. They always have the ability to remind me that I am mistaken so that I will inflict my own punishment. There, in Baghdad, I showed no resistance except through acting and dancing. My father produced roles for all of us who were new actors, newly minted graduates of the academy. Of these roles he would say, They will raise your heads high and give you immense stature. Come, you must forget everything you have memorized, for texts are prisons, they are like the prisons of the homeland, and your only recourse is to smash them by means of other performances, different performances, the kinds that shake things loose. He would stand behind me, whispering into my ear, Come out, leave your weak and fatigued body. Leave behind its nature, which is to feel guilty even before the commission of sins. Go to the bodies of others. Pry out the treachery, cowardice, and abasement from your body. Stand tall like the noblest of the ancient saalik poets, those vagabond reciters, when they were at their most fertile. Don't stand as if you are a commissioned soldier who is intent only on performing his military duty. Forget the whip of the sayyid your husband, forget his voice and his commands, even if your feet go weak and tremble, for weakness is the badge that announces the human tribe and it is the glory of actors. We do not want or intend any of you to become criminals of a theater or indeed its drunkards, filling the stage with the dregs of the steps you take. My father let slip the reins of the body and the heart. He said, You must betray that Suhaila, the defeated and cowardly Suhaila. Bite her as hard as you can and look carefully at the wound. No authorities, no rank, no battalions, no fleets of airplanes, no maps to deceive you and no uniforms to induct you into social respectability. You are an artist and not a clown.

Those years I spent on the stage enticed me and lured me on: my harshness and my torment, my crimes and my evil. As for my identity, it was fragmented, dispersed between sayyid-father and sayyid-military man. My father, too, used me for the sake of his own great glories. I will extract the pearls from you, he would say to me over and over. And I will braid them around the waistline of the contemporary Iraqi stage. But I used to distance myself from my father even as I would not come close to either my husband or myself. It was my father who gave me the nickname of "Suhaila, untamed animal of the theater." That phrase ran like fire through the dry kindling of the Iraqi press and indeed the entire regional Arabic press. That husband, meanwhile, was getting drunk and staying away. Every ascent I made in the theater was accompanied by a punishing, blasting volcanic lava in bed. I played characters in comedies and farces, but I was especially accomplished at roles that embodied miserable sadness and downright abasement. I changed my appearance, dying my hair a different shade for every role. With the help of makeup I gave myself different faces and relaxed my facial muscles and lineaments so much that I did not recognize my own self in the mirror. Then I would not be held responsible for my own demeanor, my own features. For that short span of time I would be a different creature, one whom I had created myself, one whom I had not known in the past. I invented it. It would be an unknown quantity, during those conclusive hours of my life, thus multiplying by two the risky adventure I was facing. I would always be the contrary, so that the search would continue for the face: my face. And so it was that, as my age advanced, I would bid farewell to one of those faces. Sometimes I would reconcile the two faces of myself but most of the time I did not. I was always led to something different, as if I were music that no one can hold onto but that everyone sways to as they listen hard.

❧

Ferial called. It was Sonia who picked up the phone. I was taking a bath. Tell Suhaila, she said, that Rabab and I are in Amman. I arrived from Rome a few days ago. We will try to call again or perhaps we will write her a long letter. In Baghdad Ferial used to say, Her husband's voracity doubled the number of medals that were placed on his chest. I swear to you, Suhaila, that even when he was tossing and turning in bed, his oaths would gush out over me. For he did his duty as thoroughly as one can. I knew; so did you, but you are the sort of person who keeps things under wraps. You are the opposite of me. He was afflicted with me. I am the sort of person down whose cheeks tears do not flow. Unbendable iron—if he hit me on the cheek I slapped the nape of his neck. It was all hideously, shockingly, ugly. It was me who commanded him, one way or another, to beat me. He was not endowed with patience and I would not take back my words or withdraw from battle. A blow to the head and I would kick back. I would sprout wings. Humiliation—yes, indeed!—but in the corners of my eyes my fatal charge was amassing: scorn. For how long I saw that happening, in fleeting moments! Something like joy was in it, alive and real, something that would require a whole other life if I were to truly recall and assess it and not simply be rid of it. And even then. . . . That long, long grief—that grief was what deluged my life and led me to induce those abortions. I didn't count how many there were. It's a dirty way to either freeze things in place or correct them. I know what you will be advising me to do.

When everything between them was finished, she had gone down like the setting sun. She said those words that I remember: I am exactly like my republic. I have become fragile and full of cracks. I have been depleted and ruined and destroyed yet I still feel that I have been something of value. The finest years of my life passed within a framework of a single and unchanging idea. I had the determination and the sense of responsibility and the ability to change it, but I failed. Do not envy me, please, don't you see? Our clothes are modern and the ways we beautify ourselves are in fashion, but our skins are spattered with the oil of fear and our hearts drag behind them a caravan of illnesses, misery, and obscenity. Even friendships did not come to our aid or stand with us. To my eyes they appeared threadbare, shabby, and outworn; they were not strong enough to excite respect or sincere, pure affection. Our illnesses, too, are ones we do not even seem to deserve. They are sicknesses devised by others. They are *their* invention. I was tricking you, Suhaila, and I will not say to you, I will never say to you, give me a break, when you repeat in a bashful and laughing voice as you are staring into our eyes, we friends of yours, We must not leave all of the old places to our coming maturity and old age, may it bite the dust! It commands

252

many talents for usurping what we used to imagine we were capable of preserving: nobility, self-esteem, and zeal. Why shouldn't it, when this is the sole remaining danger for us in front of them.

Ferial remained intensely feminine, continuing to attract men merely by the way she walked, her speech, and her laughter. Her appeal was like the secret police who always find exactly the right circumstances in which to inflict punishment on others. When I danced in front of them—those women—or on stage, I was acting with trained skill, and working on the roles I played, so that those meters of space would be transformed into my one and only test site. I would get to know those women better. I would sweep away all the categories of protocol and formalities, provoking their nerves. On occasion, I would feel as though they were turning or had suddenly gone against me. This state of affairs actually tempted me and generated new symbols and allusions that I used but that they did not know or connect with me. I was becoming strange to them and now and then to myself, as I emitted signals that were in no way classifiable or could be inserted into any larger image of me, signals about the movement of my soul and my body, my sex and my experience. Dance guided me to shake the whole world into moving with me and through my inspiration. Dance organized my pain and made it more resistant; dance hid my pain in a deeper place. It gave a frame to friendship and fortified my commitments to friends in trenches deeper than all those of the republic. With my first dance steps and movements I would observe my own myriad transformations inside and out. I would absorb the world instantly even if everyone were to abandon me, especially those women, for soon enough I would come back to myself as I summoned them back, one by one, steering my body toward them again and again. I lead it; I don't turn it into an obstacle. I teach it and it explains to me how it wards off the dangers from me and from them; the incomprehensible dangers that faced us and the things to which our life has led in every land and on every continent.

∽

Two letters, Mother. The first is from Amman and the other arrived from Paris. Nader handed them to me, smiling. When I looked at the handwriting I knew that the first was from Ferial and the second from Narjis. Strange that Narjis did not call to say mabruk even though a whole two and a half months had passed. I tested their thickness with my fingertips and pressed down on them with longing. I smiled at Nader in turn and he understood what I wanted: to be alone in their company.

I went into the warm, glass-enclosed space that overlooks the broad street and the carefully laid out garden. I fine-tuned the position in which I was sitting; this long and comfortable leather chair allows me to stretch my legs out all the way. It was six thirty and I longed for a cigarette but that was utterly forbidden here. For Leon's sake and yours, said Nader. I agreed, and not grudgingly. But wine—my adoration of it remained undiminished. I heard the sound of Nader's footsteps. He came in with a tray bearing hot tea and a few cookies. He had come to have an English alarm clock in him. He put the tray down next to me on the square table and went out right away. He did not let me see the captivating expression in his eyes. He was spoiling me, for my scheduled return to Paris was coming up quickly. I hastily opened the letter from Ferial and Rabab first. Rabab was our third friend in the academy and she was unique. And she had brought me under her sway by now.

Suhaila dear, here are a few lines from me before I leave you in Rabab's care. I came from Baghdad to Amman for her sake. This creature remains a hazard. It is as if we were still in those classes! To me she is like a light storm of delicate and harsh elements, as if she lived all of those years only in her underclothes. She remains pure in her relationship with herself, in the first degree, and in general her movements echo her own sculptures. And not the one she was ordered to sculpt one of those years and because of which she was dismissed from the academy. She brought me a select archive of them. She lived like those statues, in an ascetic state. Mortification of the flesh. But the fantasy erupted and returned to us our confidence in the old art, the art we used to study and dream of. Do you know, age hasn't gotten to her yet, ayy w-Allahi! Perhaps, unlike me, she didn't make it into an exclusive focus as I did and so the years have ignored her. It's an astonishing thing—unbelievable, really—for despite the terrible difficulties she suffered in Rome she still says Allah! in wonderment, even at the speck of dust she sees floating above the car which I leased for her sake, driving her from place to place. She has held onto compassion and wonder and other things of which I am not even aware. Nobility and sincerity, perhaps, which for some of us have been changed into waste. When I saw her after twenty years or more, I screamed and then I wept. I began to search for her. I searched carefully over her face and her features as I asked her, Where did you take those vile years? We are stuffed full of years. But Rabab—aah, if only you could see her, Suhaila. I cursed you as usual, and I cursed myself, my grandparents, my ancestors. I cursed all of them, between you and me. Akhkh, Suhaila, if only I were a mere ten years younger, that's all, akhkh, age would just be a dream, a phantom that went away so swiftly, that ended before it began. It wiped its hands after it ate us up and tossed us as far and as low as we could go, the lowest of the low. Suhaila, as I also said to Rabab, I still try to win myself over to myself when I am in spacious rooms or in secret rooms that are locked upon me. I am afraid of the light. I am afraid of the unknown step. In Baghdad, one after another, we incur big emotion-debts, but I don't know anyone to whom I could pass them on, and I have no son or daughter for whom I can preserve my only inheritance. Suhaila, the war has cleansed my vision: now I can see in every direction. My senses have been well-honed and I have gained what I was completely ignorant of: danger. Here, in Amman, even if it were to be a mere few days or a month, and even if I were truly removed from the dangers of those who come and go, I feel that I am living the danger in its entirety. I live it to its furthest extent. To the end. The danger of it is what renews my forces. I imagined that I was fleeing from it but I found it that it was inside of me, more than ever it was there, in this city which appears to me afflicted by the stammer of the terrified after all the original teeth have fallen out so that Baghdad put artificial teeth in its mouth. Those teeth can't bite us as they would like. Today, my dear, I feel freer than I have ever felt. In Baghdad I don't know what to do with my freedom. I tried hard, as you did, and as they all did: Tamadir, Narmin, Azhar, and Rabab. Now, would you remember her if you once forgot? Just now she is at my side, after all news of her had vanished completely. She returned suddenly like the new moon that signals the feast day and we never know exactly when it will show. She searched for my phone number and address, asking around among all sorts of people who don't know me, but she found me in the end. Suhaila, when will you return to Paris, and what are you still doing in Canada? The grandson arrived and she is the mother. You are not. Sonia has taken on all of the roles and so has the son, and he crosses the spaces between you and her like a clock hand. Return to yourself a little, return to us. I leave you now with Rabab.

∽

Suhaila, I will respond to all of those questions of yours, which I imagine are not quite formulated yet but rather still suspended between your lips and your tongue. It seems there is no escape from crossing this distance with you after I crossed it for days with Ferial. With you I will be less spontaneous and more difficult, for I was never one of your beloved women. You used to annoy me with your acquiescence but it was not up to me, or it was not my right, either before or after, to say whatever I might say not only to you but also to others. I have learned how to organize the chaos of my emotions and sentiments, like a faqih combs out his beard and trims it and plucks out the stray hairs but goes on scaring children with it, not to mention pessimists such as you. Life in the academy was my first swallow of bitterness; afterward, the cup overflowed. Your questions comprise one such gulp of bitterness. That's how I feel about it: questions coming from a past which remains strong and essential even though it has been totally annihilated. I haven't shut the storeroom door on that past and, likewise, I didn't demand forgiveness for it either. I broke off all my relationships so that I could bring to light my own condition and unearth the state that all of you were in as well. A single pit we entered, whereupon we were buried in dirt and worms, just like that, even without benefit of any riddles we would have had to solve. Who among us has been completely victorious? It appears that we have all been defeated. I am not talking about you, about your ordeal — are you really in the midst of an ordeal? I don't have the right to ask such questions — I wrote this one down as a kind of joke. Every ordeal has some appearance of begging. Even our understanding and the other person's attempt to understand us makes a sort of beggary. And here I am, watching myself begging your understanding. But why? As I am writing to you I bring you fully into my presence: your radiance on stage and your despondency in the academy's quadrangle. You were a lot, you were an abundance, you were more than we were, much more. Just now I have been discovering you but I am not reaching all the way to you and your presence doesn't allow me to bury myself in my own concerns. Just barely are we witnesses: we contracted leprosy and they came to fear our touch or any proximity to us, but we are still scratching at the site of their ugliness and their old pus and their monstrous, deformed shapes. Our heads are still bowed, and I am in the forefront. You will ask, What have you done, Rabab, in the land of the Romans? I studied, and I learned, and I got work, even cleaning the shit of some rich old women who were mere skeletons. But among them the shit had been preserved in them as a human being's strongest possible modesty and filth. From these bodies, the bodies of women in particular, emerged my sculptures and my formations and my misshapen, monstrous figures as well. From that site, and among those old women, I was born. That was the essence of my life or rather, more accurately, the core of the art. Their remains and talents are still there upon my hands, and their true insolence runs across my body. I needed them more than they were in need of me. They were very gifted with vomit and excrement, with urine and sweat, with laziness and chatting and unbearable crudeness. They were gifted with all of the illnesses of the ancient and medieval and modern world that you can possibly think of. Yaah, how much I profited from sicknesses! They were a target and they were my training and they were stubbornness and a challenge. I hunted down the ill like one of those Italian gigolos who tracks closely and patiently, and pursues the hunt, and is compelled in the end to do up the buttons of his pants and sink himself in the secret act in order just to remain somewhere above despair. All my amorous rendezvous took place in the homes of those women. I would clean and feed and perfume them and leave the light slanting in so that they would not disappear from my sight as I stole their ancient profligacy from them, and the sighs of that tyrannical ruination that was, and the moaning of the mothers over the dissolute sons. You can be confident, Suhaila, those are them, the women. Those women in whose embrace I found care and security, and before all else, adventure that was also creative. It was those women who helped me to excavate my blindness and impotence, and from inside the forest of their primitive souls they achieved for me the most beautiful sculptures. I had my first show in the garden belonging to one of them, a rich woman with the aristocratic name of Señora Clementina. She let me have a whole section of that lovely garden for my work—after all, I was a source of pride for her and her family and her wild gay grandson who had an unrivalled way of arousing me to my femininity. My sense of myself as a woman doesn't need that particular mode we all know, that calls on protection and virtues and mistakes. So I gave him my virginity as a sort of bounty to that ferocious beauty. I sculpted Mario nude and into his body I cast the rebukes, prohibitions, and insults that my notorious body attracted when I was in Baghdad. I did not plan on staying in Rome; I didn't strategize for it. Those things, those events, happened of their own accord. I saw time's existence as I left that city, and as I was leaving all of you. I was leaving the man I loved and we were saying goodbye to each other. I saw he was a trivial lie and all of those stars in the Baghdad sky were bankrupt, and those projects we dreamed of, him and me, were nothing more than a silly nightmare. That night, in that emptiness I felt throughout my body, I cried as hard as one can cry. I will cry here, I said, in Baghdad, as I am saying goodbye to it, I will cry all of the tears I have, I will finish them up and come out clean and light and pure. That is how I will come out to the airplane. I was sobbing and blowing my nose, weeping for the dust-covered city quarters and my destitute home and my eight siblings and my retired father whom I would now be obliged never to see again. I wept at the terror of those new streets that would crush me beneath them if I were to forget. For I had died as I prepared my papers for travel, and when I hoisted my completely empty suitcase I sensed that I would never return there again. Rome was the hardest. Language was not the only obstacle. I didn't have enough money, either. At the time I had no more than three hundred dollars. But when one has gotten accustomed to living at the very bottom of the pit, it is no problem to live in the bowels of a seductive and shameless city such as Rome. At the time I thought of Ferial in particular, and before I thought of you, of course, for you and I were far more thoroughly demolished than she was. Our ruin did not bring us together. Indeed, to the contrary, it tore us apart, scattered and fragmented us. It was Ferial alone who brought us together, because what is different about her, compared to us, is that she has this powerful and lightning-quick way of facing things. Perhaps it was because those who so admired her were greater in number and reputation, I don't know. My quiet demeanor was not a target in itself nor was your mute and indistinct outward appearance which stuck in the gullet. Your marriage when you were still a student at the academy infused the insanity of your inner nature with a sort of stupid wariness. This put limits on your comings and goings and on the signs you gave us at the university, even though you appeared affectionate, and the drama professors would call you the electrified ghoul. I longed to have Ferial with me in Rome, not you. I wanted her to be there so that she could regain or reorient her eyes and redo her taste in the art of décor, the specialty she chose and was so passionate about, so she would not once again grow confused as she did when she took on arranging your stupid bogus expensive furniture when you invited us to that extravagant villa in the neighborhood that was fenced in with electric wire and police dogs. I decided to forget all of you for good, but your news did reach me, bit by bit, from where I don't know. The Iraqi artists began to emigrate one after the other and so I would hear snatches of your news or hers. Ferial found herself a way by means of the homes of some of the old rich, people of influence who had emigrated for good. She began to redecorate interiors, replace furniture and carpeting, remake guest rooms, gardens, and sitting rooms. I laughed when I heard her news.

I said to myself, She has become like me. I bring back life to the skeletons of rich old women and I return by night to excavate them again and encase them in plaster of Paris. I put them into ovens, grill them, and from their most extreme moments of desolation extract suffering, shame, and their own deferred deaths. And Ferial deals with objects, everything inanimate, mute; with silk and herbage, linen and artificial flowers, with wood and steel and electricity and other things that follow. Every one of us was able to spend or perhaps to squander her life with cold, unmoving blood. She wagered on those lumps of material and creatures, and between entertainment and dream she kept going. Each of us took a small space, a tiny margin of existence, keeping it small and unobtrusive as if she were trying to conceal a nest egg from the eyes of the tax office. I know what you will say now; I can hear your raised voice. Ayy, fine, you say. Didn't life look to us more cursed than death? Precisely. What were we to do? That's how I will answer you—and you have not even asked about men and relationships, what I did there, how I handled that freedom. Not in the sense of the body only: I mean the freedom to take decisions, for a woman isn't merely a body as most men think. I doubt you know that I fell in love only twice. One of them you know, that first love. The other one was an Irish artist, a brilliant painter. The relationship ended after a year and a half when he returned to Ireland after a special study tour of murals in Florence. I did not die after he left nor did any serious fatal accident happen to me. Even so I do not personally applaud transient relationships. They stir up in me the sort of terror that death causes in us, and a sense of insult for which there is no recompense from heaven or earth. There is an inconsequentiality about such relationships that my spirit cannot bear. Fleeting relationships are life lived upside down.

You know, Suhaila, in one of our conversations at the academy Azhar was with us. Her good looks provoked admiration among the male students and professors around us, even more than Ferial did. I wonder where she is now? At the time, I felt as though we were part of a permanently ongoing hunting party and the one with the most bodily strength would master us. In response to such behavior I was always at the ready to commit a crime if I had to. My relationship with the other—with men—if it was anything at all, tended to be one of overall affection. If a certain man was not a colleague or friend, my relationship with him was governed by shared cultural interests, and that was all. I cannot feel any fondness for individuals who do not stir up real admiration in me and whom I do not respect. I know, though, what you are trying to get at. You want to know more about that miserable relationship with virginity, right? To release you from your headache, I will answer you. I know perfectly well how persistent you are behind that silence of yours. What happened to me took place without any cunning or underhanded behavior. I took it all very calmly and, later, I did not try to follow him. Nor did he feel any particular sympathy for me, as I didn't have any regrets. I did not carry with me the notion that I was a woman with a past which had killed the person I was and spoiled the future for me. In fact, he became one of my dearest friends. He always sought my help in those nervous afflictions which constantly bothered him, and I would hurry to him. Suhaila, those young men are priceless friends. Shame is not what brings us together with them nor do regrets and moaning divide us. Like most women, I believe that love is something that has nothing to do with sex in comparison to its close affiliation to the imagination. And I really do love love. The sort of love that is rare, I mean. I imagine there's a relationship here which is practically sacred, such as we feel in the presence of God. Our misery is unbounded in the absence of God, and above and beyond all of this I feel that God loves me very much, just as I love God. Suhaila, I passed through Paris often on my way to Ireland to visit that ex of mine through those time-honored years. I never thought at all about meeting you, I don't know why. Was it egotism or aversion or anger? Or as if I didn't want your help in my destructive struggle with myself? I wanted to remain by myself unendingly. I gave all of the papers to Ferial who was astounded at how I was able to record what I did, as if one of us had not been apart from the other for more than a few moments. And even so, as someone has said, I am more skilled at friendship than at love, and in this, it seems to me, you are like me.

Rabab

Dear Suhaila,

I remembered the way you put it once, when you said, in frustration, Right! What I really were problems and crises, did you suppose the opposite? You turned to us—we were at Blanche's. You and Hatim were pestering each other as usual. Suddenly you lifted your head. But you didn't look any of us in the eye as you said in a low voice, I have only realized just now that I am the problem. My son says this and here you are repeating the same words but in different forms. Blanche was saddened and angered when I told her that, ever since things have gotten tight for me, I have been working as a babysitter in my building. You kept yourself in check, though. Maalish, shu yaani, you said. So what, it is work like any other. Don't take what Blanche says seriously.

But—you told me, too—the accusation in your eyes, Narjis, challenged me whichever way I turned. Hatim was the worst. His anger was sharper than anyone's. His eyes seemed to pop out of their sockets to pour their abundant anger all over me. He got to his feet, in the middle of the sitting room, and made it clear that he was speaking directly and specifically to me. I feel the same sort of responsibility toward you as Nader does, he said, and what your son says is correct. You must close up your place and go to Canada, for the duration of this trying period at least. I know what you will say— I know all of it, Suhaila. Fine, so your son isn't the ideal gentleman for your coming life, but he must do his duty toward you. A trap. That was all you said when Hatim stopped speaking. You lit your cigarette, drained your glass, and began to lament.

I am the same, friend. I grieved and wailed when I was there— not in Canada like you, but there in Baghdad. It was a unique thing, impossible, unbearable. The world would be utterly dark but for the space cleared by dreaming. Thanks to the most tangled political situations I understood the secret of Don Quixote's appeal, I mean both the literary work and the personality as people generally understand it. Don Quixote gives us a model for the raucous dreamer, who is naïve or full of illusions, perhaps, but who struggles and fights. We Arabs will describe someone as donquihotian, Don Quixote-like; I will say it without hesitation, I will say it to you, and to some of my good friends and even social acquaintance, why not? Yet the scope of that accusation always unveils a certain amount of admiration and an admission of praiseworthy qualities. Perhaps this personality's absolute sublimity gives it a place in the world of the angels or that of those we call majadhib, crazed, those holy people who, whatever else is said about them, are always regarded as truly possessing "a piece of God," in other words, of purity and loftiness and irreality. In the arena of scientifically provable knowledge, they establish the role of fancy. They know well that fancy and imagination stimulated the truly great inventions, and they know the relationship between this sort of motivation and the energy necessary for moving from invention to application, for persistent, tireless, patient work that doesn't end until the goal is achieved. Achievements that result from positive knowledge are never ultimate or fully complete, for the door always remains open. One can always go beyond or contradict what has been done. Baghdad is leaping through that door but slipping sideways perilously: contradiction and achievement. Its vanquishing power is concealed inside of it, inside its children, in the fever of its humdrum everyday terrifying always-interrupted existence. We see this fleetingly in the eyes of an ordinary, anonymous woman as she stares at the faraway horizon but then rolls up her sleeves and bakes our bread. She cooks and washes and picks the basil from the garden and with it she lays on our hearts all of Iraq. She performs every aspect of the world's daily business that you can possibly think of, in order that she may hold onto that moment. What is that moment, my dear friend? It's the Iraqi moment, one which has stepped outside all of the familiar rules. It is different: it doesn't resemble anyone and it does not want anyone to resemble it. I left town with my friend the Saudi researcher Jawhara for the sake of that research—do you remember that? "What are the priorities of citizens, especially the women, following the horror of the war?" That was merely a marginal detail—the title, I mean. There were titles that transformed themselves

263

within a single moment, fleeing and abandoning themselves to other titles, just the way it was with us during the civil war in Lebanon. Down the entire length of the desert road between Amman and Baghdad we were questioning ourselves, Jawhara and I. We wrote the questions in the form of a questionnaire very like the one that France produced after the second world war, having to do with the divergence between priorities and results. Behind the transformation sits a movement along the ladder of values inside societies; the priorities and values that support these are not one and the same in all societies. Naturally, we can pose the same question in more than one place and make comparisons, and why not? What spurs on Iraqis today, or Palestinians or Algerians or other peoples? I don't want you to become alarmed. I went to visit your mother at home. I saw her, of course. She is a lady whom it is impossible to sum up in words, whether a whole speech or a single word or two. She sits there sewing up woolen clothes and taking them apart again, drinking tea with cardamom and muttering your name and that of your brother Diya. I believe that your father moved out and went to live with that young actress in her apartment. She was happy to have him because he was going to produce plays for her—some flops, some productions that were bordering on the indecent. In your home we heard jokes too many to count, which your mother told about him and that actress and about all that everyone is going through. She didn't smile or laugh in the way that you do. She wasn't trying to amuse herself or any of us. She would tell each joke as if it squatted obtrusively at her feet and she needed to push it to the side even a little so that she could move. We were embarrassed about the fact that we smiled and then even broke into laughter, a little. She had her eyes closed as she worked. She would put her hands on things just like a skilled professional, and she had everything right there around her, everything you could think of: tea pots, bottles of oil and vinegar, bags of flour and sugar and tea, pots and pans, plates, towels, shoes and sandals, medicines and ointments, old clothes—all old, I think, though I almost said, and new. There was Iraqi money scattered around her, dinars next to dollars, and you could count as long as God wishes without flagging. And let's suppose that you do get bored or tired: your mother never does. She has an ability to extract the special from the general, and the opposite is true as well. I recalled the words of the famous French sociologist Pierre Bourdieu when he said of language, I mean of the words themselves as they are in the dictionary, that they don't mean anything, or that the meaning they can carry in themselves is trifling. For your mother words mean nothing. She'll say a word but that's the end of it. It doesn't alter anything in her and when she says a word she does not intend that any meaning connected with her will come out of it. The word, any word, in one sense or another, has lost its fluidity, its heart, its depth. It has become like that thread which she sews and then undoes and then sews again. Threads, neither single and independent nor bound together, but lots of them, in her hands. Within the tiny and mundane spaces of her life, she toys with them and she uses them to toy with all of her time, so that in some way or other she can feel her own existence. Hence the joke. The jokes she flung out were cause for admiration and surprise, even unparalleled astonishment. Where did she get this ability to memorize and narrate? I'm not exaggerating, Suhaila, if I tell you that attending to the fund of jokes circulating among people in most Arab countries, and writing them down with the dates they emerged and spread, are tasks that must be at the heart of sociological research. What each country's jokes will say to us is certainly more telling and significant and eloquent than the information contained in the tons of articles published in the newspapers of those countries, or the speeches and serious books published there. Added proof of this is that the jokes themselves are watched; anything in them that exceeds the red line faces the possibility of surveillance, and people who tell them face defamation and interrogation. And the jokes go from oral circulation—which in itself is a potentially dangerous challenge to the authorities—into writing, which is just as serious as writing a political slogan. You know better than I do that the Iraqis are not masters of the joke quite like our brothers the Egyptians, but the wrongs, the injustice, and the terrors that have befallen them have sucked out half their lives. Thus, the other half is left to the joke. That's how it all appeared to me, anyway. They stumbled over jokes in the darkness as they were

265

calling out the names of the dead and the murdered, those who fell, the starving, and all the rest of those categories with their easy labels. I anticipated that when we saw some of our friends, men and women, we would come bearing jokes to dispel all of that sadness, oppression, and grief. But we were to discover that they had left behind distinctions such as complicated versus simple, and they were the ones who pressed us into laughter. I felt a bit afraid. I said to myself, If I tell one of the jokes that I have prepared specially, a joke about foreign leaders expressly suited to such moments as these (and as you know I am not one to memorize jokes and I don't have that special capacity to tell them well), still and all, despite everything, they will laugh. But, there, we exchanged roles. They were telling us the jokes and we needed to hold our sides, we were laughing so hard, even if it was laughter that turned before long into unending wails. Every joke told in our presence would turn into a bout of spiteful envy toward some group or other. But, alongside it all, there was also the silence and those who remained mute. That silence which is a way station between faithfully committing oneself to abstain from speaking, on the one hand, and ultimately rejecting speech as beneath one's cares, on the other. Both states were causing unbelievable pain and misery among everyone we encountered. As if speech itself was the source of mutual bad treatment on a large scale. In the best of circumstances, it was speech that had hit them with missiles and bombs rather than words and sentences; adjectives, verbs of continuing action and also of completed action, agents of action and objects and that entire rich harvest of Arabic rhetoric. That frightening silence that was never, ever absolute or total but indeed gave birth to phenomena that had no relationship in the first place to utterances. It gave birth to a sort of distension, or, if you like, a flattening. Laugh if you want to at these usages applied to things that couldn't be more serious and strange: a wholesale destruction of speech's capacity to regulate things or to pick up on reactions; to select the appropriate action or perhaps the inappropriate one, whereupon words turn into illness, epidemic, defect. Heading down a certain lane, we found ourselves in a popular quarter along River Street. Directly in front of us was a small café. It seemed to me that what the old men sitting there wanted to let us know was an unbelievable and also a brilliant thing: they wanted to tell us that they were incapable of telling us anything at all, and they were so eloquent that I was terrified. After all, there was nothing shredding their insides that they needed to talk about, nothing at all. It wasn't a matter of cleverly escaping us, of some sly set of tactics; no, and it wasn't even despair. I think I simply do not know what it is, exactly. It is something that forces our heads to bow in acquiescence and makes us powerless even to kill ourselves. As long as I live I will never forget that skeletal elderly man whom I saw in the café along the Tigris, who left an odd impact and made my anger at us, as Arabs first, stronger than the blood in our throats and our resentment toward the United States and the entire West. It was as if in my hearing he told the story of all wars: historical wars and personal ones, wars of hatred against love, friendship and absence of friendship, and wars of the separations that spouses are so good at devising against each other, wars among those who work in the same profession or craft, wars of a person with a self, wars between the noble beating of a human heart and the odium that comes to exist between human beings. The wars that happen between people are really the same wars that erupt, in some sense, between a person and his own kinds of wickedness, all his foul loathing, his triviality and cowardice. I don't know, if I were to go on enumerating for you all the wars of that creature — the human — I would have to bring into it the oppression and loss I saw in the eyes of that old man. He is the raw material for irretrievable loss, for all that is gone and will never return. That is why I was so afraid of what he would do to me, and what he would do to the rest of the Iraqi women whose names I had put on a list, and all I had to do was to knock on their doors one after the other — that is all I had to do, in the name of keeping desire and hope alive. The country was not ruined; it has not been dismembered and it has not disintegrated, corpse-like; and I will witness and reclaim all the absent ones, retrieve all those who are alive, and the sick and the elderly. And I have seen some of the pictures that were taken of young Iraqi women and men who scattered to the side streets and who were given, especially right after the war, the label of al-zahira, the phenomenon, the phenomenon of what came to be called the dance of the streets or break dance, which went on for many months. That kind of dance was born in the streets of the miserable outer neighborhoods, akin to the ghettoes of the black people in the United States or the quarters ringing the large French cities where Arab immigrants live. That variety of dance was formed, where it was born, as an expression of the cohesion of marginalized groups when faced with the prevailing, and dominant, order. An understanding began to seep into me of what it meant that young people in Baghdad were going out into the streets and becoming breakies, which was the term that had become popular especially in Algeria and spread like wildfire to all of the Arab countries, even if surreptitiously so.

The rhythms of your dancing sanctioned my view of things, I thought, when I saw the photographs of those youth as they roved the alleys and popular quarters; when you formed out of your body and with your movements a scheme for setting off anger, your own anger. I sensed, while in Baghdad, that your dancing was the life that you wanted to regain for them and for yourself, and for us too, and that what you put up against the past and the present is the goal of tomorrow's beauty itself. I understood that there are different, varied sorts of resistance now that the grand ideologies have been dislodged from their unassailable position, now that they're under suspicion, or are less and less appropriate, for they no longer provide source points for values and moral conduct. It is possible that these modes of resistance are what make everyday details more important. Life becomes a great blessing due to those disasters. You can be sure, Suhaila, that I discovered you in Baghdad, or I got to know you again. It was not chez Blanche following the evening performance at Théâtre du Soleil, when we Arabs, among us a few Iraqis, were invited so that we could attend those seven minutes for Iraq, of your dancing on stage, accompanied by that elegant Faw of whom you later said that he was one of the pillars of the Tower of Babel. We laughed that day, Hatim and I, as we were going out the theater door. Hatim turned and said to me, We never, ever saw that tower, nor did we see those gardens. Those are things that remain shadowy in the imagination. It is as if here is Suhaila saying, It is a work of deception that a person would have a single Tower for Babel. We must take Suhaila at her word, in that beautiful fête when she was there in front of us. She wants to be confident—she wants herself to believe this first and foremost—that that tower is there in the heart, her heart, and that life flows out abundantly over those who are around her, just like the gardens and watercourses of Babylon. She wants to set them off across this earth, throughout the world, at the heart of East and West. She wants to believe that life is a goal in and for itself, and does not exist for ulterior purposes. I told you that before, Narjis, when Blanche and I were preparing the footnotes and the text for Suhaila, the sources and the documents. Even Diyala worked with us, drawing mock-ups of some of the clothes or considering some backdrops for that dance we had seen not long before, which had taken seven minutes but took from us all, and from her most of all, a whole lifetime. All right, if you didn't find her dance pleasing, that is your affair. But Suhaila was waging war against hatred and enmity and despair even in you. You are one of her dear friends, more so than some others. I was sure of all of the returns I am seeing today, sure of the delightful success that inundated us, and equally sure that it all required a fiery will. I was confident that Suhaila has such determination. She is Iraqi, my friend.

I am repeating these words to you, Suhaila, for the first time. I am recording them and sending them to you, and I'm revealing for the first time in your presence what was unfolding between Hatim and me. Baghdad, going there—it was all so that I could regain you. I was the one in whose presence you kept on quoting Dostoevsky's famous line in *Crime and Punishment* about loving to see others commit transgressions. Narjis—you would say to me—I am the original authentic transgression, sayyidat al-akhtaa, the mistress of errors. Maalish, my friend, if I have given you a headache with my dancing which you did not like. That's what I sense, call it my ravings and naïveté, or call it my genuine instinct. Call it whatever you want, for in it I am defending the causes behind my life, and yours, too. I do not carry a megaphone with which I summon everyone to listen to my voice and feel the vibrations of my body. My dance is my only attachment to this world. That's what you would say.

Suhaila, before I end this letter of mine to you, I am going to recount a strange thing that happened in Baghdad. Aah, that city, what it did to me! Baghdad, you, all of you, the funeral processions in unbroken succession, the wreaths of flower and laurels—that's why my passion for Hatim burst out there, which I wasn't expecting. Imagine, I was already living tomorrow, as the city's today drowned in darkness and moaning. Hatim's voice rose in song, in Iraqi songs. I was hearing a few mawwals and bastas and some abudhiya from the radios in cafés and taxis. Possibly they listen to those songs as a daily routine until the burials end or begin again. For the dead over there are too numerous for counting, and the songs are the spiritual link between death and life. The women were wearing black, not as a mere funerary ritual, but because black as a color has become the security belt and protective collar—the life buoy that keeps you afloat. They wear black as if they are expecting worse and preparing themselves for it. Hatim's face and voice were more present for me there than my girls are present for me. Imagine that! Can you believe you are hearing this from me, who is so crazy when it comes to them? I recalled what you read of Hannah Arendt one day. You commented: It is really quite something! It seems that every human being who truly falls in love conjures up the same images and imagines that their passion is the one and only and that no other human being shares this experience. My passion for Hatim appeared to me in Baghdad: he is my very health. I wrote to him saying something close to what Hannah said to her beloved in a letter: Everything is reduced to muteness when I am not talking to you.

Mabruk to the newborn. Mabruk to Nader and Sonia, and congratulations to you as well, holder of the first link in the chain. For you to be a grandmother is a thing like having a vine planted in the heart, for everything around you no longer suffices when you see the birth of a child. How I would like to live long enough to have the same some day. Suhaila, we are all waiting for you, so hurry back to us. I brought you dates and dibis, the date syrup you love, a loofa and a bag for the bathroom, original Iraqi work which I bought for you in the Kazimiyya souqs. I brought you a handful of soil from your garden. Your mother insisted on that so I did it for her sake. It is soil that is ill—they said it was poisoned and I was afraid to believe that. It terrified me to think that the United States wants to transform this country, and perhaps the whole world, into nothing more than a graveyard. To make it thirsty—but thirsty for blood—makes no sense.

Hatim just saw the number of pages I've written, and he says, You have become a specialist in writing letters instead of research papers. Tell Suhaila that what is ahead will be finer than what is now.

Narjis

⁊⁊⁊

I stretch out to sleep on a lie: I want Nader to escape from me. I'm tired, I tell him, and I want to go straight to sleep.

He did not answer me, didn't raise his eyes off my face, as if I were gripping the menu and choosing what others would eat. As for my favorite dish, it remained the broth of Faw's sweat. Every day I was in Nader's company I would resolve to tell him the story, the chaos of that story; but I would hold back, and then it was too late: I would vacillate, and then I could not say a word. It had nothing to do with good faith and sincerity in a mother–son relationship, and nothing to do with wickedness and bad morals. It is something I find myself unable to describe, a thing of concern only to my inner self, my illness and mirth, my grief and my mourning for my life gone astray. I always used to lie to this self, a self that I see in a haberdashery shop, picking up its burdens and dragging them behind it so as to weigh down my frame, and then my position on this earth where I stand will be sedate and serious. I always feel that there is time enough for us to get old, to go soft, and to act like children with childish manners. Enough time for us to cry together about the tremblings that are fortressed-in by guards and insults. I begin to smile as I look in the mirror. My voice rises as I close my eyelids; speaking to him, my voice is low at first.

Nader, you must change the mirror. That's because it is feeble, unable to make me appear as I am. It is resisting me. I used to repeat that, whether or not he could hear me, when we had recently arrived in Paris. And when we were in Brighton, I would insist on it. And now in Canada I say derisively, If you don't change it I will. Today. Right now.

I don't hear his reply. I can't hear his voice. I changed the mirror, I add. Without your knowing. And I did it months ago. You didn't even notice. And why would you notice? Sons are like guests at court; what appeals to them is looking at the ornamented surfaces and flamboyant decorations and paintings, and the flow of water and where and how pictures and curtains are hung and the feel of objects. But they don't give their attention in the slightest to what is beneath the screaming and moaning, what is beneath and behind everything they see.

When I hear no response I go back to my room but I continue speaking to him. What is the difference, Nader, whether you are here in front of me or absent?

The light had narrowed. I told myself that here was the reason my face appeared crude, thick, even savage. What is not open to doubt is that when the lighting is so very clear, it makes a face look nearly ill, icy, and sometimes deathly. Nader, I want you to be absolutely confident that this is not my face, the face I know and you know as well. This was never my face. It surprised me and so I was upset at first. No, at first I was easily insulted because it abandoned me. It became an exhausted, emptied structure, one of those structures of which we say that it has kept on being a treasure house of the honor that gives us everything. Everything, that is, except security over honor itself. Nader, do you hear me?

I lowered the light by half as I made myself beautiful, applying makeup until my hand was dropping off, and as I began roaming around in my face and body, coming upon nothing but utter ruin. I was sad, of course, at the beginning—the start of my relationship with Faw. Time as something measurable, something in the here and now, or—according to the way physicists see it—time as something grand and all-encompassing, was, to put it exactly, swaggering along in front of me and taking pride in its qualities. When I saw Faw, in the dark, that darkness of Théâtre du Soleil, I was in need of a higher exuberance, a stronger self-abandon that would force itself out from my own internal self, something stronger than the number of years I have lived, stronger than speech and texts. Dance made the famine that was the years of my life show itself proud of gentleness and delicacy, these qualities in whose realms I was roving, to sweet rhythms, roving between my self and his body. Dance will never find its ultimate realization on the theater stage; and it will never end there. It is always beginning, even while I am embodying it as Tessa and Maria watch.

I made mistakes. I would get up from the floor, and fall, and not know where to put my feet or in what order. The exercises I did on my own seemed to unearth the worst of it. Something is stronger and more beautiful when we don't know its essence and we are unaware of what the next step is and what the reaction to that will be. Every step I took led me to him and allowed me to disembark from the train of culpability and fear that I had been endlessly riding. With his suggestive gestures and his movement and his touch, he gave me my adventure. Onstage — on that stage — I became weary of the lighting. I resisted those lights, so as not to allow him to see me at all. But I had the feeling that I had become merely a scrap of paper that he folded and jammed into his pocket: I was an identity card and he tossed me into his prison, the prison of his whole body. I would address Tessa inaudibly to get her to lower the lights; it seems that strong lights leave the veins bulging and pores open to their widest, and that's where age makes its way inside of us, in whichever way it wishes. Age refuses but to enter; it doesn't leave. It comes in and it does not come out again. I tried to let it come out even if just for a time, to delay, to be absent a little, as if it were napping or visiting someone while on its way to me, visiting Blanche, Narjis, Caroline, visiting Nur with her spreading fragrance, or even Wajd; or stopping on the way to rest a little. It goes over to tease a few lovers, those whom I see in the Metro and on the banks of the Seine and in side streets. They hug quietly, or violently, they kiss each other on the lips as if the kiss will return them to the time of their first flowering. Of the secrets of this cosmos they know only this succession of acts: swallowing your saliva, the click of teeth against teeth, and the tongue. That accursed being, age, packs them full of screams waiting to emerge. Life, age — it marches before them, ignores them, and appears not to be in any hurry. With me, though, I see it as very much in a hurry; but I changed the second mirror, too. I scrubbed my face with warm water and chemical-free soap, which is what the pharmacy manager prescribed. She is my French neighbor, and she said, This is soap that revives the skin—it's perfect. When I washed my face it suddenly looked very attractive but a quarter of an hour later it puckered and shriveled. My face collapsed into wrinkles as if the whole cosmos had sat down on top of it and then abandoned all of me. As I left the pharmacy I asked myself, What is the use of reviving it? I want to see age, life, my age. I want to extend my hand out to it and give it a friendly handshake, and wish it enough time to remove itself from my presence. Whenever I change the mirror the state I'm in is more topsy-turvy than the day before. And Faw could care less, it seems. The minute we are together he says to me, I will disburse your age in my own special way, not on the bed of sleep nor by instinct. With it I shall open a charity bazaar. Warm water and soap didn't do any good so I bought a washcloth in the shape of a hand and began to rub my face gently at first. That is what the lady told me to do. Then I doubled the motions of my hand over the temples and around the eyes, these areas I have always watched most closely. Here is where age had collected—reckless, out of control, fickle, desolate. Here is where the lies massed, along with boredom, and weariness, and bitterness, and decorous words and very faithful stupidities. What is this? I made myself into a laughing stock for I would wail and laugh and scream into the mirror's face.

I make a fist and raise it high so as not to see, as if I am putting on my age, like clothes. I impale it and I feel a soft slow twinge between my breasts which have sagged right and left and roamed unrestrained on the edges of streets and among houses and cities and rooms and sheets. Watching my mother, I used to say to Ferial, Yaa, how very old she is! But she was only forty at the time. Life, lived, itself sags onto itself, is made a laughingstock, begins to grow uneasy, to weary and get bored; age and life want something else. Age also has a life. Nader, where are you, ayni? Why don't you answer me? Come, turn the pages of my face with me, one page after another, since . . . since. . . . And don't leave me alone with my face. He would be afraid for me whenever he saw me in pain, whenever I would sing in a sad voice and go into the bathroom, whenever I remained absent for a long time. And when my silence would grow particularly heavy he would say to me, and I was certain that he was uncomfortable with my behavior, Mother, it is as if you have gone inside the mirror.

If Nader leaves me I bring in Faw. I take little sips of his blood and invite him to the banquet of my lifetime. I pull back the curtain and run dancing across the top of the Towers of Eiffel and Babel. I said to Faw, Search with me for what is left of me that you can have. Search for the overflow of the Tigris and Euphrates, the flooding of the banks and the silt on the two sides of al-Faw, there in Iraq. Dance with me for one day, for one sentence. If only my dance were translated into the living and dead languages and those that are dying! I told him that there are no rules in dance. Maria is a little overbearing, like my mother, and Tessa comes to my dreams as they all do, and she brings everyone, and she says, Do not imitate anyone, man or woman.

How can that be, Tessa? Don't you see how crude I am? I become hooliganish and bad, I move toward death walking on tiptoe. I took Tessa by the hand and said to her, Come, dance with me, let's dance, this is what the finest lineages of women do with the women who are still around. But Ferial was crossing the borders with sarcastic words; she was mocking me for having said: Acting and dancing are my birthplace: the very place where my head emerged to touch the world. No one really owns her own head, Ferial answers, so how could one possess the place where it touches the world? Who cares now about eulogizing themselves, their parents, and their ancient, first paradisiacal gardens? Suhaila, I love no paradises.

My self-abasement worried Dr. Wajd, who said, Your image is turned inside out right now. Fine, don't take this sleeping pill—I'll take it instead of you. Be confident that I will not sell your secrets. I will not be forced to do that even if I have to die at your side. I am not your personal physician; I am your faithful friend. I will not defile my duty or my oath or my fealty. I will not betray you so don't examine me like that, please. Don't be swayed by what you hear and by what is said. I am by your side, so don't be afraid. Only at a late hour did I understand her vague allusion. She began to play a tune for me and I had no help for it but to respond. I had never danced quite like this before or swayed with this simplicity. My features were in front of Faw, appearing composed so he would take me seriously and with due forbearance considering my age. I was afraid to say to him, Even the rhythm is a message. It is odd that Asma did not call with congratulations on Leon's birth, but I saw her pregnant in her last month, more or less, and she is nearly my age. I will persuade Hammada not to slip out, she said, so that he can remain close to where my emotions are hidden and so that he will not be out of my sight. I will remain pregnant with him until his birth really becomes necessary.

I think about my own death. I have thought about it a lot. My death does not cloud my serenity; it pleases me. It accedes to my commands. I deceived them, bursting into laughter. My death is amphibious; I have taken it on professionally, from all sides since having been steeped in all the poisons but without dying. It has been bewildering: I noticed that my skin looked the color of the wine my heart adores as much as Blanche does. My eyes contain many layers; my nose is stately and my hair swirls round with the swiftness of a nuclear reactor. Someone, only one someone, flares up before me like soda. Faw. He was asleep like the two tributaries, the Tigris and the Euphrates, between my ribs. He drew me out of my sleep and my bed, out of my death and my forgetting. The tears ran down my cheeks as I heard Nader's voice. Aah, it is him, and he is putting on one of my shawls that I love so much. He used to be the child, and the beautiful sad young man, and he looks straight into my eyes. I can remember his very first lines of poetry.

> *I fear death*
> *I fear life continuing without me*
> *my friends forgetting me*
> > *and my mother's tears increasing twofold*
> > *whenever her eyelids open*

Translator's Note and Acknowledgments

As a multilingual text that draws on many cultural references, *al-Mahbubat* is a transnational text and I have tried to preserve the spirit of this traveling text linguistically, although the musicality of colloquial Arabic, as well as the significance of using dialect Arabic within the narrative, can only be suggested in translation.

Every translation is a reader's interpretation, and in the end, I am of course responsible for the many decisions that this entails. The very few and minor real alterations to the text that I have made have been done with the author's agreement. Throughout, Alia Mamdouh has been a translator's dream: respectful, trusting, warm, and always generous and prompt in answering questions. Most of all, working with Alia, from our first meeting in Cairo on, has been an opportunity to get to know a wonderful person, and I am deeply grateful to her.

I want to note that in the Arabic text there is no chapter twelve: this was accidental and I have altered the subsequent chapter numbers, with the result that chapter 12 in this rendering is chapter 13 in the Arabic, and so on. There are a few direct quotations rendered in Arabic in the original, which I was not able to locate in order to quote directly from English versions; in these cases I have translated them myself or paraphrased them. The rap lyrics are my composition based loosely on the Arabic in the text, which Alia Mamdouh in turn based on lyrics by the French-based rap group NTM but which I was unable to find. The Bob Marley quotation is a quoted statement of his rather than a song lyric; this quotation was the closest I found to the meaning given in the Arabic.

"Neither spared nor left behind" in one passage of the translation ("Your theater will be a cosmic adventure that will be neither spared nor left behind, and it will cause a splitting and a rending") originates from the Holy Qur'an (74:28). For another passage ("ever since her eating of the tree of knowledge led to her discovery of Adam as an other ... and to her discovery of the principle of desire/pleasure entwined"), the author is indebted for these characterizations of the thought of Cixous to two essays by Sabry Hafiz published in the London daily *al-'Arab*: "Mafhum al-kitaba al-mu'annatha 'ind Cixous wa-l-riwaya al-misriya al-jadida," *al-'Arab* 29 October 2002, p. 14; "Ta'nith al-kitaba 'ind Cixous wa tabi'at al-ma'na al-jadida," *al-'Arab*, 5 November 2002, p. 14.

My rendering of *al-Mahbubat* into English has benefited from the generous help of several friends and colleagues as well as the fortunate yields of the internet. I am very grateful to my dear friend and sister translator, Sahar Tawfiq, for taking time out of her own work to answer questions, and also to another dear person, Ferial Ghazoul, for her willingness to help. I thank Iqbal al-Qazwini for her patient and careful help with last-minute clarifications, Carrie Cuno-Booth for checking cultural references on the internet, Nicole Côté for a felicitous French usage, Odile Cisneros for helping me think about titles, and Alex Giardino for recognizing that "Mother India" could be Amma rather than some other candidates for that appellation. Nicole, Alex, and Odile were among a magical, wonderful cohort of translators at the Banff International Literary Translation Centre, which is a program of the Banff Centre in Banff, Alberta, Canada. The chance to live and work in the company of literary translators — and among the beautiful mountains, rivers, and forests of Banff, where breathtaking walks helped me contour many a sentence herein — was, as we agreed at the time, utopian (and also real). The final version of this translation was largely accomplished at Banff. I am deeply grateful to the Centre and to its Director, Linda

Gaboriau, for making this opportunity possible. Linda's graceful, mesmeric, and always smart directorship set a wonderful tone, and I am also thankful for a most memorable climb above the Bow!